Date: 1/4/19

LP MYS CLEVERLY
Cleverly, Barbara,
Fall of angels

FALL OF ANGELS

This Large Print Book carries the
Seal of Approval of N.A.V.H.

AN INSPECTOR REDFYRE MYSTERY

FALL OF ANGELS

BARBARA CLEVERLY

THORNDIKE PRESS
A part of Gale, a Cengage Company

Farmington Hills, Mich • San Francisco • New York • Waterville, Maine
Meriden, Conn • Mason, Ohio • Chicago

Copyright © 2018 by Barbara Cleverly.
An Inspector Redfyre Mystery.
Thorndike Press, a part of Gale, a Cengage Company.

ALL RIGHTS RESERVED
Thorndike Press® Large Print Mystery.
The text of this Large Print edition is unabridged.
Other aspects of the book may vary from the original edition.
Set in 16 pt. Plantin.

LIBRARY OF CONGRESS CIP DATA ON FILE.
CATALOGUING IN PUBLICATION FOR THIS BOOK
IS AVAILABLE FROM THE LIBRARY OF CONGRESS

ISBN-13: 978-1-4328-5766-0 (hardcover)

Published in 2018 by arrangement with Soho Press, Inc.

Printed in Mexico
1 2 3 4 5 6 7 22 21 20 19 18

*To a Cambridge friend —
Heather — who joined me
in a snowy tramp around the city
last Christmas morning,
snuffling out deposition spots
for my unfortunate angels*

CHAPTER 1

Cambridge, December 1923

"Hello? Detective Inspector Redfyre, Cambridge CID here."

"There you are, Johnny!"

John Redfyre flinched. He eased the receiver an inch from his ear to take the edge off the hunting-field halloo of his favourite old relative and looked at his wristwatch. He smiled. Halfway between tea and the first gin, he might well have expected the caller to be Aunt Henrietta.

"I can't deny it, Aunt Hetty. You find me here in my foxhole. Had I gone missing?"

His voice was warm, his tone light. Redfyre's answer to any swords and lances coming in his direction was always to raise, not a shield, but two defiant fingers and skip away fast. He'd learned to greet Fate with a flirtatious smile, Adversity with a kick in the shins and his Aunt's summons with a hearty riposte. Family circumstances had forged his resilience, he believed. As the youngest of four boys of a family fallen on hard times — and not only the youngest, but the handsomest — he'd endured a childhood to rival any Biblical tale of family disharmony. He could have told Joseph where he'd gone wrong. He could have given a few pointers to the Prodigal Son.

He accepted that he was never to lead the easy aristocratic life of his forebears owing to birth order and postwar austerity, but there was one aspect of a privileged situation he still guiltily yearned for, and Hetty's call had triggered that yearning. On the occasions when she demanded his attention, he felt the need of a butler. Some suave old chap like his father's Simpson. A man who would purr blandly: "I'm so sorry, Madam. I regret the master is not at home. He is on his way to a Masonic meeting, I believe," whilst his master, in slippers and dressing gown, sat grinning shamelessly at him from his armchair.

Bloody telephone! Convenient for professional purposes, but he rather resented the social intrusion of the apparatus into his home. Anyone with access to one of these evil instruments could command his attention at a whim and the communication could not be avoided by crossing the road, affecting a sore throat or inventing an urgent engagement. Yes, here, indeed, was the Detective Inspector, caught in an unbuttoned state, glass of whisky in one hand, *Sporting Life* in the other at the end of a gruelling day — and no protective Simpson about the place to deny access. Not on a DI's salary.

Redfyre accepted the inevitable. He expressed his very real regard for his aunt and voiced his surprise that she should be troubling to speak to him by means of this inhuman device. A threepenny bus ride or a two-bob taxi fare and she could have been with him in person, pouring out her problems while he poured out a London gin and added a slug of Rose's Lime Juice. A bit of swift work with the ice pick and he could promise a tinkle of ice shards against the Waterford glass and . . . "There's still time," he added temptingly.

"Tinkling ice, eh? So there's one piece of modern equipment you don't disdain? Always a lure, of course, but, on this occasion, ice won't do the trick."

"Ah! Like me, Aunt Hetty, you've loosened your stays and settled into your evening?"

His aunt suppressed a gurgle, then gathered herself for the attack. "Now, I have to

9

tell you that your despised telephone is bringing you a delightful offer. Let's do diaries, darling. Ready? I'm looking at Friday evening. Are you free?"

"The day-after-tomorrow-Friday? That the one? Hmm . . ."

She'd caught him on the hop again. Pinned him to the page. There were several things he'd been planning in a vague way to do when his shift ended, involving a jar of ale and congenial conversation — possibly an Oscar Wilde play on the wireless — but none would survive a bald statement over the phone. He'd always found it a more fiendishly accurate revealer of the barefaced lie than the newfangled lie-detector machines he'd been experimenting with. Blood pressure pulses be damned! It was voice tremors they should be calibrating. However hard he stared, his Friday evening slot remained inconveniently blank.

"I'm free, Aunt," he admitted.

"Excellent! Then ink this in at once. I have tickets for a concert you will not want to miss. I find I can't use them — your uncle's gout again — so I'm leaving one for you at the ticket desk. Just up your street, you'll find. It's a Christmas concert in one of the college chapels, St. Barnabas. Welcoming in the festive season with a blast of traditional

10

music. Mince pies and hot punch in the interval. No pink-faced choir boys — just two soloists. Organ and trumpet . . . Oh, you know, the usual gaggle of Germans — Haydn, Hummel, Bach of course and a bit of Orlando Gibbons batting for England perhaps . . . that sort of thing. Don't worry, you will absolutely *not* be called on to sing along," she added hastily. "It's an early start — six o'clock for two hours, so you'll still have time for something of an evening and an early night."

But Redfyre was suspicious by nature, especially of Aunt Hetty bearing gifts. He broke into her chatter. "Did you say you had *two* tickets? Are you expecting me to rustle up an organ-loving chum?" He added provokingly, "At such short notice?"

"That won't be necessary, my dear. I've already allocated the other one to someone who jumped at the chance. Someone you may remember from your childhood. You'll be sitting next to Earwig."

"I'm sorry, Aunt, I didn't quite make that out. Do you know, for a moment I thought you said 'Earwig'! Ho, ho!" He shook the receiver and applied it to his other ear. "Ah! How do you spell that? E-A-D-W-I-G? Eadwig? Mmm . . . Close enough. An Anglo-Saxon acquaintance, would that be? A newly discovered Norwegian branch of the family?"

"No — English. The Strettons. Don't pretend you don't know them. You've met them all. Well-to-do family. They own much of the view to the south from the top of St. Mary's tower, which allows them to indulge their artistic compulsions. Very arty-crafty, you'll have noticed. He paints rather badly; she pots rather well. All their children were given Anglo-Saxon names: Aethelwulf, Aethelstan, Aelfhelm, Godric and Eadwig . . . Very fashionable twenty, thirty years ago. And now they're all out in the world, of course."

Redfyre groaned. "Now I'm beginning to recall the faces that go with the names. Out in the world, you say? Surprised to hear that! I'd have expected behind bars. And the place, their country seat — Melford wasn't it? Just south of Cambridge? We used to be sent over to play with them there when we were little."

"That's right. You were quite a favourite with Clarissa, I recall. She preferred your quiet, sunny nature to the rumbustious indiscipline of her own brood. And who wouldn't? Though perhaps it was ill-judged of Clarissa to say so to her own children. You spent many hours in her studio learning to handle clay."

Uncomfortable memories, long suppressed, were beginning to surface. Once, they would have stung; now they merely irritated Redfyre. "Aunt, it was safer to be in the studio with a kindly adult than to be outside in the grounds with a pack of hooligans on the loose. For the Stretton boys, 'Go out and play' meant 'Go out and fight.' I hated our visits. It was a social experiment that was thankfully cut short and abandoned. Big, blond bullies! I believe I had a particular disagreement with one of them."

"You broke his nose, darling. With your little fist. That was Wulfie — Aethelwulf. But don't concern yourself — it's been broken on several occasions since by others who shared your sentiments."

Redfyre grunted. "I ask myself what's wrong with 'Alfred' or 'Hilda,' if you're such a sucker for the Saxons? Why put modern man to the trouble of wrestling with uncouth syllables?"

Hetty snorted in agreement. "Know what you mean! It's like trying to eat a piece of overdone toast. Much noise and effort expended for little gratification. Eadwig, you'll find, is the most agreeable of the bunch, in character and pronunciation. I'm informed that 'ead' means 'wealth' and 'wig' means 'war.' Make what you will of that."

Redfyre had settled into his front row seat directly below the high organ loft — ease of access for gouty gents was always a feature of his aunt's arrangements — and scanned the program a good ten minutes before the music was due to start. He looked about him with satisfaction.

The college chapel was en fête tonight. Candles had been lit in profusion, and the air was charged with the invigorating scent of green boughs: pine and holly and ivy with, somewhere in the background, an ancient blend of incense and dark wood. Chapel officials in splendid vestments were swirling about, busily doing nothing productive and avoiding catching the eye of members of the public, punctuating this seemingly choreographed performance with an occasional genuflection to the altar. One of them disappeared behind the hangings masking the door to the organ loft and climbed the staircase up to the gallery where the performance was to take place. He appeared moments later, stage left, ostentatiously tweaking at the heavy brocade curtains, which were already perfectly draped. This was an actor manqué, Redfyre decided, impressed by the young man's good looks and his tongue-in-cheek gestures. The man even slapped a glove at imaginary dust on the gleaming wooden rail that edged the small gallery. Being at knee height, the contraption didn't impress Redfyre much as a safety feature, should some soloist, carelessly overconfident or swept up in a transport of delight, manage to lose his balance. With his trained eye and concern for public safety, Redfyre was amused to watch as the young flunky actually put a right hand on it and indulged in a bit of arm wrestling. The mahogany handrail shrugged off the attack on its integrity. So no one would be ending the evening with a headlong plunge into the lap of the law in the front row, at least.

Entertained by the performance the warm-up team was putting on, Redfyre sighed contentedly. With four Christmases in and out of the trenches of Flanders being a very recent memory, he was in heaven. He enjoyed the ceremony and respected the traditions. He offered up a silent prayer of thanks for his survival and wondered whether Eadwig Stretton had come out of it unscathed. Men of Redfyre's age (and he had calculated that this youngest of the Stretton brood was most likely a year or two younger than himself) had grown accustomed to greeting old acquaintances warily, affecting a cheery oblivion to twisted features, missing limbs and wrecked minds. With the Stretton reputation for pugnacity, Redfyre prepared himself to meet one who had led from the front and suffered the consequences. The surprise, for him, was that one of their number would have found the offer of a classical music concert ticket alluring. Or that his aunt would have considered a Stretton a likely recipient. He'd have thought those boys would have risen to nothing more demanding than a medley of Gilbert and Sullivan tunes belted out by a Royal Navy band.

Redfyre instantly scolded himself for his snobbery and his baseless pre-judgement. His aunt knew what she was doing. Always. And she had been right in his case, certainly — he knew and loved every item on the program. Though the organ was his favourite instrument, this pairing with the trumpet caused him some concern. Would a solitary piece of brass be up to the job of accompanying the magnificent medieval forest of pipes lodged up in the loft above the heads of the congregation?

He opened his program to check the credentials of the bold trumpeter and read with surprise and some disquiet the name of the soloist.

Good Lord! Was it possible? Could the audience be aware?

He looked about him, seeing the usual shining anticipation of a well-to-do Cambridge gathering. They were smiling and chattering in low voices. They must all have read the name, yet no objector had stamped out in protest, tearing up his ticket, wondering out loud what the world was coming to. The inspector's antennae constantly twitched in response to the slightest threat to public order, and he knew better than most with what speed an altercation could break out, even in this civilised town. It was, after all, full of men and women who liked the sound of their own voices and knew how to use them to good — or mischievous — effect. Debating, protesting, lampooning, even the occasional hanging-in-effigy from lampposts were skills they enjoyed and practiced, and on this occasion, someone had provided them with an irresistible target for protest.

Redfyre was struck by an awful thought — an unworthy one. Bloody old Aunt Hetty! Eyes, ears and trouble-making tongue of Cambridge society that she was, could she have got wind of an undercover plot to disrupt proceedings? The Cambridge police had dealt with several outbreaks of civic disorder in the last few months. Heads had been cracked, blood spilled, holding cells overcrowded and the reputation of the Force called into question most eloquently in the newspapers. It was clear to Redfyre that, after years of quiet, an ugly altercation was bubbling up. Town versus Gown, Worker versus Employee, Male versus Female and Everyone versus Undergraduates — all were on the menu. Small provocations could blaze up into violent scuffles within minutes, and regardless of whichever factions had lined up to do battle, the one certain outcome was that the police would find themselves in the middle of it, the unwilling magnet of ire from both sides and the condemnation of the press.

He could well imagine Hetty, over a pre-dinner sherry, grandly reassuring some college bigwig: "Don't worry, Master, I'm sure your fears are groundless, but just in case, may I offer to put my nephew into a strategic position on the night? In mufti, of course — we wouldn't want to frighten the horses with the sight of a uniform . . . No, I'm sure the Detective Inspector will be delighted."

He got to his feet, ostensibly using the last few minutes to stretch his legs. He swept the rows behind him with the mild, enquiring eye of a gentleman looking for acquaintances amongst the audience. He was even lucky enough to spot a chap he'd been at school with and gave him a swift, cheery salute. He did not, however, salute or even signal recognition of the sharp features and supercilious smile of a neatly suited representative of the *Cambridge Oracle* seated six rows behind him. Not their music critic, he noted, but their chief crime reporter. Apart from that discordant note, he was pleased to see no sign of flags or placards. No visible weaponry, apart from the hatpins still favoured by the older women.

He was being overcautious. This was a chapel, after all — a consecrated building. Behaviour would be nothing less than respectful. Nevertheless, Redfyre found his eyes flicking over the exits and counting the number of college officials on duty. It was when he found himself calculating the defensive possibilities of the organ loft as a last bastion — *Stand by to retreat on the loft!* — that he acknowledged he was being ridiculous. He forgave himself and grinned. Just let 'em try!

"Never take sides, my boy!" had been the constant advice of his boss, Superintendent MacFarlane. But he had no doubt as to where his loyalties would lie if things turned nasty. Anyone attempting to cause distress to a musician would run into Redfyre's sword arm. The arm would be flourishing a warrant card rather than a weapon, but it would be effective.

Two minutes to go and still the seat next to his was empty. Evidently, another of Hetty's victims had rebelled against her press-gang tactics at the last minute. He speculated briefly once again on Hetty's odd choice of companion for the evening. Had she planned to supply him with a strapping great bully to act as his lieutenant? It was possible . . . and inconvenient. Redfyre preferred to work alone. He was relieved that the seat remained unclaimed. He could enjoy the performance without the need for dutiful conversation with someone he knew he ought to remember — someone whose last memory of *him* could well be a black eye or worse. Redfyre had uncomfortable flashes of memory of a scene where, small, scared and deserted by his brothers, he'd been trapped with his back to the orchard wall by a pack of blond tormentors. His hosts, in full cry, had pelted him with windfall apples as hard as pebbles until, blinded in one eye but roaring defiance, he'd stormed forward with fists and feet flying, with much damage done to both sides before he'd been rescued by the chance appearance of the garden boy.

Jonas. Redfyre still remembered his name. Would never forget it. Jonas had put his stalwart frame firmly between the adversaries and threatened, with remarkable aplomb for his fifteen years, to tell Grandpa Stretton that Master Wulfie and his pack had attacked a guest and messed up the apple orchard. He didn't need to tell them that that was a beating offense. Nor did he need to mention that Grandpa Stretton would always take the word of the gardening staff before that of tale-tellers. They'd tested that out, to their discomfort, before. The gang ran off, shrieking blood-curdling threats, in search of other amusements. Young Jonas had turned to the injured boy and told him with surprising tenderness in his rough country voice, "Here, take this hanky. Go to the kitchen and ask Gertie to take a look at that eye. Never let 'em see you cry, lad! They'll tear you to bits, them little old scallywags. You were doing the right thing. The only thing." That was the first male kindness Redfyre had encountered, and he could still recall the reassuring firmness of the rough hand that grasped his, hauled him to his feet and dusted him down.

He could never be certain, but he'd always counted that as the moment when his picture of himself changed. Perhaps it happened to all eight-year-old boys? But after the rescue, he determined he would no longer be the smallest and weakest. He would be the one who helped up the fallen and encouraged the despairing, he'd decided sentimentally. "Bless you, Jonas," he murmured, half in thought, half in prayer, "but you passed on a burden I've never quite been able to put down. And here I am, still hefting it."

At the last permissible moment, there was a scampering down the aisle, and a sidesman, face frozen in disapproval, ushered Eadwig the Unknown into the aisle-side seat next to Redfyre.

Cold fingers reached out and grasped his hand in a firm handshake. "John Redfyre? Earwig. How d'ye do? Must be twenty years, eh? Talk in the interval. I think the players are about to make an appearance."

Redfyre stared, speechless for a moment with astonishment. "But . . . but you're a girl!" he heard himself burble.

The slender, fair-haired creature, silk- and fur-clad and scented lightly with Mitsouko, batted mascaraed lashes at him. "You noticed at once!" She smiled a smile wicked with lip rouge and twisted with sarcasm. "Hetty warned me you were a detective. What were you expecting?"

The inspector rallied. "The clue's in the name. Some evidence of wealth and war — an arms dealer, perhaps? A flint-eyed gent, lighting his *Romeo e Julieta* with a rolled-up fiver?"

Earwig laughed. Her laughter frothed and gurgled like champagne being poured by a generous hand.

Redfyre was charmed, but someone hissed "Shhh!" in reprimand from behind.

Earwig turned her head and quelled the hiss with a harrumph: "I say! Do settle down, gentlemen!"

The young organist entered the chapel from a door on the right. Clearly easy with an appearance before even an experienced audience, he came forward and acknowledged the welcome he was given with a wide smile, a bow and a flick of luxuriant, overlong chestnut hair. A splendid figure, Redfyre thought, and he twitched an eyebrow at Earwig, inviting her to share his appreciation.

"Goodness! He's pulling out all the stops tonight!" she chuckled under cover of the applause and dug him in the ribs to underline her joke. "That gown! What is it? Cream damask lined with cherry satin? Remind me to ask the name of his tailor."

"It's his festal gown. Only paraded on certain days of the year, and this isn't one of them. Dr. Coote must have been granted special dispensation to wear it for Advent in the name of entertainment. Good — it certainly cheers up the troops!"

Coote raised his head and gathered the attention of the distant back row, sweeping up and reflecting the warm anticipation of the crowd, before introducing himself. Redfyre checked his program: Christopher Coote, Doctor of Music. A talent from his early years, apparently. College choir boy and organist who was beginning to make a name for himself on the international circuit. Redfyre noted that he made no mention of his growing fame in his introduction, and yet he managed somehow to bring it to mind by referring, with some fervour, to his frequent appearances in this, his own college. He implied that, however strong the attractions of the venerable organs of Paris, Amsterdam and Vienna — all yearning for his touch, apparently — his Christmas would be incomplete without an interlude on his home instrument. His audience was charmed and oddly flattered.

And Christopher was delighted to be sharing the platform this year, he confided, with an astonishingly able musician, a rising star with whom he'd had the privilege of scoring pieces of Handel, Bach and Mozart for their two instruments. Rarely heard playing together, the organ and trumpet gave forth an inspiring sound. They were to experience an evening of spine-tingling harmonies, surprising interpretations of well-loved themes, but above all, music very much in tune with the season. His voice took on a jovial medieval throatiness as he promised them "a right merrie noyse."

Coote moved back to the door, opened it with a flourish and, at last, brought the soloist before the audience. He stood back, the better to assess their reaction.

All had read the program, all had been prepared to see on stage that extreme rarity: a female trumpeter.

A species as rare as the black-tailed godwit in these parts. No verifiable sightings ever made in the east of England. It was rumoured that they existed, but no one Redfyre knew had actually clapped eyes on a living, breathing specimen. People had sisters whose best friend's cousin swore that she'd seen one at the Wigmore Hall — or was it the Albert Hall? — before the War.

On reading her name, Redfyre had tried, but not managed, to censor the ribald old men's club piece of guidance on choice of instrument for musical daughters: "Remember, now! You are to have no truck with any instrument you have to put in your mouth or between your thighs, Amelia!" And, strangely, the world had complied, as Redfyre knew of no female cellists, either.

What had the audience expected? A doughty, middle-aged dame, freethinking and determined to outdo her male counterparts? Yes! She'd be clad in rusty black taffeta down to her sturdy ankles, and her gaze would be as steely as her instrument. Undoubtedly a suffragist, Redfyre had surmised. And yet, the name had not rung a bell with him when he'd called to mind his gallery of female firebrands about Cambridge. Not a name he would have forgotten: Juno Proudfoot. Now, that was a name that announced a lady who would put up with no nonsense. Reassuringly classical. Yes, a Cambridge audience would be very ready to give the lady a sympathetic hearing. She was probably the daughter or wife of one of the assembled dignitaries.

No one had expected a Florentine angel straight from the walls of the Uffizi to step shyly on stage. The beauty and grace of the young woman who now, holding her instrument by her side, stood bowing and smiling, drew first a stunned silence, then a vigorous clapping. Hair the colour of silver gilt coiled about her head in a style that would have had Fra Angelico running for his paints; pale blue eyes glinting with mischief in the candle light; her dress a slip of white silk in the Greek style, which clung in a daring way to the contours of her lithe figure. The girl was very definitely not wearing a corset.

"So that's Juno!" Earwig commented under cover of the thunderous applause. "Scheming Queen of Olympus, huh? Looks more like an apprentice Aphrodite to me!" To make herself heard, she leaned close to Redfyre, her lips brushing his ear, her fringe tangling with his eyelashes. His head was beginning to spin. Angels to right of him, angels to left. He was caught in a heavenly pincer movement.

"Lord!" Earwig made a second assault on his ear. "What an elf! She doesn't look strong enough to blow out the candles on her birthday cake!"

"I'll say! Let alone survive two hours competing with a pneumatically powered pipe organ," Redfyre agreed politely. "Recently re-voiced," he added, reading from his program notes. "Will she have the puff?"

"You must avert your eyes, Inspector, if a Hummel crescendo proves too demanding. I'm not sure that wisp of silk that passes for a bodice can cope with the lung expansion, in addition to accommodating a not-inconsequential bosom," she hissed under cover of the over-lengthy applause.

Redfyre was stunned by the boldness of the remark — he'd have thought it rather salty coming from one of his male friends — but he'd learned how to respond to Anglo-Saxon challenge. Go on the attack at once. Fists, apples, deception — use whatever came to hand. He reached for an overconfident statement, not to say a blatant lie. "Lovely gown! A Captain Molyneux confection, if I'm not mistaken? Stout English seams by stout English seamstresses. The good captain will not let her down. Or out," he said repressively.

The program got underway with the Handel trumpet concerto, a choice of opener designed to reassure by its familiarity that all was well. Here was a confident player able to take her place on any concert platform. Juno's unspoken message to the audience was, *You've all heard this before. You know how it should sound. Now listen again!*

28

An astonishing performance. The thunderous applause that followed brought a flush to her cheek and a smile to her lips. Redfyre was glad she would never overhear the remark (kindly meant) from the gentleman sitting behind him to his wife: "Great Heavens, Edna! Shut your eyes and you'd never know it wasn't a man playing!" Juno was emboldened to approach the rail, the better to take in both sides of the audience to make her own introduction to the next item on the program.

Earwig appeared disconcerted by this manoeuvre. She had begun to mumble a warning between her teeth. Leaning closer, Redfyre made out, "No, Juno darling! Not too close . . . Oh, do watch it!" Then, to Redfyre, a hasty, "So sorry, John! I have vertigo — rather disabling vertigo. It's so bad, I can't even bear to see others approach a drop."

"Then close your eyes," he advised, clapping heartily. "I'll tell you when to open them."

The angel's speaking voice did not disappoint. He'd anticipated the deep yet penetrating tone, bearing in mind her extraordinary lung capacity but the voice was also warm and intelligent. She spoke at an easy pace, giving just the right amount of information to what she assumed to be a knowledgeable audience. Having promised a piece of everyone's favourite Haydn concerto to follow, she paused and ran a quizzical eye over the rows. As though they had somehow earned her trust, she took a step even closer to the edge. (Earwig shuddered.) Head tilted slightly in a conspiratorial attitude, she spoke again, delivering an apparently unplanned confidence.

"Forgive me. I should have checked that the acoustics are all that one would wish . . ."

A concert audience was not accustomed to being consulted on such matters, but they responded at once. Smiles and grunts of approval broke out. A few soldierly thumbs were raised in reassurance. One daring and public-spirited chap even got to his feet and chirruped his assessment: Here, in the back row, apparently, the sound was well balanced and crystal-clear. Though perhaps he could use this opportunity to tell Cootie he was coming on a little heavy with the left foot?

Juno took this in the spirit in which it was offered — with amusement and an ironic bow. Redfyre was beginning to think that this musical sprite had all the aplomb of a Marie Lloyd facing a rowdy music hall audience. And they were readily seduced, caught by the casual intimacy of the exchange and warmed by the spirit of Yuletide. She held them in the palm of her hand, John reckoned. He was delighted when she decided to prolong the moment by giving an impromptu introduction to her instrument. She held it aloft and told them briefly how the shape had evolved and why it had started life as the voice of war. She conceded that, as a woman trumpeter, she was certainly a rarity, but she was not the first; she had been preceded by about three thousand years by the warrior women of the ancient world, the Amazons. There was a particularly lively depiction of one such giving a good blast on a very recognizable instrument on a black figure vase in the Fitzwilliam Museum, if they cared to go along and have a look.

"And up here, on high in this magnificent loft," she confided, "I'm taken back to an earlier time, a time when this heroic little instrument had its part to play in every citizen's life. To the very beginning of the trumpet's transformation from clarion of war into the supple and sophisticated concert performer we're hearing this evening. I'm taken back in particular to the watch towers of Medieval Europe. Mounted above the city gates in their wooden eyries, the watchmen would sound the trumpet at dusk and dawn to announce the opening and closing of the gates. And sometimes, more urgently, to warn of danger." She asked, like a kindly school mistress: "I wonder if anyone has heard the 'Hejnal Mariacki' played from the watch tower of Krakow?"

An excited young man in the third row was so carried away as to put up his hand. This was instantly hauled down with an admonishing cluck by his mother, seated next to him.

"Oh, good! Then you'll recognise this," Juno said, involving the lad and melting away his embarrassment at being caught showing a schoolboy's eagerness. "It's the warning a trumpeter of Krakow gave in the thirteenth century when he caught sight of a Mongol horde riding fast towards the city." She put the trumpet to her lips and there blared out a rousing five-note anthem, which she repeated. When she reached the tenth note, to everyone's alarm, it soared out of control and was abruptly cut off, sending an almost human shriek reverberating around the beamed ceiling.

The audience was aghast. They looked up anxiously, fearing she had played a wrong note. Had she got her tongue stuck?

32

Trapped a finger?

Juno staggered for a moment, took an uncertain step closer to the edge of the platform, wobbled, then regained her balance. As her eyes lifted to follow the wounded note into the ether she slowly lowered the trumpet and with her left hand clutched at her throat.

With perfect timing, a second before Redfyre and other alert ex-military men on their feet and poised to storm the organ loft could dash forward, she straightened up, put out a quieting hand and spoke to them again. "At this point, the sentry was shot in the throat by a Mongol archer," she explained. "Or so the story goes. An unduly harsh judgement, you might say, on a poor chap bravely doing his duty! And the townsfolk agreed, since the death note, in all its discord, has been played at dawn and dusk down the centuries to this day. And we remember that watchman."

A general release from suspense flooded through the audience at her sly humour and, under cover of the laughter and movement, Redfyre took hold of the small but strong hand that had clamped itself in terror onto his left arm and forgotten to let go. He detached it gently, patted it reassuringly and returned it to her lap.

"But the story of the trumpet bounds on," Juno pursued her theme, "particularly in the war-loving lands of the north. The mayor of one of these tough little towns noted down in the civic annals the very beginnings of the war trumpet's elevation to musical instrument. He was there on the spot!" she said, consumed with wonder and enthusiasm, further enmeshing her listeners. "This clerkly figure heard it and recognised the significance of what he was hearing. *'When our watchmen,'* he wrote, *'in the festive season play a sacred tune from the tower, the citizens gather to listen. We are very moved and imagine we can hear the angels singing.'* The mouthpiece of war and alarm had so sweetened and softened it was thought to be a voice from heaven."

She left a pause, knowing well that she had just transported every man and woman in the audience back through the centuries to a chilly central European Christmas, witnessing the birth of a new and sublime music. Then, involving them all in a confidence: "They're up there tonight, you know — the angels!" Like the rest of the listeners, Redfyre couldn't resist glancing up into the soaring oak beams, but caught no more than the impish eye of a carved Green Man keeping watch on proceedings from his niche. He could have sworn the old Pagan mischief-maker was trying to convey a grudging admiration for a fellow agitator.

Confident that they had shared her vision, she held out an invitation impossible to resist. "And here I am in my tower, halfway to Heaven — let's see if I can lure them down to make music with us." Returning to her performance spot, she raised her trumpet and added whimsically over her shoulder, "So, will any Mongolian music critics in the audience kindly leave now?"

"Tell me," Redfyre breathed into an ear that tilted readily towards him, "Exactly where did your friend acquire her stagecraft? The Royal Academy of Music, Regent's Park, or the Royal Palace of Varieties, Clapham?"

CHAPTER 2

The first half of the concert passed swiftly, ending with rousing applause from a happy audience. Redfyre noted but did not comment on Earwig's sigh, which seemed to him to be one of relief rather than pleasure. Had he communicated his own inexplicable tension to this stranger, or had she arrived trailing clouds of concern with her?

Remembering his manners, he turned to her and asked if he might accompany her into the winter-garden anteroom where rum punch and hot mince pies (just as promised by his aunt) were being served.

Earwig looked at her wristwatch. "We have half an hour," she commented. "So, yes, thank you. Easier, I think, to catch up on twenty years over a stiff drink, though I suppose a policeman, even off-duty, will feel obliged to settle for a lemonade. It's longer than the usual interval to allow the soloist time to catch her breath and change her costume, I expect."

"I thought it was extended for purposes of gossip. So much to say! Now, *I* was quite swept away in admiration. But some will consider we have just witnessed a scandalous performance," he murmured to test her out.

She glared at him. "I challenge you to spot a single empty seat when we return for the second half! No one looks in the least likely to stomp off hissing into the chilly night."

They settled, knee to knee on little gilt chairs, eyes taking each other's measure over a steaming glass of murkily purple liquid. Earwig tried it first, grimaced and took a second, more enthusiastic sip. Redfyre decided that, seen full-face, she was even more enchanting than in profile. Her short, thick hair had been Marcel-waved by an expert hand, but he was pleased to note that it was escaping the restraints of the Amami setting lotion and bouncing back into a natural exuberance to rival a feather duster. The flaxen hair he remembered had darkened to the deep gold of a newly minted George the Fifth penny. Her eyes were not the blue he had expected, but the more nuanced greenish-brown of a cat he'd been fond of. He remembered that a brown gaze signified purring affection; a green glare warned of imminent and painful retribution for some fancied slight.

"This is rather good," she pronounced. "Brandy base, not rum, I'd say. Red wine. They've managed to get their hands on some tangerines. It's well spiced — cinnamon, ginger — nice and fruity."

Redfyre recognised this for the inconsequential, nervous chatter of a stranger and was reassured. He decided to break the ice himself. "I'm puzzled! Did they keep you locked up in the nursery the day my brothers and I came to visit? On the occasion of the apple fight. I don't remember seeing you in the Stretton front line."

She nodded. "Oh, I was there all right. The smallest. I looked just like my brothers though, same haircut . . . green cord trousers and fisherman's sweater." Her grin was enchanting, full of mischief and nostalgia. "I think we kept an entire Irish fishing village busy knitting jumpers for us for years. I wore my brothers' hand-me-downs, and being the youngest, I was always the scruffiest, so people thought I must be a boy, too. My name gave no clue. I'm not sure my parents were even certain who I was. In any case, they only knew how to bring up boys — not very well, at that — and knowing nothing different, I just accepted it."

38

"But you kicked over the traces rather emphatically, somewhere along the line? I like the change! Though now I'm filled with guilt that perhaps, in all innocence, I may have aimed a windfall, or even worse, a fist, at that female nose."

The grin widened. "Heavens, no! I had more sense than to line up with the gang. I watched in a cowardly way from behind a tree, and when it dawned on me that Wulfie seriously meant to kill you, I ran off, grabbed the garden boy and asked him to come and stop the fight."

"Jonas did indeed save me from a battering," Redfyre said. "I add you to my list of guardian angels. Thank you! But tell me — Wulfie? Older than me by four or five years, I'd guess. Did he have a good war? Such an enterprising and belligerent character. He must have put heart and soul into whatever part he played." Disconcerted by an uncomfortable silence, he added with a lighthearted grimace, "You're about to tell me he's now a major-general?"

"He's a thug, you're right. Martial to the core. And he . . . um, yes, you could say he had a good war. Much decorated. Reached the rank of lieutenant-colonel." She looked thoughtfully at her punch, took another fortifying gulp and added, defiantly,

"Though fighting for the other side."

"I beg your pardon?"

"Rifles regiment, Hetty tells me you served with? Snipering? You could well have had Wulfie in the sights of your Enfield! Weren't you on the Marne? The Race to the Sea? Well, Wulfie was there too. Trying to stop you getting there. In a Saxon cavalry regiment, harrying British troops. The Tenth Magdeburg Hussars, raised in Saxony."

Redfyre was lost for words, finally murmuring: "So, Oberstleutnant Stretton was a dreaded Uhlan? Lancers regiment. Polish originally. Yes, we encountered some of those south of Rheims." His eyes clouded at disturbing memories. "The finest of horsemen. The most fearless. The most savage. Armed with sabers, pistols and lances. Ten foot long steel lances flying a pennant below the tip. Though those medieval weapons were swiftly jettisoned. They didn't survive contact with an equally determined French cavalry fighting hand to hand in the narrow lanes of their own native land." He'd reduced her to an embarrassed silence and spoke again more lightly, "Well, well! I can't imagine how Wulfie came to be recruited to the Kaiser's cause in Saxony. Magdeburg, you say? Isn't that way over to the east in Prussia, seat of Otto the Great, Holy Roman Emperor and all that?"

"It's on the River Elbe. A straight run down the river to the Baltic Sea. Next stop: Denmark and then England."

"Ah. Not so distant if you think like a Viking," he commented.

"Exactly. Wulfie . . . we . . . have . . . er, had cousins there. In Magdeburg. He spent every summer before the war there. He got on well with them. So well *he* signed up when *they* signed up, um . . ."

"In the spirit of the 'pals regiments,' " Redfyre supplied, attempting to cover his intense dislike of the entire Stretton clan. "Well, bully for Wulfie!"

"But our other brother, Aethelstan, chose to return home before hostilities broke out. He joined the Cambridgeshire Regiment," she added. Her tone, low and awkward, told him she'd picked up his sarcasm at once. She knew that her words did not go anywhere towards absolving her eldest brother of the supreme crime of treason.

"Wulfie had the good sense to stay over there in Germany when it was all over, I hope," Redfyre said coldly.

"Of course. He'd have been hanged, drawn and quartered or suffered whatever punishment they dole out in these enlightened times if he'd returned."

41

"I believe it's back against a wall of the Tower, facing a firing squad."

"Yes. Well, as you can imagine, Father went quite mad. A lot of: 'Never darken our doors again!' Went on for years. Wulfie didn't lose touch though. Pa refused to open his letters, but he didn't forbid me from reading them and passing on the gist. But in the family, we don't talk about it. I'd be obliged if you could keep Wulfie's indiscretion to yourself."

"Indiscretion! I'd have said: infamy, treachery, utter disgrace," Redfyre thought, but aloud, he said stiffly: "Of course. But I do wonder why you decided to confide in *me*? We've never been chums."

Earwig nodded. The conversation was clearly going exactly where she had planned that it should. He noted that her response was instant. "There *is* a hidden motive in seeing you this evening, as you seem to have guessed. I wanted to ask your advice. I was going to get around to it by a circuitous route, but those sharp eyes of yours tell me you're a step ahead and perhaps I should be prepared for that."

Redfyre was not an easy subject for flattery, and he didn't warn her that he was two steps ahead of where she assumed him to be. He listened, sporting an encouraging smile.

"Attacking you in the orchard was the first misjudgement of Wulfie's life. He'd never been defeated or thwarted before in any of his enterprises, and there'd been lots before you squared up to him. He thought himself invincible. It was a silly little incident, but he never forgot it, and he's a man like no other to bear a grudge. He made us children all swear a blood oath that we'd have revenge."

"Blood oath?" Redfyre asked in disbelief. He was unable to keep the distaste from his voice. "Bit of an overreaction, surely?"

"You don't know the half of it! We each had to prick our thumb until it bled, suck some out and spit it onto the corpse of a crow while saying your name and uttering a black oath."

"Ouch! Don't, please, repeat the dire phrase. You may strike me dead before I've finished this delicious brew." Redfyre saw that she was relieved that he was taking this for the nonsense it was.

"Still, that's Wulfie. Loves drama. He could have written the script for the Götterdämmerung! But I speak too harshly of him. Black sheep that he is, he does have redeeming features." She countered Redfyre's sardonic expression. "No — he does have a sense of humour. And his troubles in the war have given him a certain maturity. Like a good wine, it sometimes takes a few years in bottle at the right temperature before the true character comes out."

Redfyre had already seen where this story was leading and thought it was high time to cut it short. "I see. Tell me, when is he expected back in England?"

She gasped. Rather too dramatically, he felt. "Ah — yes. At any moment. My father, whose heir is still Wulfie, is . . . dying. At least, he's announced that he's dying. It's Wulfie's intention to return, rebuild bridges and make sure of his inheritance."

"Why didn't your father change his will if he was so displeased with his oldest son? He has several in reserve to choose from, I understand."

"He's never mentioned it. I've no idea what the terms are, nor has anyone I've spoken to. But daddy's lawyer has been about the place quite often recently. Nearly as frequent a visitor as the doctor. Getting things in order, you'd say. So there you are. Trouble ahead! I thought I should give you fair warning, since you're very much a local figure — and a policeman. That really is something Wulfie would despise. As you've guessed, he's on his way back home from Germany. You could well run into each other. I'm probably being unnecessarily cautious about this, but, well, it's the least I could do! I can't guarantee there'll be a Jonas on hand at the next encounter."

"What a load of piffle!" was Redfyre's judgement, but he censored it and replied pleasantly. "No need to fret, Miss Stretton, I'm sure. Your brother and I are both grown up, and we've both learned to survive. I've worn the bull's-eye on my back many times and lived to tell the tale! I'm sure Aethelwulf won't want to draw the attention of the law down onto himself, bearing in mind the personal circumstances you've revealed to me. He'll keep his head well below the parapet. So unless you ask me to tea again, our paths will never cross. We move in different circles socially, so the worst that can occur is that we will encounter each other by chance one dark night down by the river in Laundress Lane and only one of us will make it out to the Anchor for a restorative pint."

"Laundress Lane? Sinister little alleyway! Wulfie wouldn't be caught dead or alive down there. Not his style at all. No, you're more likely to meet by appointment on Jesus Green, at dawn — your choice of

45

weapon, a doctor and two seconds standing about, biting their nails."

Catching a genuine agitation disguised by frivolity, he gave her a warm smile and told her, "All will be well, Miss Stretton. But feel free to contact me again. I'll give you my card, should anything else be troubling you."

He looked at her steadily, wondering if this was the moment she would come clean and tell him the real reason for this contrived meeting with an officer of the Cambridge CID, but she merely smiled, her cat's eyes narrowing briefly before she accepted a mince pie from the plate he held out. All in good time. He guessed that her real problem, the one that had provoked Hetty's strange ticket distribution, remained undisclosed, was still worrying her and, in some way he had not yet fathomed, involved *him.*

The second half of the concert took on a party mood from the first moment of Juno's reappearance on the platform. She had changed into a shiny, dark-red ankle-length gown, low cut, and the white slopes of her upper bosom were covered with an unashamedly extravagant piece of costume jewellery: a cascade of rubies in a gold setting. On her head, in place of a formal tiara, she'd jokingly placed a wreath of dark holly enlivened by bright red berries. The Angel of Purity had changed into the Spirit of Christmas, and the audience responded to the change with warm applause. The program for this part of the evening had taken on a seasonal flavour as well, and one riotous and well-known anthem followed another. Aunt Hetty's assurance that Redfyre wouldn't be called upon to sing proved ill-founded, as after the first piece — a jolly "In Dulci Jubilo," it was clear that Juno could not rein in the audience's enthusiasm a moment longer. With perfect judgement, she invited them to join in with the words of "Deck the Halls."

Redfyre looked at Earwig and grinned in delight. He plunged in, offering up his warm baritone unselfconsciously, years of school choir training buoying him up. Earwig sang squeakily, hitting one note in three, he estimated. She knew all the words, but was not having the happy time that the rest of the congregation was enjoying. Carried away by the jaunty tune, the punch-fired, unbuttoned humour of the crowd and not least by the joyous trumpeting, Redfyre seized the hand next to him and boldly gave it a squeeze. She smiled nervously in acknowledgement, but delicately detached it and struggled to catch up with the chorus.

At the end of the piece he leaned to her and murmured, "I think I must have died and gone to heaven! I don't think I want this banquet of the senses to end."

Earwig frowned and looked at her watch again. "Do you suppose they'll keep her up there playing lots of encores?" she asked, her voice thick with concern.

"No! It's hardly the Alhambra. It's a Cambridge crowd. Well-mannered and aware of how exhausting playing the trumpet is. They won't insist."

The close of the program was, like the rest of it, well managed by both audience and players. There were polite but enthusiastic cries for more, and these were dealt with by a smiling Christopher Coote, who stepped forward to explain that Miss Proudfoot had borne the long program with exemplary stamina, but there was a limit to even her prowess and lung power. Nevertheless, he knew (he turned to Juno for a nod of acknowledgement) that she would not be able to tear herself from such a wonderfully responsive audience without leaving them with one last bonbon. Were there any suggestions?

As skilled as Juno at handling the crowd, he skated over all the well-known tunes proposed from below until he heard the one he was waiting for. " 'Hark, The Herald Angels Sing,' did someone say? Excellent suggestion! That's it. First and last verses."

Five joyous minutes later, that was that. The musicians waved a final goodbye to their noisily appreciative audience and remained up in their tower, pottering about packing up their instruments. Wasting time, Redfyre guessed, until the crowd had put on its gloves and scarves and moved out, calling to friends, giving and accepting invitations for nightcaps and a little last hot savoury on toast. "Welsh rarebit do you, Wilfred? A little oxtail soup? Cook's waiting up. Join me in a snifter? You'd be very welcome," Redfyre overheard behind him, and would at that moment have gladly swapped places with Wilfred, whoever he was. Two by two, they began to shuffle out, still humming the ancient tunes and pausing in the archway to run appreciative eyes over the medieval fairytale setting the frost-spangled courtyard offered them. Following the pale gold puffballs of light from the line of Victorian lamps leading to the great gate, they began the tramp back to the hearths they'd left carefully banked and guarded to provide a warm welcome home.

So, Aunt Henrietta! What on earth had been the point of this unexpected evening? He could only infer: matchmaking. Another failed effort to fix him up with a suitable girl. Fearing worse, his suspicious nature had unnecessarily put him through two hours of increasing tension and, while he'd much enjoyed Juno Proudfoot's performance, he now found himself with a prickly stranger on his hands. On his arm, rather. He extended the arm with automatic good manners to escort her from the chapel. To a taxi? Had Daddy sent the car for her? That would be the ideal end to the evening, releasing him to wave goodbye and nip into the Blue Boar for a pint on the way home. The singing had given him quite a thirst. He was deciding between Greene King and Guinness as they began to move forward at the pace of the crowd around them when his pleasant state of anticipation was shattered by a piercing dread.

The evening was not yet over, and these last few moments when crowds were milling about in an uncontrolled way with all the exits wide open could be exploited.

Redfyre would never rightly know what instinct, what subliminal sound had triggered his reaction. He dropped Earwig's arm and pushed his way towards the staircase to the organ loft. The door was closed, the brocade hangings in place over it. Fools! The two players would at any moment now be attempting to come down those high, narrow stairs in pitch blackness. Some attendant should have eased forward, cleared the exit and brought in a light as soon as it was evident they had reached the end of the performance. He tore back the drapery and seized the handle to the door.

The thud and the scream from the stairs rang out as he threw the door open and stood in alarm, trying to penetrate the darkness and make sense of the series of bumps and jagged cries cascading towards him. He rushed at the staircase, blindly reaching out his hands to break the momentum of whatever alarming avalanche was about to engulf him. To his horror, before he could climb a step, he was knocked backward, his outstretched arms filled with the slippery, satin-clad form and flopping rag-doll limbs of Juno Proudfoot, falling headfirst, bloodied and senseless, to the ground.

CHAPTER 3

He dragged her body into the light and set about searching for signs that she was still alive. Through his concern, he was aware in the background of a clutch of elderly gentlemen responding urgently to the situation. A cordon of chairs was being set up around the scene, and the departing audience urged to keep clear and leave without panic. Someone called loudly up the stairs, "I say, Doctor Coote! Bit of a problem down here. Miss Proudfoot has sustained a fall. Do not attempt to descend yourself until further advised."

A second self-appointed lieutenant, young and limber, announced he was going to run to the Porter's Lodge to make a phone call summoning an ambulance from the hospital. He merely raised an eyebrow and sketched a salute when Redfyre shouted at him, "And the police as well. Request Sergeant Thoday, will you? Say Inspector

Redfyre is already in attendance at an incident requiring their instant attention."

But it was Earwig's response that surprised him. No screams or palpitations. The girl who had appeared to him brittle and distracted — antagonistic even — was now all calm and focus. She threw herself to her knees opposite Redfyre, peeled her fur coat from her shoulders and placed it decorously over the undefended curves of Juno's body. She pushed away his hand, which was indecisively hovering over potential pulse points. "Behind the ear is a good place to start," she said, firmly tweaking aside the holly wreath lying crushed and displaced on the girl's head. "She doesn't seem to be breathing, but I could swear her eyelid fluttered just now. Yes, here — check this for me. I'm sure that's a pulse." She guided Redfyre's hand to the small white ear and placed his finger on exactly the right spot.

"Confirm," he said, with memories of countless battlefield checks for life coming back to him. They had been devastating, but expected and dealt with methodically by firm, steady fingers. His current emotional state, faced with the warm but ominously still form in front of him, was washing this way and that. His instinct was pushing him, incongruously, to gather the girl up in his arms and hug her back to consciousness, murmuring, "There, there, little one, that was a nasty tumble," as he had done many times for over-adventurous nephews and nieces. A potentially fatal manoeuvre. A glance into the challenging green eyes opposite him stiffened his spine. He resorted to soldierly brevity. "Pulse confirmed," he repeated. "She's alive." He stilled his fingers and gently palpated her neck. "Nothing broken there, I'd say, wouldn't you? Skull?" A further gentle exploration, then: "All in one piece. No bleeding of the scalp. No swelling yet. The dribbles of blood on her face are caused by scratches from the holly leaves, I think, nothing more sinister. Still oozing — another good sign. Abrasions to arms and shoulders."

"Nothing a little arnica won't cure . . . and her back?"

"I won't risk an examination by turning her over — it might make a bad situation worse."

"Of course. We should leave that to the medic to verify."

Their hissed exchanges were interrupted by a polite cough. The gentleman with the stentorian voice who'd called up to the organist had been keeping an eye on proceedings, efficiently deflecting the public's attentions. They appeared to accept his authority without demur. He inquired of Redfyre, "May I announce to all and sundry that Miss Proudfoot is still with us? The crowd is congealing, feet dragging — not out of morbid curiosity, but because they would like to be of assistance. I've collected offers of handkerchiefs, smelling salts and a lift home in a Rolls Royce. If I could re-assure them that all is well, they might get a move on and clear the hall before the authorities arrive."

"Good thought! Certainly say she appears unharmed by her . . . let's call it a 'tumble,' and they may leave everything to us. Miss Stretton here is her friend — and a nurse," he improvised, "and I'm Detective Inspector Redfyre with the Cambridge CID. You are Mister . . . ?"

"Doctor Henningham. Sadly not a doctor of medicine, but you seem to be managing quite well. Ladies! Gentlemen!" He turned a smile that beamed comfort on the people shuffling by. "All is well! And in good hands. We have professional staff in attendance. Miss Proudfoot will soon be up and tooting again after her tumble. Please hurry to clear the gangways now! The ambulance crew will be appearing at any moment."

A wail from the loft distracted Redfyre from his attentions and he looked up, anxious and angry. Henningham read his thoughts and reacted at once. He turned and projected his fine voice up to the loft. "Doctor Coote! A little patience please! There may be a fault with the staircase. You would be most unwise to venture on to it before its structure has been checked. I will arrange for your rescue."

Looking back at Redfyre, he added thoughtfully, "And perhaps when he descends he will be able to enlighten us as to why we have, playing Humpty Dumpty at our feet, a Miss Proudfoot rather than a Doctor Coote. I do wonder why he did not precede his partner down the stairs. Remind me of the etiquette, Redfyre. I was always taught to take the lead when escorting a lady up a staircase. For obvious gallant reasons. Checking the way is clear, avoiding glimpses of underwear and so on. But also to precede her when *descending,* to prevent just such occurrences as this evening's. Or have I got that wrong?"

Redfyre almost smiled. "I shall enjoy hearing you put it to him. We'll leave him where he is for the moment. There are many questions I have to ask that young man. Now —

did you mention smelling salts? Any chance
. . . ?"

Doctor Henningham turned out his pockets. "I thought you bobbies were supposed
to carry supplies with you. Let's see, they've
thrust all sorts of goodies at me. Hankies, a
tin of Wintergreen ointment, a hip flask of
cherry brandy and — yes, here it is. Might
be just the thing." He produced a tiny silver
bottle attached to a chain, twisted off the
lid and sniffed the contents warily. His head
jerked back in automatic revulsion. "Argh!
Yes, that's the stuff! Ammonia. A whiff of
that — it takes your head off!" He handed
it to Earwig. "Here, you're meant to insert
the pointed end into a nostril, I should
imagine. Clever little device!"

Earwig took one look at it, snatched it
from him crossly and put it away in her bag.
"Exactly! More likely to kill than revive! An
abrupt evasive movement in an unconscious
person can do damage to muscles and
bones. This chemical can burn the mucous
membrane of the nose and the lining of the
lungs. And *that's* something she wouldn't
thank you for! Hand me the brandy." She
took her own handkerchief from her bag
and poured a stream of brandy onto it,
folded it into a point and pushed it into the
girl's mouth. No one tried to stop her. To

Earwig's great satisfaction, Juno stirred, moaned and began to flutter her eyelids. Earwig withdrew the brandy-soaked linen and began to murmur reassurance. The movements grew stronger and more purposeful as consciousness returned until the eyes opened fully and Juno looked about her in puzzlement. Redfyre thought he'd just witnessed a textbook recovery.

At this point, the professional lawman asserted himself, keen to hear the all-important first reaction to the plight she was in. "You're safe, Miss Proudfoot," he told her. "I'm with the police. What have you to tell me?"

Her mouth opened, but no sound came at first. After a deep breath, she tried again. "I'd like some more brandy."

Earwig offered the flask and skilfully dribbled a further shot of the bramble-coloured life saver between the eager lips. A sigh of what sounded very like contentment followed this process and then: "Why am I lying under a fur rug? Fur makes me sneeze. I say, do move aside and let me get up. I can twitch my fingers and waggle my toes so I think there's nothing broken. Though my head hurts." She pushed aside the fur and brought one of her hands into view. "Hell's Bells! What's this?" she exclaimed, holding something towards Redfyre.

It was still tightly clutched in her hand, twining down her white arm like the asp on its way to Cleopatra's bosom. A length of twisted dark green satin rope of the kind you'd use to make a curtain tie-back or a bell-pull, Redfyre judged. Three feet long with a loop at each end. He extricated it from her grasp, rolled it up and put it in his pocket. "Possibly the reason for your fall, Miss," he said. "Thank you for hanging on to the evidence!"

The medical crew arrived with gratifying speed, to no one's surprise since the hospital was just a quarter of a mile's distance. Juno Proudfoot had been recovering at such a pace that Redfyre thought she might well spurn the stretcher, declare herself walking wounded and set off down Kings Parade under her own steam but after only the slightest hesitation, she smiled her gratitude and allowed herself to be lifted aboard. "No need to alert anyone," she confided to the doctor in charge. "Miss Stretton here and I are acquainted. She will act as my representative, signing me in and out, making telephone calls. She'll do whatever's necessary — except pay the bill, perhaps!"

The doctor was glad to hear her make a joke, however feeble. He seemed to be warming to this girl. Provocatively clad in satin and rubies, bruised and bloodied in her battered head wreath and reeking fruitily of brandy, she looked like nothing so much as the survivor of a Saturnalian orgy and had made an unfortunate first impression on the young man, though the concerned chorus of detective inspector, college don and female companion in elegant evening attire had gone some way to reassure him.

"We'll keep your friend in overnight for observation, Miss. Sometimes a blow on the head shows delayed symptoms. It's not necessary for you to accompany her, but if you wish . . ."

Redfyre firmly drew the doctor aside and spoke to him quietly. "I'd rather she didn't skip off. Miss Stretton will be staying with me for the moment. She's a witness to what may well turn out to be a crime."

"A crime?" The doctor looked back at Juno in some puzzlement. "Falling down a dark staircase is hardly a crime, surely?"

"Attempted murder is a crime in my book," said Redfyre. "This apparent accident will be investigated as such. A stair tread tampered with, a push in the back, a trip . . . not unfamiliar. I would be most grateful if you could bear that in mind when

60

you carry out your more detailed examination at the hospital."

"Indeed? Well, of course. A sort of 'antemortem' report? Understood."

Doctor Henningham, still serenely in the role of master of ceremonies, approached to say goodbye to Juno as they prepared to cart her off, tucked up in hospital blankets against the cold. "Don't worry, Miss Proudfoot. The College will do whatever it possibly can to see that this matter is accounted for and resolved."

She gave him a meltingly lovely smile. "I'm so grateful, Mister, um . . ."

"Henningham. Doctor Henningham. Master of the College."

"I might have guessed!" She spoke with the saucy grin of one who is confident that sickness grants a license for overfamiliarity. "I say, Master — could you have my trumpet found and returned to me? I must have left it up on the platform."

As soon as she was out of earshot, Earwig turned on him. "Now! Staying with you — a witness to a crime? What was all that nonsense about? I'm going home to Melford or to see Juno at Addenbrooke's, as and when the fancy takes me. You will not try to stop me."

"I'd prefer your cooperation, of course,

but if necessary I'll handcuff you to a pew," he said in a playful tone intended to assure that he was joking for the moment, but that she would regret testing him. "The next hour or so is going to be boring for you as we set up a crime scene, and I don't want you slipping off when my back's turned. Here comes Sergeant Thoday, and — ah, good man! — he brings a police constable and my murder bag."

Another desperate cry from above made them both raise their heads.

"Ah, yes, the essential witness to all this . . . Doctor Coote! Prepare to descend!" he yelled up to the organist. "Here comes your means of exit." A vertiginously tall, scaffolding-like piece of equipment was being trundled towards the loft by a team of porters in aprons. "I think they use it to climb up and dust the candelabra," Redfyre said. "I hope the chap has a head for heights. But regardless, I can't have him trampling on evidence or putting his foot through a duff stair tread."

"Impressive and ingenious," said Earwig, dusting herself down. "And the spectacle of Coote in festal gown and polished Oxfords scrambling down promises to be entertaining! Almost sorry I have to miss the show. Well, you know where to find me, I think.

Good luck, and please thank your aunt for an unforgettable evening, will you? I'll be writing to her, of course." She clicked shut the catch of her handbag with finality and turned to leave.

Redfyre had been prepared to be cast aside like a soiled glove all evening, but the arrogant finality of the gesture annoyed him. He felt that this girl had made use of him (and perhaps his aunt, as well) in the pursuit of schemes she had certainly not revealed to him, and he was determined to find out much more about little Earwig before she quick-stepped out of his life. Redfyre seized her arm and, beckoning to the advancing sergeant, told him, "Sarge, this is Miss Stretton who is an important witness. She's under police protection and not allowed out of my sight. I want you to keep an eye on her, and if she tries to sneak off, use your cuffs to restrain her."

The young sergeant appeared unsurprised by the order. He looked Earwig up and down coolly from his intimidating six-foot height and nodded. "Understood, sir. Cuffs it is."

"Now listen." Redfyre turned back to his witness, who was beginning to splutter and hiss like a kettle on the front burner. "I will hear what you have to tell me, including a full account of your presence here this evening, but, unlike a crime scene, *you* are transportable and do not decay. So, you must allow me to give precedence to the staircase. I'll do what's necessary here, and then we'll leave to conduct the interview in more comfortable surroundings."

He realized he'd unwittingly turned up the gas when his promise was greeted by what Redfyre considered a boiling-over.

"Comfortable surroundings? *Huh!* Police headquarters on Saint Andrew's Street, I expect you mean! The Old Spinning House — is that what you have in mind for me? Good Lord! A night on the treadmill until I confess to something? How dare you. I refuse to go there!"

"You know as well as I do that the medieval torture that occurred in the Spinning House ceased when the Police Force took over the building twenty years ago." Redfyre was trying for a patient reply to the insult, but his annoyance that he'd allowed her to trip him into a testy riposte broke through. Countering the often-repeated jibes — even only jokes — that came his way regarding the sinister origins of the local force had grown wearisome. He could well appreciate that a period of three hundred years of horrific and unjust punishment carried out in the forbidding prison building in Saint Andrew's Street had so deeply etched itself into the town's psyche that a mere two decades of change and improvement had not gone far to erase its memory.

The more so since the replacement public building failed to raise spirits. Squat, meanly appointed and insignificant though it was, it still managed to be threatening. Unsurprisingly, in most people's minds it remained the hated "Spinning House," and Cambridge women still crossed themselves when they hurried by in front of it. Redfyre crossed himself when he hurried into it.

His irritation led him to add, tight-voiced as any schoolmaster, "The treadmill and the spinning machines are long gone, Miss, and females are no longer swept up off the streets and punished for prostitution."

"And I have your assurance that no police minion with dirty fingernails will shamble forward to ascertain the state of my virginity? Are you saying the Town Crier is no longer paid to discipline ladies of pleasure with his whip for ten bob a session?"

There it was again: the Stretton challenge. The unnecessary confrontation. But why? He decided to ascribe her bad manners to shock and concern for her friend.

Faced with her insistence on open warfare,

he decided to reply lightly to her contrived and, he judged, deliberately provoking indignation. "Oh, these days, the bobby on the desk is more likely to give riotous ladies sixpence for a taxi ride home to their Mum's and glad to be rid. I'm sure you know that. Please don't waste precious time making feminist points that are so easily demolished. You devalue the currency of your argument."

"Pompous prat!" Earwig said, voicing his own estimation of his performance. He grinned, unabashed, and continued, "I promised 'more comfortable surroundings' for our chat and you may hold me to that. Now, do you want to come and examine those stairs with me? Or will what we find up there be no surprise to *you*? Flashlight, Sarge? Thank you."

While Sergeant Thoday set about assembling and taking down names of witnesses in his notebook under the supervision of the master, Redfyre undertook the first examination of the lethal staircase alone, his invitation to Earwig having been coldly rejected, as he calculated it would be. No woman in her senses would have agreed to a scrummage on a dark and dubious set of stairs with an equally dark and dubious police inspector. He dug about in the large Gladstone bag his officers referred to indulgently as his "murder bag" and took out a pair of thin rubber gloves, which he proceeded to slip on with no sign of awkwardness, though some curious looks were exchanged amongst those remaining in the hall.

The uniformed police constable directed the powerful beam of a police torch upwards from the base, and Redfyre held a smaller one in his hand as he climbed the stairs slowly, checking each step for stability and signs of tampering. The handrail was also a subject of his scrutiny, but he was careful to touch it as little as possible. When he descended, he addressed the sergeant. "Interesting! That's all I can do for tonight, Sarge. Too many shadows." His eyes flashed around, checking his bearings, and located the south windows opposite the stair. "Order up the usual team, will you, for fingerprinting? Tomorrow — we want the best light on this. I'll have a word with some of the witnesses right now. Got their addresses? Some I'll have to visit later for statements. If, of course, this proves to be a crime of some sort. After a chat with Miss Proudfoot tomorrow, it may be we can all come off watch and go back to stirring our

Christmas puddings."

He ran an eye over the concerned half dozen men who had stayed behind. He was disturbed by a presence and an absence. He failed to spot the face he was looking for. "Master?" He caught the ready attention of Henningham, who was quietly talking with an agitated Christopher Coote. "The young gentleman whose job it was to arrange for the lighting of the stairs prior to descent — I don't see him here. I didn't see him at the *moment critique,* either!"

"Bunked off early, are we thinking? Deserted his post and left the lady in the dark?" The master frowned. "Not his style at all! Thomas Tyrrell. A most meticulous young man. One of our music scholars." He looked about him and asked loudly: "Anyone seen Tyrrell?"

The general opinion, muttered in puzzled tones, seemed to be that young Thomas had been lost to sight immediately after he had ushered the performers up the stairs for the concert to restart after the interval. The sergeant flourished his notebook with eyebrow cocked and pencil poised.

"Note that he is a member of this college but, being in his second year, lives out in the town with a landlady. He's in digs. His lodgings are somewhere out on the Newmarket Road I believe . . . Or was it Maids Causeway? Enquire at the porter's office, will you? They'll have all the details of domicile you need there." He rested a large hand on Redfyre's shoulder and said confidentially, "I say, can I leave all this in your capable hands, old chap? I'm not feeling too good. Bit wobbly, don't you know! Should never have had that second glass of punch. There's nothing much I can add, I think, so I'll leave you to your witnesses and clear off back to my roost."

Redfyre said his farewell and took over. "Sarge, get a message delivered. I want Mister Tyrrell found and warned that I shall need urgently to have a word or two tomorrow morning. I'll see him in his college. Now I'm going to have a few words with Doctor Coote, and then, Master, if you don't mind, I'll leave my team here to cordon off the area and tidy up. The constable will remain on duty for the night, but everyone else may go about their business. Thank you, everyone, for your help with this distressing situation." He glanced around, seeing the bright, open expressions of men eager to help dimming with disappointment at the lack of resolution, a feeling of deflation at the end of what had been such a triumphant musical performance. He was keen to avoid sending them home with a sour taste in their mouths, so he added, chin raised, "How fortunate we are that the heroine of the evening appears unscathed by her fall, in both body and spirit! I'm sure we'll all be hearing from Miss Proudfoot again before long." And he added, flooding them all with a warm optimism, "Entertaining the angels in Cambridge!"

"Hear! Hear! Look forward to that!"

"Wonderful evening, apart from the . . . um . . ."

"Lucky escape, what!"

"Addenbrooke's will see she's all right."

"Glad you were there, old chap! Well done!"

One by one, they shook Redfyre's hand with a cheery, distancing comment and went on their way, duty done, hurrying now to escape to their warm homes and their suppers with a dashed good story to tell — a story in which they'd played a part. It even had a happy ending to please an eager audience.

The last man had deliberately hung back and now stood silently, waiting to take his leave. A figure designed not to draw attention to itself, Redfyre reckoned. Of medium height, dark-suited, fedora in hand, a polite smile enlivening his pale features, the man put out his hand with exaggerated ceremony, clearly anticipating a rejection by the inspector. Redfyre seized the hand offered and retained it, holding it in a tighter grip than circumstances warranted. He drew the man aside and murmured in his ear. "Mister Scrivener, I believe? I'm rather surprised that you've chosen to make yourself known. The sixth entry in the sergeant's list of interesting parties? I see you failed to state your profession, sir. I think I have the pleasure of addressing Sebastian Scrivener, chief reporter on the Cambridge Tittle-Tattle? The particular slant of the articles you put out in the summer might well have warned of a frosty reception from the law. I'd have given me a wide berth if I were you."

"Pleased to meet you too, Inspector, at last. You're a rather unapproachable fellow." The smile was easy, unimpressed by Redfyre's sarcastic growling.

"*Crime* correspondent, if I'm not mistaken?"

"I just report on life — and death — as I find it, Inspector," was the bland reply. "In an impartial way, of course."

"And I just arrest troublemakers, wasters of police time and tormentors of the English language. In a likewise impartial way."

71

Icy smiles were exchanged.

"A trumpet enthusiast like me, I was astonished to note," Scrivener said. "I wasn't aware our local plod had musical sensitivities. An ear for the classics? I wouldn't have thought they knew their Arne from their elbow! But crime — of special interest to both of us, surely? Was there crime done here this night? Was there bloodshed?" he enquired innocently, eyes scanning the medieval tiles under his feet in mock disbelief.

"You have a lot of questions, sir, and I'm not answering any of them. There's nothing for you to report. Unless you think a patch of gore streaming from the nose of the newshound who'd upset the chief plod would be of interest to the readers? There, I can oblige. No?" Redfyre asked easily. "Then do at least let me help you with your copy. That much I am able to do, knowing what your readers expect — indeed I *am* one of them — I suggest:

A delighted audience was treated to a memorable concert by two up-and-coming young musicians. Miss Proudfoot (trumpet) wore a gown by Captain Molyneux of London and Paris. Doctor Coote (organ) wore a gown by Messrs. Ede and Ravenscroft of Trumpington Street, Cambridge.

A Christmas cornucopia of ancient music by composers from Albinoni to Zieleński was much enjoyed. The evening ended with a rousing rendition by soloists and audience of that old favourite: "Hark! The Herald Angels Sing." We all went home humming the tunes.

"See if you can squeeze that on to page eleven. If you need any help with the spelling of 'Mikolaj Zieleński,' just give me a ring."

As he left, Scrivener breathed a comment on the inspector. Amused, Redfyre added "toffee-nosed toss-pot" to "pompous prat" in his evening's haul of appreciative reviews.

A weary hour later, Redfyre dismissed Christopher Coote and turned to his uniformed staff to deliver final instructions, then looked about for Earwig, certain that she had disobeyed him and gone off without permission. He had no right to detain her, and he was sure that she'd seen through his bluster. He was quite sure also that she had a good deal of worldly knowledge and experience outside the repertoire of most women her age.

Suddenly, she was out of the shadows and

at his side. "Somewhere more comfortable, I think you promised?"

Any other female speaking those words while linking her arm through a gentleman's in such a familiar way would have been thought to show flirtatious intent, if not erotic promise. From Earwig Stretton, the words carried all the allure of an invitation to tea with the Spanish Inquisition.

Still, at least she'd decided to stay. "Yes, shall we get this over with? The taxis will all have disappeared." He glanced at her feet. "How well are you shod?"

She stuck out a foot for inspection and gave him a derisive smile. "I never wear anything I can't outrun a policeman in. These shoes are the softest of leather, but they'll take me anywhere you may suggest, unless you're proposing a spot of night climbing over the rooftops. For that, I should have to find my gym shoes."

"And conveniently *lose* your vertigo?" he asked, not expecting an answer and not disappointed when he didn't get one.

Once out in the courtyard they both stopped, speechless — breath caught by the sudden onslaught of cold air, hearts stopped by the unearthly beauty of the December night. They looked up silently at the roof-tops of the colleges. Elegantly frosted by a slight fall of snow, a Gustave Doré landscape of pinnacles, turrets, domes and cornices unfolded above them, outlined against the dark sky by a three-parts-rounded, hunch-backed moon.

Redfyre broke the too-long silence. "Ah, moon be waxing gibbous!" he said, affecting a practical countryman's voice in an awkward attempt to avoid any comment that might have been interpreted as romantic. He couldn't imagine an evening and a place more conducive to romance and with the right girl on his arm the possibilities would have been intoxicating. Instead of resorting to the words of his wartime sergeant, a Suffolk man who'd announced the weather and the phases of the moon over No Man's Land every night, he'd have selected some choice words of Shakespeare, because no other poet would have been equal to expressing his feelings. But, present company being so clearly the wrong girl, he found his ragbag brain had come up with Sergeant Rose's "waxing gibbous."

Earwig shuddered. At his verbal clumsiness? Probably, but at least she echoed his unromantic mood. "Spooky!" she said. "The moon in any shape has always scared me stiff. Have you noticed it always comes up in a direction you weren't expecting? It slides in and spies on us. You turn around and there it is, whispering, 'I know what you did!' It drives people mad."

"I think Mark Twain must have had the same feelings of foreboding," Redfyre said, reaching for a writer he thought he could count on to be a favourite with a girl brought up with boys and much in tune with Redfyre's own good-humoured skepticism. *" 'Everyone is a moon,'* he said, *'and has a dark side which he never shows to anybody.' "*

"Oo! Do you have a mysterious dark side you never show to anyone, John? I mean, as well as the mysterious dark side you present to the world."

"Me? Side, front, back — all as clear as a mountain stream."

Breaking the mood, he urged her to move on. "No night climbing tonight. It's the off-season, even for those with a head for it. So how about a little night walking? What do you say to a quarter of a mile through the most civilised streets of this fair city?" he said with a bonhomie he didn't feel. "A few cobbles and a haunted lane to negotiate, but you have a chivalrous right arm to fend off the drunks and a chivalrous left to hold on to, should the pavements have iced over while we've been in here communing with

the angels. Or was it the devil? I'm hoping
you'll tell me, Earwig."

CHAPTER 4

In the parlour of the Blue Boar, nineteen-year-old Thomas Tyrrell was kissing his first girl.

If this *was* kissing? He couldn't be certain, but she'd allowed him to apply his eager lips to her ear and remain there in contact for longer than was quite proper. The ear was silky and cold and smelled of an English herb garden. *Pears* soap. At least he recognised the scent. The brand's advertising jingle came reassuringly to mind: *"Preparing to be a beautiful lady . . ."* Yet another indication that the girl he was nuzzling like an over-eager colt was indeed a lady. A girl from his world, where the ladies' bathroom was supplied with Pears soap, the gentlemen's with bars of bracing Coal Tar. He'd heard that "girls of the town" put Soir de Paris or something equally bold behind their ears and on their necks to ensnare innocent young scholars. Rouged cheeks and lipstick were another indication of a loose woman. He glanced down. The full pink lips were alluring, but their sweet curves owed nothing to artifice, not even a sheen of Vaseline.

Lois, she'd said her name was. And her appearance was as smart as her name. Fashionably short calf-length dress, bobbed hair under a cheeky fur toque, matching fur wrap slung casually over one shoulder, giving her the air of a dashing Hussar from an earlier age. Very pretty, and too young for such a sophisticated outfit, he reckoned. The kind of girl who normally turned her nose up at undergraduates. Thomas had often wondered how on earth you found such a girl. And now he knew. You didn't. She found you. Barely five minutes into the interval, he was still adjusting the curtains on the stairs when she'd approached him, looking quite distraught. He'd hurried to offer assistance, and she'd asked him to help her find her handbag, carelessly left under her seat.

He'd calmed her girlish flutterings with a confident male optimism that the bag would turn up. No one in this audience would dream of walking off with it, and if it had been picked up, it would have been handed in to him as he stood on duty at the door. But someone might well have unintentionally displaced it with a clumsy foot in the rush for the refreshment room. If the worst occurred, he promised her that he'd give her a shilling for her taxi fare home. In a show of efficiency, he had established in which section she had been seated and suggested they start their search, Lois at the front, himself at the back and working towards the middle.

It was surprising what people had chosen to temporarily abandon under and on their seats, Thomas thought, encountering a pair of gum boots (what on earth did the owner currently have on his feet?), a thermos flask, a copy of *War and Peace* and many hats and scarves. On his second row, he came upon a lady's bag. Black leather, as she'd specified. He called out Lois's name and held it up triumphantly to show her. To his disappointment, it was received with a pantomime he'd seen employed by his little sisters. The thumb of one hand went down, while simultaneously the thumb and forefinger of the other pinched her nose in a gesture of disgust, usually accompanied by "Yikes! Smelly!" or some such. He looked again at the bag and saw his mistake. He'd fished out an up-from-the-country, district-nurse bag, capacious and battered. He put it back where he'd found it.

A moment later, he came upon another bag, lurking unseen under a fallen striped college scarf. Not an evening bag, but small and neat, like the girl herself. Not wishing to look the fool a second time, Tyrrell was in a dilemma. He resolved it quickly by ducking down below the seats and surreptitiously opening the bag. He'd no idea what he was looking for, but as soon as he turned his torch on it, he knew he'd found the right one. The beam skipped over a reassuringly rich and predictable female clutter, highlighting a gleam of silver, a wisp of white lace handkerchief, a glint of enamel from a tiny implement he recognised as Cartier perfume spray. Better yet, in plain view was an envelope addressed in bold writing to a Miss L. Lawrence at "Midsummer View" on de Montfort Avenue. One of those big, red-brick houses across the river, occupied by bank managers, city councillors and other overblown characters — nouveau riche, he'd heard them called.

Smiling relief and gushing gratitude, she'd settled down with him in a pew and he watched while she opened her bag, on his advice, to check that the contents were intact. A silver powder compact, a key ring, a diary, the perfume spray, a bag of mint humbugs, a purse with rather a large number of pound and ten shilling notes folded into it, all proved to be present and correct. No wonder she'd been concerned! Even then, he'd wondered about the cash. Could she be a working woman? Friday was payday, after all, in the mysterious world outside where people, some of them female these days, had jobs.

They'd talked on long after it was necessary. It had been surprisingly easy. A brief exchange of names and they'd plunged into a discussion of the performance. She seemed to know a lot about music and was flatteringly interested in his own musical career and his tastes. All too soon, the ten minute bell sounded the approaching end of the interval, and they had turned to look at each other in dismay.

"You must excuse me, Miss . . . er, Lois." He'd stumbled through a swift account of the duties he had now to perform to ease the progress of Miss Proudfoot to the loft and get the second half of the concert underway.

She'd clutched at his arm. "You must do your officiating, of course! Never neglect a duty. But I won't leave you there, Thomas," she'd said, "in the middle of a sentence. It's 1923, not 1823, and I won't behave like a Jane Austen heroine. We have lots more to say to each other, so why don't we continue our conversation somewhere else? I'll wait for you at the main door, and when you've finished whisking about, scattering rose petals and making safe the way of Her Ladyship, we can slip out together! We'll have an hour all to ourselves."

They'd sneaked out together. It had been her idea to come here.

Discreetly seated in the parlour of the Blue Boar, it suddenly occurred to him that, having dashed out in his academic dress, he had absolutely no money on his person. A frantic search of the sleeves of his gown, which sometimes turned up the odd half-crown, this evening offered him no more than an apple core and an inch of fluff. He'd leapt up in dismay. She'd laughed as she passed him a ten-bob note. "Don't worry, Thomas! You can pay next time. I'll have a glass of amontillado sherry, please. I'm sure they have one. Oh, and can you bring me a pickled egg and a ham sandwich? I'm starving! Have one yourself."

And here they were, two pints of strong, manly ale, two elegantly feminine sherries and a pickled egg and ham sandwich or two later, canoodling.

A sudden inrush of gentlemen, chattering volubly about music, cut through his alcoholic haze and, in dismay, Thomas began to wail. What was the time? Good Lord! He'd missed his cue! Had they all managed without him? Had the master noted his absence? Old Henningham was a stickler for the formalities.

Lois tried to calm him. Of course they would all have managed! It really wasn't important. No, they obviously hadn't set the bulldogs on his trail. Probably, no one had even noticed he wasn't there. What a fusspot! Too late, he noticed that her comforting tone had soured to scathing. She rose and announced she was going to see if the establishment had a decent ladies' room.

Ten minutes later, it dawned on Thomas that she wasn't going to return.

He'd been ditched, rejected, cast aside. How dare she? It was all her fault, if you thought about it! Hurt was turning to resentment, the sting of betrayal to the heat of righteous anger. He desperately needed to have a word with the uppity Miss Lois. Teach her some good manners! If he moved off quickly, he might overtake her before she picked up a taxi in the Market Square. She couldn't have gone far. He took a moment to try to still his whirling brain and his queasy stomach. In a moment of clarity, he remembered with a surge of waspish triumph that he knew where she lived. "Midsummer View" indeed! How pretentious! How typical of hoi polloi! Who did these city girls think they were? Taxi? There were no buses out to the wilderness north of the river at this hour. The girl was alone. A woman would never be attempting the long walk along the river bank unaccompanied. He wouldn't have attempted it himself. Town was full of ghastly thugs who'd chuck an undergraduate in the Cam and laugh their socks off when they heard him scream. If he missed her in the Market Square, he could simply take the next cab and direct it to de Montfort Avenue.

Adding to his confusion and devastation, he tuned in to the loud and alarming conversation of the group of men who'd just entered and seated themselves with their drinks at the next table.

"Awful scene! Are we sure she was dead?" said one round-eyed gent, downing a whisky.

"Not polite to linger and stare, of course, but I'd say she was a goner," opined a voice from behind a half of bitters. "I was in the front row. Witnessed the whole thing! That scream — more like a death rattle! Poor child! Do you suppose she saw it coming? I mean, all that throat-clutching and teetering on the edge? Made out she was having us on, but I don't know . . . A portent, would that be? Did she know she was doomed?"

"At least that policeman chappie seemed to know what he was doing," said the whisky, trying for a less lurid approach. "No fuss, army type. All safe in his hands, I'm sure."

"Indeed! Good fellow! But *why,* perhaps we should ask, was a policeman there at all?" a dry sherry wanted to know. "Instantly on hand to catch the body as it fell? How likely is that? Bit queer that, don't you think? Dirty work at the crossroads?"

"Don't be ridiculous, Monty!" the whisky expostulated. "It was that bloody old staircase, I expect! Medieval and wormy as hell! Doesn't always show on the surface, you know . . . Solid as a rock one minute, a pile of dust the next. It can happen to the best staircases. My father once put his foot through a tread at the Earl of Aldeburgh's seat."

"Mungo, it *was* the *back* stairs, and your father had no business being there in the middle of the night," the dry sherry pointed out slyly. "Still — death traps, I'd agree."

The body? Death trap? Policeman? Thomas staggered to his feet, gripped the table to steady himself, looked at his wrist-watch and set out to make his way into the night. There was something he had to do before the unexpected, berserking heat of a long-lost Viking ancestor faded and left him once again Thomas Tyrrell, the subservient music scholar. If only he could steer a straight course between the tables and keep down the two pints of beer he'd unwisely quaffed.

CHAPTER 5

"So? Did he confess?"

Redfyre took three more strides along the pavement of King's Parade before he answered.

"You must be more precise when you speak to a police officer. A few linguistic clues like nouns come in useful to us plodding members of the force," he prevaricated. "Who? Confess to what?"

"Come off it! Did Coote push Juno down the stairs? Did he say so? He was the only person around when she came tumbling down. I'm surprised you've let *him* stroll off back to his room free as a bird, when you've got *me* clamped in an arm lock on my way to heaven knows what interrogation scene. My only questionable act the whole evening was sitting down next to you. Coote was within an arm's stretch of Juno when she fell headfirst down the stairs. I say again, did he come clean?"

"I'm surprised that you need to ask. I could have sworn I saw you skulking behind an adjacent pillar when I drew him aside to put the suggestion to him."

She shrugged. "I couldn't make it all out. You were talking deliberately quietly."

Redfyre smiled. "How inconsiderate and annoying of us! Well, you didn't miss much. He says he didn't touch her, and I believe him. According to a very distraught Christopher, they were packing up amicably when Juno announced that she wouldn't wait for him to be ready — it takes far less time to put one small trumpet in its carrying case than it does to put a pipe organ to bed, and she had a train to catch. Don't bother to escort her down, she told him — she could manage. He wasn't even aware that the stairs were still swathed in darkness when he heard the scream and the thumps as she fell. Next thing, the master was yelling at him to stay put. It was an accident, and bad enough, but that's all it was. He was certain that there was no other presence on the organ loft or the staircase when they made their way up to the performance area after the interval. After that, the whole scene was the centre of attention for over three hundred pairs of eyes — including yours and mine. No one entered that staircase. The stair treads themselves were jolly sound, he remembered — didn't even creak. He'd been thumping up and down them all day rehearsing, after all — he'd have noticed. Juno must have simply missed her footing. Caught her heel in her evening gown? He had noted her shoes — red satin, Spanish heels. Women were tripping themselves up all the time with dresses the length they currently were. It had happened to Coote's own grandmother, apparently — with tragic consequences."

"I expect you come across that quite a lot — rich, elderly persons falling down stairs?" Earwig asked.

"It's the weight of the gold sovereigns in their pockets — they overbalance," he said. "But yes, I take your meaning. Juno is young and agile . . ."

"And hasn't a penny to her name. No, really — she wasn't joking when she raised the matter of the doctor's bill. It would be a concern. I shall offer to pay it, of course, but there'll be a rush to oblige. Juno's loved by all; no one would want to kill her. That's the puzzle. I'm wondering how long it's going to take the great detective to work out just what it is about her that someone wanted to obliterate." Her hand tightened on his arm as she turned to him, face pale with concern. "And as she's survived, may *still* want to obliterate."

The wretched girl had voiced his fear and his dilemma.

If someone wanted Juno Proudfoot to die, they might try again. If Redfyre allowed that the fall was an engineered attack on Juno, then it was pre-planned and spectacular. It was comparable to a well-directed stage effect. The man whose mind was vile enough to have conceived such a deed was unlikely to simply accept defeat and creep back into the shadows. He would be looking for acknowledgement. He'd insist on taking a surreptitious bow, surely? But why Juno? What was it about this excellent girl that had incited a murderous attempt? An answer had occurred to him much earlier in the evening, but he had swatted it away instantly as a ridiculous and unworthy thought. When he had a case to solve, Redfyre stuck to common sense, modern scientific techniques and if all else failed, the Scotland Yard handbook. The victim of this possible assault was unknown to him. He had much to do before he could proceed with the investigation: a further interview with her in the morning, the doctor's report on her injuries, a check on her background and contacts. One of the first things he had learned to set aside in murder cases, however, was the reaction of friends and family. There was nothing like an assault, successful or bungled, to confer instant sanctity on the victim.

He slipped his free hand under his overcoat and into his jacket pocket. The coiled silk curtain tie still lurked there — cold, slippery and surprisingly repellent. It ought by now to be safely in an evidence bag on its way to police headquarters. An oversight? No. Redfyre could explain it away as such, but he needed to have it safe in his pocket. It still had a role to play. The wide, innocent eyes of Juno as she'd handed it over to him with unquestioning trust had stirred and quite disarmed him. An entirely proper response on his part, he judged, understanding and approving his initial reaction to an attractive girl in very clear distress. Man that he was, he'd been caught by her beauty and her childlike assumption that he would help her out of her unpleasant situation. Caught? Transfixed was closer to the truth, he admitted. But the policeman he was would have none of that. Redfyre would set aside his masculine urge to protect and go, as he always did, straight for the truth.

Earwig seemed content to maintain the silence her comment had caused. She was quite like a canny old sheepdog, he was coming to realise, startling him into movement with a show of teeth and a gentle growl, only to belly down in the long grass, still and unthreatening, when he moved off in the direction she'd chosen for him. He was relieved when her attention was distracted by one of the buildings on their route.

"This is my favourite façade in Cambridge," she said, stopping to admire the elegant columns of the Pembroke College Chapel, gleaming in the moonlight. "By Sir Christopher Wren. His first completed work of architecture. Commissioned by the Bishop of Ely, who just happened to be his uncle, you know."

Was the girl incapable of saying the simplest thing without an undercurrent of bolshevism or feminism? "So I understand. And how lucky we are that his talent was spotted and encouraged to bloom," Redfyre said easily.

"And there's Peterhouse, and opposite the college, there's Addenbrooke's. Ah, are you taking me to visit Juno? Already? I was under the impression that we really wouldn't be welcome at the bedside while the examination was being done, and they were planning to give her a sleeping draught to settle her until morning. What are you up to, Inspector?" After a moment's thought: "Oh! I've guessed your secret! Have you fallen victim to her charms, too?" Earwig gave a shout of laughter. "Using me as a means of getting close to her? You wouldn't be the first, or even the twenty-first man to do that!"

"Not at all," he managed to say equably through his surprise. "It occurred to me that it might be useful for you to be close to your friend — just across the road, you might say, in case of unforeseen problems. The doctor has a number to ring. Oh, we're nipping down this little lane. Come on! It's just by Little St. Mary's Church." His tone brightened as they homed in on their destination.

Earwig hung back. "Are you sure? I know that lane — it leads down to the river, it's awfully dark down there. There's nothing but the back bits of Peterhouse, a graveyard and some run-down little houses for college servants."

"Drat! The gas lamp's out again. I'll shine my torch. It's only a few steps, and at the end of them I promise you there'll be electric lighting and a glowing fire to warm your toes by. Here we are!" He flung out an arm in welcome. "Magnolia Cottage, I'm afraid. Sorry about that! It's a conceit of the owner. It's no cottage, you'll find, and it doesn't possess a single magnolia, but it does have a view of a magnificent specimen opposite in the graveyard. You must try to see it when it opens its sails in May!"

He put a key in the lock of a green-painted door and pushed it open a careful inch. "Allow me to push ahead of you — there's a fierce dog to negotiate, and it's right by the door, waiting for an unsuspecting foot to be inserted."

A throaty growl was rising to a hysterical rage.

"Snapper! Down, boy! Grrr!" Redfyre growled back. "Supper in two minutes! Basket!" He lifted the tiny dog, to its evident delight, on his toe, clearing it from the doorway and projecting it across the room.

They entered from the lane straight into a living room in which lamps in Tiffany shades had been switched on and a fire glowed in the hearth, secured by a sturdy fireguard. The small black and white terrier whimpered with delight, dashed up again, licked Redfyre's hand vigorously, then wagged his stump of a tail all the way to his basket by the hearth.

Earwig stood for a moment, taking in the scene and smiling gently. "So that's all I have to do to get the inspector's attention? Kiss his hand and waggle my derrière? I've done worse, I suppose. Which is my basket?"

Without waiting for an offer, she flopped down into Redfyre's own armchair opposite Snapper and proceeded to hold the dog in conversation while Redfyre took off his coat and shoes. Uncannily, the dog seemed to be replying to her overtures in strangled whimpers. Finally, abandoning good manners for duty, he jumped out again and went to fetch Redfyre's slippers one by one from where he'd secreted them under the table and delivered them to his feet.

"I'm sorry he doesn't have any your size to offer, but do take your wet shoes off — we've seen a lady's feet before, and he won't nibble your toes. May I take your coat?"

Earwig removed her shoes and put them by the fire to dry out. She tucked her feet up under her, still snuggling under her fur, and made herself look completely at home. "I'll stay inside my coat, thank you, till I decide whether I'm staying."

Redfyre wondered which unfortunate animal had made the final sacrifice to provide the pelt now gleaming and undulating in the firelight as she wriggled herself into a comfortable position. Knowing nothing of furs, he thought that "golden minx"

96

sounded about right. He found himself listening for a contented purr when the uncomfortable feeling that he'd invited an oversized and malevolent marmalade cat into his home struck him. "Beware my teeth and claws," was the unspoken message he was receiving from the sleek creature now surveying and assessing his domain. "I may be honouring you with my presence for the moment, but I can strike out and run from you whenever I please."

"The comforts extend to a telephone." Redfyre pointed to his desk by the window where the gleaming black and gold instrument sat in solitary state. "Do please ring anyone who needs to know that you've been detained and assure them that you will be returned to base with a police escort before . . . shall we say, ten thirty?" He unleashed his most disarming smile. His show of confidence hid the disturbing knowledge that in making her come here to his home, he had overstepped boundaries. What he was doing was probably unlawful, and most certainly morally unacceptable. Would his behaviour be described as caddish? No, thuggish was nearer to the mark. He couldn't depend on his sketchy charm to win her over; she'd seemed impervious to the few feeble attempts he'd made, preferring a salty challenge. And yet, he'd persisted in keeping her alongside in spite of what he told himself was her token resistance because he sensed that she had more to reveal to him in private than in the very public bustle and discomfort of a police interview with a yawning sergeant taking notes.

"Telephone? That won't be necessary. I've taken a room at the Royal Cambridge Hotel just down the road. Daddy has an arrangement with them. Whenever I'm in Cambridge and friends can't put me up, they always find me a room. I was planning to stay overnight and divide my Saturday between Heffers bookshop and Vogue Fashions. I must say, I'm relieved to find that the prisoner still has access to a telephone call. May I assume that the traditional fish and chip supper's included in police perks, too?" She looked about her quizzically, as if expecting a duty officer to step forward, enquiring, "Would you like salt and vinegar on your haddock, madam?"

"So, here we are, in more comfortable surroundings!" she conceded. "Is this your home? Your house?"

"It's my home, yes. Not my house. I rent it from a rogue called Barnwell. My landlord owns several houses of odd sizes in various parts of the city, mostly named after the nearest tree."

"I'm surprised you didn't offer for 'Linden Lodge' or 'Mulberry Manor.' This is rather small, isn't it?"

"Your butler at Melford doubtlessly has much more spacious accommodation," he said smoothly.

"Sorry! That was rude. I should have said 'cozy.' It is. But I like it! A space of your own, where you're at no one's beck and call. That's wonderful! And you've filled it with such pretty things. It's a Bruton Street salon in miniature! Willow-green walls, and such a daring use of white. 'Darling! It just shrieks Sibyl Colefax,' " she said in a very convincing Mayfair accent. "Have you invited The Prince of Wales, Cecil Beaton and Noël Coward to your little soirée, too? I'm honoured!"

Redfyre was fed up with Earwig's ragging, but he didn't retaliate, sensing that she was disguising a genuine appreciation of his valiant attempt at decoration. He ascribed the new glimpse of a cheerful Earwig to the dog. The wretched animal had that effect on people. Insane good humour and bounding energy were infectious. It had been a mistake to choose a dog for his small size. Snapper might well be in proportion with the house, and his fur blended well into the general colour scheme, but Redfyre should have remembered that, for all other qualities, a Jack Russell terrier was off the scale. Courage, intelligence, endurance and a manic joie de vivre — Snapper had them by the sackful. He normally showed good judgement on visitors to his home, and his instant acceptance of the unfriendly Earwig was a bit disconcerting. He'd been led astray by the misleading allure of her fur coat, Redfyre decided. An Earwig in a stout gabardine raincoat would have had quite a different reception.

"Now, Inspector! If you're expecting me to *sing* for my supper, I'll go along with that and make a full confession to anything you like, but may I have the supper part first? Sorry to bang on about it, but it occurs to me that I've had one mince pie to eat since breakfast and I'm prepared to fight Snapper for his biscuits. A crust of bread will do . . . perhaps you could spare a smear of butter and jam?"

"I can do better than that. How about beef stew and dumplings with a baked potato, followed by apple and blackberry pie? It's all on the stove in the kitchen. The stew may have dried out a bit, as I'm later than I expected, so give me a moment and I'll slosh a glass of red wine in there to slacken the gravy."

For one brief moment, he basked in the expression of something very like adoration in Earwig's expression.

Such was her curiosity about his domestic arrangements, she left her armchair and followed him into the kitchen, helpfully holding up the lid of the casserole and offering advice while he added red wine from a bottle already open, a handful of herbs and a grating of pepper. He decided to treat her as one of his mates and handed her a cloth with instructions to get the potatoes out of the oven while he laid the table. He pointed out the bathroom where she could wash her hands and, by dodging around each other and good-humouredly doing whatever seemed necessary for the next ten minutes, they were able finally to settle down to dine. Earwig had warmed sufficiently to allow him to take her coat and, laughing, pointed out that, dressed as they were in evening clothes, they could almost be dining at the Ritz.

"Your green silk would be better complemented by foie gras and turbot than stew, I'm thinking," Redfyre said.

"Indeed. In deference to my outfit, we'll say *daube de boeuf à la provençale!* Which it is! My compliments to your chef. It's as good as any I've had in Provence before the war." She looked at him enquiringly. "Wine? Herbs? Do I taste garlic? Now, where on earth in Cambridge did you come by garlic? We'd never persuade our cook to indulge in such foreign nonsense! If it's not in Mrs. Beeton's, she'll have no truck with it."

"No chef, alas. But you're right — I don't claim responsibility. Mrs. Page at Number 10 used to work as a cook at the college over the road before she retired. She has some fancy banquet-night recipes in her repertoire carried over from the spacious Edwardian days before the war, and she still practices her skills. Stealing garlic from the pantry and smuggling it out in the pocket of her pinny is one of them. Her poor old husband and I daily risk gout, dyspepsia and embolism, I fear, as one dish after another comes steaming out of her oven. This is one of her plainer efforts. She's accustomed to me bringing congenial company back home with me on Friday nights, so she keeps it simple, copious and English. She also keeps the place clean and looks after Snapper when I'm working long hours."

Earwig gave him an inscrutable smile. "A room of his own, a telephone and a live-out housekeeper — what more could a man wish for?"

Redfyre had the self-restraint to wait until she had put down her dessert spoon, following her second helping of apple pie, before he asked his first question.

"Are you ever going to tell me why you twisted my aunt's arm and arranged for an officer of the law to be sitting next to you when your friend performed this evening?"

"You didn't believe what I had to tell you about Wulfie? No? Thought not. Hetty warned me you were a jolly handsome bloke, but she didn't tell me you were quite sharp-witted, really . . ."

"For a policeman?"

"For a man."

"What story did you tell her?"

"The Wulfie saga. But she refused to believe me, too. Skepticism seems to be a family trait. Hetty thought I was trying to get alongside one of the most eligible bachelors in Cambridge . . . That's you! You clown." She sighed with impatience as he dismissed the compliment by casting a joking look over his shoulder to locate the eligible bachelor. "Ladies of her generation keep lists, you know. And you feature in pole position in one of them. They are quite firmly of the opinion that those men lucky enough to have survived the war in reasonably good shape should do their duty by their species and marry one of the superfluous girls left on the shelf through no fault of their own." She paused for a moment, then added with a slight smile. "You're looking at one such, I'm afraid. Twenty-six next birthday. An old maid. Worse, I'm very choosy. Worst of all, I'm penniless. Or shall be soon, when Pa kicks the bucket."

"Surely he'll have made provision for his daughter?"

"You don't know him! In his world, daughters are farmed out as quickly and as cheaply as possible onto some well-to-do, obliging chap of the same class." She gave a world-weary sigh that would have gone over well onstage, playing opposite Noël Coward. "You know — over the brandy and cigars, some young Percy or Cecil will be drawn aside and sounded out. 'My gel Earwig? I hear you've been paying some attention? Interested, are you? If you'd care to take things further, I wouldn't stand in your way. Could do worse, you know!' "

The bitterness in her voice roused Redfyre to strive for a cheering antidote. He gave a theatrical shudder. "Don't! I have been that Percy, that Cecil! Though it takes an increasingly desperate father to pencil in a policeman on his list of approved suitors. But your allowance — will it be protected, do you think?"

"Interested, are you?" Her lip curled. "I don't think my allowance was at the fore-front of his mind when he drew up his new will. In any case, he's struggling, things being what they are in these austere times." She glanced at the fur hanging casually on a peg behind the door. "The coat is very much pre-war. It was my mother's. The silk dress, I wore for my coming-out party five years ago. I've altered it to look fashionable, thanks to the skill with a needle I acquired in the war."

Redfyre recognised a diversion and a lie when he heard them. "But you're flush enough to pay for your friend's medical attention?"

"Just about. Juno's very welcome to what-ever I have."

"Right. Next layer of the onion, please. What exactly were you afraid would happen this evening? I think you were aware that Juno was in danger of some sort. There was a Beware-the-Ides-of-March twitchiness about you all evening. But the moment the accident happened, you were calm and unafraid, and displayed all the sangfroid of an unflappable sergeant-major. I admired

105

the brisk way you made a decision on the smelling salts! I don't suppose the master has been dealt with so peremptorily since he left the nursery. By the way, I'll relieve you of that little silver holder, which I believe you slipped into your bag. An antique vinaigrette, if I'm not mistaken, though of an unusual shape? It looks valuable; I'll undertake to have it returned to its thoughtful owner."

He extended his hand, calmly ignoring the hackle-raising that signaled she'd taken offense, and held it steady until she placed the holder into it. He dropped it into his pocket.

Conscious that he had asked too much too soon, inadvertently having accused her of stealing, he added a shorter, more straightforward question that could raise no prevarication: "Where did you acquire your medical knowledge?"

"At Elmleigh Abbey, a cycle ride from home. I volunteered as a nursing assistant there in 1915, when Lord and Lady Elmleigh converted part of their house into a military hospital. It's conveniently on the rail line to London, and the ambulance trains could get there easily. I was a Voluntary Aid Detachment girl — a VAD. On a short three-month contract — renewable, which suited my parents better. They didn't quite approve of what I was doing, but as I was doing it only a few fields away from home and could leave at any moment, they didn't object too strongly. Living under the grand roof of one of their friends and surrounded by other young girls of good family, I was in a socially secure, even admirable position, they judged. They could say that even their daughter had rolled her sleeves up and joined the war effort. Thank God they never came to visit! It would have shattered their comfortable Arts and Crafts world. The blood, the screams, the filth, the ribaldry, the comingling of ranks, classes and sexes — they would have been horrified."

"Ribaldry? Comingling? I'm shocked to hear you were party to any of that!" he teased. "So, with your nursing experience, you recognised as soon as I did that Juno's condition was in no way serious. But, I say again, you had been anticipating an attempt on her safety or well-being all evening. Why?"

With a sigh and an obvious dragging of feet, she got up and retrieved her bag from the armchair. "You'd better see these," she said.

"These" proved to be a slender brown

cardboard file containing three or four sheets of writing paper. Earwig cleared a space on the table and put it down in front of Redfyre. "They're in date order of receipt, starting from the top," she told him, and sat back watching his face to assess his reaction.

"Ah! This begins to make sense," he said grimly, on reading the first.

"Words and letters cut out of the local newspaper. The evening edition of November the fifteenth. I checked the print with their editor," Earwig said. "He was very helpful."

"He usually is when he scents a story," Redfyre commented. "What promise did he extract from you in return, I wonder? This seems to be arranged and stuck on with Cow Gum to a clean sheet of writing paper — the kind you can buy at any W. H. Smith."

"Does it qualify for the description of 'poison pen,' in your professional experience?"

"Hardly! This message appears to be rather milder than the usual offerings."

He read out. "*Ladies do not play trumpets.* I'm more used to the *Sally the Slag is having it off with Filthy Fred* variety. Who was the recipient of this little billet-doux?"

"Juno. She showed it to me. She thought it was quite a laugh. I stopped her from chucking it in the fire. It seemed to me to have more importance than she was giving it credit for. Someone went to quite a lot of trouble to do all that craftwork. It looks grotesque! Is this the common way of communicating bile these days?"

Redfyre laughed. "In fact, it's not at all common outside of the pages of the penny-shocker press."

"Well, I was glad I'd preserved it when another appeared in the next day's post."

"The correspondent seems to have given up on the tedious business of cutting and sticking and opted for handwriting in capital letters," he said, studying the second. "A person leading a busy life, do we infer from that? Impatient? Too much to say to be able to convey it by means of scissors and paste? Or a time-on-his-hands busybody who's run out of detective novels to pass the time, but remembers the barmy techniques he's learned from them? The content is more alarming. He seems to have given up on the mild rebuke, as well. He — shall we say 'he' for brevity, while acknowledging that it's quite likely, possibly even more likely to be a 'she'? Anyhow, he is more explicit in number two, not to say downright crude.

"ONLY SLUTS APPEAR IN PUBLIC BLOWING ON MALE INSTRUMENTS.

Disturbing. And oddly phrased, don't you think? Is the writer throwing light on a lapse in social etiquette or musical taste? It's a vulgar notion conveyed in rather high-flown language. It's a thought that could be expressed by either a man or a woman, but one with ... er ... a certain knowledge of the ways of the world," he finished delicately.

"A knowledge that makes the writer almost certainly a man," Earwig said firmly, "since the arts of trumpetry and fellatio do not generally feature in the repertoire of a Cambridge lady. Even the married ones."

Redfyre looked aside, embarrassed by such loose talk and annoyed by her lack of logic. "And therefore a *correspondingly* small number of Cambridge gentlemen, I'd have thought. It still takes two to tango, I discovered when I last took to the floor with a lady in my arms. But perhaps I operate in morally elevated circles — there's always that. Whatever the underlying meaning, this nonsense hardly constitutes a threat. It could be dismissed by any half-competent barrister as a personally held opinion. You'd find that at least ten out of the twelve male jurors would sympathize with the sentiment. The other two would fail to understand the innuendo. The Public Prosecutions Service would advise against pursuing a case."

"You're hard to please. But look, he's just getting into his stride. Here's the next one. Received two weeks before the performance was to take place." She fell silent and waited for him to work his way through the sheets.

"And we have number three? Mmm. Leaning towards what I'd call the biblical proscriptive style: THOU SHALT NOT ENTERTAIN HARLOTS IN GOD'S HOUSE! No case there, either. I believe some Puritan households have that in needlework above the fireplace, masquerading as the eleventh commandment."

Earwig was frowning at him, but said nothing, clearly waiting for him to move on to the next note.

"Number four, again in capitals. This one's more promising! ENTER THE ORGAN LOFT ALIVE, LEAVE IT DEAD. Now, unless this is a carpenter's report on the outbreak of a bad case of *Anobium punctatum,* here we have a clear threat! It's very silly, but it's clear all right. Something we can work with.

"Hand me number five. This is more like it! It's even more specific and bluntly threatening. I'd say he was getting angrier. The strokes are thicker, less controlled. *YOU WILL BE THROWN FROM A HEIGHT AND*

YOUR BODY DEVOURED BY DOGS. How nasty! But why dogs?"

Redfyre was acquainted with the biblical reference to the point that he could have given chapter and verse number for it, but he wanted to hear her interpretation of the threat. With a bit of coaxing and trickery, she might even hand him her theory on the motivation of the culprit. He was quite certain that Earwig knew much more about this sordid affair than she was letting on. He'd draw her out, entangle her in the thread of truth and — he admitted to himself — take shameful satisfaction in hobbling her with it.

"It was the punishment meted out to Jezebel, Queen of Israel. Kings 1 and 2. I thought all spotty little boys knew that lurid story?"

"Forgive my ignorance. I'll put my hands up to the spots and the callow youth, but I'll have you know I spent my formative years under the blankets with a torch in the company of Huckleberry Finn, Rob Roy, Blackbeard the pirate, and other clean-cut villains. Kings 1, you say? Old Testament — Historical Bible Studies, my parents called it. Both scientists who swore by New Testament stuff in these post-Darwin days. I'm Church of England, of course — you had to be in the army, but all I can be counted on for are the hymns and prayers. Does this reference to Jezebel hold significance to you?"

"Of course! He's shown his hand, revealed his motive!" She looked pityingly at Redfyre's blank expression and sighed. "Let's pick up our coffee and drink it over there by the fire, shall we? This is definitely a fireside story. No, don't pull that face! It's utterly fascinating, I think, and a likely clue to the diseased mentality of the oaf who composed this."

He plumped up the cushions of the two armchairs, threw Snapper back into his basket and poked up the fire, sending a dazzle of sparks up the chimney and a gush of warm air over the hearthrug.

Earwig gave proper lip-smacking attention to her coffee before embarking on her story, he was pleased to see. He brewed his coffee with care in a silver contrivance he'd brought back from France with him, and he always ground the best beans he could find in the ancient brass-handled grinder his father's cook had been about to throw away. Earwig savoured every drop and held out her cup for more before beginning.

This was to be no "once upon a time" told-to-the-children account, he realised from her opening. He was not to be lulled into a passive role. She started with a question: "Do you know what the name 'Jezebel' means?"

"Um . . . Well, I know it's synonymous with 'harlot,' but I expect I've got that wrong."

"Funnily enough, it has exactly the opposite meaning: 'chaste and virtuous.' An equivalent to 'Virginia,' perhaps. A good name for a queen, you'd say. She was a beautiful, intelligent and talented princess of the Phoenician people, who were neighbours to the Israelites. A sophisticated, seagoing, clever race, the Phoenicians were admired and feared in equal measure by the dwellers in the Promised Land. In a political arrangement, Ahab the king married her, and seems to have been completely dazzled by her. Sadly, she was of a different religion. Rather than worshipping the one god, Yahweh, she set up altars to Baal and the goddess Astarte. She worshipped idols. Instead of converting his new wife to his faith, Ahab surrendered to her polytheism, building altars to Baal in his capital, Samaria."

"Oh, dear! Never a people to lie down unprotesting, the ancient Jews, if I remember correctly. And didn't they have a nifty knack with a war trumpet?"

"You're right. This surrendering of the faith went down very badly with the people. They also despised Jezebel's flighty foreign ways — she painted her eyes with kohl and dressed her hair. It was said that, in spite of the ardour-dampening presence of a pair of guardian eunuchs provided by the king, she was lecherous by nature and took many lovers."

"Sounds fun!" Redfyre said, unguardedly. "But I take your meaning. Queen Jezebel was quite a strider! And just the kind of villain we can expect to see when a strong woman steps onstage with painted face and tiddled-up hair: Lady Macbeth, Cleopatra, Helen of Troy, Mata Hari, my cousin Joan. Becky Sharp — would she qualify?"

"Probably. But I'll tell you who doesn't. Juno Proudfoot!"

"In someone's mind she does. What, in Juno, has triggered this comparison, would you say?"

"She's very pretty. Lovely hair. Wears makeup on stage. Her dress was a bit . . . well, showy, as you noticed. Though if it had been Marie Lloyd or Gertie Gitana wearing it, no one would have batted an eyelid. Juno was so cross when she saw these notes, in defiance she borrowed a daring evening dress from one of our friends who shops in Paris, and we sewed it down to her size." Earwig grinned. "If I seemed nervous about the gown holding out for the performance, it was with good reason! I sewed the seams!"

"Well there you are! The world is full of fuddy-duddies. They see a good-looking girl who's taken trouble with her appearance and think the worst of her. Forget them! They aren't worth knowing. But, I'm thinking that alone wouldn't trigger such a nasty explosion of hatred. In any case, even our psychologically disturbed chum would have no way of knowing that she wouldn't appear shrouded in a layer of black bombazine over a woolly vest for the performance."

"There's her talent. She's streets ahead of any male trumpeter in the country."

"Somehow I don't think we're looking for a jealous musician at the bottom of all this."

"No. I think it was a cocktail of unintentional provocation. Sex, talent, looks but also . . . would it be over-interpretation to suggest that her very position that night — up in the loft, looking down on the audience — might have conjured up in the letter-writer's mind a picture of Jezebel?"

"Ah. We're back to the throwing from a height and the devouring by dogs?"

"Yes. And to the vengeful mind behind

that. Jezebel may have wound the king round her little finger, but when Ahab died, she ran into the stony fist of the prophet, Elijah, who ordered the queen's priests, supporters and sons to be killed. Bloody battles between the two strong wills ensued: Israelite male versus Phoenician female."

Redfyre sighed. "Now, there's a pair of contenders the Cambridge CID had quite overlooked. I'll put them on our watchlist."

She arched an eyebrow at him and said: "Yes, you should," before continuing her story. "Unusually for a female in the Bible, Jezebel is given a voice: 'If you are Elijah, so I am Jezebel.' Her very words and their meaning couldn't be clearer. She's thrown down the gauntlet, and is gunning for him in a fight to the death. Elijah blinks first and flees in terror."

Redfyre smiled at her imagery, which seemed to him to owe more to the Wild West than the Ancient East. This girl certainly relished a good story. "But it doesn't end there?"

"Leaving a woman in power? Certainly not! Elijah plots that one of the king's generals, Jehu, will exterminate Jezebel and all her descendants. Jehu drives about Caanan like a whirlwind in his chariot, hacking and slaughtering everyone on his list. Finally, he screeches to a halt in front of the palace, his hands still red with the blood of Jezebel's eldest son. As she sits at the window of her tower, preparing for the deadly encounter, Jezebel dresses her hair and paints her face. A seductive ruse? Is she readying herself for quite a different sort of encounter with General Jehu? That's the typical leering masculine interpretation! They accuse her of a last desperate act of harlotry. Rubbish! The woman was a grandmother by this time! Facing the man who had just killed her sons and grandsons, she was simply performing her last defiant gesture in the face of death in accordance with her own tradition — 'If I'm going down, I'll go down looking stunning.' I'd have done the same."

Earwig's voice wavered and she gulped down emotion, reaching into her bag for a handkerchief.

"I understand," he said gently, filling the gap until she could recover. "I always polished my buttons and waxed my moustache before going over the top."

"But you don't wear — oh!"

"Carry on. If it gets too dramatic, I'll put my hands over Snapper's ears."

She rewarded him with a watery smile and pressed on: "Jehu sees her up in her window, flanked by her two bodyguards. Jezebel leans out and taunts and abuses him. Jehu calls up to the eunuchs, who are his countrymen, after all, to do their patriotic duty. They seize the queen and throw her from the window, down to her death under the hooves of Jehu's horses. Her body is trampled, and the dogs of the town tear it to pieces and consume it entirely, apart from her skull, a lock of hair and the palms of her hands."

"And all we have left of this astounding woman is a few words," Redfyre said. "And lucky to have those after — how many? — three thousand years?"

Earwig looked at him in scorn. "We have her story. But a story told by a man. A male scribe, a historian on the side of the victor, perhaps is even the victor himself."

"But even he can't eradicate the pride, the style, the intelligence and the strength."

"Some men will always feel demeaned by that. Some men will always call out the execution squad."

They had reached, finally, the point she had been steering him towards but he decided to allow her to make the accusation.

"I think, John, there was one such in the audience tonight. A Jehu who was seeing

Juno, not as the exceptional and talented individual she is, but as a dangerous threat. A woman! Sordid. Unclean. Immoral. A man's downfall."

"Surely a medieval monkish attitude we wouldn't find in today's society?" His tone was only mildly challenging.

She pounced on his response with scorn. "Do you have any idea how many men in Cambridge still live the medieval monkish life? They seek it out; they relish it. They would go to any lengths to preserve it." She waved a hand vaguely in the direction of his bookshelves. "Even *you* aspire to some aspects of it. There are thousands of such men. They are at every level of society, in every family. But they are especially present in this city, making their rules, smothering female talent, gagging and belittling their wives and daughters."

"Hold it right there, Earwig!" Redfyre was finding it increasingly painful to play the chosen scapegoat for his sex. "I've no wife or daughter to gag, and I'm sure I've never smothered a female talent in my life, so please, won't you point your arrows elsewhere? I'm one of those state-appointed soldier-ants who stand in a thin blue line between the angry crowd and the feminist firebrands who set out to annoy them. We're attacked from front and rear, and pretty fed up with both sides."

Appearing regretful, she reached over and took hold of his hands. The gesture came not out of affection or a rush of good feeling, he suspected, but from a determination to make the point she had been working up to all evening. "I know that, John. And we thank God you're there! A modern man, a man of the new century. Approachable and rational. But listen! One of these monstrous men I'm speaking of was in the audience with us tonight. He clapped and smiled, he sang along with the carols, he shuffled in procession past what he'd planned would be Juno's body. Perhaps he even murmured words of condolence or offered assistance, attempting to stay close by his victim until it became clear — to his chagrin, no doubt — that she'd survived the fall. He realised he'd have to try again. Perhaps he's plotting his second attempt as we speak! And, as I'm in a biblical mood tonight, I'm going to give you a clear command, inspector! Before he can do any more damage, give me that man's head! In a noose, on a plate, or in a bag. I'm not fussy."

"Earwig, if there's a guilty head to be severed, you shall have it. And I'll ensure Caravaggio is standing by with his brushes to record the moment. Would Scrivener of the *Cambridge Oracle* with his trusty Speed Graphic and magnesium flare be a satisfactory stand-in?"

CHAPTER 6

Redfyre hurried downstairs to answer the telephone. Seven o'clock! It wasn't even daylight yet, and no one ever rang before dawn with good news. Was this the hospital ringing to tell him something he didn't want to hear? Earwig Stretton, attempting to relight his fuse? He was almost relieved to identify the gravelly tones of his superior officer, Superintendent MacFarlane.

He'd got as far as "Detec—" before the familiar northern voice began its onslaught.

"Just read the notes you sent me via Sergeant Thoday on that fiasco at St. Barnabas. Good thing you were there on the spot. Ringside seat, no less! And perhaps you'll tell me, when you decide to put in an appearance, how you managed to pull that one off. Now, this girl — the one who died in the night? Tell me what you know."

"I'm sorry, sir — girl? Which girl?" Redfyre dragged the phone across the desk and sank down into his chair.

"Why are you still there instead of at the scene of the crime? I sent Constable Whatsisname with a message half an hour ago! Good thing I chased you up. The doc's first impression is not long dead, and not suicide, but murder."

"No message yet, sir. I say again, which girl? Who's died?"

"Good Lord, man! No need to shout! Now, if I knew her name, I'd have had the courtesy to use it. Loosen your tie and tell me, how many dead girls have you got on your books this weekend? I'm talking about the one we dragged out of the Cam an hour ago." He growled for a moment in a holding manoeuvre, then launched crisply into his briefing, reading from notes. "Female, eighteen-ish. Unidentified as of yet. Body spotted by a Sewage Works employee. On his way to work? Dunno. Anyhow, floating in the river, the body was, about ten minutes he calculated — and he would know! — from entering the city sewage system. So thank God for small mercies. It could have been worse. All the same, I'd advise gum boots."

"Have you checked the list of missing female persons?"

"Course I have! Nothing corresponding in

124

the latest alert." Paper crackled as he read and summarised: "Two elderly ladies sought by their nephew. Having met their young relative, I'd judge they've probably done a bunk to Brighton to avoid him, though I have sent Matcham to check out said nephew's back garden for evidence of fresh diggings . . . you never know. Fourteen-year-old girl, been missing two days. Most likely hopped on a train to London to stay with her older sister, who's thought to be leading a livelier life than Cambridge can offer. So — duty doc's already there at the scene, as I said. We're all just waiting for our fancy-pants inspector to finish his early-morning star jumps, take an invigorating swig of his Earl Grey and bugger off down there. North bank of the river, opposite Midsummer Common. Got it? Good! On your bike, man! The cycle path is the best way to go. Take your best torch. Now, where the hell's Whatsisname got to?"

"He seems to be at the door right now, sir. I'll keep you posted."

MacFarlane had rung off.

MacFarlane grinned and shook his head indulgently as he replaced the receiver. He called down the corridor for a mug of tea, emptied his full ashtray into the wastepaper basket and lit a Senior Service, frowning thoughtfully through the puther of blue smoke. He knew he didn't need to keep so close behind his star inspector, treading on his heels. He just got a kick out of being the governor of a subordinate who was patently a toff. And this was all right, he reckoned, just so long as he reminded himself occasionally that the satisfaction derived was certainly self-indulgent and probably reprehensible. And so long as the subject of his bullying — the patent toff — was toff enough to affect a complete indifference to class and rank. Regardless, Redfyre whatever his class — and this was, for the most part, a mystery to the superintendent — was a bloody good copper.

Unlike some of the newly appointed officers coming straight into the force from the war, Redfyre had done a formative year on the beat before rising swiftly up through the newly fluid organization to his present rank. Rumour had it that one of his great-uncles was the present Director of Scotland Yard, a fearsome old general who'd retired from the army, enjoyed a week of retirement and gone straight back into harness as head of the police. The old tiger had excelled on the battlefield and was now cutting a swathe through the organisation that purported to be the national force of law and order, rebuilding its reputation. Or rather, since that reputation had always been dubious, setting out to swing the demolition ball about a bit and build up from the very foundation a new reputation for efficiency and probity.

Smart young men like Redfyre had been promoted, while corrupt coppers — and there had been many, especially in the capital — had been sacked or pensioned off. MacFarlane approved. He liked to run a tight ship, but he acknowledged that he had his own demons to deal with. A Yorkshireman, grammar-school educated and with few social graces, he was, nevertheless, intelligent and ambitious. He strode the deck of his tight ship keeping order, and sent other, more fleet-footed crew members up the rigging.

MacFarlane's deployment to Cambridge — a university town, and the most ancient and lovely in the east of England — had confounded him for a while. The townsmen were, to his relief, the kind of law-abiding and not so law-abiding mixture of common folk you'd meet anywhere in the land. As far as he could work out, they were a three-part cocktail: largely the indigenous East Anglians, fair-haired, easy-going and ponderous of speech; a sprinkling of dark, tight-lipped Men of the Fens from downstream towards the North Sea; and, adding a sharper note, a dash of Cockney from the incoming Londoners bringing their yapping voices, quick wits and flashy style of dressing. All contributing to the usual mongrel mix that somehow always managed to blend, balance and be British.

It was the other lot, the gownsmen, he had a problem with. They lived, largely unobserved by ordinary folk, in a land of their own behind ornate stone walls and thick oak doors, a land they called Academe, where they made their own rules, employed their own officers to enforce them and looked down on the efforts of the civil constabulary. If there was an outbreak of bicycle stealing and it was suspected by the colleges that townies were responsible, the superintendent's immediate attention and interest would be demanded. But a police presence, even the highest officer's, was otherwise discouraged in their domain.

To gain access, he would have to alert the porter at the front gate and be directed round to the tradesmen's entrance. He'd be parked, ignored, in some busy corridor, waiting for an escort to take him through a labyrinth of courts and staircases to find a supercilious official who would barely put down his toasted crumpet long enough to give him his instructions and dismiss him. It was trickier than negotiating a passage across the Styx. After one or two humiliating episodes when he'd attempted to investigate young ruffian undergraduates who'd inflicted severe injuries on lads from the town, he'd admitted he'd been outtalked, outsmarted and set aside.

And then, two years ago, he'd been allocated this secret weapon: John Redfyre, MA, DSO, CID.

Here was a bloke who spoke their language, was related to not a few of them, had a good degree from a Cambridge college and was much decorated for gallantry in the recent war. He marched into these institutions through the front gate with a smile on his face, a spring in his step and who knew what token for Cerberus in his pocket. He took on the masters, the deans, the whole boiling, and addressed them, as he would have said — *de couronne en couronne*. MacFarlane wasn't quite sure and never bothered to ask what he meant by that, but he approved. The inspector got some interesting results. Not always by the book, and on one occasion, his inspector had explained to him the meaning of an-

129

other pertinent foreign phrase, Latin this time. *Quid pro quo* was familiar territory to MacFarlane, and he let it pass. So long as no 'quids' in the currency sense of the word changed pockets, he had no objections. He knew when to look the other way and let his officer take the lead.

The superintendent glanced down at his scribbled notes. The drowned girl, he could have sent any one of three inspectors to investigate. He knew Redfyre was up to his ears in last night's melodrama in the chapel and he ought by rights to have spared him, but there were some details here that alerted him. This was no street girl, the kind of woman who usually ended up by suicide or violence in the Cam. What had the constable said, reporting the doctor's comments? "Found in a well-to-do part of town. Large private houses all about, university boat-houses nearby, nice little park . . . The victim is well dressed, manicured hands, expensive boots, smart hairdo —" Mac-Farlane had interrupted to ask bluntly, "Lady of the Night, was she? Doc find any sign of sexual aggression?" The constable's reply had been a stiffly delivered, "No sir. And none found." Into the silence on Mac-Farlane's end, he had relented and added, "A girl from a good background, to all appearances. Doctor Beaufort quickly established that she was *virgo intacta,* and her underpinnings similarly untouched."

Good background? In Cambridge, chances were that meant a university background. Two upper-class girls attacked in one night? How likely was that? MacFarlane knew it was as likely as a snowstorm in June. Not unheard of, but come on! Instinct told him to send in Redfyre. Already involved in the first attempted murder, he'd be in a position to find out whether the second — and this time, successful — attack was somehow connected.

Experience told MacFarlane they probably weren't. The first attack (if that was what it proved to be) was staged in front of several hundred people in a brightly lit chapel. This second was a secretive piece of nastiness committed on a deserted towpath under cover of darkness, where the victim was alone. And what the hell was she doing out there on a freezing river bank at that hour?

Still, two young, upper-crust ladies in one night? MacFarlane remembered that Jack the Ripper had attacked twice in the space of an hour, on the occasion when his first killing and mutilation had been interrupted by passersby. He'd had to scarper and find another victim round the corner. Couldn't rest until he'd had his fill of blood. Unresolved murderous urges, psychological deviance — was that what plagued the culprit? Was this some upper-class loony loose on the Cambridge streets? MacFarlane groaned. Cyril the Slasher?

The superintendent couldn't be doing with the new psychological insights into motivation that he was supposed to consider. A killer was a killer, no matter what excuse he put forward for the blood-dripping dagger in his hand. And no matter what his family and connections.

And where would it end? Worryingly, the superintendent recalled murders of women which seemed occasionally to happen one after the other. For the reason that the perpetrator had it in for a certain class of female and, being of the weaker sex, these females succumbed easily to male violence. The name "Whitechapel" still sent shivers of dread and guilt down the spine of any conscientious policeman. But these poor wretches had died in the hunting grounds of the criminal classes: the red-light districts, fairgrounds and cheap boarding houses. And their attackers came from the same lowly social class. To MacFarlane's knowledge, no one ever cut a swathe through the ranks of educated, upper-class women, however great the provocation. He spent a brief moment taking the pulse rate of his own response to provocation. Worse than the average man's, he estimated with honesty. He loathed any uncontrolled outpouring of emotion in male or female members of the public, but shrieking women put his teeth on edge. And that jab with a sharpened six-inch hatpin wielded by a Newnham College harpy had lowered his tolerance a few notches.

Worse — you couldn't lay a finger on them, even in your own defense. With a crowd of men, you could pick out the troublemakers, knock 'em down and sit on 'em to achieve a bit of order, but when the gentler sex stabbed you in the bum, all you could do was offer the other cheek.

"Sir! Your copy of the *Oracle,* sir." The duty bobby swept into his office, disturbing his lugubrious train of thought. He put the morning's newspaper down on the desk. But instead of leaving at once as he usually did, Constable Barnes loitered, casting a critical eye on the paper and sighing with discomfort of some sort.

"What's up? Ulcer giving you gyp again, Barnes? Or have you seen something you don't like the look of in the rag?"

"Page three, sir," Barnes said and shot off.

MacFarlane picked up the paper hesitantly. Printed during the small hours of the night, there was no way they could have got wind of the body in the river. Surely?

He turned straight to the recommended page, read a few lines and his roar of outrage was audible even to the retreating back of Barnes as he hurried down the stairs to the security of the front desk.

MacFarlane lit another cigarette and sat down to make a dispassionate reading of the article by one Sebastian Scrivener. He realised he was talking to himself but, judging no one else on his staff deserved to be made to listen to his foul-mouthed comments he decided not to call in his sergeant to hear them.

Under an over-emphatic headline: FALL OF AN ANGEL? there appeared to be an account of the very events witnessed and reported by his own officer the previous evening at the Barnabas concert. Shit! Was no place safe from the weasels of the press? A tedious old carol concert in a college chapel, for Gawd's sake! What possible excitement could have drawn one of them there? A tip-off? How do you give someone a tip-off about an accident?

It started off factually, if quirkily:

134

A delighted audience in the Chapel of St. Barnabas was treated to a memorable concert by two up-and-coming young musicians. Miss Proudfoot (trumpet) wore a gown by Captain Molyneux of London and Paris. Doctor Coote (organ) wore a gown by Messrs. Ede and Ravenscroft of Trumpington Street, Cambridge.

MacFarlane considered this. No words wasted here. But — "gown by Ede and Ravenscroft"? The University outfitters? Purveyors of ermine-lined hoods and long-sleeved academical dress? This was what the well-dressed organist-about-Cambridge was wearing this season? What the hell had got into Scrivener? Was he auditioning for a transfer to the Ladies' Modes page? He read on. This was more like it:

A Christmas cornucopia of ancient music by composers from Albinoni to Zieleński was much enjoyed. The evening ended with a rousing rendition by soloists and audience of that old favourite: "Hark The Herald Angels."

He should have stopped right there. 'Nuff said. A balancing piece on the annual Advent concert for the elderly and needy by the Sally Bash in the Market Place would have been welcome, but MacFarlane read on and growled in dismay.

The audience — of which your reporter was a member — might surely have expected to walk out into the December night with the joyful tunes ringing in its ears? Alas, it was the disturbing — nay, shocking — sound of an unfortunate girl's screams of pain that rang out as the crowd left. Not just any girl: the soloist herself, trumpeter par excellence, who had only moments earlier been smiling in appreciation of the audience's delight in her performance, mysteriously lost her footing as she descended the stairs from the organ loft. She came crashing down, screaming for help as she bumped from stair tread to stair tread down to the bottom.

Her bloodied, seemingly lifeless body was stopped in its fall at the last moment by the stalwart frame of none other than Detective Inspector Redfyre of the Cambridge Police Force, who, by a stroke of extreme good fortune, was right on the spot. He had occupied a front-row seat at the foot of the organ loft, ostensibly to enjoy the music. So, it is to a taste for classical music on the part of its guardians that the town may attribute the speediness

of the setting-up of an official police enquiry.

Indeed, so concerned was this officer to
discover the cause of the lady's non-fatal
fall that the scene was cordoned off, a
medical officer called in and members of
the audience (including the master of the
college himself) detained for questioning.

MacFarlane tutted critically. He appreciated the "flowers of rhetoric" as much as
the next man — they'd been beaten into
him in English grammar classes at his
northern, penny-a-day grammar school. He
knew his *nonne* from his *num;* he could
identify a spot of litotes and hypotaxis when
he came across them. But the unintentional
result of this severe schoolmastering had
been a determination on the part of the
pupil to avoid at all cost using the verbal
tricks he'd learned. He left that sort of elit-
ist nonsense to soft, overeducated southern-
ers.

There was only one flower that Mac-
Farlane had plucked from that bouquet of
rhetoric and sported defiantly in his buttonhole, and that was a little beauty called
parataxis. Keep it short. Be clear. Avoid
subordinate clauses. His own reports were
couched in hand-thrown prose. They left

nothing to the imagination. Proper and frequent use was made of the full stop. His puritan ways with prose were extended to his staff; he'd had occasion to take that cavalier wordsmith DI Redfyre to task for committing acts of wilful alliteration. And the superintendent had nothing but scorn for the way Scrivener, this weasel of the press, was using innocent words to misdirect and inflame his readers. He forged on, his suspicions growing darker by the line:

One of these witnesses suggested to your reporter that this was not the heavy-handed and over-officious reaction it might at first appear. In his view, the police were right to be suspicious. Did she fall, or was she pushed? Tripped? Doubtless all will be made clear, but those of us who heard her pitiful screams were left in a state of extreme unease. An attempt on the life of a gallant and beautiful young woman had been made, some felt. Possibly an organised attempt. A conspiracy? But why could anyone possibly wish to destroy such talent? Unless, it has been whispered, the coils of masculine envy and hatred had been stirred into venomous, possibly collegiate action, roused by the question of her sex. No one objects to beauty and courage, but many — very many in this town and further afield — object to the display of a talent which has hitherto been regarded as the province of the male sex.

"Ladies do not play trumpets." That very warning was, according to a close friend of the injured girl, sent to Miss Proudfoot anonymously before the event. With typical bravery, she insisted on continuing with the recital. She had been denied a platform for her talents on every other college and musical stage in the city, and this appearance at St. Barnabas, playing alongside its world-famous organ, was her first chance of revealing her skills to the world.

Could it be that some interests had decided that it should be her last?

Readers will remember that, hitherto without exception, the male colleges of the university have consistently voted to deny the granting of a degree to female students, however outstanding their talent.

Miss Proudfoot is at present being treated for her injuries at Addenbrooke's Hospital, where she is expected to make a complete recovery.

Bloody Hell! Was this idiot trying to start a civic war? How much of this guff was actionable? Better get a lawyer to look at it. This slimy Scrivener had just managed, by deceitful flattery, to avoid overt criticism of the police force, but he'd surely trodden on someone's toes? The notoriously sensitive toes of a powerful academic institution, one of the wealthiest and most powerful colleges in the university? St. Barnabas was not an establishment to take such an accusation lying down. And if anyone was going to be handing out accusations of attempted murder and collegiate conspiracy, it was going to be Superintendent MacFarlane, CID, in his own good time.

Raging, MacFarlane called downstairs to the desk. "Get me a squad car! No drivers? Sod it! I'll drive the bugger myself! Tell anyone who's interested I've gone down to the river. To chuck myself in," he yelled, delivering his communication in decidedly parataxical style.

CHAPTER 7

In the gray murk of pre-dawn, Redfyre became aware of a small group of people huddling disconsolately around a tumble of clothes and limbs a few yards away from the towpath. A copper in uniform confirmed he was expected by waggling his torch about excitedly. The PC greeted him and came forward to take his bicycle.

"Who've we got officiating, constable?" Redfyre asked before joining the group.

"Doctor Beaufort. The best, sir. Two blokes from the hospital standing by with a stretcher and the bloke who discovered the body — a sewage worker out walking his dog — awkward old so-and-so."

"Inevitably!" Redfyre smiled. "Where would detection be without dog walkers?"

The copper handed over his notebook. "All there, sir. All that's known, anyhow — names, addresses, times, initial statements, geographical location, the usual."

Redfyre took it and read the single page by the light of the officer's torch, appreciating the brevity and neat handwriting. He handed it back with a nod and unhooked his murder bag from the carrier on his bike. He cast an eye over the group, kneeling uncomfortably on the frost-covered grass.

"We won't bother defining the crime scene," he instructed the constable. "We haven't got enough tape to cordon off a whole common, river bank and half a dozen boathouses! It would probably attract gawpers, anyway. Look, I've asked for reinforcements. Until they arrive, I'd like you to stand by the towpath and direct traffic past. There's no one about at the moment, but in an hour there'll be cyclists and people going to work. I'll be taking a look at the body first, then organizing a sweep search of the immediate area as soon as we have light enough to see what we're treading on."

"Sir. Yes, sir!"

A stocky, short-legged figure in a trilby hat broke from the group as he approached and hailed him with a disrespectful "Oi! You! 'Bout time too! Officer, are you? I need permission to take my hound home for his breakfast." He pulled forward a forlorn-looking dog that echoed its master in general physical makeup. On cue, it uttered a pitiful whine and scrabbled in the grass with frozen paws. "Your bloke in uniform has been damned difficult! If Toby turns up another corpse, I shall tell him to just leave it! And we'll pass on by. Let some other fool suffer a police interrogation for a full hour on an empty stomach."

"Good morning, sir! Mr. Hanley, I believe? Manager of the sewage works?"

"That's director of the pumping station to you."

"Well, thank you for reporting the find and cooperating with my constable. PC Somerton tells me you have been very helpful and patient. I've read your statement." He bent to fondle the long velvet ears of the puzzled-looking basset hound. "You're a clever chap, aren't you? Finding a body in the dark? Ready for brekky, old mate? Aren't we all?" He straightened and addressed Hanley again. "Do feel free to go home now, both of you. I have your details in case I need to bother you again. I'll take it from here."

He began to turn away.

Mr. Hanley was suddenly disposed to linger. " 'Ere! 'Arf a mo'! Don't you want to know how he came to find her?"

"I'd love to hear, but don't let me keep you."

" 'Cos he's a *hound,* that's why."

"I noticed. A basset, I believe. Good noses on them, bassets!"

"Right on! Best scent hounds in the business! One minute he's pulling for home, the next he's dragging me over to the river, howling and whining. Lucky I had my torch with me." Even in the gloom, Redfyre saw the bluff face tighten at the memory of the discovery. "Your man marked the spot. Stuck, she was, snagged and frozen up against that old wrecked punt. Can't have traveled far downstream — there's not much of a flow in this freeze-up." He began to back away. "Well, must be off — got a works to run. Must keep the filth flowing, mustn't we?

"We must indeed! You and me both. Thank you again, Mr. Hanley. Enjoy your breakfast! And have an extra sausage for me!"

Redfyre's smile was returned, to his surprise, and a hesitant hand extended to shake his. Muttering a quick promise of help if there was something else he could do, the dog walker made off down the towpath.

Doctor Beaufort's greeting was brisk and affable, and then he fell silent. The two men had dealt with each other to mutual satisfac-

144

tion on several occasions. The doctor knew it was wise and time-saving in the long run to hold his report until Redfyre had studied the body and the surroundings. He looked on as the detective — young, he knew, but looking older than his years — approached the body. The doctor conceded that the situations in which the man chose to put himself were hardly conducive to a fresh, unwrinkled face; he saw distress, concern, enquiry and resolve chase each other across the handsome features as he watched. "Cause of death, doctor?" the inspector finally asked.

Beaufort pointed to the throat of the young girl. "Bruising here and here. Thumb marks?" He had learned to skip all the business of slathering his speech with concessive clauses of a "provided that . . . unless . . . later examination may show . . ." nature, designed to cover any misunderstanding or initial misdiagnosis. With Redfyre, he was confident that there would be no unfair retribution for that. He knew he was dealing with a soldierly outlook on the task at hand. One that decided on the objective and went straight for it. "There may be water in the lungs, but I doubt it's of drowning that she died. I'd say she was killed by someone taller than herself, and considerably stronger, who attacked her from the front, strangled her and threw her into the river. With this cold weather I shall have to make a few calculations in the lab to tell you when she died, but the initial estimate, and a vague one, is sometime late last night or early this morning. Honestly, John, it'll be not much more than guesswork."

"Wristwatch? Have you looked? Surely it would have frozen up at the critical time?"

"She's not wearing one." He added lugubriously, "Or perhaps she was and the perpetrator took it off her body. Robbery? Or to keep the time of her death a mystery? Perhaps that's why he took the trouble of heaving her into the river? To foul up the usual methods of calculating time of death? Well, I must say he knew what he was doing. The river iced over in the night — coldest evening in half a century, they say. Poor chicken! I wonder whose daughter she is?"

"Any indicators of her identity, doc?"

"Nothing apparent. She must have had a bag at one point, but it's not on the body. It may be in the water wherever she was chucked in. Some poor sod will have to go in there after it."

Both men looked gloomily at the crusted, grey-green murk just sliding into view in the dawn hour and shivered.

■ ■ ■ ■

Redfyre could put off the moment no longer. He knelt by the body, thankful that the doctor had closed her eyes and arranged her as decorously as possible in this ghastly scene. The face was stiff with death and hoarfrost and told him little. Her youthful features seemed at odds with the silvering on the black strands of hair that had trailed across her face, frozen there like a mask. To him, she was Edmund Dulac's Snow Queen: chilling in her beauty, as distant as a star and as mysterious.

Redfyre tore his eyes away and examined her left hand.

"No wedding ring," the doctor commented. "She's quite young. I've looked at her teeth. Nothing much in the way of wisdom teeth. I'd say eighteen to early twenties. Well nourished. I removed her gloves. The hands, as you see, are well kept. I doubt this girl ever held a scrubbing brush; she was no working girl." As Redfyre turned the left hand over and looked at the right hand as well, Beaufort added, "So, no signs that she defended herself. That's a pity. No broken nails or skin under them to tell their tale."

147

"No visible signs of violence then, doctor, other than the strangulation marks?"

"None. I've checked the fingers and wrists for sprains and breakage. Nothing. As far as I can tell, she put up no resistance. She may not have expected the attack."

"Or she might have been completely unafraid — trusting of whoever it was she came face-to-face with in this god-awful spot. She was a girl of some consequence, I'd say. And local, wouldn't you think?" He looked about him at the lights beginning to twinkle through the gloom. "Someone will surely know she's missing. Anyone . . . ?"

"No missing person reported answering this description," Redfyre said. "We're in free fall. But doing well so far! Without her bag, we're not likely to make much headway at the moment, but I do like to appear to be one step ahead of the grieving family. What else offers? Clothing — have you?"

"Only to establish that she wasn't the victim of a sexually driven attack. I thought I'd wait for you to take a look with me. I did notice a maker's label — a London one — in the cape she's got buttoned on around her shoulders, but there's no name tag stitched in. Girls give up on those habits as soon as they leave school and swap their uniform gabardines for a mink."

Redfyre's swift fingers checked the collars of her cape and dress and found nothing new. "Hang on a minute. It was a damned cold night, wasn't it?" Digging more deeply, he grunted with satisfaction. "She's got a vest on! Sensible creature. Chances are, it's been bought locally. Girls don't go to London to buy boring old vests; they pop into Eaden Lilley's. And that store keeps good sales records. Look here! It's a what-do-they-call-'em body protector, the sort they wore at school before the war."

"A liberty bodice!" the doctor corrected. "That's what that is. They have to wear them at school, but some girls choose to keep wearing them on the quiet. Not so much as a 'waste not, want not' effort, but because they flatten the chest, and these days what every girl seems to want is a flat chest. According to my eldest, who swears by them," he finished awkwardly. "Alice. She's twenty now." He gazed with barely concealed emotion at the dead girl's face.

"We'll have him!" Redfyre placed a hand on the doctor's shoulder in comfort. "Somewhere in the town, there's a shite tucking into his bacon and eggs after his night's work, one who's going to be having his Christmas dinner behind bars." Not professional or eloquent, but the doctor responded

149

to the feeling expressed and nodded firmly, unable to speak.

"And here's a name tag! On the bodice," Redfyre said, eager to reestablish calm procedure. "Thank God for Cash's name tapes. They've been of inestimable help to the police over the years. And, woven as they are, they never run in water. She's a Miss Shelley, Louise. Louise Lawrence Shelley."

"Hang on a minute." The doctor flashed his torch over the letters again. "You missed the full stop after Lawrence. Cash's never gets it wrong! Her name, or more accurately, the name of the owner of this piece of underwear is Louise Lawrence. Full stop. 'Shelley' is, I'd say with some confidence, having sewn on dozens of these over the years for my girls, the name of her house in school. Useful for laundry-sorting purposes. Mine were all in Raleigh House, after Sir Walter. They're usually Englishmen, heroes of 'our rough island-story' . . . Percy Bysshe Shelley House, would you say? The poet?"

Redfyre smiled. "No. I'd say Mary Shelley, his less famous wife. The novelist. And I think I can make a guess at the school. If we were to ring up the headmistress of an educational establishment just south of the river and ask her how she names her houses, she may tell us: Shelley, Wollstonecraft,

Nightingale and probably bloody old Boadicea!"

"It's the famous school for harridans you have in mind, isn't it?"

"An excellent establishment! And it could well be this girl's old school. It's a thread to pull on, anyway. Where's the nearest telephone?"

"We've been using the one in the vicar's parlour. See the church over there?"

"All Souls?"

"If you say so. The vicar had his lights on. They get up early to officiate or whatever it is they do, even in this weather. He said we could make free with his instrument in the name of the law. He's got quite pally with our constable — oh, Lord!" he broke off, his attention distracted by a stirring and a shouting on the towpath. "Now what? Look behind you, Redfyre. Isn't that the body-finder and his dog? Coming back, and at a fast trot. He's waving frantically, wouldn't you say?"

"I'll head him off," Redfyre said, and loped down the towpath to intercept him.

"Ahoy there! Told you he was a good hound! He's just made his second strike of the day. We'd gone about a couple of hundred yards — got just past St. Barnabas boathouse when he slung his anchor out and wouldn't budge an inch. Dragged me over to the side of the path, making his seeking noise the whole time. I finally let him run his course and found this!"

He reached inside his overcoat and, from a concealed poacher's pocket, pulled out a handbag.

"Good Lord, man! Do you remember where he found it, exactly?"

"Course! Some lout had stuck it upside down on one of those white hitching posts by the towpath. Just opened up the bag and jammed it on top. You could have missed it in the dark, but certainly not in the daylight; it wasn't exactly hidden. It's that post down there, in line with the bottom of de Montfort Avenue where it comes out on the river. I tied my hanky 'round it to it to mark it out. Red, with spots one. You can't miss it."

Redfyre took the bag and slapped him on the shoulder in delight. "Well done! You and Toby have done a dashed good day's work already, and the sun's not even up!"

"Glad to be of help, officer. Has the Force thought of equipping itself with a squad of bassets?"

" 'Scent hound times six: detective officers for the use of.' It'll be on the next requisition list," Redfyre assured him.

"Stroke of good luck?" the doctor said, cocking a questioning eyebrow when Redfyre showed him the bag.

"Nothing to do with luck, I think," Redfyre said, affirming his colleague's suspicions aloud.

"A setup? It would have been simpler to chuck it in the river with the body. Why leave a marker? A message? A taunt? Couldn't it just have been found by a third party, emptied and abandoned?"

"I'll settle for all of those for the moment. Let's take a look inside, shall we?"

Redfyre slipped on his gloves and handled the bag with care. Before he opened it, both men took a long stare at it.

"Goes well with the victim's outfit," Beaufort commented. "Sleek. Expensive. That's crocodile skin, and the fittings are silver. Distinctive. A lot of people would recognise it, I'm sure."

Redfyre clicked it open and they peered inside.

"Cheeky bugger!" Redfyre growled. "He's emptied it of whatever the contents were. Purse? Compact? Not even a bus ticket stub. Nothing!"

"Odd, that!" said Beaufort. "Bag like this, girl like this, you'd expect the contents to be worth making off with. And I'm sure we're expected to assume it's a common or garden robbery that turned violent. But any criminal type would recognise the value of the bag itself. Worth a quid or two or even ten in any back street pawnbroker's. Probably worth more than the contents, unless she was carrying something really special with her."

"Hang on! He's left us with one item." Redfyre drew an envelope from a side pocket inside the bag. "It's used. There's no letter inside. It's addressed to Miss L. Lawrence, Midsummer View, de Montfort Avenue." He looked up, his grey eyes glinting in the winter sun with an edge of steel that made the doctor look aside in concern. "Arrogant shit!" Redfyre spat. "When we examine that post, do you suppose we'll find a helpful arrow chalked in, directing us up the road to de Montfort? 'This way, Plod! You're nearly there!' "

The doctor turned and looked about him carefully. "Wouldn't be surprised. And I'll tell you something else — at this moment, I'd bet you a fiver he's watching us!"

"Second sight, doc? Cold trickle of foreboding, eh?"

"Put it down to experience. I call it my graveyard intuition. Because, on at least six occasions that I'm aware of, the bastard has been at the scene of a murder or even present at the funeral. In the graveyard — lurking, watching, enjoying his moment while he still can. One of the blokes who eventually confessed to the murder had actually hefted the coffin at one of these sad events! Yes, a coffin bearer! Getting close to his victim for the last time. Concealing his villainy behind a pious face and a strained shoulder."

Redfyre, spooked by the doctor's evident unease, swept a glance about him and groaned. "Don't look now but we're about to be accosted by a villain with a pious face. And the voice of a sergeant-major. You know my governor, DS MacFarlane, I think."

Beaufort grinned. "We've worked with — and against — each other on many a case. Good officer, I always say. You could do a lot worse, believe me!"

The three men exchanged grunts and nods of recognition and settled on their haunches to examine the victim in silence. Having taken in the scene, MacFarlane shot out a series of questions to which he received convincing answers. When he asked what progress they had made on establishing identity, Redfyre replied levelly, without a flicker of triumph in his voice, that they knew who she was and she most probably lived a hundred yards away across the road in the avenue. He produced the evidence of the handbag.

"It was where? Good Lord! You happy with that, Inspector?"

"No. Relieved — but suspicious — to have the information so soon." His voice trailed off and he looked again at the river, remembering its direction and trying to calculate its speed of flow.

"Makes no sense to me, but then, I'm a rational man," MacFarlane offered. "Get into his head, Redfyre! Why waste time and go to all the bother of heaving her body into the river? It's not as if he was trying to disguise it as a drowning by suicide or accident. He could have just left her to be found on the bank where he killed her. He didn't need to mark the spot with the bag. He didn't need to leave that envelope in there. He wanted us to know who she was, and what happened and where."

"But not when," Redfyre said thoughtfully.

"So why the hell put her in the water?"

Redfyre continued to stare at the river. "He wasn't calculating on a sharp-nosed hound and inquisitive riverman on the other end of the lead passing by. I'm not sure yet, and I'll sketch it out when I've had a chance to do a bit more ferreting. But whoever did this made a miscalculation, I'm thinking. His victim was discovered before she'd completed her journey. Another half hour and he'd have made his point, I fear."

"Mmm." MacFarlane had learned not to push his inspector when he had that introspective look on his face. "But you think you have a sure handle on her ID?"

"Yes. Apart from the envelope, we were well on the way to tracking her down via her school." He explained the name tape on the item of underwear. "And would have got there even without the beaten path he offered us. But, like you, sir, I feel we're being made monkeys of."

"Right. So get me the organ-grinder and I'll have his guts for garters. Next thing: a trip down de Montfort Avenue. I've shanghaied a sergeant to help you. Thoday was just coming on duty, so I nabbed him. He should be finished parking the car." He stood, put his fingers to his mouth and whistled. "Here he comes. He's a sound bloke; you can leave him in charge of things here. You'll want to check for footprints around the hitching post, I expect. Fat chance of finding anything! Ground's frozen, but go through the motions. He may have dropped a calling card in his excitement."

MacFarlane broke off and stared again at the dead girl. He gathered their attention and spoke more deliberately. "Look here, I want this poor lass taken straight to the hospital where her family can attend for purposes of identification. They'll clean the river filth off her and comb her hair. Make her look pretty again. Damned if I'm going to drag anybody who was fond of her out to this miserable scene. I mean, look at it! It's the entrance to Hades!" He added in stricken tones, " 'The wide, silent places of the night where Jupiter has buried the sky in shadow and black night has drained the colour from things.' " He ground to a halt in embarrassment. "Or something like that . . ."

The doctor had looked up, alarmed by the change in tone, but relaxed on receiving a reassuring wink from Redfyre. With a natural Yorkshire aversion to expressing sensitive feelings and a meager working vocabulary, the super would, on the rare occasions when emotion caught him out, dredge up something remembered from his classical schooling to supply his deficiencies. As he usually did, Redfyre covered for him by picking up the baton and running with it, capping his quotations. "Right on, sir! I expect any moment to see the grim ferryman, dreadful in his squalor, sticking out his awful old hand to relieve the wailing dead of their pennies."

The doctor shivered. "Know what you mean. A good thought, superintendent. It would haunt them for the rest of their lives. Hard enough to lose a child in any circumstances, but we can at least spare them this hellish sight. I'll summon up the blokes and escort her to the police morgue. I'll do my best. All we can do now."

Reverting to his customary no-nonsense tone, MacFarlane gave his final order. "Inspector, you go and break it to the parents or whatever poor sods are waking up now in that nice house over the way. You've got more words than I have, and they come out smoother. Take the bag with you for them to ID."

After exchanging a few words with Sergeant Thoday, he set off back to his car.

Redfyre left his bicycle in the care of the sergeant and set off across the river bank, striking out not for de Montfort Avenue, but for the welcoming lights in the church of All Souls. Putting off the inevitable? Wasting time? He was always ready to accuse himself of these shortcomings, but countered by telling himself firmly that a few minutes given over to reconnaissance and preparation were rarely wasted.

The vicar answered his halloo from the open door at once and understood what he wanted. No, the inspector would not be detaining him. He was staying on anyway to greet Mrs. Andrews and her ladies, who were bringing in the greenery to decorate the church for Christmas. Redfyre was invited to follow the Reverend Denton through to his office, where a telephone could be placed at his disposal. He declined a polite offer to take his hat and coat; the temperature in the stonewalled cell of a room next to the vestry where they fetched up struck him as lower than that in the frosty realm outside.

But the warmth of the welcome took the chill off. A cushion was plumped up and put onto a chair in front of the telephone, which was sitting at the ready on the right hand side of a tidy desk. A notepad and pencil were at hand. "Glad to be able to help in the dreadful circumstances," murmured the vicar. Responding quickly to the slight unease in Redfyre's expression, he hurried to add, "Not that I know a great deal about the circumstances — let me assure you that your constable was the soul of professional discretion. And so, I may say, am I! Nonetheless, I shall make myself scarce while you conduct your conversation. The best I can do, I'd say, is fetch you a mug of the coffee from the flask my wife sent me out with this cold morning. It's Old Brown Java from Matthews in King Street. Will that do you? Milk? Sugar, if I can lay hands on some?"

Redfyre decided this was a man after his own heart. He even liked the eccentric look of him, or the little he could see. Ecclesiastical robes seemed to have been flung on over a furry brown dressing gown, and a red woolly comforter was tied around his neck. A pair of mud-stained gum boots completed the picture. The face belonging to this teddy bear in fancy dress was appropriately round and benignly smiling. He returned the smile. "Ah! It'll be the best thing that happens to me today!" he said. "Just black, please. Nothing with."

"Another man who's learned to do without the frills!" The simple words told a fellow soldier that Denton had been an army padre. Coffee of uncertain provenance was sometimes available to the men, but milk, hardly ever and sugar, never. The vicar was in early middle age, Redfyre reckoned, and as well as being a coffee-lover, the man had the energy and confidence to carry on unabashed and without apology when caught in a doubtful state of dress at an unearthly hour.

He reached gratefully for the telephone.

The operator put him through at once to his number. A cool and youthful female voice answered.

"Hello. This is Saint Agatha's School, Cambridge, and this is the headmistress speaking."

"Miss Sturdy? So glad you're at your desk already! Detective Inspector Redfyre here."

"John Redfyre! How good to hear from you again. Though, on second thoughts, I can't imagine why I've said that! I don't suppose you're ringing to wish me a happy Christmas?"

"You're right, as usual. Look here, I have a question or two to ask, and the answers may lead to a sadness for the school, but if there is bad news, at least I shall be the one who delivers it. And I know you're not in the habit of shooting messengers."

There was a gusty sigh from the other end. "Go ahead. My best hope would be that Lettice Rumboldt has been caught shoplifting again but I'd guess from your tone that

162

it's more serious than a few stolen sherbert squibs."

"Indeed. And I only wish it were something I could solve as simply, but I'm afraid this case involves the discovery earlier this morning of a young woman who was murdered. Her body was fished out of the Cam. We're trying to establish her identity from a couple of clues we've turned up. My first question is, can you tell me if one of the houses in your school is named Shelley?"

"Shelley, the poet? Sorry, no. My predecessor opted for an inspiration of scientists. We have Curie, Herschel, Anning and Garrett-Anderson."

"Oh, dear! Wrong girls' school . . . I'm sorry to have troubled you, though pleased not to be burdening you with bad news."

"Hold on a moment. Shelley? Mmm — it's possible you're looking in the wrong place. I'm acquainted with a school that has Shelley as one of its four houses. The others are Byron, Jonson and Rochester."

"A dissolute foursome! I'm surprised to hear you keep such company, Miss Sturdy."

Suzannah Sturdy gave a blast of hearty laughter. "I try not to imagine the conversation of that rackety lot assembled around a dinner table comparing notes in Heaven! I hardly need to tell you that it's not a school for girls. It's one of those scandalous co-educational boarding school establishments that are all the go at the moment. Boys and girls occupying the same building, mixed staff, pick and choose your own syllabus — you know the sort of thing. The one that comes to mind is in Surrey, in a fold of the hills near the village of Shere. It's called Branscombe School, after the founder. But I'm too harsh. Friends of mine have sent their offspring there and been delighted with it."

After a pause she asked, "Do you have a name for this poor girl?"

"Tentatively. She could be a Louise Lawrence. A local girl. We have an address in de Montfort Avenue."

"Lawrence! Oh, no, not the Lawrences!"

Alarmed by the sudden silence following this outburst, Redfyre waited.

She reined in her emotions and the response came, tight-lipped. "The pharmacologist Lawrence is a well-to-do businessman, you'll find. We have the two younger daughters here in school — boarders, both. Read what you like into that. They're due to be going home for the vacation next week. They adore their older sister. Listen, if there's anything I can do or say to help —"

"I'll let the parents communicate with you

— once the identification is complete. We could just be jumping the gun; it's information I need at the moment."

"Of course. The girls' older sister, Louise, I have met once or twice. She was never a pupil here. She refused to be interviewed for a place back in the days of the old headmistress. She is a — er, a strong character, apparently, and insisted that her parents send her to a mixed boarding school a longish way from home. One of her older cousins was an alumnus and sang its praises. A determined young lady by all accounts. In retrospect, I'm sure she made the right decision for everyone concerned. Oh, dear! So it *is* to be bad news for the school after all . . ."

"Suzannah . . ."

"It's all right. I understand. Please offer my condolences if the moment ever seems right. I shall say nothing to anyone until you or her father communicate with me further. What a tragedy! What a waste of talent! I can't bear it. Oh, I'm so sorry, John. What an unpleasant task you have before you!"

"I'll say all the right things, don't worry. It's never easy breaking the news, but — I've never said this before, and it's an odd thought — the bereaved can be unbelievably considerate and generous. They try to set *me* at my ease, understanding through their own grief and shock that the messenger too must be suffering. Others, of course, try to punch me on the nose. I shall just have to hope that Mr. Lawrence is of the former persuasion."

"Good luck, and let me know what I can do. Oh, there's the assembly bell! Must fly. I toast crumpets at five every day, if you can manage — oh, dear!"

The phone went dead on a suppressed wail, and Redfyre was replacing the receiver with a gentle smile when the Reverend Denton coughed loudly from the doorway and came in carrying a fragrant mug of coffee.

"So, it's the Lawrence girl, is it? Dear, dear! Oh . . . I was loitering by the door trying to judge the right moment to come in, and I'm not going to pretend I didn't hear. This is no time for silly etiquette. Look, inspector, if you're going to take off for the Lawrence house, there's something you ought to know about that family before you go putting your foot in it. The two younger girls are wonderful, cheerful and thoroughly nice children — choir members, both. The father is agreeable enough, for a commercially-minded thrusting business man. But I ought not to speak in that

166

pejorative way, since his business is a very worthwhile one, he tells me. He has built himself a laboratory to the northwest of the city, and there, with university cooperation, he is carrying out research and development of a number of drugs and treatments which the medical profession desperately needs. He won't talk about it, apart from saying what a pity it is these medicaments were not available to mankind during the recent war. It is a valuable enterprise from which humanity will derive great benefit, I'm sure."

He looked shrewdly at Redfyre. "The conversation with Lawrence will be painful, but he will be rational and helpful. I have noticed this with businessmen — they don't waste their own time or anyone else's. No — the problem, if you have one, will be with his wife."

CHAPTER 8

Redfyre stood in the shelter of the deep porch of the Victorian house on the corner of de Montfort Avenue and tugged on the doorbell. As he waited for a response, he glanced about him, trying to estimate the quality of the reception he might receive from the family who lived here. He'd learned that an impressive setting was no guarantee of a civilised welcome.

Dangerous places, doorsteps! Especially for men in uniform. He remembered examining with pleasure the delicately carved Art Nouveau framework and ravishing stained-glass panels of an entrance by Macintosh (or his equal), a splendour behind which lurked a slavering bullmastiff with no pretensions to civility. He winced at the memory and reached automatically for the twelve inches of stout English oak truncheon he no longer carried in his long-pocket.

No expense had been spared on this

building; the architect had been given his head. He'd indulged in pillars, porticoes, leaded panes in wide low windows, and topped off his creation with a mansard roof-line that, taken with the rose-red brick decorative details, gave the whole capacious house the flavour of an oversized ginger-bread cottage. Rather sweet-toothed for some, perhaps, but Redfyre was no Puritan. He anticipated a well-decorated and comfortable interior suited to the needs and comforts of a modern family. Perhaps, he fancied, there would be a lingering sentimental attachment to the style of William Morris expressed in the furnishings and drapes. These would have been supplied by Liberty of London — all sweeping curlicues involving birds, fruits and foliage. But the traditional Englishness would be under-pinned by a severely twentieth-century approach to plumbing and electrically driven machines of one kind or another.

He caught himself indulging in what he admitted was a personal fantasy and shook it off.

He sniffed the air, wrinkling his nose. The ornate chimney pots were already contributing their dark reek to the skies over Cambridge, but he detected an underlying unpleasantness and made a swift check on the position of the weathercock, whose gilded tail was just glinting in the rising sun on the roof of the house opposite. It told him what he wanted to know. A northeasterly wind, though still too slight to loosen the grip of the frost, was oozing over north Cambridge, spreading not only an Arctic air stream, but a reminder that out there, a mile or two distant in the fenland, lay the infamous Cambridge Sewage Farm. Mr. Lawrence had chosen to call his house "Midsummer View." He could equally have called it "Milton Miasma." The local press had covered every irascible word uttered by the inhabitants of the harmless Cambridge village, which had had imposed on it the runoff from the open sewer that had been the River Cam for generations. And it was his new friend Mr. Hanley, Director of the Cheddars Lane Pumping Station just down river, who had the task of keeping running the massive engine which strained the river waters and diverted the glutinous product through two miles of underground pipes. The resulting effluent ended its journey in the fields of Milton, where it was dried out and prepared for reuse as fertiliser. "Well, that's something we have in common, Hanley! Shit-shovelers, both. And proud to do it," Redfyre was thinking when the door opened.

He found himself face-to-face with the servant girl whose domestic duties, beginning at some unearthly hour, had most probably awakened the house and set it on its feet. She was small and young, with bright eyes in a face red-raw from washing in cold water and harsh soap. Her lips were chapped from biting, but she managed a smile warm with welcome and curiosity as she twitched her pinny into place, bobbed and told him cheerfully it was the postie she'd been expecting. Redfyre grinned, apologised for the disappointment he'd caused and showed her his warrant card. He explained that he needed to have a word, rather urgently, with the master, Mr. Lawrence.

He was hesitantly asked inside and told, after a concerned glance at his damp brogues, to wait on the doormat while she went to find out whether Mr. Lawrence was down yet. He detained her. "Before you dash off, Miss, if I can just check a small matter with you to save time. A matter of lost property. I'm in possession of an item belonging to Miss Louise Lawrence. Is she at present under this roof?"

"Miss Louise? Oh, yes, sir. She finished her schooling last summer and she's back

171

home again for the foreseeable. Would you like me to take it up for her?"

"I must hand the item over to her directly and receive her signature for it, I'm afraid," Redfyre persisted. He was always uncomfortable winkling information from domestic staff without the master's permission, but one or two embarrassing incidents where close links between staff and employer had led to unforeseen collusion and worked against him had taught him to be less sensitive. Employers these days would go to any lengths to retain scarce staff, and staff would loyally support any good master or mistress.

The maid lowered her voice. "Um . . . not at the moment, sir. I got her fire going when I took up her morning tea, but . . . well, the bed hadn't been slept in. She's not here — somewhere else at the moment. I'll go and get the master." She was glad to shoot off about her business.

After an interval just long enough to convey the message that a visit from the police at this time was unexpected and inconvenient, the maid was sent back to tell him that Mr. Lawrence would see him in the breakfast room, but could only give him a few minutes, as he was going in to work.

Lawrence was seated by himself at the table, and he was clearly in the last stages of breakfast. A napkin trailing from his neck down to his corpulent bulge showed the progress of the meal from porridge, through egg and bacon to buttered toast. His chubby fingers hesitated in a marked manner between a choice of honey and marmalade to top off his last triangle of toast. The gesture told Redfyre that he was about as welcome at the breakfast table as a wasp at a picnic.

In understanding and pity, he watched the last piece of natural, if annoying, behaviour before shattering the man's world with his news. He gave his name and rank again and showed his warrant card.

"Mister Lawrence, I'm afraid I have some very bad news regarding your eldest daughter, Louise —"

"Well of course you have! You always do — Hold it right there, inspector." The tetchy command was delivered with an accompanying traffic-stopping gesture. "I will not be pursued into the intimate recesses of my own home by the police. What is it this time? Cycling with disregard for public safety? Knocking a bulldog's bowler off?" He opted for the Cooper's Oxford Thick Cut and continued as he reached for it, "How about showing disrespect for an officer of the law? That's one I always enjoy! Have you fellows really nothing better to do on a Saturday morning?"

"I only wish I *were* the bearer of such vexatious and trivial news, sir," Redfyre said sternly. "But what I have to tell you is of the most dire nature."

Lawrence's attention was captured at last. He tugged the table napkin from his neck and got to his feet to put himself on eye level with the inspector. A very male struggle for superiority ensued as Lawrence's bulbous dark eyes engaged with Redfyre's brown. Irrational anger gave way before cool authority.

"Carry on, man!" Lawrence barked.

"At about five o'clock this morning, the body of a girl was spotted in the river. Police aid was called upon, and she was taken onto the bank and examined by a police medic, who pronounced that she had been dead for possibly more than six hours. No bag and no identity papers were found with the body and, in accordance with practice, she has been taken to the police morgue at Addenbrooke's for clinical processes. It is believed that she was the victim of murder, not suicide. I have managed to trace her identity through a marker in her clothing and believe her to be your daughter Louise, who was in Shelley House at Branscombe and was still wearing one of her school undergarments. We would much appreciate it if you and Mrs. Lawrence would come to the hospital, where you may identify her formally in complete privacy."

It was impossible to tell how this was being received by the father, whose features had settled into a mask, stern and inexpressive. There they remained, his first line of defense against unpleasant matters outside his control. It seemed that, like the majority of bereaved fathers, Lawrence was choosing the stiff-upper-lip response to tragic news.

Redfyre gave him time to reel from the shock and regain his balance. Instinctively, he poured out a glass of water from the jug on the table and held it out to the silent father. To his surprise, Lawrence accepted it and drank it down. Quietly, Redfyre began to go through the rest of his litany. He enquired as to whether Mrs. Lawrence would prefer to be told the news by her husband. Redfyre was quite willing to —

At the mention of his wife, Lawrence found his voice. The inspector's services were abruptly turned down. He would take that sad duty on himself. His wife was an invalid. She was frequently unwell, and as her condition stemmed from a mental rather than a physical disorder, she obviously had to be handled with care. She and her daughter had not got on particularly well, but Ella would nonetheless be devastated by her death. His younger daughters, both expected back home now for the holidays, would likewise be informed by their father. They were devoted to their older sister and would be greatly affected.

Lawrence asked incisive questions about the circumstances and listened with care to the answers.

The father had no idea that his daughter had been out and about late at night. He had last seen her when she popped into his study to say goodbye before she went out with friends — lady friends, of course — to a shindig at St. Barnabas. Advent carols or some such. Lawrence had rung for a taxi to take her there. It was a long walk for an unaccompanied young woman. She had plenty of cash in her bag to take a cab back from the Market Square. She'd promised to be back home by ten o'clock and told him not to wait up. No reason to assume she hadn't; she'd always kept her promises. He'd spent the evening working in his study at the rear of the house and wouldn't have heard her coming in anyway. He'd gone to bed himself at eleven. His daughter had received little in the way of discipline at that wretched school, and Lawrence had taken it upon himself to lay down and enforce, even at this late stage, a few rules of behaviour. It had seemed to be working, as she had been much less rebellious of late. Seemed to have settled into her life.

Yes, she'd always been popular. Apart from school friends who visited all too often, she had friends in the town. "Town" was pronounced with a dismissive sneer. Lawrence suspected they were all rather louche, as she'd never invited any of them to the family home to meet him and his wife. Her girlfriends, of whom she had quite a collection — he frowned as he recalled them — haunted the place. Always giggling in corners. In fact, to go further, he was afraid some of them were in rather a fast set. He knew for certain, as he'd paid the subscription fee, that she was a member of a tango-dancing club. He was sure the inspector must have its name and address on his books, run as it was by a pair of dubious — Redfyre knew he was about to say "dagoes" to enjoy the alliteration — "South Americans," he finished. "Or so they claim. It's the home of the tango, you know, Argentina," he added helpfully.

Names of her friends? No idea! In the modern way, they arrived with no formal invitation. They'd usually pass one or two on the stairs on the way to her room. "This is Flora, Daddy. This is Victoria, Mummy." Giggle, giggle.

Louise had been in employment. Of a sort. One of his business associates had offered her a position in his company. Perhaps he'd heard of it? Messrs. Benson and Uppingham? Their HQ and offices were just over the common in Midsummer Place. Redfyre wouldn't have noticed it, camouflaged as it was in the row of grand houses for the gentry of Cambridge, such as they were. Redfyre thought he detected a tinge of property envy. The desirable setting was a mere ten-minute walk for the girl over Cutter Ferry Bridge. The factory where the medicaments were actually produced was out on East Road, the factory hands all came from over there somewhere, and the management (and Louise, of course) had no contact with that side of the operation. Responding to Redfyre's bemused look, he elaborated, "Purveyors of Perk-You-Up Pills to the Pallid, don't you know." This snatch of information was delivered without a touch of irony, and Redfyre took it for an advertising jingle he was not aware of. Not being one of nature's pallid people, there was no reason why he should be. "The pills . . . Surprisingly effective, I hear . . .

Some swear by them, Mrs. Lawrence included," Lawrence was grinding on. "Oh, nothing too demanding, the job. She sat about for five hours a day in Benson's office answering the telephone, keeping her employer's diary in order. No, not a secretary — never let her hear you call her that. She didn't even know how to type, I'm afraid, and refused to learn. Oh, dear . . ." He looked aside for a moment, gathered himself and continued, "At first, she was actually allowed to tot up the figures. The accounts." Another pause. "She must have made a faux pas, however, because she was relieved of accounting duties pretty sharpish. Surprising, that — my Louise was always very good at tots. Clever with figures, when she was a little thing. Taught her myself." A misting of regret was wiped away by a brisk stroke of resentment. "Yet another useful skill to rust away at Branscombe!"

At this point, Redfyre produced the handbag from his inner pocket. "This was recovered near the scene," he explained. "I wonder —"

"That belongs to Louise. It's her best bag. The present she chose for her eighteenth birthday. She always used it in the evenings. Could never be bothered with those little dangly things."

"It was empty when found. Do you have any idea of what it might have contained, sir?"

"Not the foggiest. Whatever girls carry about with them. Powder compacts and such like? Her house keys. She was allowed her own set. Cash — she was never short."

Sensing that his information lacked the precision that Redfyre had been hoping for, he harrumphed a bit then said, "Look here, the maid will know more than I do. Girls keep diaries and such, don't they? All the names you want are probably written down somewhere in her room. Beth will take you up and show you around. You'll have to tell her why you're snooping about, of course. Go carefully — the girl was very close to Louise, and she'll be as devastated as her sisters. In fact . . ." Suddenly the shrewd businessman, he paused and added, "Word of advice: you'll get the best out of Beth if you don't let on just yet that her mistress is dead. As soon as you announce that, you'll sink under a tide of tears and a hurricane of hysterics. Stiff upper lips never much in evidence amongst the servant classes. They enjoy their drama too much. And you'll be exposed to three acts of it if you're not careful. No — if you ask her help to track down her *missing* mistress, she'll tell you everything she knows, calmly and as a matter of urgency. Women!" Redfyre didn't care to hear the scorn in his voice. "Got to know how to handle 'em, don't you know. They can be as cunning as a trout." He tugged at a bell-pull, then sank back down into his seat, dismissing Redfyre and allowing him smoothly to carry out the next task on his list.

Beth's bright little face showed concern when the master told her to escort the policeman up to Miss Louise's room. "Miss Louise has chosen to do a bunk again, Beth. You're to do your best to help the inspector find clues to her whereabouts. Answer all his questions, there's a good girl."

Redfyre breathed deeply and found that he was clenching his fists as he followed the girl upstairs. Torn between the temptation to land a punch on Lawrence's arrogant nose and the annoying realization that the old rascal probably had it right, he tried to calm himself and take professional advantage of the easy ball he'd unaccountably been bowled.

The first thing he did on entering Louise's room was to explain that the young mistress had failed to return home last night, as Beth had discovered. Her handbag had been found and handed in. It had been identified as Louise's, and he was here to investigate further.

The girl was concerned but ready to do her best to help. She confirmed that the bag was indeed the one Louise had taken out with her the previous day. She was intending to go on to some musical event after work. It was her best bag. She gave him an account of the items Louise normally carried about with her.

"She was robbed, sir, wasn't she? Is that what you're saying? And it was a Friday night, too."

"Friday, Beth?" Redfyre picked up on the precision. "Is that important?"

"Payday. Her boss gives her her wages — never a cheque, always cash — on Friday afternoon. Banks being shut until Monday morning, she always carries it about with her at the weekend. I tell her it's a barmy thing to do, but she always says the same thing, laughing an' all. 'Not on your Nellie! This house is no safe place to leave anything precious! My bag's my bank.' "

"Have you any idea how much she earns, Beth?"

"No, sir. She never did say. Enough to bulge one of them brown pay envelopes. And seeing as she's living here, all found, whatever she gets is just pin money. What she doesn't leave in the bank I reckon goes to clothes she buys in London. She goes up on the train about once a month with her smart friends, and sometimes she stays over. That's why I wasn't too worried. But if her bag's been taken, well . . . She wouldn't give it up without a fight, sir. P'raps she's been knocked unconscious and left in a ditch on the common, sir. In this cold!"

Redfyre cut short the beginnings of gloomy speculation, assured her that the common was being searched, and drew her attention to the room and Louise's belongings. A diary was located and placed confidingly in his hand. "You'll find names and addresses and telephone numbers and such like at the back, sir."

He began to look about him from the doorway, quartering the space as he had been trained to do when dealing with a crime scene. The pretty room was decorated in fresh shades of green and yellow and predictably furnished by Heal's of Tottenham Court Road. The eye-catching draperies hanging at the two windows were of printed cotton in a design he thought he recognised — Charles Voysey? Amongst the swirling shades of jungle green, he could just make out the mysterious shapes of exotic birds. Parrots? Peacocks? Despite the lack of occupant, Beth had faithfully gone about her duties; the fire was cheerfully taking the edge off the cold, and the curtains had been drawn back to reveal a pleasant view over the stretch of common and on down to the river. The tree-lined river path, he thought, must be a wonderful sight in the summer with its constant parade of boat crews, cycling coaches and loafers. With a stab of belated concern, he approached to check whether the scene of the discovery was visible from the house in the now-watery sunshine that seemed to be dispelling the gloom. How appalling if the family had been able to catch sight, unwittingly, of the body of a loved one being carted off on a stretcher to the ambulance. He stopped a few paces from the window and stared. Something nagged at his attention. His eyes were sending him a message that his brain was too stunned to make sense of. He looked again more carefully, filled with foreboding.

"Sir? Sir!" Beth was calling him over to the wardrobe. "Come and look! I can tell you what she was wearing, because it's missing. Would that be any help?"

Although he had personally inspected the outfit on the girl's body all too recently,

Redfyre took out his notebook, wrote down the clothes Beth listed and thanked her.

"Mmm, all smart lady-about-town items. She wasn't planning an evening at the tango club, would you say?"

"Lord, no sir! That's Tuesdays and Saturdays. These are her tango frocks on the other side." Beth pulled out one or two skinny, silken, brightly coloured dresses. "These ones with fringes on them must look lovely when you're shimmying about in them," Beth sighed.

"And the other days of the week, Beth? How does Miss Louise spend her time? Does she enjoy reading? Knitting?"

A gurgle of derision greeted this suggestion. "Course not! She can't keep still a minute! Always something on the go. She plays tennis, goes off on walking holidays. Skiing — she's off to Switzerland next month. On her afternoon off work — that's a Wednesday — she packs her sporting gear and bicycles off into town for a couple of hours. She gets back in time for tea and sometimes brings back her . . . teammates."

"Team, did you say? What sort of team are they in, these girls?"

"Not really sure. Would it be netball? Indoor tennis? Not something outdoors, because her kit's never wet. Or dirty."

"Kit? What does she wear for these events?"

"White trousers like boys wear for cricket and her old school gym shirts. What she must look like!"

The response was rather scornful, Redfyre noted.

Suddenly conscious that this quiet, agreeable man was in fact recording her words, Beth applied a correction: "But that's not to say she hasn't a serious side to her nature. No, sir! She's a member . . . Is that the right word? Dunno. It may not even be a club . . ." Beth lapsed into thought and uncertainty.

"I'd like to hear anyway. It would be very helpful to know what societies she's joined, whose company she enjoys, what activities she's engaged in. Somehow, I don't picture your Miss Louise as a member of the Band of Hope Temperance Movement or a recruit to the Women's Institute."

Beth grinned at the idea of the Women's Institute. "Well, it sort of is that, sir. Not the regular one that meets to pass on jam-making recipes and bake Victoria sponges. Nah! That's of no interest to Miss Louise! But there *is* something she and her friends are nuts about. There's a group of them, and they go round each other's houses for a natter. At least once a week. It's not regular. Sometimes they see each other twice or three times when they've got something important on. If you can find them, they might know what she's up to."

"How many of them? What do they talk about, Beth?"

Beth hesitated, perhaps wondering if she had been unwise to have spoken out. "There's about eight of 'em, though they don't all come at once. Between eight and a dozen, I'd say. They always talk private, sir. When I'm around handing the tea, they just talk amongst themselves about fashion and men and what's on at the Alhambra. But I have overheard them gabbing on about politics . . . if that's the right word for cursing the government?"

"It's spot on, Beth. Names? Do you know the names of any of these girls?"

"Not their surnames. I've never heard them." Beth hung her head and looked aside. She was regretting opening up this line of thought. "Look, sir, perhaps I've got this all wrong. It sounds so silly now you make out it's important. It's rubbish, really. A right daft, kiddies' playground thing to do." She took a deep breath and rushed on. "Well, there's: Diana, Flora, Vesta, Victoria, Laetitia and Luna — such a pretty name. If ever I have a daughter, I'll call her Luna."

"Well, that's a relief! They don't exactly call to mind a witches' coven, do they? Very proper English names. Do they all end in an 'a'?" Redfyre asked with a smile.

After a moment's thought, Beth came up with, "No, sir. Venus. There's a Venus. She doesn't come round much, and she's . . . different, not like the other young ladies."

"In what way is she different, Beth?" Into the frowning silence that greeted this, he added, "Dress? Speech? Manners?"

"All those. She's a Cambridge girl, sir, judging by the accent. I mean, a town girl, not like the others who all talk posh. Not that she has much to say for herself. She's a year or two older than Miss Louise. She wears nice clothes, but they're always a bit . . . bright, if you know what I mean. Off the peg rather than bespoke. Gamages catalogue, not Harrods. But she must be something special — the others all treat her with respect. You know, pour her tea out first, offer her the last cream bun. I did wonder if she was in the Salvation Army . . . you know, some sort of do-gooding God Squad. The master's a big supporter of the Sally Bash."

"Are there any others who don't quite fit the mold, Beth?"

"Oh yes, there's one who stands out. She's a bit older than the rest, and bossy with it. I actually heard her giving Miss Louise a good wigging when she'd done something silly. This one's called Minerva."

"Ah, yes she would be. Goddess of wisdom and warfare. You'd want her on your side," Redfyre said softly, beginning to see a pattern.

"Minerva! Sounds to me like somebody's headmistress. Bit stiff and old-fashioned. Still, it suits her."

"And Louise?" Redfyre pushed her, seeing a connection and an exception.

"Um, Miss Louise was called plain 'Iris,' sir, for purposes of these club meetings. That's what makes me think they were all using . . . er . . ."

"An alias?"

"That's right. That's young ladies for you. Never satisfied with their given name! What's wrong with Louise? Not much you'd say, but it was never quite good enough. She started calling herself 'Lois' when she got down to that school in Surrey. Sounds much smarter, she said. And she had a right to all the letters anyway, she'd just chucked away two she didn't need. But when it came to these ladies' club meetings she was 'Iris.' Why? There's dozens of Irises in Cambridge. Nothing special." Beth shrugged her shoulders and rolled her eyes in exasperation of such infantile frivolity.

"That's eight names with something in common, though." He sighed. "A self-regulating group with a common purpose? And they've awarded themselves seats at the very highest table, it would seem. Higher even than the highest table in Cambridge!" He added mischievously to lighten the mood, "I begin to suspect Miss Louise has joined something more terrifying even than the Women's Institute, Beth!" He lowered his voice and confided, "I think she may be a member of a pantheon!"

"Is that against the law, sir? Can they lock you up for it? Sir, I never meant to — she'll kill me if she ever finds out I've blabbed and made her out to be an *agitator.*"

Alarmed to see that he had genuinely scared the girl, he quickly said, "Just joking, Beth! A 'pantheon' is a collection of ancient gods and goddesses. I couldn't help noticing that all the names you remember — including lovely Luna, goddess of the moon, are those of Roman deities. Iris is goddess of the rainbow." His voice lost its school-masterly tone as he added quietly, "Shimmering, colourful, a fleeting, misleading presence. But it's no more a crime than joining a gentlemen's club, I assure you! Perfectly harmless! Perhaps they gather to read each other extracts from classical literature, eat dormice stewed in honey, or worship Astarte . . ."

"Nothing like that, sir!" Beth looked at him in puzzlement for a moment, then, coming to a judgement about him, decided to confide. "I think perhaps you ought to take a look in Miss Louise's special cupboard. It might help you to find her. I know where she hides the key."

CHAPTER 9

MacFarlane was loitering by the reception desk when Redfyre hurried in to headquarters.

"He's been waiting half an hour for you! Says you told him to present himself for interview at nine." The superintendent narrowed his eyes and gave a triumphant bark. "Hah! Thought as much! You'd forgotten you'd booked him. The Barnabas man from last night's show. The lad who should have been officiating when your lady trumpeter took a dive — remember *him*? The sergeant got his address from the college and left him a message. Glad *one* of my men at least appears to be doing what's expected of him. You can probably do without this interruption to your busy day, so just get him to sign something and pack him off. I managed to detain him for you in the holding pen. But he's getting twitchy!"

"Thomas Tyrrell! Light-bearer to Juno

Proudfoot — Lord! I *did* forget. I'll take him up to my office."

"Tyrrell, Thomas. Post-graduate student at St. Barnabas," the chap announced the moment he sat down opposite Redfyre. He checked his wristwatch. "I have a confession and an apology to make."

He'd have him out of his hair faster if he went with this seemingly controlled flow of narrative, Redfyre reckoned, and he smiled encouragement.

"I was distracted and deflected from my duties at the concert last night. Had I attended to them more rigorously, the accident to the young lady — the fall she suffered — would most probably not have occurred. I was meant to pull back the curtains to the organ loft and light her descent with my lantern. The staircase is not wired for electricity, you see. I have reported my omission — my sin — to the master, and he recommended that I come to confess all to you personally."

At last, he was hearing a straightforward account. Redfyre noted the earnest expression, the handsome young features sculpted by guilt and a sleepless night into the image of a penitent saint. Flushed. Inward-looking. Otherworldly. For a moment, Redfyre was glad flagellation had gone out of fashion; then he remembered the theatricality of Tyrrell's performance early the previous evening and warned himself that he was dealing with something of a poseur. He suspected the man had already obtained absolution from a higher authority than the Cambridge CID and was now free to indulge in a show of noble contrition.

"Well, thank you for coming. I can well understand your predicament," Redfyre said. He decided to bowl him an easy ball to test his strength. "Um, this distraction and deflection you mention —"

His question was interrupted by a torrent of words from Tyrrell.

"Lois Lawrence! That's her name! Daughter of Eve! She tricked me and seduced me from my duties with blandishments and alcohol!"

Redfyre sat up in his chair with a start on hearing the name. "What? Wait!" He held up a hand. "Hold it right there! Would this be the Lois Lawrence who lives in de Montfort Avenue? Eighteen years old? Dark-haired?"

"That's the one! Though she's older than eighteen. She's the one to blame for landing me in this hot water! And for nearly getting that poor woman killed. The master tells me Miss Proudfoot survived and was taken to hospital. How is she doing?"

"First, Mr. Tyrrell, I'd like you to go back over yesterday evening and tell me exactly what transpired."

The official request to hear his story calmed Tyrrell, and a succinct account from the hunt for the bag and the fortuitous glimpse of its contents, through to their escape to the pub, followed smoothly. Slightly irritated by Redfyre's insistence on knowing, down to the grains of salt on her pickled egg, what Lois had consumed, he filled in the details with a puzzled brevity.

When he reached the moment where Lois had left him alone in the back parlour, Redfyre tugged on the reins and required him to be as precise as possible regarding the timing of his subsequent actions. "So, an hour's performance after the interval takes us to eight-thirty, eight-forty if we add on the encore, to the moment when you were scheduled to do your stuff, but with time flying in the company of a young lady and a couple of beers, you missed your cue. When exactly did you become aware of this?"

"When the audience — a selection of it, all male, of course — began to arrive at the bar, discussing the drama."

"So, at about eight fifty-five?"

"I would think so. About nine. Yes, it was nine o'clock — I looked at my watch. Couldn't believe the time had passed so quickly. Miss Lawrence went off at that same time or seconds after and didn't return. Ten minutes later, I guessed she'd ditched me and gone off to get a taxi. I decided to chase after her. But then I thought: 'What on earth shall I say when I catch her?' And I couldn't think of anything that didn't sound peevish and juvenile. I wandered around the Market Square for a bit, but couldn't spot her. It would have been easy to miss her — there were crowds gathered to hear the Salvation Army band playing carols. And so many people jostling for taxis home. Perhaps someone had given her a lift? Invited her to share their cab? People do that when they're feeling jolly. It's quite accepted, you know. I was getting cold by then, as I'd gone out without my overcoat and was beginning to feel rather silly. And guilty, too — I'd ratted on my job and probably been the cause of a serious accident. Only one thing I could do in the circs. So I bit the bullet and came straight back to college to make a clean breast of things. I went to the master's lodge, saw that his lights were on, and asked to see him."

"Timing, please Mr. Tyrrell? Can you be precise?"

"Well yes. You can check it yourself. The porter makes a note every time you go in and out. It was nine-thirty."

"Doctor Henningham agreed to see you at that inconvenient hour?"

"Oh, yes. He's very modern in that way — always makes himself available for the students. It was especially good of him to give me a hearing, considering . . ."

"Considering what?"

"He was taken ill. You didn't know? He was actually in rather a bad way when his man showed me in. I was told to be quick about it and not be surprised if the master did a sudden bunk because he had the trots. One of those Delhi Belly interludes. He's just back from India — been there for the last six months. They say these things sometimes catch you just when you think you've got away with it! I must say, he looked foul! Rational enough and his usual genial self, but green round the gills. Having trouble with his breathing, but luckily he didn't need to sprint off before I'd made my confession."

"And you left him at what time?"

"Nine-forty. I've told you — check the porter's book. Then I went back to my digs on Maids Causeway —"

"On foot or by bicycle?"

Impatiently, the reply came. "Well, on foot, of course. My bike's laid up with a puncture in the shed at the back of Mrs. Luscombe's, my landlady. I let myself in and went straight to bed. Before you ask, it was ten o'clock. I have my own keys, as Mrs. Luscombe is often out in the evenings. She's a war widow on a pension, but a very sociable type of person. I couldn't sleep and I heard her come back in, drunk as a skunk, giggling and tripping over the stairs at about — oh, it must have been after midnight. Well, it was. She told me when she served my breakfast she'd been out with a gentleman friend for a special pre-Christmas dinner at that new Motoring Inn that's opened on the London Road, and they'd 'heard the chimes of midnight' as they drew up outside."

Redfyre made a note.

Tyrrell looked at him sideways. "You *do* go on about the time. Does it matter?"

"Oh, you know what policemen are like. We try to plot every witness's movements within a time frame for the record. Especially when we're dealing with an attempted murder and an actual murder, occurring within hours of each other."

198

"I beg your pardon? I thought we were discussing one accidental fall . . ." Tyrrell's voice lost its confidence and he gulped. "I say, would you care to elaborate on that surprising last statement?"

"Certainly. I'm almost sure that there was an attempt on the life of Miss Proudfoot in the chapel at about eight-thirty. An attempt which would have been neutralised, had you done your job, young man. And a second person with links to the attempt, Miss Louise — or Lois — Lawrence, was herself murdered, probably by midnight, and her body discovered at about five o'clock next morning."

"Lois? Murdered?" Tyrrell fell silent, his eyes starting from his head. He began to tug nervously at his blond quiff and breathe shallowly as the enormity of his situation stunned him.

"We are left with a scenario where a jilted young man who confesses a degree of animosity towards the girl who has deceived him has hours of time on his hands to go in pursuit, track her down, kill her and return to his empty digs at his leisure. Apart from the short time you were talking to Doctor Henningham, you do not, it would seem, have an alibi. I shall be speaking to your landlady and to the master in an attempt to establish an accurate picture of your movements last night. Meantime, I'm sure you understand, I must keep you incommunicado until I have spoken to your two witnesses. Therefore, if necessary, I am prepared to put you under arrest on a charge of the murder of Miss Louise Lawrence and possible involvement in the previous attack on Miss Proudfoot. You may avoid this measure by agreeing to stay in a holding cell. If you try to leave, I shall issue the arrest warrant. I'll have you escorted downstairs. The superintendent will probably want a word. Sarge! Ah, Sergeant, will you take Mr. Tyrrell to cell ten. And fetch the lad a cup of tea."

Tyrrell appeared for a moment to rally. He raised his head and called out dolefully. "Wait a second, Sergeant! Would you make that two sugars, please?"

"Good man! We've got 'im bang to rights then? Selfish little berk! I'll just ring the chief back and let him know the good news. No communication as yet with the press." MacFarlane was cock-a-hoop as he ran an eye over Redfyre's interview notes.

"No sir! He didn't do it. I'm reasonably certain of that. My instinct is telling me he's involved only to the extent that he's been put up to mischief by others — used as a cat's paw. There's a deeper conspiracy in play here, and we're not near to unraveling it. If you must, you could tell the chief that we have detained a suspect who is helping us with our enquiries and we may confirm identity by the end of the day, or some such. That should hold him."

MacFarlane glowered and muttered, but he knew better than to mistrust messages from Redfyre's gut. He reluctantly returned the receiver to its hook.

"From where I'm sitting, sir, it looks as though the chosen scene for this debacle, the university body, is the rich but rotting medium from which this nasty fungus has spawned."

"Right! For once I'll grant you a metaphor, and remind you that spores are airborne, free to blow about and settle anywhere. Go for the master, Redfyre, before worse occurs. Pin him down and interview him straightaway. I bet he knows something! It happened on his watch. And be prepared to be hoodwinked — you know what these university types are like for protecting each other. He'll swear the young toad Tyrrell was in bed with Mrs. Master all evening if he has to, to get him off a charge . . . He's got the what? The squitters, eh?" Mac-

Farlane gave an evil grin. "Perfect! That'll learn 'im not to go gadding off to foreign parts in term time. Use it, Redfyre! Catch him off-balance. Square your shoulders, block his exit to the jakes and stand no nonsense."

"Doctor Henningham! It's very good of you to see me, bearing in mind your, ah, delicate condition, sir. I'll make this brief."

"Not at all, Redfyre. We've all seen worse in the trenches, what! Just stay clear of the doorway, in case I have to go rocketing through. I'm not expecting it — the worst, I'm sure, is over. Unless the worst turns out to be malaria." He sighed and grimaced. "There's always that fear. Nasty payload satisfactorily jettisoned last night, however! Sorry I had to bail out early. I knew I was leaving matters in capable hands." He managed a wan smile. "Can't say it was unexpected — the medics always warn one. It's just that, having made it through six months of secondment to India unscathed, one begins to feel one is immune."

Redfyre peered at the master, who was lying shivering on a chaise longue, rugged up to the chin in a tartan blanket. The ruddy features he remembered from the previous evening were pinched and pale, and there hung in the air a faint trace of vomitous effluent.

"You got back last week, I understand?"

"Last Monday. Not a day too soon! Much picking up of threads to be done. And a fair bit of heavy-duty darning, you might say. I could have well done without this present piece of drama. I can tell you!"

"So, I hadn't appreciated that the arrangements for the concert were not within your —"

"No, indeed!" was the swift response. "I'll make it clear, Redfyre. Have you read the local paper? No? Take my copy and make what you will of it . . . The idiot reporter is ascribing to me a generosity of spirit to which honesty does not permit me to make a claim. Here." He handed over a folded newssheet. "Take a look. 'Miss Proudfoot' — to whom the feller seems to have lost his heart! — 'was denied a platform for her musical talents by the whole university,' he asserts. Apart, as he would have it — from this college chapel. St. Barnabas. People are congratulating me on my farsightedness and liberality! Others are condemning me for breaking ranks and betraying the principles of the University. Men whom I had considered my friends are in a decidedly black-balling mood!"

He shuffled about in discomfort for a moment, sighed and confided, "It was not *my* decision to offer the girl a platform in the chapel. Not mine at all! I was in Calcutta, up to my ears in financial arrangements for an offshoot college over there at the time, and completely unaware of — or at all concerned by — box-office politics back home. Permission for the event was wrung from my deputy, Dean Herbert, whom I had left in charge. We'll probably find that *Mrs.* Herbert was the driving force behind it. Manipulative lady, Honoria! Awkward, what! In all honesty, Redfyre, I should say that, had the request been made of me, I would have declined it. I'm a traditionalist when it comes to the granting of degrees to women, and look with disfavour and dismay on the terrorist tactics certain feminist agitators use in their efforts to change the structure of our society. My stance on such matters is well-known, understood and supported. However, I want to make it clear that, presented with the *fait accompli* of the performance booking, I would have gone to any lengths to avoid harm coming to the talented young lady, who, as you must have noticed, is charm itself. I will help in any way possible to establish what happened to her. I cannot claim, however, that she performed in my college *sub auspiciis praesidentis.*"

His lungs or his patience, exhausted by this speech, gave out, and he broke off to cough into a large handkerchief.

"Thank you for clarifying that, Master." Redfyre took advantage of the pause in delivery to take up the matter he was really interested in. "But I'd like to hear what you have to say about your Thomas Tyrrell and his activities yesterday."

"I've given him a bollocking already!"

Redfyre enjoyed the spirited expletives which occasionally spiced the academic's expression. Clearly this man had spent time in rougher company than the effete fellows he rubbed shoulders with these days.

"The young twerp's well aware that Miss Proudfoot came tumbling down owing partially to his dereliction of duty. When she's strong enough to survive the awful sight, I'll send him along with a bunch of hothouse roses to grovel."

Redfyre explained that he needed to check the time of Tyrrell's arrival back in college and the time he'd left. He produced his notebook.

The master grimaced. "Of course. I can confirm both those times he gave you. It was a very brief encounter! Ten minutes at the outside. I was in no state to be able to grant him longer. The curse had just come upon me, and I had bellyaching enough of my own to suffer without dealing with an emotional music scholar ranting on about a girl who'd stood him up."

"Of course." Redfyre closed his notebook and got to his feet. "When did you realise you'd fallen victim to Vishnu's Vengeance, sir?" he asked, smiling politely. "My last sight of you was of a commander in chief, organizing his squad with aplomb."

The tough old face relaxed into a thoughtful expression. "You're right, inspector! It came upon me all of a sudden. One moment I was helping Coote down from the scaffolding, then I was handing back unwanted offerings — handkerchiefs and suchlike. An old lady came to retrieve her hip flask of brandy from me. Did you notice how effective that was, Redfyre? Something to keep in mind, eh, what?" His voice trailed away as he tried to reconstruct the later events of the evening. "Then, I suddenly felt sick. Could hardly get my breath. Headache, shivery and the rest of it. You'd got your witnesses lined up by then, so I pulled everything in tight and made a dash for the Lodge." Silence again for a moment, then, "I say, thinking of people's kindnesses, do you happen to know what became of that rather pretty little inhaler — the silver device that someone handed over. Smelling salts, she said it contained?"

Catching the appalling import of the thought, Redfyre took his time replying and chose his words carefully. "Yes, I do know. It's quite safe, sir. If I remember correctly, you unscrewed the top, took a sniff and identified it as smelling salts. You handed it to Miss Stretton, who was attending to her friend and she, rather ungraciously, you must have thought, snatched it from you, declared it an unsafe medicament and put it away in her bag." He smiled reassuringly. "She later handed it to me. It is at present locked away in the police safe in St. Andrew's Street," he lied. He had controlled the automatic movement of his right hand towards his right trouser pocket on the mention of the inhaler and hoped that the slight bulge of the object at present digging into his thigh could be taken, if noticed at all, for a cigarette lighter. He'd been about to hand it over to the master. "If you can give me the information which will identify the kind lender, I'll see that it's returned to her, sir."

"Two things, Redfyre. I think we both value precision in our work, so you won't think me pedantic if I clarify: I couldn't positively identify it as smelling salts. But don't take my word for it, as I have never actually had the experience of sniffing at such things. No idea what to expect. The ladies of my family are not the shrinking violet type, and things like that are unknown in my household. But I can tell you that it was disgusting! And to think that you're supposed, from the design of it, to insert it into a nostril and breathe in the fumes! The fumes from a substance which derives from the charred shavings of a deer's horns, they tell me! Argh. The very thought makes me retch! Glad I did no more than wave it under my nose!"

They fell silent for a moment, recalling the scene, then the master resumed. "Secondly, Redfyre, every instinct would be to avert one's nose when offered those salts. Believe me! No *unconscious* person, I am persuaded, would be physically able to make that life-preserving evasive movement had someone attempted to insert it into a nostril . . ."

Redfyre shuddered. "And Miss Proudfoot was at that moment out of her senses and immobile — but breathing."

"We should thank God for Miss Stretton's intervention! Lying here, feeling useless, I've had time to think this through. And now I'm going to voice the thought you are too professional to utter, Redfyre: I fear a *second* attempt was made on that young girl's life last evening. By someone who was prepared to activate a backup plan. Someone who was lurking, observing, manipulating others, riding on circumstances." He shot a penetrating glance at Redfyre and asked, "Are these fevered speculations? I rely on you to tell me if I've fallen into a state of delirium."

"If you have, sir, you have company. This is a path I'm treading myself."

The master nodded and continued, gathering confidence. "I fear we must contemplate a man or woman who was in no hurry, and ready to seize an opportunity if and when it offered. They had the means to hand and the nerve to use it. A cool game-player. The worst kind of opponent for a lawman who plays by the rules."

Redfyre nodded, his expression sober. Though impressed by the master's perspicacity, he was not ready to share his further thought: "Two unsuccessful attempts, perhaps. But another attempt on a young Cambridge girl's life has succeeded." He would keep this up his sleeve for the moment. He sensed that Henningham was tiring and was determined to keep the master's fevered and swivelling eye on the finishing line.

"And the lady who handed you this silver device?" he asked.

"Never saw her before in my life. Nothing out of the ordinary. Usual Cambridge lady on an evening out. But I must do better than this for the police!" He frowned and went on with precision: "She was five foot, four inches tall — a bit overblown, you'd say. Busty, corseted. Looking like anybody's aunt. No distinguishing features, unfortunately. She was wearing a straight-cut dark woollen coat — navy or dark green. A cloche hat, with a rather cheery spray of holly berries on the side," he finished in triumph. "Just the sort of trustworthy old trout you would accept help from. I didn't think twice!"

"Did she have anything to say to you?"

"Yes. She spoke well. Educated . . . low register. She knew who I was, addressed me as 'Master.' Said something like, 'Do give the poor girl a sniff of this. It will have her conscious and on her feet in a trice.' "

He gave Redfyre a concerned look, which was returned.

"Inspector, may I ask you to examine carefully that silver inhaler when you can get your hands on it? It *is* locked away, you say? Thank God! We wouldn't want that being passed around for sampling in the officers' mess!"

"Even with the lid on, it pongs!"

With the end of his pencil, MacFarlane poked at the silver cylinder that lay between them in the middle of his desk. "You feeling all right, Redfyre? You've been trotting about round town with this in your pocket all morning." He peered at it dubiously. "Is this what you'd call a 'vinaigrette,' by any chance?"

"No. Please don't fiddle with it, sir! It's the wrong shape and has a slightly different purpose, I think. Vinaigrettes are small, slab-shaped decorative containers and they have a lid that you lift. They give out sweet, strong odours — oils like lavender or eucalyptus dissolved in vinegar, I suppose."

The third man present in MacFarlane's office nodded agreement, his brown eyes twinkling with amusement over his face mask. Tall and silent, the masked man wore the green lab coat and gloves he'd rushed out in when he received the call for help at the hospital.

MacFarlane had wasted no time and pulled no punches. "We want your best man over here in two minutes. I've sent a car for him. That's it arriving now. Poisons! We need an expert in poisons to take a look. No, we're NOT sending it over in a bag! It's . . . *volatile,*" he improvised. "And an immediate danger to life. We could lose the whole force and the station cat if it gets out!"

Professor Henderson had arrived with a bag of precautionary pieces of equipment that had appeared to be snatched up and tossed in hurriedly as he'd left the laboratory. He'd put up the mask dangling around his neck in the doorway before entering and swiftly giving them a rundown on his impressive qualifications. These included, as well as one or two degrees, wartime experience in poisonous gases. He now carefully picked up the silver inhaler with a pair of tweezers and put it away in a glass vial with a tightly fitted stopper. He placed this inside a wad of cotton wool, packed the whole bundle into a steel box and again fitted a lid.

"You're right," he said calmly, "about vinaigrettes. The gentry would sniff them to combat the stench from the river or the crowded ballroom. But smelling salts, which this purports to be, can be carried about in any small container. Anything from a disused glass salt pot to a bespoke gold Fabergé confection carrying the family coat of arms. This one is a clever design that enables the contents to be delivered straight up the nostrils. I say — I must check, you haven't . . . ? Thank God for that! It may be quite innocent of course, you never know until it's tested."

"Bit of an old-fashioned device, I think?" the superintendent suggested.

"It's a very old-fashioned substance," the professor said. "Ancient. Known to us from Roman times — sal volatile," he went on conversationally as he stowed the box away in his bag. "Pliny the Elder mentions it: *hammoniacus sal.* Ammonia salt. No recorded cases of it being used by Roman ladies, who seem to have been made of sterner stuff but one sniff would give a lift to a fading wrestler or a faltering boxer. So I expect it was an essential item in the *materia medica* of any Master of Gladiators worth his salt." Straight-faced, he added, "Never ones to miss the chance of an unfair advantage, the Romans. And the well-trained, experienced gladiator represented, after all, a considerable investment to his *lanista.* No, this stuff has always been useful for anyone requiring an instant boost to the sympathetic nervous system. The Victorians abused it, and the habit is taking a long time to die out. I blame novelists for its overuse. It's a more dramatic device than a tap on the nose with a fan, and they have their overwrought characters reach for the salts to emphasise their emotional state and even to raise a laugh. Dickens has one of his characters — in *Hard Times,* I think — order some inhalers to be made up specially to be offered round to startled friends and family when he announces his wedding engagement."

"But can you tell if there's anything else in there besides ammonia? We're dealing with the case of a gentleman who has actually sniffed at that bottle and, we believe, was taken ill as a result."

"His symptoms?"

Redfyre supplied the list. "Breathlessness, headache, nausea, diarrhea — symptoms he naturally assumed to be due to a tropical stomach condition he picked up abroad. He's just returned from India."

"Well, I'd say he's probably right in his assumption. Sounds like gippy tummy to me. It's becoming fashionable to call it 'European cholera' these days. Still, murder is what you blokes have to deal with, and I expect you know your job. Let's take no chances, shall we? I'll bring this back to the lab and let you know if there's anything in here that shouldn't be as soon as I can."

The professor paused in the doorway and spoke again, thoughtfully. "I'm not a pathologist, but, you know, if I were, I'd take especial care in investigating the *nasal* tissues of any victims of heart attack, lung collapse and pneumonia that fetched up on my slab."

"Not sure he was taking us very seriously, but the feller's right, you know," grumbled MacFarlane. "All too easy! You can imagine the conversation: 'Aunt Matilda's had one of her turns . . . Heart attack this time, would you say, Brenda? Then we're all agreed? It's a heart attack! Send for the doctor. It'll take him ages to get here so, meantime, why don't we try to bring her round with a sniff of this stuff I got from the pharmacy? Still unconscious? Try again — the other nostril this time. Oops! Oh, dear! Never mind the doctor — send for the priest!' "

MacFarlane's voice trailed away, his black humour silenced by the dire implications of the theory he was forming. "By Gow! I wonder how many we've missed? When you think how many dodgy substances are available over the counter in a pharmacy! All it

215

takes is a little ingenuity to put them to lethal use. And it's worse in France! *La pharmacie* means 'what's your poison?' You just stroll in and take your pick! Even their tonics are nothing other than red wine with a hefty slug of cocaine. Ever tried Vin Mariani, favourite pick-me-up of Queen Victoria? Even endorsed by Pope Leo!"

Satisfied with Redfyre's stricken nod, he advised, "Stick to your whisky, lad. Now I'm wondering how many death certificates hastily signed in the presence of weeping relatives should have triggered a searching look up the nose of the corpse!"

"Lucky young lady, Miss Proudfoot. Doubly lucky. High time I went down there and asked her a few searching questions, I think, before she hares off back to London." Redfyre got to his feet.

"Sit down a moment. She'll keep for a while." MacFarlane smirked.

"How can you know that? She's a free agent and a very determined young woman. She's probably on the London train as we speak."

"Hardly! I've given instructions to the matron. They've managed to mislay the suitcase her friend Miss Stretton took along for her this morning. She has no clothes or shoes to put on, poor lass — she arrived in evening dress and a woolly blanket last night, of course, but that won't get her on the train to London. Her things will be found again only when Inspector Redfyre gives the all clear." MacFarlane's granite features cracked into a fissure that Redfyre interpreted as his grin of triumph. "So give her a good grilling when you see her. Find out what her connection is with Louise Lawrence. Get to the bottom of the first attempt, and the business of the second girl will soon unravel. And see if there's anything to be gained from tugging at this university thread while you're at it. I don't much like the sound of the dean's wife the master mentioned. Or even her name. Honoria Herbert! What's the betting she wields a six-inch hatpin?"

"I wonder if at this point we ought to ask ourselves if we may be barking up the wrong tree, sir. Are we getting ahead of ourselves? We can't be sure at all that Louise Lawrence didn't fall foul of some passing footpad or pickpocket intent on robbery. It wouldn't be the first time a villain has panicked and decided to silence his victim."

"Come on, Redfyre! Chancers of that type seek out crowds in busy places, not deserted river banks. I've read your notes. Who would have known — apart from Tyrrell — that she was carrying an unknown but suspiciously large amount of cash in her bag? Where did she get it? Why cart it about with her?"

"Waiting for the banks to open on Monday morning when she could pay it in over the counter . . ."

"At her local branch, we assume? We'll get Thoday in and brief him — he can do the legwork. Check where her account was held and the payment pattern. Why would she take her pay in cash, are you asking, Redfyre? Girls of her class would expect to be paid by check, wouldn't they? And allowing for the evidence from Tyrrell that she was flush, so to speak — why would she be wandering about after dark by herself on the tow-path? Shows a high level of recklessness to me."

"Not sure I'd say that, sir. She was stuck without a taxi and avoiding him. He may not have clapped eyes on *her* in the Market Square, but she could well have spotted *him* and made off. Allowing for the slippery conditions underfoot, it would take a healthy young girl thirty minutes at the most, I reckon. She would have returned home just before ten. A ten o'clock curfew sounds like a reasonable arrangement for a daughter, wouldn't you say?"

"Depends on the parents. Mrs. Mac and I have three little 'uns, two of 'em females. You wouldn't catch me letting one of my lasses out by herself at any hour. Not in a town full of randy young, usually drunken, undergraduates." He thought for a moment, then asked, "Is all well in that family, Redfyre? Go back and dig a bit further. And this friend of the family who hires a girl who doesn't even type . . ."

"I thought so too, sir. He's on my list."

MacFarlane grunted, scratched his head and resumed. "So, we've got the two of them in the Market Square, playing blind man's bluff round the Sally Bash band before they both take off into dark streets in different directions. Or did they? Tyrrell could have overtaken her easy-peasy if he'd run. Or used his bike. Or someone else's bike — any reported stolen? I still fancy Tyrrell for it. When you see his landlady, Redfyre, check the condition of the bike he says he has. Punctured, he claims? Have it brought in and looked at. Check the wheels for mud, gravel, dog shit, cow pats, whatever you like. And his shoes. If he crossed Midsummer Common, he's bound to have something interesting and distinctive stuck to them."

"Sir. I'll have it compared with the victim's

shoes, as well. I'll go myself on foot over the route she must have taken."

MacFarlane moved over to the map of the city pinned to his notice board. "Easier said than done. There's about ten different paths she could have taken."

"It's not really difficult when you understand the girl and her circumstances, sir. I think she would have correlated safety with distance, factored in familiarity, and come up with this track." He pointed at the Market Square. "From here, she nips down Sidney Street and turns right into Jesus Lane. King Street would have been more direct, but for a single woman out and about on a Friday night — never! It's one rowdy pub after another, all the way down to the Four Lamps crossroads. No, she'll get to Four Lamps along Jesus Lane. Her only problem here would be running the gauntlet of being accosted by members of the Pitt Club loitering effetely amongst their ionic columns on the steps of their classical Temple to Nobility. From what I've discovered about Miss Lawrence, she'd have had them ducking for cover with a few well-chosen epithets and perhaps a wolf whistle."

"She's still on course for Four Lamps though," MacFarlane commented, poking a stubby forefinger at the notorious junction of four main roads. "Our very own Red Light District, with the houses of ill repute along Maids Causeway, the taverns in King Street and the wide open, unlit spaces of Midsummer Common. Wouldn't like to think a lass of mine was negotiating Four Lamps without an armed escort."

"I agree it would take some nerve, but nerve I think our girl had. And, let's not forget, she's now almost in home territory. Her office is here, on the other side of the crossroads, overlooking the common. She could skirt around on the north side and nip down Brunswick Walk, close to the parade of posh houses, then follow along to the Cutter Ferry Bridge. After that, it's past the boathouses and she's home and dry."

"But someone distracted her. Between her office on Midsummer Place and the bridge, she met her killer. By chance? Possible. Was he waiting for her? If he was, he knew her regular route. Did he come out from the city centre? Following her? Trailing her and putting off catching up with her until the moment was favourable for a lethal encounter?" MacFarlane summarised with a sigh. "I dunno. It still takes a lot of pluck for a girl on her tod to do that."

"Courage derived from drinking two sherries?"

"Hardly! Not with the size of the shots they dispense at that pub! You'd need half a dozen to get you going. Perhaps she picked up an escort along the way? Someone she knew?"

Redfyre nodded. "The doctor said she might well have known the man who strangled her. She was facing him at the time of death and put up no perceptible struggle. Any sightings, I wonder? I'll get the blokes to do a knock house-to-house along her route."

Detective Sergeant Thoday was summoned to the office and briefed. He produced his own map of Cambridge from his pocket and spread it on the desk. "Got it, sir," he said and pointed a finger north of the river. "Here's Miss Lawrence's home. Here's the nearest bank on Chesterton High Street. It's a branch of the Midshires. I'll try them first." He traced her route back from the place her body was found along the river bank. "Not many houses along her route, in fact. And the ones there are in old alleyways, with back gardens running down to the river. I'll start knocking here," he pointed again, "and work my way along. I know a few characters in these streets from my beat-bashing days, and they're always ready to have a chat. At that hour, there's always somebody about, letting the dog or cat out, nipping down to the outside loo before retiring for the night. Worth a try."

MacFarlane smiled with satisfaction at the bluff confidence of the Cambridge man. "Excellent, Sarge! That will free the inspector to do his hospital visiting." He turned to Redfyre. "Give the young lady my regards, will you? And remember — she gets no shoes until you're satisfied you've squeezed everything you can from her."

CHAPTER 10

Redfyre introduced himself at the reception desk, where he was warmly welcomed by the nurse on duty.

"Yes, Inspector Redfyre, I'm pleased to report that Miss Proudfoot is doing well. Though I should warn you that since you saw her immediately after the event, the contusions have become evident. She's quite a picture this morning! All the glorious colour of the *Fighting Temeraire*! Luckily, no bones are broken, and other injuries are superficial. However, Matron asked me to pass on a request. In cases of blows to the head — and clearly we have one here — we really prefer that our patients spend a day or two under observation. But Miss Proudfoot insists that she is perfectly well and intends to leave our care as soon as she can arrange to sign herself out. She leads a busy life, she tells us."

"Indeed she does. And she's a strong-minded young lady. I'm grateful that you've managed to detain her as long as you have."

"Matron is hoping you will be able to exert some influence with our patient to encourage her to stay on at least one more night, Inspector."

"I'll do my best, Sister." Redfyre smiled. The hierarchy was as meticulously respected in the nursing profession as in the military. Constant observance of rank and use of titles was drummed into the women who staffed the hospitals from their first day in uniform. The best talent rose to the position of "sister," which Redfyre translated as "captain"; the supremely able rose to be "matron." And where in army ranking would one place a matron? "General," at least, he decided. Though in the case of Stella Foxton, "field marshal" might have been perfectly appropriate. With a matron of her calibre in charge of the Great War, it really would have been over by the first Christmas, with all sent home with a flea in their ear, guns and footballs confiscated until they could behave themselves.

"Matron can make herself available, should you wish to consult her, Inspector."

"Ah. Well . . ." He hesitated. He'd fenced with this matron on one or two occasions and lost each skirmish. "No need to distract her from her more pressing duties, I'm thinking, Sister." he lowered his voice and confided, "Just a routine visit. I shall be in and out in no time."

Her slanted smile and nod told him that was what she wanted to hear.

Before going up to see the patient he was careful to ask if any other visitors had presented themselves. Yes, at nine o'clock that morning Miss Proudfoot had had two callers, he was told.

"What? Two?" he questioned. "You were asked to admit no one but Miss Stretton before I arrived."

"The first was, indeed, Miss Stretton, bringing a suitcase full of clothes for the patient as we had requested, Inspector. The second was her brother."

"Brother?" Redfyre reacted with alarm. "Miss Stretton's brother?"

"No, no!" The nurse produced the visitors' book and pointed to an entry. "The *patient's* brother."

He made out "E. Stretton" in an illegible flourish and "S. R. Proudfoot" in a neat, clear hand. Just asking to be read, he thought with suspicion.

"The gentleman accompanying her was Mister Proudfoot." The sister gave a defiant shake of her flounced linen cap and fixed him with a challenging eye. "The request was referred to Matron, of course. Miss Stretton is well-known to her and Matron had no hesitation in admitting her in the company of the patient's own brother. He left twenty minutes later with Miss Stretton. He brought such a pretty little vase with one white rose in it. So elegant!" Her eyes closed, her nostrils flared and her starched pinny heaved in a sigh. Mr. Proudfoot, it seemed, had made quite an impression on the sister. She collected herself and carried on. "We've put our patient in a single private ward on the third floor, rather out of the way. I'll call a porter to take you up, Inspector."

"Thank you, Sister. Before I go up, I shall need a description of Mr. Proudfoot. Pernickety, time-wasting nuisance you'll think me, but I always say to myself, 'Better safe than sorry!'"

"That is quite understood. We have our own watchword: 'A stitch in time saves nine.' We count the benefits of that every day in catgut inches."

"Were you on duty at that time, Sister? . . . Good!"

He produced his notebook and wrote down every word of the succinct description she gave him, pausing only slightly in surprise as she confided the last telling detail in a discreet undertone.

Large south-facing windows were flooding the room with sunshine when he opened the door to the small ward. Juno was sitting cross-legged on the bed, swathed in a voluminous and very unbecoming gray cotton hospital gown which seemed to have been designed to slide off her slender shoulders. Her face lit up at the sight of him, and she closed the newspaper she'd been reading.

"Ah! At last! My hero!" She chuckled. "I've just been reading the paper's account of my fall yesterday and the stalwart part the Cambridge policeman played in cushioning me from disaster. So it was *you* I bounced off and swooned over?" She gave him an appreciative look.

"Inspector John Redfyre," he murmured. "Glad to be of service."

"I'm sorry to greet you looking like less than the contents of last week's laundry basket, but I thought red satin and high heels were a little outré for a Saturday morning. And if I had a wardrobe in here, that's all it would contain, I'm afraid, seeing that they've scuttled off with the supplies Earwig brought in for me. But since you're here, you can tell them to stop horsing around and hand it over." Her bobby-dazzler of a smile beamed again, and Red-fyre was duly dazzled. "They seem to think I'm trying to escape! As though I'd leave before I'd seen and thanked you. Now, don't stand about in the doorway, John — do you mind if I call you John? You did save my life, so it seems a bit unfriendly to call you inspector in the circumstances."

" 'Inspector Redfyre' will do to start with, Miss Proudfoot. When you know me better, you can call me 'Inspector.' And I can't claim to have —" His smile must have defused his brusque comment, since she grinned back and interrupted him.

"Oh yes you can. It says so in the daily rag. And anyway, I remember your face looking down at me when I came to my senses. You were holding my hand in such a reassuring way."

"I was searching for a pulse, I believe."

"Well, of course you were. So glad you found one! Now, I expect there's lots you want to ask me. Come and sit on this chair."

He approached and found that, with his knees in a state of quivering indiscipline, he would be glad enough to sit down. He restrained himself from loosening his collar. The atmosphere in the room was over-heated, over-bright and heavily scented by a

229

parade of bouquets of flowers lined up on the windowsill, each one accompanied by a florist's card. The girl's chattering liveliness added to his discomfort, as did her unconvincing attempt at flirtation. Any assumption of intimacy from a subject raised his hackles and shortened his responses. He turned the chair round so that he could face her and avoid squinting into the sunlight. A petty manoeuvre, but it was all he could do in this alien territory to assert his authority. When in doubt, move the furniture around.

A dour detective inspector in size ten brogues, overheating in his trench coat and agitatedly turning the brim of his fedora in nervous hands, was no match for this sunlit, barefooted imp. She had all the moral advantage of the injured party, which she quite literally was; he could just catch sight of (and suspected he was being *granted* a sight of) a sticking plaster on one scraped shoulder. Her left wrist was bandaged, the forearm streaked in the purple of iodine and the yellow of an ointment of some description, and on her left eye was a shiner equal to any he'd seen on a bar brawler on a Sunday morning. The other eye, blue as he remembered, shone back at him, full of mischief. Her fair hair, which had been plaited and coiled elegantly around her head the previous evening, hung loose in waves on her shoulders.

In Redfyre's artistic fantasy of the model before him, Rossetti had replaced Botticelli as painter of choice. She would be fitting as Fair Rosamund, The Blessed Damozel, Lady Lilith — any Romantic Lady of Sorrows who had ever fallen victim to man's malevolence. He was quite certain that, from the top of her shining head to the two pink feet showing below the drab hospital gown, she was offering him a calculatedly alluring picture of innocence. What was it about her that put him on the defensive, that triggered his instinct to pull down his visor, seat his lance and take aim?

The lies, perhaps? Her assumption that his profession was an indicator of a lumbering intelligence?

"Wonderful flowers," he commented as he settled. "Heaven knows where they find them at this time of year."

"Oh, in hothouses," she explained. "That's where. We have roses and lilies in December! Hyacinths from Holland! The Dutch are *so* clever with flowers."

Clearly, any conversational crumb he threw out, however dry, would be picked up and chewed over.

"And what it must have cost! People are

so kind," she added, her good eye swimming with tearful emotion.

Redfyre would have liked to take a closer look at the signatures and messages attached to the various bunches. Who knew about her narrow escape? Whose concern was sharp enough to prick him or her into ordering an expensive mark of esteem so swiftly? There came to mind Doctor Beaufort's story of the coffin-carrying villain, reveling in a final closeness with his victim. Redfyre put forth the question to himself: if *he'd* arranged this girl's death, but despite his best efforts, she'd lived on to play another day, would he then have sent a fragrant token of his regard and wishes for her swift recovery? Celebrating his chance to try again? To enjoy a second bout? It was always unpleasant to dive into the depths of the criminal psyche, but yes, he rather thought his criminal alter ego would have done just that.

The would-be killer's name could well be written *en clair* within arm's reach, and the only thing preventing Redfyre from seeking it out was crippling good manners.

"I didn't bring any flowers — I thought you might already have an overload." He fished in his pocket. "Thought you might prefer these."

She took the brown paper bag from him with the exaggerated expectation of a little girl at a birthday party. "Oh, you shouldn't have! What is this — a police bribe?" She stuck in a hand. "Ah! A bag of sherbert lemons! Not a bribe, then. Four ounces of sherbert lemons won't buy you much in the way of corruption. And there's something else — what's this? A book! Oh, thank you!"

"Something tells me that you like a good mystery. Do I have that right? That's the latest Agatha Christie. I'm not much of an admirer myself, but this one looks entertaining."

She read out the title. "*The Secret Adversary*? Hmm . . ."

"We all have one," he said blandly. "Some of us even *are* the adversary."

Her playfulness evaporated. "You think I don't know that?" she said in a sharp tone he would have thought her incapable of. Evidently, he'd touched a nerve. "Almost *all* of you are the secret adversary, the undeclared enemy of the female sex. Unscrupulous cheats who will resort to any underhanded tricks to prevail! To come first, to carry off the prizes, to win!"

"Well, that's croquet players for you! We'll risk our reputations to be first to strike the centre peg," he said, jovially obtuse. "You're

233

right. When it comes to a game of skill with the mallet, we just can't bear to be out-croqueted." He hoped that his frivolous comment would lower the developing tension, but he suspected it might provoke another outburst.

"There! You see! You're a fine example! Devious and dismissive!"

He put his hands up, miming surrender. "Not to add: defeated! I admit to pegging out first on many occasions using under-handed methods. Though never so frequently or duplicitously as my Aunt Henrietta. I tend to play games as though my life depended on it; sometimes it does. It's a reprehensible, though notably successful, technique we must all adopt in these lean times, I'm afraid. And, miss, I have noted that it's not the exclusive preserve of *men* to stake life and limb to achieve an essential goal or to win the laurel wreaths they deserve."

She looked at him in surprise and mistrust. "Not many men have that self-knowledge. They will never admit that they are adversaries, in life or games. Not many can even grasp it. But those who are aware are the ones to be feared. They understand, but having understood, they accept and condone. The very rare one amongst you takes up arms — secretly. Now, what is this? A formal interrogation?"

"Miss Proudfoot, you must know by now that your friend, Miss Stretton, has shown me the anonymous threatening messages you received before last evening's performance at St. Barnabas."

"Yes, Inspector Redfyre, she told me she had. I know what you're tying yourself in knots to say, so I beg you to be more direct and stop tangoing about the topic. I hate the tango! All averted gaze, dramatic poses, sporadically kicking your partner in the shins while pretending to be dying of lust!"

Redfyre was growing weary of the barely disguised derision, but nevertheless, the corner of his mouth twitched in suppression of a smile. Very well, if directness was what she was looking for, he would supply it. "Sorry to hear that! We must have learned the dance in different classes, you and I. I do the version I learned in Paris night clubs after the war. It was called the 'one-step' there. Teeny-tiny dance floors they have in Montmartre! And always crowded. No space for dancing — bodily interaction was just about all that could be achieved in the circumstances. You had no choice but to cling closely to your partner. Anyone posing dramatically or delivering a scissor kick would have been thrown out. Though dying of lust was not discouraged."

He was pleased to see the small feet retreat under the hem of her gown. Instinctively, she tugged the fabric up to cover her exposed left shoulder. Annoyingly, this caused it to slide off her right. He could have sworn she was trying not to laugh.

"Message received," she said simply. "Very well. Suits me. Dance on — but let's do a two-step rather than your version of a one-step, which sounds a bit indelicate to me."

"Starting with the first letter . . . Where precisely did you receive it?"

"At Earwig's. I was staying with her, as I often do. We were at school together, same dorm, and we've been friends ever since. Sometimes she stays with me in London. My family has a house in Bloomsbury. Nothing smart like Earwig's place, but it's on the underground now and very handy for Oxford Street. The letter came in the post addressed to me 'care of Melford Manor.' Cambridge postmark. It arrived, oh, three weeks before the performance. Very shortly after — about a week after — we'd been granted permission to stage the concert. Christopher had been trying to get it for ages — St. Barnabas being his own college, he thought they could hardly refuse, but the master had always dug his heels in. Said Christopher could perform whenever he liked, but it was the femaleness of the trumpeter half of the duo that stuck in his craw. In the end, there was only just time to arrange the tickets and advertising. We were thrilled to have pulled it off. Quite a coup! Pity it had to end like this. Still, the ice is broken. A precedent has been set. More women will feel able to perform in public now. My sacrifice was worth it, every scratch."

"How greatly would it spoil your achievement if it were to get about that the master of Barnabas had not himself granted permission?"

"Oh, you know about that? My! You've learned an awful lot in a very short time, Inspector." She shook off momentary dejection. "Very well. I admit that the master was incommunicado in the middle of the Indian Ocean at the time, and I know it must look as though we took advantage." She encountered his raised eyebrow and instantly became the rebellious child caught with a hand in the biscuit tin. "But it still counts! The dean was his appointed stand-in and he came up with the consent — after much cajoling. Christopher is a wonderfully persistent cajoler, and found just the right moment to approach him."

"The right moment? And what would be the right moment to approach a dean? Do tell! Sounds like a useful piece of knowledge to have in this town."

"Oh, I don't have dealings with deans. You'd better ask Christopher. They probably exchanged male shibboleths." Seemingly growing uncomfortable, she retaliated with a blunt question. "How did *you* find out?"

"Henningham told me himself."

"Urgh! Is he angry? He was very kind to me when I came tumbling down. I was hoping . . ."

"I didn't get the impression that he was after your blood. He's discreet. I'm sure he won't make a fuss or denounce you in the local press. He may have a sharp word for the dean, however. And I wouldn't hold out any hope for a repeat booking if I were you. But to continue with our one-step — give me, will you, an account of what happened on the darkened staircase? You decided to make the descent while the crowd was inconveniently milling about and on its way to the exit, and despite the fact that the non-appearance of the gentleman officiating had left the stairs in complete darkness. Some would have thought it prudent to wait. Or to call for assistance."

"I had a train to catch. The audience wasn't likely to get in my way; Cambridge people are very sensible, you know. Not the types to bother you to sign their programs or stand about, ogling. I'd been up and down those stairs all day rehearsing. Knew them well. No problems at all. They were very sound. Did you inspect them?"

"Yes, of course. Sound as a bell."

"So I set off. I was carrying my trumpet case in my right hand. I suppose I could have caught it on something and knocked myself off-balance, but I don't think so. I think I dropped it."

"You did. I retrieved it four steps from the bottom of the stairs where it had settled, and handed it to Coote for safekeeping."

"Thank you. Then I'm left with my strongest impression: Something tripped me. It was high up on the stairs, so I had farther to fall. Makes awful sense, I suppose. I'd just started to feel my way down. It must have been at shin level. If you think about it — and lying here, I've had time to — any obstacle stretched across the stairs at waist level or above would have resulted in a *slide* rather than a trip, don't you agree? I'd have come down feetfirst, slithering on my satin-sheathed bottom."

Redfyre stared. Such language! Was she teasing? He looked into the innocent blue eye trained on him and decided — yes, she was playing him like a skillful angler. Though he had no quarrel so far with her reasoning, which corresponded with his own.

"Ah, yes. A well-rounded assertion to which I cannot possibly object," he murmured and waited for her to go on.

"A very undignified entrance into the hall, but I wouldn't have been so bashed about. Pride heals faster than a sprained wrist. No, it must have caught me below the knee."

"What exactly was it below the knee?"

"Well, you know! I'm sure I handed it to you when I became conscious again." She concentrated and went through a series of mimed gestures to help her memory. "Yes, I did. It was wound round my arm. The left one. I must have grabbed it as I fell, wrenched it from its moorings and dragged it down with me. What on earth was it?"

"This? Is this what you remember?"

Redfyre produced from his pocket a dark-green length of shining, twisted fabric with a loop at each end and laid it across the foot of the bed.

"Hah, that's it! Some villain stretched it across the staircase. Thought as much!" She gulped. "Inspector, this could have been — it was intended to have been much more serious, wasn't it?"

"I have yet to inspect the scene in daylight, but for the moment, I'm thinking that if what happened was as you describe and had been successful, you could indeed have died of a broken neck or a cracked skull. If this was the method, we have to establish at what point of the evening it was fixed in place."

"I can tell you exactly. I've been going over and over it. The interval was half an hour long for the audience. Christopher and I took twenty minutes. I changed into my red satin in the robing room they'd set aside for me, and Chris brought along a flask of tea, which we shared. Then we went back into the hall together rather early to get up to our places in the loft and tune up our instruments so that we could make a snappy start on the second half. I had a train to catch and didn't want the performance to trail on."

"Remind me — did Coote climb the stairs before you?"

"Of course! A gentleman always precedes a lady on a staircase, up or down. We wouldn't want to risk inflaming him with a flash of ankle, now would we? There's no chance that Christopher could have laid a trap."

"You and Doctor Coote work together with the professional ease of a vaudeville double act, I observe. Though which is the stooge and which the straight man is hard to say. It's not even clear to me whether I'm dealing with a comedy turn or a magic act."

She chose not to be offended and replied calmly, "We have a certain ease of communication because we've known each other for years. We went to the same music school. And we've performed together abroad once or twice since the war ended and travel to the continent became possible again."

"Ah, those wonderful organs in ancient northern European towns you spoke of?"

"Yes. Christopher has the entrée to the very best. Germany, Poland, Bavaria — they've always welcomed good musicians. Some of the audiences don't even care if one of the players is wearing a skirt. And if she has fair hair done up in plaits reminiscent of a Nordic goddess, that's nothing but good news. People forget that young Mozart toured the European capitals with his very talented sister, and no one ever attempted to trip up Marianne! And while we're speaking of the other half of the duo, Christopher did not push me, trip me, or try to kill me in any conceivable way! You're to write that down. And I'd like you to tell Christopher I've spoken up for him."

"Thank you. If we can return to the evening's routine? The college official with the lantern did his stuff following the interval?"

"Yes. Don't ask me to describe him. I wasn't paying attention, and there were two or three . . ."

"Five on duty, in fact. I have their names. The man who attended you was a musician named Thomas Tyrrell, and I've already spoken to him."

"Well, Tyrrell shone his light and we went up. After that . . ." She shrugged. "We were making so much noise with our tuning, we wouldn't have noticed if the Grand Old Duke of York and his ten-thousand men clattered up the stairs after us. But in the eight or so minutes before the bell rang, anyone could have slipped through the curtains, crept up the stairs and fixed that thing across them. You'll have to check for fixing points when you go up again. People were drifting back into the hall, wandering about greeting friends, swapping places, generally stirring about. Would anyone have been aware of someone ducking between the curtains and reappearing a few seconds later? You were on the front row, Mr. Policeman. Surely you would have noticed."

"Almost certainly not. Not if he or she moved with confidence, looking as though they were at home there or had a job to do. Many of the audience *were* at home there — college members. Some were on duty, and not a few were flouncing about in gowns. Look, as you say, I was sitting on the front row with Earwig. Would I have paid attention to anyone looking confident enough to climb those stairs? No. I'm sharp-eyed and suspicious by nature, but if I'd even noticed, I wouldn't have questioned. If I'd questioned, I'd have found an easy answer: 'Hey, Chris! You left your lucky rabbit's foot in the gents — here it is.' "

"Someone dressed as Father Christmas? A man in a gorilla suit?"

"All part of the Cambridge scene! You must have noticed the general weakness for fancy dress! Ermine-lined gowns, rusting chain mail, Eastern robes — ten a penny down King's Parade on a Friday night. Over cocktails, I once paid a delicately pointed compliment to a friend of mine on his fashion sense, and he said to me in surprise, 'Oh, this little number? I'm going on somewhere afterwards.' The Queen of the Nile is always a popular character at some of the loucher establishments in town."

"Really? I shall have to take your word for it."

"So, we have eight minutes available and about a hundred unremarkable characters on hand to fix the booby trap. Hmm. The world and his wife had the opportunity, so we'd better look for the motive. Finding that should reduce the candidates."

She shook her head sadly and handed him the copy of the newspaper. "If you're seeking a motive, look no further. Here, take this. Have you seen it yet? The reporter makes a rather startling claim. But it appears less startling when I hear you making your own deductions. It's bubbling again, isn't it, John? The hatred and violence. The college — or some element of the college — tried to contrive my death last night. Not because they object to me, Juno Proudfoot. They don't know me or wish to know me, but they hate what I represent. I'm a woman. Despicable creature! An unclean, incomprehensible victim of the moon and her courses! And worse, I'm a woman with a particular talent, which in their minds, is reserved for the male sex. Jezebel was thrown to her death from her tower, and the righteous rejoiced. Three thousand years later, and still out there in this sophisticated city is a soul of iron. A cold, unbending Jehu. A man who would delight in my death."

She looked at him for the first time with fear in her expression. "I've made it easy for them. Shown my face on their tower top and blasted out a challenge. Right there in their inner sanctum. I've been chosen, haven't I, John, as a symbolic victim? I've flaunted myself, like Jezebel. And the only person who has seen through them, deduced their — what does he call it? — their collegiate conspiracy, is this reporter. What's his name?"

"Sebastian Scrivener. But look here, misogyny is only one of several possibilities," he said cautiously. "And I wouldn't put it at the top of my list. Scrivener ought to know better than to stir up trouble in the town. I shall have a word with him, but the best way of quietening the press is always to ferret out the truth and make it available as fast as possible. It's fevered, baseless speculation that does damage. Look again at this length of silk, Miss. Did you ever see this object before the event?"

"No, I don't think so, though I can't say I go about checking the haberdashery before every performance." She studied the exhibit thoughtfully. "It's made for curtains. There are curtains draped all over the organ loft — bit of a fire hazard with all the candles they use, but it can be a very draughty place in winter. I expect it was used to fasten back one or another."

"The chapel curtains are all in heavy woven red and gold fabric. No one would have chosen dark-green silk to fasten them back. I would suggest that, in a premeditated act, someone brought in this length of fabric from elsewhere for you to become entangled with it."

"Oh, for goodness sake! Red? Green? You're making such a meal of this!" At last, the irritation he'd sensed bubbling beneath the surface burst into the open. "It's just a bit of fabric! Its colour doesn't matter more than the identity of the person or persons who planted it on college premises, and whom you can't begin to identify. I was their victim. And I say 'their' deliberately, because this reporter chap has got it in one while you're fussing about. You should be thinking of protecting *him,* the voice of free speech. Scrivener is the only man who dares tell the truth in this submissive town. It's a conspiracy you're dealing with. The college authorities probably held a planning meeting to outline and sanction the decision to take action against me, followed by the selection of executives who would take on the practicalities of the operation, keeping the method secret so as to absolve anyone else of guilty knowledge. You know how these people operate."

"No, I'm afraid I had no idea that douce Cambridge had been invaded by a branch of the Spanish Inquisition." He managed a polite nod. "I bow to your inside knowledge, which I expect you have already shared with the gentleman of the press."

Her frown deepened, and he tried not to smile at the increasingly thunderous colours gathering on her face.

"I have. You will read his account on Monday morning. It's high time for this place and its sheeplike inhabitants to be jerked out of their submissive state. If you can't find out who nearly killed me, I shall have to rely on Sebastian to do it."

Redfyre sighed. Time for the scissor kick. "Look again at this tie-back, will you? They're usually found in twos, I'm sure you'll have noticed." She nodded. "I came upon the pair to this one only this morning." He took a second slender dark-green rope from his other pocket and placed it beside the first. "There. Haberdashery as provided by Messrs. Heals of the Tottenham Court Road, frequently supplied to accompany and restrain swathes of 'Dreams of the Jungle' fabric by Voysey. I can vouch for its provenance. The upstairs maid, whose task it is to draw back the bedroom chintz in a certain Cambridge residence, was disconcerted this morning to find that one of the ties was missing. She was even more disconcerted when I took away the second in evidence. But in evidence of quite what, I'm wondering, Miss Proudfoot? Have you any idea?"

He almost rang for the nurse. Juno had turned rigid. Her blackened eye showed up livid against her pale skin as she looked from one length of silk to the other with disbelief, unable to say a word. Alarmed by the change he had brought about, he reached out and seized the hand nearest to him.

"Ouch!" she cried out in pain, shaking him off. "Go away! I'm ringing for Matron! I have nothing more to say to you. Are these the police intimidation methods we've all heard about? Earwig told me you'd be sympathetic! She may have known you years ago, but she doesn't understand you! She called you a gentleman."

In the face of this noisy bluster and bell-pulling, all Redfyre could do was get to his feet and dash for the door before Matron bore down on him. Ignominiously, he had to retrace his steps to gather up his evidence from the bed before he left, murmuring polite leave-taking phrases. At the door, he steeled himself to turn again and ask hurriedly, "One last thing. How many brothers do you have, Miss Proudfoot?"

Surprise overrode her anger. "Brothers? What are you on about? I have no brothers. No sisters, either. I'm an only child."

CHAPTER 11

"Wimmin!" MacFarlane could turn two syllables into a double-barreled explosion of derision. "They certainly have you tied in knots, Redfyre!" Then, relenting, "Still, the threat of Matron chasing you down the corridor would be a stick of ginger up any bloke's bum. A lesson for you, Sarge. Were you taking note?"

He exchanged a meaning look with Sergeant Thoday, who had joined them in the inspectors' offices ten minutes earlier, breathless and with his cycle clips still firmly clamped around his trouser legs. Redfyre failed to spot reciprocation of MacFarlane's scorn on the sergeant's face, since any emotion was filtered out by the sergeant's luxuriant moustache, a magnum opus which outdid in size and glossiness Field Marshal Horatio Herbert Kitchener's own. The chap was far too young to be sporting such a growth, Redfyre thought, but he understood that a policeman did whatever he was capable of to assert his authority over a hostile public and was not always aware that he was making himself ridiculous. He wondered what quirk he unconsciously adopted as his own protective measure. His smile! He thought the unemphatic baring of his impeccable teeth was disarming, but also likely recalled a great white shark.

"You were probably wise to scarper, Redfyre," MacFarlane conceded, "though I'd have liked to hear what she claimed was her relationship — if any — with the Lawrence girl. Which, if you remember, was the main point of your visit. I'm leaving these two files with you, Redfyre. You're right — there's a connection. Work the two cases together and put everything else aside until you get to the bottom of it. You need urgently to grab Miss Lawrence's killer, as she appears to have supplied the means of sending Miss Proudfoot base over apex to her death. What in hell are we looking at? A would-be murderer who becomes a corpse herself, all in the space of an evening?"

"Is there a protocol, sir, for charging a corpse with attempted murder?" Thoday asked innocently.

"Never needed to find out, Sarge. We may have to write it ourselves. I'd like to know what was Miss Lawrence's grouse against Miss Proudfoot. That business with the curtain tie — I'm not prepared to laugh that off as a bit of female wrist-slapping or hair-tugging. It's calculated and fatal. Attempted manslaughter at the very least. What sort of belly-aching provokes a performance like that?"

"Someone snatched someone's boy-friend?" the sergeant offered. "Women'll put up with all sorts, but if someone nicks their bloke, that's when they reach for the frying pan."

Redfyre sought to encourage but gently enlighten the sergeant. "Exactly. Spur of the moment, weapon to hand. But we're looking at a different scene entirely. 'Malice aforethought' sums it up neatly. There's a brain behind this, one that's been plotting since . . . Now, when did that first anonymous letter come through? A month ago?"

"That's no flash in the pan. Or bash with the pan," MacFarlane finished for him.

"Whatever the relationship — and I have an idea for throwing light on that from a different angle, sir — Miss Lawrence could not possibly have administered the second, backup attempt on Miss Proudfoot's life," Redfyre reminded him. "If, indeed, we hear from the laboratory that the inhaler contained more than the advertised sal volatile. She was in the pub, sipping sherry to relieve the tedium of an evening spent in the company of Thomas Tyrrell before, during and subsequent to the time of the fall. The unloved Tyrrell, in fact, makes the very best of alibis, should the corpse find itself in need of one."

MacFarlane turned to Sergeant Thoday, who was beginning to stir restively. "Was that your hand up, Thoday? Let's have your thoughts, then. Are you making any sense of all this?" he asked.

The sergeant was only too pleased to be involved, Redfyre thought, and reminded himself that it had been Thoday on hand last evening, witness of Juno's heartrending deathbed performance. Like every man who had filed past the recumbent figure, tactfully looking aside at the last moment, he must have been stricken by the sight of such beauty laid low.

"Yes, sir. Seems to me that the business of the curtain tie is an amateurish bit of jiggery-pokery. The sort of trick undergraduates play on each other in their first term up at college. Goes along with apple-pie beds and the bucket of cold water over a doorway. Kid's stuff, done for a laugh or at worst a snigger. Only noteworthy when it all goes wrong. The inhaler I think will turn out to be just that — an inhaler kindly lent by someone's granny. We could always try the milliners' boutiques for . . . what did you say her hat had on it, sir . . ."

"Holly berries, Sarge."

"Right." Thoday sighed and pressed on. "Nothing like the case of the second poor lass, who died a violent and, I think, calculated death. It may have an element of opportunity about it, but — oh, I dunno, I have the feeling there was a sense of serious purpose there. It was never intended to make anybody snigger." Before MacFarlane's attention wandered from him, he hurried on. "Besides, sir, I think I've found out from Miss Lawrence's bank a reason why someone might want to top her."

"Go on, Sarge."

"It was a hole in one! Her account was at the nearest branch. Midshires in Chesterton High Street. She opened it on her eighteenth birthday with an initial deposit and guarantor documents signed by her father. All shipshape, in Bristol fashion. It's been meticulously maintained ever since — never in the red, and the manager had no concerns. He examined it with me and, in the light of her suspicious death, looked at it with closer attention than usual. I told him we would need more than a quick glance at the positive sums at the bottom of every page of her statement."

"Quite right, Sarge. What did he spot?"

"Two things. Her pay, for a start. He knew she was a girl who worked for a living, and assumed that she was employed by her father at his pharmaceutical business, so he rather expected that she wouldn't exactly be on starvation wages. It's an accepted way of squeezing as much profit out of a firm as you can and avoiding taxes — pay your offspring for work done at the firm. Lots of people do it. She started out on a good rate for a young girl. More than I earn! And after a month, the weekly rate suddenly shot up. Doubled, in fact. After the third month, it went up again and remained steady. Outgoings were, on the whole, negligible — she was living at home, all expenses found. Her earnings were 'pin money,' as the manager called it. Trips to London once a month with associated spending on clothes and shows."

"How does he know that?"

"Well, he hadn't clocked it until I started ferreting about and he took a look at the checks she'd paid out. They keep ahold of them for twelve months. Tax returns and such. But the buildup was interesting. The girl was putting in twenty quid a week! And moving fifteen of that sideways into a savings account with a good rate of interest, always calculatedly staying in the black. Twenty quid! That's four times what an experienced secretary gets in her pay bracket. Now, in my book, there's only two ways for females to get their hands on cash like that."

"She was on the game or blackmailing some poor bugger!" MacFarlane muttered.

"Often the two skills go together." Thoday nodded.

"Come off it!" said Redfyre. "You're forgetting that the girl was pronounced *virgo intacta* by Doctor Beaufort."

"Oh, right. There's that," MacFarlane grudgingly agreed. "Doesn't rule out the blackmail element, though. I've known nuns who could extort your last penny with such skill and charm, you'd feel you'd done yourself a favour handing it over. Redfyre, it's time, I think, someone paid a call on her employer. Established what it was about young Louise that earned her such a generous remuneration. Thoday?"

The sergeant looked up eagerly. "Yes, sir?"

"Good work, lad! Now you can get on with the rest of your tasks. Pick up where you left off on that door to dooring on her route to the place where she died. And have uniform comb the common, just in case. Ground's frozen, but we might find something."

"Right, sir. Good thing I didn't bother to take off my cycle clips, then."

"Was it something I said?" MacFarlane asked with a shrug when the sergeant had left amid a flurry of pointedly polite salutes and an exquisitely soundless closing of the door behind him.

"He's keen," Redfyre said. "And able. I rather think he was hoping to be given the chance of grilling Miss Lawrence's employer himself."

"Horses for courses. He's a good lad — grammar school boy, and bright with it — but he's young and homegrown. The owner of a thriving Cambridge business is likely to be either well-off or well-connected, probably both." He riffled through his notes. "You'll find him at Number 1, Midsummer Place. Very smart. He lives above the shop, so to speak. Discreet offices in the basement, apartment on the floors above. Very continental! Hmm . . . Well, after him, lad! Now! Ditch the bike and take the Riley. You can't arrive there in cycle clips and balaclava; he'll think you've come to rob him.

Go in and disarm him with your posh accent, then finish him off with your fox's cunning. A chap who'll pay out eighty quid a month to some young chancer he's not even having it off with has something deeply dodgy to hide!"

"After him, now!" had been MacFarlane's command. To Midsummer Place. Redfyre always questioned orders — frequently, he disobeyed them. He looked at his watch and saw that it was one o'clock, a businessman's lunchtime. Policemen had no such perks. He grimaced and came to a decision. He snatched up the keys to the Riley, rejoiced that it started when asked, and set off in the opposite direction, heading south once again down Trumpington Street.

"Inspector Redfyre! Back again so soon? I'm terribly sorry, but you've missed her. Miss Proudfoot left an hour ago. You did give us permission to return her suitcase to her, yes? Did I misunderstand the instructions?"

He reassured the sister that all was well, though he had carelessly left his notebook in the ward and would like to dash up there to retrieve it.

"Then you'd better hurry," the sister said. "The staff will be setting about the room with mops and buckets and fresh linen."

"Of course," he said easily. "If I'm lucky, they may already have laid hands on my book. Oh, the flowers, Sister? Wonderful showing! Did Miss Proudfoot make arrangements for them to be given away? Far too good to be put in the bin, I'd have thought!"

The sister smiled indulgently to hear his concern. "They wouldn't have been wasted. We would have given them across the road to decorate Little St. Mary's, or to the orphanage. Miss Proudfoot could hardly take them with her — she had her hands full with her suitcase and hatbox, and was intending — against all our advice — to jump aboard the twelve o'clock bus to Melford. The bus! In her condition! Of course, we couldn't allow it." She leaned forward and confided, "We had to do a certain amount of bargaining with her! Matron agreed to allow her to sign herself out on condition that she accepted the offer of a taxi to take her to her destination. It was either that or an ambulance. Matron was implacable. The taxi was already paid for, if that was a concern — one of Miss Stretton's insistences. She agreed to the taxi. But she was in such a hurry to be off, I think she'd quite forgotten about the flowers.

When I asked her what she wanted done with them as she climbed in, she was quite flummoxed. She asked me to put them in a box and send them on." Sister exchanged an indulgent shake of the head with Redfyre. "We're at a bit of a loss as to how to get them to her. Flowers are not the easiest things to pack."

"Let me solve your problem," Redfyre said. "I have the Riley outside, and I'm motoring out to Melford to pay a call on Miss Earwig Stretton this afternoon. Why don't you have the flowers collected up and put onto the back seat of my car, and I will ensure that they get there safely?"

He hurried upstairs to carry out the inspection he'd been unable to do that morning. The room had not yet been entered for cleaning purposes, but he could hear the clank of approaching buckets in the distance and went swiftly about his business. When he saw that the notes were still attached to the offerings, he breathed a sigh of relief and began to read them, starting with one that accompanied a flamboyant bouquet of red roses.

Darling! So brave! Ease your poor eyes by looking on these.
I stole them from Daddy's greenhouse.

261

We always have red roses brought on (or is it held back?) for Christmas.

What a joy! Come to us the moment you feel strong enough!

Earwig hadn't needed to sign it.

A dozen statuesque white lilies were next in line.

My dear! I so enjoyed your concert last evening and was devastated to witness your fall. If there is anything I can do . . .

I left my number at the reception desk.

Your devoted servant and admirer,
Colonel Sir Reynold Brandon

God! The stage-door Johnnies were everywhere! Bloody old Brandon! Redfyre remembered they'd kept a file on him at HQ. And classical music did not feature amongst the many esoteric enthusiasms of the ghastly old pig-sticker.

He recognised his own Aunt Henrietta's copperplate hand next to a starkly elegant green and white bunch of hellebores from her own garden, whimsically fastened together with a twist of raffia.

My dear child! I hear from Earwig that you have survived to toot another day!

Well done! I'm designing a medal to pin to your brave bosom!

Christopher Coote had sent a single pink hyacinth in a pot with a typed florist's note:

Juno,
We must speak as soon as you are up and about!
I'm worried about you. I'm worried about me!
The Peelers think I pushed you! CC

A bunch of mixed freesias gave out much strong perfume, but rather less information:

A close shave! Well survived! Remember:
"A friend loveth at all times, and a sister is born for adversity."
Your loving sissa,
M

Redfyre reminded himself to give a good shake to Juno's family tree.

The Master of St. Barnabas had managed, in spite of his own tribulations to communicate. No flowers, Redfyre assumed, as the handwritten note stood by itself.

We met in near-tragic circumstances

last evening. I was delighted to hear you are doing well and send good wishes for your speedy recovery.

May I say how very much I enjoyed your performance?

Richard Henningham

Lastly, the white rose in a Lalique vase that had so touched the nurse at reception.

The single white bud stood proudly in a four-inch-high glass vase of great beauty. The cameo pattern of gray over a white background was a misty swirl of Art Nouveau wild flowers. Lovely, but was it actually Lalique? He didn't think so. Puzzled, Redfyre lifted it from the shelf and peered at it more carefully. With satisfaction, he saw between two curling petals a signature in cameo: *Gallé.* Émile Gallé, a Frenchman whose workshops in Nancy in northeast France had produced last century what Redfyre considered to be artwork superior to that of the better-known Lalique.

Frowning, he replaced it and turned his attention to the handwritten florist's card propped against it.

Angels are bright still, and when the brightest falls . . .

264

My arms are outstretched.

A

Another well-wisher who felt confident enough to take liberties with the original text, adjusting the Bible and Shakespeare to carry their own meaning. "M" and now "A." Well, "A" of the Outstretched Arms, he reckoned, must be a well-heeled chancer. Redfyre knew the value of the vase and had a good idea where "A" might have found it. He looked about him to be sure he wasn't being observed. He took out the rosebud and popped it in amongst the freesias, poured the water down the sink, wrapped the vase in his handkerchief and slipped it into his inside pocket.

"Oh, sorry, sir! We thought the room had been vacated."

The two puzzled girls in trainee nurses' uniform were standing hesitantly in the doorway, mops in hand, dragging a trolley laden with clean linens.

"Ladies! Come in and carry on! I'm just organizing the removal of these flowers. I wonder, could you have them put in a box and ask a porter to bring them down in the lift to the car park? He'll find my car just to the left of the front door."

He swiftly gathered up the cards and slid

265

them into his other inside pocket before returning to the reception desk, where he brandished his notebook briefly in comic triumph and told the nurse that he would be in his car awaiting delivery of the box of blooms.

"Oh, Inspector . . ." She reached under the desk and gingerly brought out yet another floral offering. "This arrived while you were upstairs. By courier. You might like to put it with the others. And here was the envelope with it."

"Why not! I'll take it off your hands right away."

"Careful now! It's awfully prickly!"

He put on his gloves to handle the object and made his farewells, eager to take the latest piece of florist's art off to the privacy of the Riley's front seat where he could examine it at leisure.

Settling into the deep security of the leather interior, he shivered not with cold, but at the sight of the wreath he had just been handed.

It was well constructed. But, having conceded this much, his admiration lapsed. It was an intricately contrived weaving together of winter greenery. He recognised the dark green of holly, ivy, cypress, mistletoe and yew. Unusually, there were no cheery red holly berries or mysterious milky white of mistletoe to enliven the wintry foliage; these had been stripped away to give place and emphasis to a trail of purple-black berries borne by a small, glossy-leaved plant that twined its way between the sprays. Unpleasant. Repellent, even. What was it? Buckthorn? Some garden version of the wild English hedgerow plant, he decided. Whatever it was, it had the slick, deep colour of poisonous deadly nightshade. Analyzing the contents and structure helped him to dampen the overlying sinister effect of the whole. And the sinister intent could be in no doubt, taken together with the black satin bow and ribbons that trailed from it. It was a funereal wreath. The sort of thing you'd throw on a coffin before the first shovelful of earth fell. Or weave to decorate Satan's altar.

Recoiling in disgust, he noted that the envelope was addressed to Miss Proudfoot in black-inked block capitals. He opened it. He saw one line, in the same hand:

PRIDE GOETH BEFORE DESTRUCTION AND AN HAUGHTY SPIRIT BEFORE A FALL.

When a porter appeared, carrying a box of Juno's flowers, he helped him to lower it onto the back seat of the Riley and put the additional offering on top. He would suppress it. She'd suffered enough; no reason to frighten the poor girl any further. But, with anger beginning to burn bright, Redfyre knew at that moment that if he could have laid hands on the soul who'd sent the wreath, he would have made him eat it. Every poisonous berry and sharp prickle.

He reflected for a moment on the quality of a girl who could inspire, on the one hand, a carefully contrived black-hearted curse and, on the other, a flawless beauty spontaneously offered by — surely? — a lover?

Redfyre had to see a man about a vase. He checked his watch. Only two o'clock! God, it felt like midnight! But with a bit of luck, Marcus Milsom (Antiques and Objets d'Art) only a few strides away opposite the Fitzwilliam Museum, would be behind his counter and ready to talk about French art glass.

Milsom's welcoming smile froze when he recognised Redfyre.

"Stand at ease, you old rascal! I haven't come to tell you that last seascape you sold me wasn't by Buttersworth. Because I'm sure you already knew that. Well, so did I, so no harm done. I shall be keeping it. The price wasn't too bad, and I like it. Now, I'm assuming you'd like to creep back into my good books, eh?" A gulp and a widening smile gave him his answer. "Right-o. Take a look at this. I think you may recognise it."

He produced the French vase and watched as the antiquary greeted it like a long lost son.

"No, I'm not selling it back to you. The lady who was given this as a gift this morning is very happy with it. I just need to find out who was the generous gentleman who bought it here before popping a choice rosebud into it to present to her in hospital."

The information he received was readily given. The description matched exactly the one Sister had given him for the gent masquerading as S. J. Proudfoot, and included a detail which would clinch any future identification. One of those outstanding characteristics which polite witnesses only remember to mention at the very last, blurting it out almost as an afterthought for a run-of-the-mill account of height, weight, colouring and age.

Mr. "A" had apparently bowled over old Marcus with his good looks and charm, and gone on to impress him with his instant appreciation of the Gallé — well, who wouldn't just adore the Gallé? Marcus had another one, its twin, out in the back if Redfyre was interested. The customer hadn't bothered to bargain when a price was quoted, just coughed up in cash like the gent he was. No, nothing odd about that. Many transactions were conducted in cash rather than checks. It was encouraged in the trade, checks being such bouncers after the war. Couldn't trust anyone these days . . . The price Marcus confessed to asking made Redfyre flinch and purse his lips. He remembered with a flush of embarrassment that he had offered the same girl a bag of sherbert lemons. But, he reminded himself, she had left this gift behind on the window ledge and fled to safety with Earwig in the country.

Could he be misinterpreting the intentions of this admirer? Mashers who hung about stage doors hoping for contact with a girl who'd taken their fancy were a scourge in London. Had one of these pests pursued Juno to Cambridge? Sir Reynold Brandon was homegrown and a nuisance rather than a danger, but Redfyre knew of one or two cases where a determined masher had tracked his target as a huntsman stalks deer through the heather. Unnerving behaviour for a woman whose profession exposed her onstage to the public's eye. Six nights a week plus matinees. He knew that the danger point was generally reached when the deluded stalker finally woke from his fantasy and boiled over with rage and shame.

Such a man knew exactly where and when his prey would appear within range of his knife, bullet, bottle of face-scarring acid. He would enjoy the performance for one last moment of bittersweetness and make his way to the stage door for his lethal confrontation.

Had Juno rushed away in fear, knowing that the man who stalked her had suddenly closed the distance between them, even wormed or tricked his way into the confidence of her best friend?

Eager to be on his way, Redfyre left Marcus Milsom with the promise of a return visit to examine his glass stock in greater detail and made his way back to the car. He needed some lunch and thought he could find a congenial partner to eat it with very close by. Keeping his gloves on, he picked up the wreath again, then set off back into Addenbrooke's.

As a visitor to the morgue, he felt he cut a suitably funereal figure. All he lacked was the tall top hat. He peered through the glass pane at the top of the door to the postmortem facility, saw that his quarry was up to his elbows in his work, and walked in.

271

"Great Heavens!" Doctor Beaufort exclaimed. "What's this? The New Compassionate Policing? Every corpse the recipient of a funerary token of the Force's esteem?"

"No, I'm inviting you to lunch. Bet you've eaten nothing since breakfast?"

"Not so lucky! It was Friday supper, if we're being precise. Glad of the distraction. Give me a minute to finish here, and I'll wash and be right with you. On one condition: that you leave that hideousness behind in the bin. I can't afford to be seen out and about, bristling with floral tributes. Bad for business."

"Gladly — but it's evidence. I'm just about to drop it off round the back at the labs. I don't want to send it with a note."

"Forensics?" He looked again at the wreath. "Who needs forensics? I can tell you from here, those black berries aren't poisonous, if that's the bit you're curious about. *Rhamnus cathartica* is what you've got there. *Common buckthorn.* Tiddled up a bit and tamed for horticultural production. The berries look jolly dangerous and they taste vile, I'm told, but are actually rather good for you. The Anglo-Saxons used to boil them up with honey to kill the bitter taste and use that as a laxative. Hence, *cathartica.*"

"Thought as much. In fact, it's the *rib-*

bons I'm interested in with their lovely satin finish."

"Oh? Ah, I see."

"I'll drop this off, then go and get us a table at the Anchor, shall I, while you're scrubbing up?"

"Good. Mine's a pint of IPA and a steak and kidney with mash."

Beaufort dabbed the foam from his moustache with his napkin and sighed with satisfaction.

"You've been well-behaved and not asked me once if I have any results yet. So I'll tell you — I have. Want to hear? I'm just about to dictate a preliminary report for Mac-Farlane, but it won't do any harm to stay one step ahead of the old bugger."

Redfyre grinned his encouragement.

"Look here, I haven't quite finished yet, I hope that's understood —"

"Of course. We hadn't hoped for anything before tomorrow."

"I had a bit of luck. The Lawrence parents were quick off the mark and arrived for the identification at eleven. We were only just prepared for them. No tears shed. Stony silence between them — I didn't hear them exchange a word. The parents usually grasp each other's hand for mutual comfort.

273

These two didn't. She chose to stand opposite her husband and fix him with a glare I wouldn't have been able to sustain myself.

"But this is about their unfortunate daughter." His voice took on its customary formal tone. "Louise Lawrence. Initial survey: I confirm everything I mentioned this morning in the semi-darkness on the riverbank. No evidence of a sexual motivation, none of any activity in that direction. Strangled. Left-handed? Right-handed? Impossible to say. Equal — and great — pressure exerted by two strong thumbs. Traces where his fingers dug in at the back of the neck so I can tell you his glove size. Same as yours. Big. Seven and a half. But, John, he wasn't wearing gloves. His nails had left scratches and indentations. On a night like that, he would have been wearing gloves. Why take them off? To make his grip more certain? Or the better to enjoy the experience? Stinks of premeditation to me. The perpetrator left no physical sign of his presence. I say 'his' because the chances are nine out of ten that it was a man, based on hand span and strength necessary to accomplish the task of killing. It wouldn't have been all that easy. The victim, under all those clothes, was a well-muscled girl. Did you have any idea? Rather odd for a girl who spent her working day behind a desk."

"Which muscles do you mean? Running? Tennis?"

"Tennis, yes, possibly. Or fencing — that would fit the bill. The right arm is more developed than the left. But I'm thinking of the body in general. I'd have said: dancer, but more bulky, less willowy. If she were a horse, you'd say she was bred for speed and strength. A good hunter. If a man, well, a pentathlete or something of that nature. Broad shoulders and long strong legs."

Unguardedly, Redfyre grimaced.

"Oh, nothing untoward. No, no! She was an attractive girl, but it's unusual to see muscles most girls have never used in their lives in a fine state of development. She could have put up a fight, I'd have thought. And there's the heaving and pushing involved in getting her body into the river. The average woman wouldn't be able to undertake it."

"Do you have a clearer idea of the timing?"

"Oh, yes! Very clear! Body temperature was a useless indication — impossible to calculate with any accuracy given the freezing conditions. I've taken a few readings, but I've not had the time to do the calculations and make them sound impressive for

the record yet. They'll tell you nothing useful. But the stomach contents? Now they
were revealing. Sherry, a hard-boiled egg
and a ham sandwich! And, to top it all off,
very shortly before death, a cup of cocoa.
Puzzle that. Do they serve cocoa in Cambridge pubs these days?"

"*Pickled* egg, would that be?"

"If you say so. Urgh! Still, the state of
progress through the digestive tract tells me
she died at about ten o'clock, give or take
half an hour either side. If you can find a
pub that served such a combination last
evening —"

"We've got it! At least, three out of the
four items. I can't account for the cocoa.
And we have the lad who was drinking with
her."

"Crikey, that was quick! He must have
been waiting for you on the doorstep at the
nick to hand himself in!"

"In fact, I'd booked him in already the
night before. Minutes before the murder
was committed, if your calculations are
exact." Redfyre laughed. "Now, that's what
we call the New Policing!"

"You have him under lock and key?"

"No. I let him out. He doesn't have the
stomach, the head or the hands for it."

"Well, read my report when it comes

through. There may be something in there that has more meaning for you than for me. Hairs on clothing, human and dog — that sort of thing. Scrapings from the soles of her boots we're still waiting for. Oh, and — I think I can divulge this, she's your case isn't she? — the other girl, the one who fell down the stairs at St. Barnabas Chapel?"

"The trumpeter? She's not a corpse yet. Only just evaded your clutches, though."

"That lady. Well, a professor of toxicology nipped down to confer with me. A lot of cross-pollination goes on between them and our pathology department, you can imagine. He was rather keen for me to understand the underlying dangers of a common folk remedy for shock — smelling salts, no less! He delivered his lecture and illustrated it with an interesting exhibit. A little silver inhaler job that you'd made off with from the scene of the near-crime? Certainly made me think, and what he'd found had quite unnerved him. He's rung in a report to MacFarlane, so you might as well hear it."

"Yes, yes!"

"Mainly salts of ammonia, but with an added ingredient. Mercury cyanide. It's an innocent-looking, though toxic, white crystalline powder. Similar to the ammonia. A very small quantity ingested or inhaled will kill you. And here's the intriguing bit — it's tasteless and odorless! All you'd smell is the sal volatile."

"And that's bad enough! A perfect camouflage, you'd say. Frightening! How does anyone get their hands on a supply of this mercury cyanide?"

"Well the odd thing is, it's used in one or two perfectly innocuous ways. In the manufacture of antiseptics, for instance. Photographers use it in their dark room hocus-pocus activities. It's also thought to have been prescribed with some success in the treatment of syphilis, though this use is very hush-hush and known only to members of the medical profession and the well-heeled clients they're using as guinea pigs." He fell silent for a moment, then shrugged. "You know what my profession is like when it comes to discretion. The first we ordinary mortals hear of a breakthrough is in the pages of *Nature*. No, this stuff's not generally available. Different story in France, though! Stroll into any French *pharmacie,* and you can buy a box of ampoules over the counter. Monsieur Leclerc, Rue Napoleon in Calais, would probably be your nearest supplier, or you can make a weekend of it and pop over to Paris. No shortage there of helpful corner chemists."

Carefully, Redfyre said, "No wonder the professor was issuing dire warnings! Did he mention the symptoms of anyone who might have been unfortunate enough to inhale the stuff?"

"Yes. Breathlessness, nausea, dizziness, headache, confusion, quickly followed by coma and death. Not really alarming until the two final stages are reached, of course. The earlier ones are not uncommon and are symptoms of a variety of other less sinister medical afflictions. In fact, they are closely associated with exactly the type of female complaints which normally call forth the use of smelling salts. Clever, eh? Redfyre, that cocktail was lethal. And the last thing you'd want anyone to shove up your nose if you were already unconscious, I think?"

"No. And of course, if the worst should occur, in the case of a girl who's just tumbled dramatically down a dozen steep stairs headfirst in the view of a hundred people — well, one would ascribe her death to the bleedin' obvious, wouldn't one?"

Beaufort gave his evil pathologist's grin. "Unless she were lucky enough to end up on *my* slab!"

Chapter 12

It was past three o'clock, but the skies over Cambridge had cleared. Redfyre calculated that he had at least an hour of useful light left in this interminable day as he parked his Riley on Maids Causeway and paused at the edge of Midsummer Common to get his bearings.

His eye was caught by the caped figures of four uniform branch constables working their way across the cropped grass along the route Louise Lawrence might well have taken on her way home if she'd cut a corner. Backbreaking work, and Redfyre watched with sympathy and pride as, bent double, they nosed their way over the tussocky ground. The Common — the name this land had come by in the early Middle Ages was still appropriate. It was held in common ownership for the town. Any Tom, Dick or Harry was free to graze his cows here, to walk his dog, court his girl, chuck away his cigarette ends, vomit out the excess of beer downed in any of a dozen nearby pubs. Free to dump a body.

One of the officers broke off on catching sight of him and waved with an urgency that made him hurry over.

"Sir! Something here you might like to take a look at. Sergeant Thoday briefed us, so we know what we're looking out for." He led Redfyre to a narrow patch of earth, clear of both grass and snow. "Emergency water pipe repair. The workmen finished yesterday last thing. They kept at it by lamplight until the job was done. Six o'clockish, they put their spades away, the gaffer says. Loose, sandy infill. It can't have been fully frozen over when a lady with a size six boot put her foot on it. Now, in the daylight, I reckon you'd stride over a patch like that — if you wanted to walk off the path anyway. It looks messy, and the sandy colour would stain your boots. But in the dark, you'd never notice it."

Redfyre peered at the clear imprint. "As you say, constable! Right foot, right size, right place, right time!" He touched him lightly on the shoulder in congratulation. "Stand up and take a butcher's at this with me, will you?" He lined up the direction of the footprint with a forefinger and pointed.

"Well, I reckon that, unless she did an about-turn, Miss Size Six is heading straight for that big house over there. The one on the corner."

"As you say! And it just happens to be next on my calling list." His eyes narrowed as he focused on the grand house on Midsummer Place. "I wonder if she ever arrived. Perhaps someone knows."

Stirred by the excitement of the chase, the constable drew his attention back to the footprint. "If she ever got there! Sir, sir! Look again at this! It's frozen over now and crisp as a plaster cast. But look again to the left edge of the heel. There's a bicycle tyre print that just catches the edge of the boot print. Cutting over it! Someone riding or pushing a bike passed right behind her very soon after. Not walking *with* her, or the prints'd be some inches apart. He was tailing her, sir!"

"Well spotted, constable! Make a sketch in your notebook for now, will you, and I'll tell the sarge to get it photographed. Better take a plaster cast, too. Take steps to protect it overnight. Got plenty of tape, have you? Good. That's vital evidence! Find me some more while the light lasts!"

The semi-basement floor serving as offices

for Messrs. Benson & Uppingham, Purveyors of Medicaments to His Majesty King George V and the royal family, were in darkness and clearly unoccupied late on a Saturday afternoon, but the three floors above where Mr. and Mrs. Benson lived were in use. Lamps were already being lit and, as he watched, Redfyre saw curtains being whisked across windows, preparing to keep out the twilight. Someone anticipating a cozy Saturday evening at home was shortly to be disturbed by a police presence. He tugged on the bell and waited. In the depths of the building, or perhaps in a courtyard behind, a dog gave a startled and menacing warning howl. He rang again, and after an annoyingly long interval, he heard someone approach the door.

A young footman opened up, surly faced and suspicious, and announced, "Mr. and Mrs. Benson are not at home."

"Oh dear! They forgot to tell you." He stepped inside, offered up his warrant card and added, "You may show me in and tell them that Detective Inspector Redfyre of the Cambridge CID is paying them a call. They are expecting me." Firmly but politely, he handed the man his hat.

Moments later the door to the drawing room on the first floor was being opened for him, to reveal Mr. and Mrs. Benson still at the tea table. He declined the offer of a cup of Assam, pleading a late lunch, but accepted the offer of a chair to sit on. Mrs. Benson, he noted, avoided his eye and continued to butter her crumpet, applying a thick layer of raspberry jam in a marked manner. A visit from the police was unwelcome at any time in a civilised home, but a teatime appearance was beyond acceptable. Mr. Benson at least gave Redfyre frowning attention.

The inspector established that the pair had received the news of the death of one of their employees in the environs of the Common the previous evening, news conveyed by the girl's father, who was both a family friend and business associate. Was Redfyre aware? Redfyre was. Customary phrases of condolence and sadness at the loss were exchanged.

"I should like to establish as many facts as possible about the movements of your, um —"

"She was my deputy office manager, Inspector. She answered directly to and was supervised by my manager, Mr. Philpott. George Philpott. He will show you when he returns to work next week that she signed the passbook and left the premises at her usual hour of five P.M. yesterday. I have already checked. We have no information regarding Miss Lawrence's subsequent movements."

"I see, sir." Redfyre made a note. "And your Mr. Philpott left at what time?"

"At six, his usual time."

"Will you give me the names of any further employees who work regularly on the premises?"

"I keep two typists, local girls. Miss Ada Drake, aged twenty-one, and Miss Grace Jewell, aged twenty. They also left at the earlier time of five o'clock."

Redfyre took down their names and home addresses while Mrs. Benson glowered at him over her teacup and enlarged on the information. "Having a concern for our staff's welfare, we think it right to dismiss the ladies earlier than might be accepted as the usual, so that they may reach the safety of their homes before the evening sets in. Ada and Grace live on the same street, ten minutes' walk away. They come and go together."

"We are a relatively small concern, but growing," her husband supplied. "Here on these — what you call premises and what I call my home — we undertake the clerkly business of the operation. This is the official address for the company, but we naturally maintain a completely domestic appearance, en suite with the other houses in the terrace."

"Quite understood, sir. This is a sensitive and well-regarded part of town."

"Exactly! My factory in the east of the city, where our product is made and shipped, has a much more fully staffed office under the direction of a Works Manager."

Redfyre noted that the address he had for the factory at Frog End, Newmarket Road, would have sounded a lot less prestigious to clients, be they royal or plebeian, than Midsummer Place, Cambridge. He went on to ask the routine background questions on Louise Lawrence and her terms of employment, which were answered succinctly by Mr. Benson. He made a point of hearing a response from both husband and wife when he asked at what hour they had each last set eyes on Miss Lawrence. Mrs. Benson had not seen her since half past five on Thursday, the day before, as Mrs. Benson had left early on Friday morning to spend the day with her sister in Ely, where both ladies were involved in money-raising efforts — a knitting bee on this occasion — on behalf of the cathedral. She had commandeered the family motorcar for this expedition and returned with her chauffeur at six o'clock precisely. One's servants worked to ever tighter schedules these days, she confided to Redfyre. Employers who disregarded their wishes in the matter of time-tabling found themselves deserted. Supply and demand, she admonished him, had absolutely to be born in mind. One hardly needed the economic astuteness of Maynard Keynes to appreciate that.

Redfyre wondered silently whether Mrs. B's economic astuteness told her that the cost of her chauffeured expedition to Ely in working hours and fuel amounted to many times the sum she had raised from knitting woolly scarves for the indigent poor as he listened on. Exhausted by her philanthropy, she had come straight upstairs to change as she normally did and had been lucky enough not to encounter any of the office staff. That must have been just after six.

Mr. Benson had last seen Miss Lawrence when their paths had crossed at nine in the morning on Friday. She was arriving for work as he was leaving for the factory, and they had exchanged greetings in the hall.

Redfyre interrupted him at this point to ask: "Friday. Payday, I believe? Indications are that she had received her pay packet.

How was this managed?"

"In the usual manner. I had left a sealed envelope in the drawer of her desk the previous evening, as she requested."

"Was this a perfectly secure means of transferring the pay?"

"Of course. It has never yet failed. And why would it? My staff are chosen for their reliability and one hundred percent honesty. Philpott I pay by check, which he prefers. The girls, who are on a considerably lower rate of pay and may not even hold bank accounts, prefer cash."

Redfyre let him ramble on, thinking it was no bad idea if the man were to infer a suspicion on the unimaginative policeman's part of intra-staff jiggery-pokery.

"And how would you describe Miss Lawrence's success in her post?" he asked blandly.

"She did all that was asked of her and more," Mr. Benson replied after a moment to reflect. "On a professional level, she was quick, insightful, able — and she was an excellent timekeeper, never once late. Always a good and surprising quality in a female." His watery gaze skittered without emphasis over his wife.

"My dear," Mrs. Benson interrupted him, "you are being too kind. Inspector, my husband has an optimistic and forgiving nature. He picks out everyone's best qualities for mention. I fear Miss Lawrence was very likely to be a temporary appointment. Without a degree, she could not expect to make much progress in a young industry which demands the very best scientific brains on one side and the most skillful business abilities on the other. With so many able young men released from wartime duties and emerging from their university courses, the connected firms of Lawrence and Benson have a large pool of talent to choose from. Miss Lawrence, Inspector, was not swimming in that pool."

"I'm wondering why her father arranged for her to work in the menial capacity you hint at, Mrs. Benson."

Marion Benson looked surprised and irritated that he should expect an answer to such a question. "She is — was — young, strong-willed, pernickety and thought herself better qualified than she was or ever could be. She expected to be successful in the cut and thrust of a man's world, a flaw in her character which should have been eradicated by her parents at an earlier time. When she finished her expensive, and in our view, over-indulgent education, she came home and — oh dear — our families have been on friendly terms for decades, and I feel disloyal when I say it, but she made her parents' life unbearable. She was not a girl to sit in a corner stitching and peacefully helping her mother run the household, no. Her father, at least, was aware of the problem and asked Sidney if he would take her on for experience at this, the commercial end of the business. She had already spent some time familiarizing herself with the work of the laboratory where, I'd inferred from certain things her mother breathed to me, she had outstayed her welcome." She sighed and gave a tight, sour smile. "We did our best to employ in our office a girl who was never prepared to learn typing and stenography."

Had Miss Lawrence made a call at the house at sometime after nine that evening? Redfyre next wanted to know. The pair looked at each other in puzzlement for a second, then replied in unison: "Certainly not! Why would she?"

Did they remember their guard dog barking at any time during the evening?

Again, the response was an instant and mutual "No!"

Whilst jotting down his notes, Redfyre had also been taking in details of the couple and their surroundings. He'd decided at once that Louise's employer was certainly not love's young dream. In early middle age, he was tall, but slim and pale, his graying hair at odds with his unlined and rather scholarly features. He looked, Redfyre reckoned, like a plant artificially forced along in a cellar. Someone had neglected to bring him into the light at the right moment, and now it was too late.

No attempt to place him in a romantic liaison with the lovely young Amazon, Lois, was successful. Redfyre could barely envisage Mr. Benson in an intimate relationship with Mrs. Benson. She was a clear ten years his junior, in her mid-thirties he guessed, and undeniably the more forceful of the pair. Though Benson was doing most of the talking, he constantly referred to his wife. Redfyre had seen the same strained expression on faces in the back row of under-rehearsed amateur choirs as they glanced too often at their conductor for reassurance.

His first impression of Marion Benson had been one of pink plumpness. She did not have the clear-cut features he might have looked for in a dominant partner. She had the ill-defined look of one whose chin would, in middle age, melt and flow like candle wax down into an undulation of chins. A more searching look revealed widely-spaced brown eyes, attractive and expressive, and the mouth that he had at first sight dismissed as a fitting destination for Charbonnel's violet creams was capable of expressing firmness and derision. But humour? He couldn't be sure. Impossible to tell. The situation was hardly conducive to light conversation.

"Sidney was working out there at the factory until quite late, as he frequently does and returned here well after the staff had left," his wife supplied crisply. "At about — oh, what would you say, Sidney — eight o'clock?"

"At ten minutes before eight, my dear. I remember you asked me if I had time for a gin and tonic before dinner was to be served, and that's always at eight. I hurried to change and accepted a dry sherry instead and went straight in to dinner clutching it. My wife and I spent the evening together. We have formed the habit of spending Friday evenings at home for the last year."

Redfyre shied away from any account he perceived to be a preconstructed alibi, and he sensed that one was about to be laid out for him. He decided to throw a spanner into the oiled works.

"Miss Lawrence was very attractive. I would guess that such a fine-looking young girl must have acquired followers, admirers. I wonder what you have to tell me about intrigues in her personal life."

It was Mrs. Benson who replied with a laugh. "You want to know her secrets? 'Well, I will tell you, if you solemnly promise to tell everybody else!' " she trilled.

Her husband thought this hilarious and joined in what seemed to Redfyre a game for two players. "The inspector says thank you, and he will make a point of repeating it. Ho! Ho! Ah, do I guess, Redfyre, that you're not a fan of Oscar Wilde? My dear wife was quite the thespian in her youth and played the part of Mrs. Allonby, one of whose lines she has just given you. Well remembered, my dearest! And well delivered!"

Marion Benson dimpled and smirked. "*A Woman of No Importance,* Inspector. It was on the wireless last night. We listened to it after dinner with our brandy and coffee. Second act. Five minutes in," she explained.

"The evening drama performance is something we have taken to hearing every Friday, as I was saying." Mr. Benson was set on picking up his prepared speech. "Perhaps you yourself are an admirer of the British Broadcasting Corporation?" He drew Redfyre's attention to a copy of the *Radio Times,*

293

or *The Official Organ of the BBC,* as it proclaimed itself on the cover. The journal was sitting on a table handily alongside a magnificent nut-brown bakelite wireless set. "What a wonder it is to be able to tune in whenever one wishes to the very best of music and drama the country has to offer — and in one's own drawing room! My dear wife risks becoming addicted to the pleasures on offer, I'm afraid, and I seriously suspect the wireless may be killing off the art of conversation."

"Sidney! I protest. Addicted? I always manage to resist *Kiddy-Winks* bedtime stories when the wireless starts up at five o'clock. And the hour they devote to ladies' interests at six rarely fixes my attention. Yesterday's subject — you'll never believe this, inspector — was 'Bringing Succour by Sleigh to the Outcast Siberian Lepers.' A whole hour of soul-searching and wither-wringing as we were invited to struggle along with an intrepid lady adventurer by sledge over the frozen tundra! I switched off while still a thousand miles from our goal and didn't retune until seven when 2LO broadcasts the first news of the day. I continued to listen whilst waiting for Sidney to return. The 2LO Light Orchestra was playing a selection of Russian favourites.

Interspersed with contributions from the Savoy Light Opera Group . . ." Her annoying little voice pattered on, and Redfyre tried to hang on to the thread.

He shook off a sudden attack of drowsiness and resigned himself to hearing out what he sensed was a carefully prepared joint alibi. He read nothing sinister into it. Many entirely innocent witnesses did the same, and with the reputation the police force still had for thick heads and heavy boots, he didn't blame them. But such a performance did on occasion offer him an irresistible opportunity for mischievous questioning. He would let them play out their scene.

"The Savoy Opera, eh?" he said with enthusiasm. "My favourite! I hope they at least kept up the Russian theme of the evening by giving listeners a snatch of 'The Volga Boatmen' '?" He calculated that one call to the BBC would establish whether her response was a lie or a confirmation of her overworked alibi.

"Of course they did! How could they resist? Dreary nonsense! Though they lightened the mood by following with a selection of lollipops from *Iolanthe* and *The Mikado.* Supper was cleared by half past nine when the play started. We dismissed Vincent

295

— our butler — and Sidney and I settled in for the rest of the evening to hear it."

Redfyre closed his notebook and sat forward in his seat, suddenly companionable and smiling contentedly. "And prepared for an hour and a half of superb entertainment! I too am an ardent admirer of Oscar Wilde. I bustled home to hear it," he lied cheerfully. "Splendid performance! The station repertory company did awfully well! Sylvia Scott made a particularly good Mrs. Allonby, I thought. Don't you agree? Such a shame she blotted her copybook by fluffing her lines towards the end of the second act. Disaster! My heart went out to the poor lady. Did you catch it? Lord Illingworth was delivering his wonderful line: 'All women become like their mothers. That is their tragedy.' Awful silence from Mrs. Allonby, who clearly missed her cue, and poor Lord Illingworth — quick thinking, Lord Illingworth! — had to complete his own witticism: 'No *man* does. That is his.' Her best line, and she dropped it! What do you suppose went wrong for her?"

While smiling agreeably, Redfyre took in the changing expressions of the faces opposite. Sidney Benson was flummoxed, mouth opening and closing, failing to find a response and looking towards his wife for guidance. Redfyre turned his attention to her as well and noted how coolly she received the double-barreled challenge.

"As a thespian, Mrs. Benson, you must have a professional solution?" he said, sticking in a barely disguised challenge.

"Naturally," she said. "Such lapses are more frequent than the average listener realises. You, I am supposing, Inspector, are quite knowledgeable about the theatre. Are you familiar with the texts? On the wireless, the acting techniques are rather different from those one employs on stage. Reading from scripts standing bunched together around a microphone, it is surprisingly easy to miss one's cue, even to slip a line — or indeed a whole page! — of text. Luckily, this goes unobserved by the general public, and the other actors are so skilled they can always come to the rescue of their erring company member. Sidney — as you see — was quite oblivious of any fault."

Sidney mimed bafflement.

"In fact, Inspector," she confided, "my husband was half asleep by then. He leads such a tiring life. I'm surprised to hear that *you* had the energy and concentration to apply to a dramatic performance after the long day I think you must have had yesterday." She picked up a copy of the morning's newspaper, which happened to be lying, neatly folded, between them on the table. "I read that you were up to the armpits in that very serious incident in St. Barnabas Chapel. You were quite the hero! Poor man! What a shattering experience. I don't wonder that your concentration may have wandered and you may have misheard."

Redfyre laughed. "I think you have it exactly right, Mrs. Benson!" He gave a sideways nod of his head to indicate his surrender. The questions he most urgently wanted to ask concerning the large amounts of cash the murder victim was extracting from Mr. Benson would have to wait until he was not being fed lines by his formidable wife. This was not the time to pursue them.

He left with politely friendly farewells from both Bensons, reflecting that the alibi they had established for the time of the murder could either be one hundred percent solid or completely worm-eaten, crumbling into dust as soon as he applied pressure.

What most intrigued him was that they had so obviously thought it necessary to establish an alibi.

As he took his hat from the manservant in the hall, he looked into the impassive face and said cheerfully, "Vincent, clear something up for me, will you? Mr. and Mrs.

Benson are at odds on the question . . . Last night, while you were on duty, the doorbell rang at nine o'clock, according to Mrs. Benson, and at nine-thirty, according to Mr. Benson. Which one is correct?"

The response was instant and clearly delivered. "I'm surprised to hear you say so, sir. Can you have misunderstood? No one was expected that evening, and no one called unexpectedly. They dismissed me at nine-thirty, as they usually do when there are no guests. The master and mistress were alone listening to the wireless when I returned from the Champion of the Thames public house in King Street at eleven to lock up and check the windows."

He smiled blandly and threw the door open with a wide, dismissive gesture. Redfyre knew the man was savouring the image of a boot up the retreating police rear end and tried not to flinch.

He had taken three steps towards the edge of the common when a voice called after him and Vincent hurried up to him, his back to the façade of the house, waving a pair of gloves.

"Inspector! Do accept my apologies," he said. "You left your gloves inside your hat when you arrived. I took them out to warm them through, they being quite damp, and I clean forgot to hand them to you."

It was a moment before Redfyre was able to identify the sinister contortion of the left-hand side of the man's face as — of all unexpected expressions — a wink.

Hiding his bemusement, Redfyre took the gloves from him with a good-natured bellow of forgiveness, just managing to stop himself from chirruping that his own gloves were at that moment safely stowed away in the depths of his pockets. Vincent muttered briefly, "I'm usually in the Champ by nine thirty-five, where and when I'm able to speak freely."

A polite half bow and he was off.

CHAPTER 13

At last, Sergeant Thoday had struck lucky.

He had become dispirited by the abrupt closing of doors in his face and the bad-tempered comments. He'd had enough of:

"No Hawkers! Can't you read!"

"Come back when Mum's in."

And even, yelled through a letterbox, "Bloody bailiffs! Bugger off!"

He had almost reached the end of Trafalgar Street. A few more strides would land him in the river. It surprised him that so much leftover Victorian squalor could exist within yards of swish, heavily ornamented boathouses like Goldie and John's.

But here, at Number 27, the door was opened fully by a sweet-faced girl with a kind voice who looked him in the eye and smiled. Thoday gulped. Her eyes were huge, glistening with tears, and they were hazel. She put her handkerchief away hastily in her pocket, sniffed and spoke to him again.

"I said, Thank goodness you've come! You *are* the policeman they said was doing the rounds, aren't you? You took your time!"

"Er . . . I'm Detective Sergeant Thoday, Miss. Here's my warrant."

"I'm Grace Jewell, officer. I don't have a warrant — you'll have to take my word for it."

Thoday collected himself and asked, in what he thought a shrewd tone: "You were expecting me?"

"Of course. It's about Lois, isn't it? My friend Ada at number thirty-two and I worked with Lois at Benson's. We're typists. Just the two of us, though he calls us 'the pool.' We thought you'd want to speak to us about her last movements."

Thoday could not suppress a smile. "Certainly do, Miss. May I come in?"

"No. Sorry, but no. My dad's on night shift this week and he's asleep in the upstairs front. Talking down here in the parlour wakes him up; the ceilings are as thin as paper. Look, if you're going to speak to Ada as well, why don't I give her a knock, and we can all go for a walk and have our chat? There are things she and I would like to know."

She hurried a few doors down the street and banged on a green front door. A net curtain at the window was raised and dropped and a second later, a large, apron-clad bust appeared, jutting out over the doorstep.

"Hiya, Mrs. Drake!" Grace said. "Can Ada come out to play?" The two women burst out into peals of nostalgic laughter.

"So long as you're back before the corner gas lamp's lit," came the expected response. "And who's this handsome bloke you've got in tow? Never seen him before!"

"He's a copper, Mrs. Drake. A detective! We're going to help him with his detecting."

"Well, don't go playing hide-and-seek round the boathouses with him! I've warned our Ada about men with moustaches . . . Ada! You're wanted!"

"We'll go across Cutter Ferry Bridge and walk on the Common," Ada decided as they set off. "The scene of the crime," she added darkly. Before she pulled her cap on, Thoday noted that Ada had curly red hair and she seemed to be a year or two older than her friend. The two girls, well muffled up in serge coats, woolly scarves and gloves, stationed themselves one on each side of the tall sergeant and set off at a brisk pace. They seemed so small he almost offered them each a fatherly hand. He crooked his arms, and they took one each without comment in an entirely natural manner. "Watch it, ladies!" he advised. "The pathways are still a bit slippery. With two anchors I should be all right, though."

With misgivings, Thoday remembered MacFarlane's rambling comments in the briefing room, comments directed at Redfyre. "Interview the women she worked with. Here's the list of people at the workplace. Two of 'em are typists. Now our Lois was a cut above that. Manager of some sort, was it? Although she was a year or two younger than them, and fresh out of school, Daddy a friend of the boss. Ooh, and let's not forget all that cash she had to flash! Bound to be a bundle of resentment there. Nothing like a bit of female jealousy to release the gossip. Stir it up until they give you the lowdown on Miss Snooty Boots Lawrence. See them both together if you can — face-to-face, they're less likely to tell lies and exaggerate."

This interview was meant to be Redfyre's task; Thoday knew that and was concerned. But the girls had fallen into his lap and, whatever the protocol, he was not going to miss this chance. For the sake of the investigation, he told himself, he'd risk MacFarlane's wrath. It wasn't often that two spiffing girls decided to give the police a helping hand. He'd handle them with extreme care and respect.

"Now then, Mister Plod, come clean!" Ada told him with a street urchin's cheek when they were out of earshot of any passersby. "Before we tell you anything, we want to know what on earth happened to poor Lois. All we know is we were sent home early by Mr. Benson because she'd been murdered on the riverbank last night on her way home from town. That's it — take it from there."

He looked down at the bright eyes fixed on him and realised that they were dealing with a tragedy by putting on a brave face. They were both upset, near to tears, hiding fright under a brisk insouciance.

He patiently gave them the facts he thought he was able to reveal, which he admitted was about as much as he knew himself. The rest, he would have to dig out of them and commit to memory. He didn't want to produce a notebook. He'd realised early on in his short career that the production of a pad and pencil led to a seize up of information flow. No one felt comfortable talking at dictation speed. Quite often, people missed out on important details because they did their own mental editing and rejected the wrong items. Some clever dicks even corrected your spelling.

"So she was strangled then, and her body thrown into the river? And you need to know who she met on this riverbank sometime between nine and ten," Grace summarised with a shudder. She looked about her. "Any crimes reported in this area lately? I haven't heard of any. Policing is much better than it was before the war, at least around here. Back then, my parents could have pinpointed half a dozen scallywags who'd rob a girl on her own and led you to their door. Not any more."

"We are inclined to think Miss Lawrence knew her attacker," he admitted.

"Family then, or work. Or a friend who wasn't so friendly," Ada said. "Can't think of anyone she knew who'd have it in for her. Can you, Grace?"

"No, everyone liked her. She was lovely."

Surprised by the assertion, Thoday decided to check whether this opinion was honest or merely polite. People could be annoyingly misleading about the newly dead. On breathing their last, the biggest rogues were suddenly up there with the saints and martyrs, and as MacFarlane often pointed out, "Wimmin! Nothing they like so much as a good cry. Mind they don't blub all over you."

"She was younger than the two of you, but earned considerably more. How did you feel about that?"

Grace smiled. "Cross! Very cross indeed, when she first arrived. And did you know, Sergeant, that her father is a family friend? Nepotism! Is that the word? Raises the hackles. But it didn't last. She was so nice. Never thought to give us orders, though she could have done. She helped us out. Made us think we were all in the same boat, working towards the same thing. I don't think the Bensons really thought about what they were doing when they took her on, so she made her own job. Called herself 'assistant office manager.' Kept old Philpott off our backs!"

"At first, she was given the books to do," Ada told him. "She told Philpott she had a good head for figures. Big mistake!"

"He put her on to tracking down a sum that had gone missing from the records. She found it, no bother. But she carried on examining the books. Never said a word, but I think she found something in there she didn't like the look of."

Ada added thoughtfully, "And right after that, Lois decided it would be a good idea if she went off for a day to the factory to learn what went on there. 'Staff liaison,' she called it. 'Shared knowledge leads to increased efficiency,' or something like that."

"She got away with things like that because it jolly well worked," Grace said. "She'd caught on that she had better abilities than any of us in writing. She set about answering the correspondence and giving us copies to type up. It was a lot faster and more pleasant than taking dictation from Philpott. She cleared a week's backlog in no time. She always knew exactly the right phrases to use, the correct grammar and punctuation. And she could write to anyone."

"She had to compose a letter to the queen one day!" Ada remembered. With an assessing glance at the sergeant, she added with a gurgle of amusement, "Can you imagine? She had to sell — or offer, rather — a sample of our latest wonder pill, developed to overcome monthly aches and pains in females to Her Majesty!"

"Even queens have the monthlies," Thoday said, determined to show he was unshockable. "I'd have thought Her Maj was a bit past that sort of thing, though."

"Her daughter isn't. Her maids aren't. Her sons have wives. But that wouldn't have occurred to Mr. Philpott. That's when we realised how clever Lois was. Just the right tone, but persuasive and informative with it. Anyone would have dashed out and bought a bottle," Grace said.

"And she wrote it in five minutes! I'd have been chewing my pencil for an hour," Ada commented.

"Even the boss — that's Mr. Benson — started listening to her advice. She had the knack of correcting him and pointing him in the right direction, though he had no idea he was being steered one way or another. She got to know the production side of the business. She said understanding the processes would help her with the correspondence and with the books."

"Makes sense to me," Thoday encouraged.

"As the weeks went on, she had him more and more firmly in her pocket," Grace told him. "I still don't know quite how she pulled that off — it was all very professional — but she had him all right. And before you ask, Mr. Plod — no, there was no hanky-panky going on."

Ada giggled. "You'd be looking a long time at Mr. Benson before you thought of Ramon Novarro! No interest in ladies. It's hard to think what he *is* interested in, but it certainly doesn't wear a skirt."

Thoday filed this away for future reference.

"And the other gentleman in the office?" he asked without emphasis. "Mr. George Philpott? The office manager?"

He was pleased to see the girls exchange looks. Finally, Grace spoke. "Well, I'm afraid he was outmanaged. Lois didn't set out to annoy him — quite the reverse — but he came to realise that she had more talent than he did. There was nothing he could do, because in the event of a difference of opinion between them, Mr. Benson always came down on Lois's side."

"Ouch! Sounds uncomfortable. Surely Philpott resented that?"

"He hid it well if he did."

"Possibility here — imaginary scenario: Philpott meets Lois by chance by the river. Resentment bubbles over. He seizes her by the throat, kills her and disposes of her body. How likely would that be?"

Both girls, in spite of the appalling scene suggested, burst into nervous giggles. "You've never met Mr. Philpott, have you?" asked Grace.

"Philpott is a weed! A right softie! He wouldn't say boo to a goose," Ada exclaimed.

"Hang on, now. He's not someone you'd want to be stuck in a lift with, is he?"

"Well no, because he has bad breath. He

smokes, but pretends he doesn't, and eats mints to cover it. Yuck! But I don't think he'd go trying to put a hand up my skirt. He may have been taller than Lois, but physically he was no match for her. She'd have just laughed and thrown him over her shoulder. It would have been Philpott's body you had to fish out of the Cam if he'd laid a finger on Lois."

Seeing his bemusement, Grace explained. "Lois took lessons in jujitsu, Sergeant. Every week on her afternoon off — Wednesday. She was very fit — played a lot of sport, danced and so on, but that Japanese fighting stuff was her real enthusiasm. She learned it from a Japanese couple who hold classes in the Cornhall. I was going to join up in the new year."

"And she was good at it. She won a black belt to hold her trousers up, or something."

"Most importantly, it gave her such confidence. She didn't exactly swagger when she walked, but people seemed always to move out of her way."

"Oh, tell him, Gracie, about the thug with the dog!"

Eyes gleaming, Grace was eager to oblige. "Why don't we all rest on the seat over there for a minute — that's where it all happened." When they had settled, one on either side of the sergeant, she launched into her tale. "We were down here, the three of us, eating our sandwiches for lunch one day in September when a town ruffian came ambling by. Showing off at the sight of three girls in a row. He whistled at us, but we took no notice. Then he shouted something rude, and we went on munching our sandwiches. I could see that Lois was getting cross, but she did nothing about it. Didn't even shout back. Not many would have been foolish enough to do that anyway, because he had a big dog in tow. And it looked as evil as its master."

"It was a Staffordshire bull or a mastiff or whatever they call them," Ada said. "Ugly, scarred, growly thing. The sort they keep for the dog fights behind the Wrestlers pub."

"The lout wasn't satisfied with our reaction, so he proceeded to find some fault with the poor animal and hitched it to that tree, right in front of us. He picked up a stick from the ground and started to beat it. Well that did it! Lois sprang up and moved in on him. She kicked the stick out of his hand faster than you'd believe possible. Pow! That made him yelp! I think she may have broken his wrist, because it went all floppy. And then she took a step back and waited for him to turn and come towards her. Well, he did. He was a lot bigger than Lois, but" — she shook her head in wonderment — "she caught him off-balance, grabbed him by the front of his jacket and threw him in a somersault onto the ground. He landed with quite a thump! I thought he might have broken his back, because he just lay there, groaning, Lois bending over him, grinning like a mad person. She kicked him in the shins and told him to get up, that she'd do it all over again."

"Lord! Silly girl! Brave, but silly! That could have been dangerous!" Thoday said.

"That's what we thought, and it was. She wasn't dealing with other jujitsuists who knew the rules and bowed politely at the end of a bout. This was a big backstreet scrapper in a rage. I went and picked up the stick and threatened him with it, and Ada started jumping up and down and pointed across the park, shouting that the police were coming. They weren't. Good bit of acting though. *I* was convinced! He picked himself up, swearing all the while. When he made towards the dog, Lois shouted at him. 'Leave it! You're not fit to own an animal!' He did as she told him and went off at a quick trot."

"I hardly like to ask, but what became of the dog?"

Grace grinned. "He's still with us. Lois spoke to him nicely, shoved a potted meat sandwich into his mouth and took him back to the office. She told Mr. Benson that he really needed a guard dog for the house. And there he still is." She glanced across the common towards the grand house on the corner of the place and looked saddened as a further thought struck her. "We walk him every day in our lunch hour."

Ada also suddenly seemed stricken. "He'll miss her, Bruno will. We all will." The brave face crumpled, the tears started, and Grace joined in the hiccups and snuffling and dabbing and the passing of handkerchiefs to each other.

"Watch it! Grief is always catching," Thoday told himself sternly, biting his lower lip, "but a police officer is immune. Oh, what the hell!" Without even bothering to look about him for witnesses to the scandalous scene, he flung an arm around each girl and hugged them both.

"I say! So sorry to break in on an emotional scene but — needs must!" a warm baritone interrupted the wails and sniffles. "That's my sergeant I believe you have in your joint grasp, ladies. Would you mind awfully releasing him to his duties?"

■ ■ ■ ■

Redfyre had been on his way to his next interview with Louise Lawrence's mother via Cutter Ferry Bridge when he'd caught sight of his sergeant flanked by two young women, apparently out for a late afternoon stroll. In a spirit of mischief fueled by the depressing half hour he'd just spent with the Bensons, he'd dodged from tree to tree like a trainee plod honing his clandestine surveillance skills. So absorbed were they by their conversation, his three targets had not noticed his arrival until he was close enough to breathe down their necks. They all squealed and exclaimed in a very satisfying way as they sprang to their feet.

To his credit, Thoday was swiftly in control of himself and the situation and, of all things, was performing an introduction. "Sir! Good afternoon, sir! What a stroke of luck meeting you here. I don't believe you've met Miss Ada Drake and Miss Grace Jewell of Trafalgar Street? Miss Drake, Miss Jewell, may I present my commanding officer, Detective Inspector Redfyre of the Cambridge CID? Sir, the ladies were fellow workers of Miss Louise Lawrence and knew her well. They have been giving me a very useful witness account of her character and circumstances."

"Indeed! And there was I, suspecting the sergeant of double dalliance whilst on duty. I should have remembered that he is not an officer to be distracted from his task."

To his surprise, the girl Grace squared up to him. "Yes, you should. The sergeant stepped out here with us to have a bit of privacy. To hear our statements and view the scene of one of Miss Lawrence's exploits. He's been nothing less than correct and respectful."

Redfyre gave a deferential nod of the head. "I'm delighted, though not surprised, to hear that, Miss. He is indeed a rising star in the police force and a credit to us all."

She held his gaze long enough to satisfy herself that this imposing man meant what he said and then spoke to Ada. "Now, Ada, love, I think we've had our say. We ought to be going back and getting the tea on." Grace turned to Thoday. "Nice meeting you, Sergeant. You've got our addresses and are welcome back to Trafalgar Street any time. Just say you're a friend of Gracie's."

Watching the girls hurry off, Thoday turned to Redfyre and murmured, "Thank you, sir. And thank the Lord it wasn't the gaffer creeping up behind me! If Mac-

Farlane had caught me in a flurry of female histrionics, I'd never have heard the last of it!"

"Not sure that's much of a compliment, Sarge, but I'll take it as one."

"Sir, they did have some surprising things to tell me about the victim. How are you fixed? Do you want to hear them now or wait for my report?"

"Now! Sit back down again and tell me how you managed to run to earth the very pair of girls I'd just put on my 'to-interview' list. And what on earth you said to be granted the Freedom of Trafalgar Street! I've got five minutes to spare before my next date with a lady. It would be useful to have another angle on Miss Lawrence before I talk to her mother."

CHAPTER 14

He was met in the hallway by Beth, who managed to be both conspiratorial and alarmed. Her eyes were reddened, he guessed, from weeping, and she had changed into the appropriately dark uniform of a parlour maid. She was wearing a cap with black ribbons in recognition of the sad circumstances and the trembling of the ribbons echoed her state of agitation. "There's no one home but me and the missis," she said, getting down to essentials. "She'll see you upstairs in Miss Louise's room. The master went in to work to take his mind off things and he's not returned." She leaned close, and in spite of the assurance of privacy, whispered, "But it can't be long before he gets back. The missis has taken it very bad but wants to see you. Says she's sure she knows who killed Miss Louise. She's pulled herself together and seems to be a bit — well, clearer in the head than she usually is."

He found himself whispering back, "I'll make the most of it. Thank you Beth. Will you take me up?"

The curtains were drawn, and the room was lit by one solitary bedside lamp. Entering from the brightly lit landing, Redfyre found he had to rake the dark shadows before his eyes made out a darker shape moving towards him from the window, murmuring a greeting.

Clad in a mourning dress from another age, Lois's mother unnerved him. He took the cold white hand he was offered and spoke to the cold, expressionless white face. He had no recollection of his words, but was certain that the habit of years had stepped in and spoken for him, since she nodded sadly in response and clasped his hand in a not-unfriendly way.

He took a deep breath in an attempt to shake off the senseless terror which had seized hold of his mind. He accounted for it the moment he realised was looking at a negative photographic image of his worst childhood nightmare: the ghastly figure of Dickens's Miss Havisham. How many children of his generation had grown up haunted into adulthood by that tragic character? Crumbling away in her loneliness, tormented face floating above an equally decaying white wedding gown from another age, Miss Havisham was still a troubling presence. Here, inches from him, was the same pale, aging face, but the gown below, covering her from throat to ankle, was unrelieved black.

Redfyre pulled himself together. He was meeting a bereaved mother in difficult circumstances who wished to see him, according to MacFarlane.

"You may call me 'Ellen,' " she told him in a surprisingly low and controlled voice. "I have never enjoyed being 'Mrs. Lawrence.' "

"Of course. Ellen it shall be," he replied easily.

"I see you are alarmed by my dress, Inspector. Very old-fashioned. Edwardian, I'm afraid. It's first — and, until today, last — outing was on the occasion of King Edward's funeral in May 1910. Stiff, formal, outdated and dusty. It suits me perfectly; I shall go to my grave wearing it. And unless you can help me, that grave may already have been dug. He will take one look at me, know what I have done, and put me in my coffin. He has the means — means which will outwit the best of your pathologists,

Inspector. His knowledge and skills are superior."

Mad, clearly. Several people from the local vicar onwards had warned him. He reminded himself that his main purpose in being here was to get ahold of the key to Louise's mysterious cupboard. Beth had waved under his nose an opportunity. What had she said? "It might help you to find her" if he took a look inside. She claimed to know where Louise hid the key. But it proved to be missing, to the maid's chagrin. "Must have taken it with her — she always had a ring full of keys in her bag. But wait a mo'! Her mother has a copy. Perhaps she'll unlock it for you?"

Redfyre doubted that very much, and for a desperate moment, he'd toyed with the notion of prising it open with a shoehorn, but he had no warrant for any such behaviour and held off. Though perhaps he'd been mistaken. Had she summoned him here to produce the key? There was no sign of helpfulness and cooperation in her demeanour. She seemed more set upon accusing some unfortunate gent of planning her own imminent demise. He rather thought it within his detective's capabilities to guess the bloke's identity. Poor old sod! Lawrence was a pharmacologist — a modern-day alchemist, pushing the frontiers of scientific and medical knowledge, a figure who attracted mistrust and fear. He was bound to be dangerously exposed to both suspicion and exploitation. Add a dash of marital disharmony, and he had a potentially explosive mixture on his hands.

Redfyre decided to calm the situation. "You were so kind as to offer to unlock Louise's cupboard for me, I understand. Do you have the key?"

She sighed and produced a small silver key from a pouch attached to her belt. "Beth assures me that you are discreet and helpful, quite unlike the usual run of policemen. The girl shows good judgment as a rule, and who else is there I can trust?"

She handed him the key and he went at once to the corner cupboard, closely followed by Ellen Lawrence.

Disappointment was his first reaction. If he'd had sisters, he was sure they'd have all kept such a private Holy of Holies in their rooms. A toppling pile of outdated diaries occupied the whole of the topmost shelf. Below that, old letters were filed away alphabetically according to sender in brown cardboard envelopes, and on the third shelf down was a fascinating if higgledy-piggledy mixture of well-thumbed books. He noted nursery rhymes and fairy tales giving way to the even more stirring sagas of the ancient Norsemen. Tales of Ancient Rome surrendered to the romances that every girl read, Jane Austen and Charlotte Bronte seeming to be favourites. Conan Doyle and Wilkie Collins were next along; swift, undemanding reading for a girl with little time to spare. These English novels were supplanted by the latest deposit in these ordered strata of literature: a vein of yellow-backed French novels, some of which he'd enjoyed himself. *Madame Bovary* now lay cheek to cheek with the young *Don Juan,* he noted, and hoped both parties were satisfied with the arrangement. One or two were plainly filthy and completely unsuitable for a young girl, the rest were the latest crime mysteries and thrillers. Redfyre smiled. He would have had a lot of views to exchange with Louise Lawrence, if he'd ever had the good fortune to meet her.

He was suddenly aware that the girl's mother was looking at the contents with as much curiosity as himself. Could it be that she had never bothered to open the cupboard before? His question was answered a moment later when she reached in over his shoulder and picked out a slim volume.

"Ah, I wondered where that had gone! It's

my copy of *The Book of the City of Ladies*. Do you know it? By Christine de Pizan. The first woman writer in France. Fourteenth century." She put it in his hand. "Here, take it. It was written for men like you." Then, more doubtfully, "You *do* read French? It's impossible to come by an English translation, unsurprisingly."

"Thank you, Ellen." He leafed through the book and added, "Modern French, which I see this is, is no problem. I wouldn't care to attempt the medieval version! I'll return it with my thanks when I've digested and been improved by the contents."

She almost smiled. "That is by the by. What you ought to be interesting yourself in, Inspector, are the items on the lower shelves."

Redfyre had been trying and failing to make sense of the piles and boxes, which looked like nothing so much as the leftover stock at the end of a very hectic jumble sale.

"Start here, will you?" Ellen Lawrence pulled a length of fabric from the top of a pile of newspapers. "It's important for anyone who wants to understand Louise and why she died. Do you recognise it?"

He put out a hand and touched the length of silk. "A scarf of some sort. Green, purple and white, and it's embroidered with the words 'Votes for Women.' How could I *not* know it? The force has confiscated many of these from over-enthusiastic ladies attempting to disrupt the normal flow of traffic in public places. They were waved about by supporters of Mrs. Pankhurst, I believe? Many were stripped down from the pinnacles of Cambridge colleges and incinerated in the station boilers, largely before the outbreak of the war. Thankfully, though there have been rumblings of dissatisfaction since the war, outbreaks of hostility are quite rare."

"But that particular scarf is very special. Look more carefully. You will note that it still carries smudges and stains. Mud and grass and — see here — that brown smear you will recognise as blood. Blood spilled by a martyr to the cause."

"I can guess the cause, Ellen," he said with a trace of weariness, "but you're going to have to give me a stronger clue to the martyr's identity if it's important that I know it."

"Clue? I can do better than that! I can show her to you." She rummaged in one of the boxes and extracted an envelope of photographs. As he removed the topmost one for inspection, she spoke again. "This one records the moment of her death. Her name was Emily. Emily Davison."

"Ah. That Emily Davison."

"I'm sure you know the story — the popular myth — but may I ask you to look through the rest of the photographs without disturbing their order? They are in series. Press photographs taken of that infamous scene from different angles. Scrupulously collected together by my daughter and presented in filmic sequence."

To push things along and establish his unprejudiced knowledge of the Davison affair, he said crisply, "She was a clever woman, Miss Davison. Studied at both London and Oxford universities —"

"Though no degree was awarded her for six years' study and work. Because she was a woman."

"So, understandably disgruntled, she joined Emmeline Pankhurst's lively faction?"

"The Women's Social and Political Union? Yes. You may call them 'suffragettes' if you wish, Inspector. They did not regard the name as an insult, though as such it was certainly intended."

He began carefully to leaf his way through the prints as she turned on the strong overhead light.

"Taken by both professional press photographers, carefully positioned, and by amateur members of the public standing about with a Kodak in their hand on the thirteenth of June, 1913. At Tattenham Corner on the racecourse at Epsom. The occasion of the Derby," she commented as he silently worked his way through. "Emily had been watching the race from a vantage point behind the rails with the rest of the crowd when, several horses having raced by, she ducked under the rail and ran onto the course, spotted her target — the King's own horse, Anmer — and, well, what exactly did she do? Look closely."

"The record tells us that, physically damaged and mentally deranged by force-feeding and other tortures in Strangeways prison, she dashed onto the course deliberately to throw herself in a suicidal gesture under the hooves of the King's horse. By bringing it down and killing herself in the process, she would gather the greatest possible press coverage for her organization. Presumably she was hoping also for a certain amount of public sympathy." He raised his head and looked her straight in the eye. "In that respect, she made a fatal misjudgement. The vast majority of the British public would always instinctively show more concern for a downed horse — and a royal horse, what's more — than for a strident, law-breaking woman protester."

"Oh, dear! Not so impartial a man of the law, then!" She sighed. "Though I grant you are telling me no more than the blunt truth. Or are you trying to hurry me on? I see I must come to a conclusion which will open your eyes. Look at the evidence in your hands, Inspector! And admire the insight, intelligence and sheer doggedness of the person who collected it together in the teeth of much opposition. My daughter!"

Sombered, he turned again to the evidence.

"There, you see, Emily's movements are not wild and uncontrolled. This is not a suicide attempt. She's carrying something in her hands, do you see? She steps out deliberately seeking out a particular horse, easily distinguishable by the bright colours worn by its jockey. But she does not attempt to pull the horse down or harm it in any way. Have you identified the object she's carrying yet?" She passed him a magnifying glass, and he took it closer to the light and peered.

"Good Lord! It's . . . it's . . . are you telling me that it's this scarf? This very one?"

"Your own eyes are telling you that. The object she held in her hand is the one you now have in yours. If you have it tested in your laboratory, you will identify soil and grass from the Epsom Downs and the blood of Emily Davison. It's a suffragette scarf, bearing their message in large letters along the bottom. Emily had planned that she would throw it over the horse's neck so that it would gallop over the finishing line in front of the battery of news cameras bearing for all to see: 'Votes For Women.'"

"Nonetheless, a suicidal gesture is the best interpretation a disinterested witness could put on her actions."

"Unless you know, as I do, that the week before, she had been practicing on the downs with colleagues this very gesture of throwing a scarf over a galloping horse. She did not intend to die."

"A clever woman. She must have known the risks."

"She did. And accepted them. She was very ill, Inspector, a result of the infamous treatment she had suffered at the hands of the police and prison staff. I believe she knew she had not long to live and wanted to use her last resources of strength to make an impression at a time and in a place when the attention of the whole country would be on her."

"She certainly got the attention of the

poor jockey who was unseated when his mount did what any horse would do naturally and tried to avoid contact with a human. Here, look at this photograph. The beast is terrified. He wrenches his head away, and in the entanglement of reins and scarf, he falls and drags her down with him, pounding her — involuntarily — with his hooves."

"The jockey bounced up again and was fit enough — and moved enough by Emily's brave sacrifice — to attend her funeral."

"And what bearing does this fascinating bit of history have on your daughter's murder, Ellen?" he asked quietly.

"Emily Davison became a fixation for Louise. Most girls of my daughter's age collect photographs of film stars and crooners or air aces. Louise was fascinated by women like Emily. Just as seven hundred years before, Christine de Pizan was fascinated by Joan of Arc, who was her contemporary. Christine died two years before Joan was betrayed by her own people and handed over to the English army for torment, trial and death. She was found guilty of witchcraft and burned at the stake. The knowledge of such brutality at the hands of men would surely have rendered Christine's book less hopeful and joyous, if indeed she had retained the will to write the book at all. Listen, Inspector. For an eighteen-year-old, seven hundred years is too long a time to wait for reason, justice and rights to prevail. Seven *days* is too long. Louise's school encouraged her in her enquiring attitude and taught her scurrilous tricks for advancement in the modern era. She corresponded with national newspaper editors and members of Parliament. Masters of colleges in Oxford and Cambridge were her targets; lord mayors trembled at the mention of her name."

Ellen took the pile of photographs from him and replaced them in their packet. She tapped it with her finger. "Louise saw these as the template for her own campaign, Inspector. Emily Davison did not succeed but she saw before her death that in the modern age, the tools for advancing a cause had been forged. The media of the newspapers, the wireless, the *ciné* film. This is the way to inform and sway the national conscience, to convince and persuade the people who elect the lawmakers."

She fell silent and studied him critically, clearly wondering whether she was giving away more than was good for her and her deceased daughter. "She learned early on that the men — for it is only men who disseminate this information — are not all men of integrity. Many abuse their position as it pleases them or their paymasters to tell lies. Outright lies. And because their words appear in printing ink or are broadcast via the wireless, the credulous public believes them without question. We still venerate the word, be it written or heard over the ether. You yourself have just admitted you accepted the published version of Emily's death, without question! And you are a man in the business of questioning. An educated, thinking man!"

Placated by his silence, she ironed the note of hysteria from her voice and spoke with greater urgency. "Louise reckoned that, once you knew the newspapers' strength, you could use it against them. I know she was planning to apply the rules of the jujitsu fighting she was so good at to a mental tussle with the press. She intended to use these weathercocks, these jackals, as an instrument to convey the lies or truths *she* wished to tell. 'All these words come from the hand of a *man,* mama,' she told me. 'Even the text of the *Times* is not handed down from heaven already inscribed in stone.' Physically, men can be thrown over a girl's shoulder, Inspector, and equally, they can mentally be diverted by a clever woman to her own use."

"Indeed! It happens to me two or three times a week," Redfyre tried to counter the venomous tone she was developing with a touch of humour. "I rather think it may be happening to me now."

Ellen Lawrence merely stared at him, irritated by his interruption. "She was energetic and right-minded and — for one so young — unusually ruthless. There are several men not a million miles from here who would have gladly pushed her into jail, under a horse, or off a cliff. Now one of them has done it."

Before she blurted out the name of her suspect, bringing the hunt to a premature end, Redfyre decided to head her off and make his final assault from firmer ground. "I've just come from the home of the Bensons, the pair who were employing Louise in their family business. A business in which I understand your husband has more than an interest — an association."

"Yes. The two concerns are compatible as you must have established. They have a simple joint aim: putting pills in mouths. Which pills, whose mouths, and for how much profit are their only concerns. My husband employs the very best of scientific researchers in his enterprise and is, he assures me, on the verge of making a discovery that will improve the capabilities of medicine a thousandfold. He stands to become a very successful, very rich man over the coming years. He would normally, of course, count on handing the business over eventually to a son. Unfortunately, he has only daughters. Clever and able, all three. But female. Had Louise been a boy, she would have fitted at once into the hierarchy, would have learned the routines and been respected as the next owner. Instead, she was sent away to a peripheral school, denied a university education and parked with a safe employer until such time as she might marry. Hopefully, and with a little direction, her choice of husband would have been a man who would himself take up the reins of Oliver's business."

"Cambridge being a pretty good place to embark on such a selection?"

"Oh, yes. Oliver had a few local candidates in mind, one or two already in his employ."

"Enough, if true, to start any girl on the road to insurrection," Redfyre agreed.

"She plotted and planned to fight back. She had gathered about her a group of like-minded women. They were not members of any existing suffragist group. These had all failed, according to Louise. They'd called a truce for the duration of the war. Even rolled their sleeves up and joined in the war effort at home. Yes, Inspector, they kept the home fires burning, but afterwards, were unable to rekindle their own."

"The war ended in 1918 and, that very year, women were granted the vote," Redfyre pointed out. "Perhaps that went some way to cooling the ardour? Perhaps we could even say that Emily Davison had not died in vain."

Her response was scathing. "Women *over the age of thirty* were enfranchised, and only those who were property owners and financially secure in their own right. A tiny percentage of the population. Men merely have to attain the age of twenty-one. Not many women were taken in by this empty gesture. Not even rich old birds like your Aunt Henrietta, who is my last remaining friend from the old days. Louise and her young colleagues hoped for better. They accused the suffragist groups of throwing in the towel, of failing in particular to represent the rights of women of the underclass — who are the vast majority, after all. They formed an action group of their own. Not entirely drawn from the literate and learned upper classes, either. Louise deliberately sought out strong-minded women in the lower ranks of society. A class of women, she maintained, who had even greater grievances than their well-to-do sisters. And they had an invaluable part to play in her schemes. They were — are — an unknown quantity."

She anticipated his next question and rushed on. "No use asking me who these women are, Inspector. They scarcely know it themselves, I think. Much secrecy. They even took false names when together and knew each other only by those. They have not gone so far as to name their organization. The moment you fly your flag and rally round it, you become a visible target. It's easier to spot and root out a single wasps' nest than deal with a cloud of midges. But they can both ruin a picnic."

"Mmm. It's hard to discredit or lay information against a movement that has no identity," Redfyre observed. "Not even a catchy set of initials. Now, the press does appreciate a set of initials. It saves space and makes them appear to be in the know. They might even have invented one for the group . . . 'Women's Association for the Suppression of Paternalism,' perhaps? 'WASP'?" She was looking at him strangely, so he gathered himself and asked more formally, "May I ask, Ellen — you tell me

Louise could be ruthless. Would she have been capable of making an attempt on the life of a woman, possibly someone she knew? Could she, at the least, have recklessly endangered another girl's life?"

Ellen frowned. "I can't say. Not unless you are willing to be more precise." Thinking carefully, she added, "She was a life force, Inspector, not a death dealer. Oh, I know that's an easy, overdramatic expression, but it summed her up. She had the utmost respect for her fellow men, women, all creatures. She was the sort of child who rescued mice from the cold bathroom and installed them in the airing cupboard with a dish of nuts. But she was equally hot-blooded and would never have ruled out a passionate and physical reaction to cruelty and injustice."

"Why did Louise not confide in you? You were of the same mind and could have helped her in her struggle."

"I was of no use to anyone. She knew my condition, and from the time she returned from Surrey, she worked to identify the cause. Once she ferreted it out, she conspired with me to overcome a very dark force. What you are hearing from me now is a relatively sane voice. Some weeks ago, I was mute and senseless. Within a hair's breadth of being carried off to a mental institution. Two signatures from the medical profession is all that is necessary for such a step. And my husband — the fiend who has made me into the mental and physical cripple I am — has many, many friends and dependants in the medical trade."

"This is a very serious accusation you are making, Mrs. Lawrence."

"Of course it is!" she snapped. "Do you ever say anything original, man?"

"Hardly ever. I react, I enquire, I uphold the law with all the patience I can muster. Cleaning up the messes made by others calls for a certain steadiness, a plodding approach that may well be out of step with the emotional flights the suffering and guilty are experiencing."

"I'm sorry. I'll try to plod along with you. Please understand that I make this accusation using a mind that has only recently regained its ability to think. For years, he has been giving me pills to counteract the depression that fell on me after my last child was born. Increasing the dose and changing the formula at his whim. He didn't use me only as his guinea pig, he declared me an invalid and kept me deliberately out of sight in a darkened room for years. Louise, when she returned and looked about her, realised what was going on, and instead of making a fuss, challenging him and putting him on his guard, used subterfuge and deception to wean me off the doses whilst hiding the fact from Oliver. He still has no idea that we know the villainy he is up to, the criminal damage that he and Benson are inflicting on the women of this country. Louise found out. She worked for days in her father's labs, and at the factory at the other end. She used her own contacts outside the businesses to check her findings. She gathered evidence that would send them to jail! Right where they ought to be. And Benson's appalling wife with them. She knows, and she encourages and instigates!"

The overstuffed pay packets. The secret savings account. Suddenly and shockingly, these were accounted for, his suspicions confirmed. Blackmail. The only way to escape it was to take the Duke of Wellington approach: "Publish and be damned!" Or to kill off the blackmailer. Because once started, blackmailers never stopped. No wonder the Bensons had jumped through hoops to establish that they'd been spending a quiet evening with Oscar Wilde at the moment Louise had met her death. Though her own father was every bit as much exposed and stood to lose his career, his livelihood and his reputation if Louise chose to spill the beans. Or the pills, to be precise. He had more questions to ask about the pills.

"The Bensons and your husband are still unaware that Louise acquired this dangerous evidence?"

"What do *you* think! No, they found out! Louise was very excited these last few days. Her schemes were about to be launched. She didn't tell me anything about them, so I wouldn't give anything away. I still have my low moments, Inspector. She was planning to take me away from this house and set us up in a small apartment somewhere. A refuge for her younger sisters. She had a little money in reserve, she said, though goodness knows where that had come from. There was a small bequest from her grandfather five years ago, and I know she put that into a savings account. The money I brought to the marriage is all gone — Oliver's used it to develop his business, though I still have some jewelery to sell. She was always expecting to move away and on and up, and made provision for it. She could have done without the extra baggage of a sick mother holding her back. But that's Louise. She has a heart of gold if you care to look for it."

"*Had* a heart, Ellen. Until someone stopped it beating last night." Cruel and insensitive, but Redfyre was running out of time and did not want to leave without hearing the name he sensed was trembling on her lips. Uttering a denunciation was the hardest part for most witnesses, and some needed a sharp push in the right direction. "Are you going to confirm what I have already worked out for myself?" he asked, smoothing her path.

She nodded and looked anxiously at the clock. "It's past six. My husband will be here at any moment. Beth won't say a word if you can get away before he arrives.

"It was Vaudrey. The creature who strangled my daughter — his name is Vaudrey."

CHAPTER 15

The inspectors' meeting room stank of fish and chips. At eight o'clock on a busy Saturday night, Sergeant Thoday had had to use his police clout to get to the front of the queue in Stan's Fish Supper Parlour to place his order for cod and chips with salt and vinegar times three.

Even Redfyre had not complained about the lack of plates and forks, but had tucked into the newspaper-wrapped packages of hot food with his fingers. Upon finishing, the three men crumpled their sheets into balls and threw them into the distant wastepaper basket.

"By gum, we all needed that after the day we've had!" MacFarlane announced, wiping his hands on his handkerchief. Thoday allowed his eyes to swivel sideways and run along the lineup of seven used tea mugs on the superintendent's desk in wordless comment.

"Now, Redfyre, don't keep us waiting. Tell us how you got on in the house of horrors."

"Would that be the one at Midsummer Place or de Montford Avenue, sir?"

"Both, in time sequence. I'll shut you up when you start to repeat yourself. Hiccups and belches are acceptable, but I can't be doing with tedious."

He managed to avoid all three pitfalls as his story flowed, dovetailing acceptably with Thoday's own account of his meeting with the girls.

"So, what I'm hearing from the pair of you is a useful but surprising account of this girl Louise's character and activities. And on a quick count, you've between you collected four more people who would cheerfully have strangled her. That's five, if we reckon with some bloke on a bike crossing the common last night." MacFarlane interrupted his own account and paused for a moment in reflection. "A potential nuisance to the Force, that little Miss, I'm thinking, if she'd stayed alive and active. All that jujitsu rubbish! A London colleague of mine ended up hanging from the railings of Buckingham Palace by his braces when a certain Miss Garrud of the self-styled suffragette bodyguard squad had done with him. And now they've set up shop in Cambridge, you're telling us. Go round and throw your weight about, Redfyre. Well, metaphorically speaking, of course, and tell them they're not welcome — under surveillance — whatever comes to mind."

"Would that be ditto for the tango school she frequented as well, sir?"

"Inspect them first, Redfyre. We're not unreasonable." MacFarlane glowered and carried on. "She's an even worse problem now she's dead. But what a lass, eh? Has anyone done as I asked and thought to get hold of a photograph for the scrapbook?"

Redfyre bent and retrieved his briefcase. "Sir, her mother willingly handed this one over. It's her school-leaving photo. It'll come in useful for identification in interviews with other witnesses."

"What a corker!" was MacFarlane's verdict. "Shame she didn't have two proper parents who kept her on the straight and narrow. Couple of loonies like the pair you've described, Redfyre, could turn anyone into an agitator. Now, what's next out of the hat?"

"A scarf. A suffragette scarf."

Redfyre told the tale as Ellen Lawrence had recounted it.

MacFarlane appeared unimpressed. He refused to touch the fabric, pushing it about with the end of his pencil. "You are aware, Redfyre that these things are two a penny in Epsom High Street? Curio and memento shops? Never more than one on display at any moment, of course. They have to convince every punter that he's being sold the one and only."

Redfyre didn't believe him and said stiffly, "All the same, I should like to have it examined by forensics."

"As you wish. Waste of their time. They'll find mud and manure and grass all scraped from the hallowed turf, I'm sure, and a dab or two of tomato ketchup for effect."

"Sir, the scarf in question did exist. It's here in the photographs. It was abandoned on the course when Miss Davis's body was carried off on a stretcher. There were racecourse officials instantly on the scene, and I'm sure one of them would have dutifully picked it up and removed it, not being aware of its significance at the time. It could well be in existence somewhere, and I would like to find out whether this is the one."

"Suit yourself. It doesn't advance our case, whichever. Dead end."

Thoday, who'd been listening with increasing exasperation, stirred and nodded in agreement. "Sir! Don't you think we're clutching at straws in the wind?"

"It's possible. What is certain is that you are hybridising your metaphors, Sergeant. Not just mixing them, but breeding from them. Don't do it. Now, Inspector — have you got anything else in there? Something more solid?"

"Try this. A group photograph. At the last moment, Ellen remembered that just one photograph had been taken of Louise's unnamed gang of anonymous girls in the summer. Not all the regular members are there — it was an impromptu meeting, and there are naturally no helpful names written on the back."

He placed the print on the table in front of his two colleagues and waited for them to study the exhibit.

MacFarlane extended a stubby, nicotine-stained forefinger and counted up the faces. "One, two . . . seven of 'em. It's just an innocent tea party," MacFarlane scoffed. "Straw hats, cucumber sandwiches and jugs of lemonade on the terrace in the shade of a horse chestnut. Conkers just starting to form, I see, so — late August, early September. Louise is easy to spot. But — 'girls,' Redfyre? I can see a couple here who are nearer fifty than fifteen."

"Louise wasn't running a Girl Guide troop. She recruited with care, according to her mother. She valued experience and wisdom."

"Mmm. Who recruited *whom,* though? We shouldn't assume Louise was the leading light just because she's our subject of interest. Perhaps she took her orders from above? Could be that her house — the one she seemed to have the run of — tucked away over the river away from, let's say university eyes, was damned convenient for a bunch of militant ladies. Out of the academic orbit and off the map for townies, but only a few minutes' walk from both. And all the wimmin have bikes these days. Do we think Miss Louise was playing the adjutant, the facilitator for some other, more experienced old biddie? An agitator-in-chief? Here, take a look at this boot-faced harridan — the one with the teapot. Bet she packs a six-inch hatpin!"

"Sir!" Redfyre could barely hang on to a tone of reprimand through his amusement. "The lady you are speaking of is my Aunt Henrietta."

He enjoyed MacFarlane's discomfort for a moment, then explained, "Aunt Hetty is an old school friend of Mrs. Lawrence's, and godmother to her daughters. She is the only one to have stuck by Mrs. Lawrence over the years in the face of Mr. Lawrence's maltreatment. I was unaware that she visited every Wednesday to check on her friend's welfare. It would be the most natural thing in the world for my gossipy old aunt to preside over the tea things and, finding herself surrounded by a gaggle of grinning girls, all friends of young Louise, entertain them with the stories of her gilded youth. And yes, she does indeed pack a hatpin that she would not hesitate to use on you, sir, if you offended her."

"Thanks for the warning. You'd better get over to hers and confront her with this. How well does she know these other girls? Can she give us their names?

"I doubt it! According to young Beth, they each chose a name from the pantheon of Roman deities to disguise their identities."

MacFarlane's eyes opened wide in disbelief, and he looked again at the smiling faces. "Then I think I've just spotted 'Venus,' " he said with a chuckle. "Have a gander at this little bundle of fun on the front row! Blonde hair, cheeky grin, neat ankles. Do you recognise anyone else in this lineup, Inspector?"

"Yes, one for certain." He pointed to a girl sitting on a swing hanging from a tree bough, one leg saucily extended and showing her petticoats in deliberate imitation of the Fragonard painting. "That piece of mischief! And this lady over here on the left, hiding half her face behind her teacup. Obviously, she's uncomfortable at the idea of being photographed. If my identification is correct, she has good reason to be. I'm marking her down as Minerva!"

MacFarlane peered more closely at Minerva. "Mmm . . . she'd be my pick! What a smasher! Big lass, though. Look at those muscles! She'd know what to do with an oar."

"Indeed. I understand she rowed at stroke in her women's college crew, some years ago," Redfyre replied stiffly.

"Take a posse if you're planning on arresting her. Any more take your fancy?"

"If I caught sight of the *eighth* girl, I might well be able to greet her by name."

" 'Arf a mo'! Eight? There's seven here."

"I mean the one holding the Pocket Kodak, sir. People always forget that someone is looking through the viewfinder and pressing the button. Of the party, but not recorded. The one of this crowd who would not wish her features to be recognised amongst such a gathering. The one with a reputation to make and uphold."

His theory was received with a measure of

skepticism, followed by the orders he had hoped for to "Get your aunt in a corner and give her the third degree! I want the low-down on every face in this picture and the one taking it."

And then: "Come on, Redfyre. Your bag's still open, I see. Pull out a few more rabbits, will you?"

He produced a box of Swan Vestas and rattled it. "Another job for our long-suffering Forensics!"

He pushed it open, and they all peered in at the multicoloured collection of pills and tablets.

"Mrs. Lawrence had got herself together sufficiently well — or perhaps Louise had done it for her — to present a sample of all the medicaments her husband had imposed on her over the last five years. Some, but not all, are stamped with the commercial imprint of Benson's factory, B&H. The H of the old firm being long dead, apparently."

"Well done, Redfyre. She saw you coming, it seems. Just remember what the old bat said about mental jujitsu — I don't want to see my best inspector hung out to dry. Get these over to the hospital labs with a note."

He looked keenly over the desk as Redfyre closed his case. "Aw! That all?"

"Not quite, sir. There was one more thing Mrs. Lawrence handed me. The name of the man she is convinced killed Louise."

"Redfyre, you've got handcuffs. Why isn't he wearing them?"

"Time enough." Redfyre smiled. "I'm meeting this gent in an hour's time down the pub, at his suggestion. If he coughs up, I'll make the arrest, but I'm not expecting it. I'd rather like to take the sarge along with me, if he can stay awake long enough."

Thoday grinned and mimed awakeness.

"His name's Vaudrey."

They looked at each other in puzzlement. "Not her dad, Lawrence, then? Not Benson?"

"No. Vaudrey. As chance would have it — no, routine procedure had it! — I'd spoken to the very man on entering and leaving the Benson household. He's the butler-cum-footman. Vincent Vaudrey. Ellen Lawrence is quite sure that he is the creature, the pair of strong hands used by either or both Mr. Lawrence and Mr. Benson."

"Makes sense to me. The first bit of sense you got out of that nutcase. The father and the employer both wanted her out of circulation, neither having the physical or mental strength to do the dirty deed."

"So they look about them and ask —

351

'Who will rid me of this turbulent daughter?' Vaudrey is a London man, possibly a villain on the run, according to Mrs. Lawrence. She blames the postwar servant shortage."

"Hear this, Redfyre. With the stakes as high as I'm beginning to think they are, you ought to get your skates on and nab this bird before he goes missing. He'll be under the ice in the Cam or on his way to the Riviera in no time — they won't want him being interviewed by CID. Paid assassins have the shortest survival rate of any villain, largely because they're never local and nobody's interested in tracking them down. If he's still running free, nick him and put him in the cells. Tell him it's for his own protection. It's Saturday night — I'll tell the duty sergeant to reserve cell number ten. Solitary occupancy, so no one'll get to him."

And in a rush of concern for the late hour and the extended day his officers had worked, he muttered, "Better take the Riley." He promptly spoiled it by adding, "Easier to transport a prisoner in the back than invite him to walk along back to the nick with you, even if there's two of you. Conversation might become a little stilted."

It was well managed. Thoday had entered

the Champion of the Thames ten minutes before Redfyre, and he was five minutes before he expected Vaudrey to make his appearance.

Thoday was settled at the main bar, elbow to elbow with a couple of the regulars whom he seemed to know. The pint in front of him was already half empty. Redfyre noted that the sergeant had chosen a spot where he could cover the whole of the small-panelled room with one glance in the mirror behind the barkeeper. Redfyre approached, ordered two pints of the best bitter and looked about him while they were pulled. The "Champ" was uncomfortably crowded. He decided the best way to establish a space in which he could conduct an uncertain conversation with a dubious character was to pick that space and clear it. He gathered up his pints, selected a table which would be well within the sight of Thoday and approached the pair of town roughs who were lounging there looking disconsolately at their empty glasses.

"Finished here, have you, fellers?" he said jovially. "Bit quiet in here for you? Why don't you join the funsters in the public bar, eh? And have one on me." He winked and put a half crown onto the table. This seemed to take the edge off the riposte they had initially been about to summon up, and they moved off, taking their empties with them.

Vaudrey came in at 9:37, greeting several of the men in the bar. He caught sight of Redfyre sitting behind his two pints and steered a course through the crowd to join him.

"Vincent Vaudrey," he said politely, extending a hand.

Redfyre felt in his grasp the calloused palm of a gardener, a trench digger, or a hard-worked footman. "Recently of London?" he enquired with a smile. "I believe you know some friends of mine down there in the Smoke."

"I think you mean 'am known to' some of your pals. The ones with a lovely view over the Thames," he said with bluff openness. "Don't believe a word they tell you. Those lying turds fitted me up. For something that got me a year in the Scrubs. If you're ever on the blower to them again, say Vincent sends them a two-fingered salute. That he's working a cushy little number in Cambridge, where he's enjoying the unpolluted air. Even the coppers up here are clean." The voice had the speed and jerky rhythm of an Eastender. The sharp eyes and intelligent face were making a swift assessment of him.

"Happy with your employment, then, are you?"

"What do you think? It's bearable." He took a deep swig of his beer. "At least, it was until very recently. I've packed my bags. I'm getting the first train up north tomorrow morning to where my sister lives in Sheffield. They were lying to you, did you know that? The old trout and her weasel husband."

"I knew. What I want to establish is why they felt they needed to lie."

"I'm not sure myself. It's probably not safe to know. They're up to something, and Lois had an idea what it was. Look, do you want to hear what really happened on Friday night?"

Redfyre nodded.

"The dog knew she was there. It barked a warning. At about, oh, I was just locking the back door, so it would have been nine twenty-five. He's made a good watchdog, Bruno. But Lois was special for him, he could get wind of her a hundred yards off. I wasn't surprised to see it was her on the doorstep a second later when the bell rang. Least, I was surprised that she was there at all. She'd gone home at the usual time. Told everybody she was going to a concert at one of the colleges. Never came round in the

355

evenings. She shot inside when I opened up, looking over her shoulder. Scared like.

" 'I didn't know what to do, Vincent,' she says. 'There's someone following me. Can I use the phone to ring my father and ask him to come and fetch me? Don't bother the Bensons. I'll just sit quietly here in the hallway and wait.'

"It wasn't like Lois to be scared of anything, but she did seem rattled. 'Who is it? Any idea?' I asked her. I walked out to the end of the path and shone the torch about. Didn't see nobody. Nothing stirring. Still, it's impossible to spot anybody who doesn't want to be spotted amongst the trees. Too many hidey-holes on the common, that's why it's so popular of an evening. You let yourself be spooked by every squeal and squeak, and you'll never get across it. But it was brass monkey weather last night. You'd have to be desperate for it to go out canoodling in that."

"Could she give you any details of her follower?"

"Yes. He was on a bike. She'd clocked him halfway down Jesus Lane on her way to Four Lamps crossroads. She'd moved over under the trees by the wall to pull up her stocking. This bloke shot past on his bike. She watched him to the end of the road, wondering where on earth he could be going in such a hurry. Decided it was probably an undergrad rushing back to his digs out of town before curfew. He stopped at Four Lamps and looked around. She wondered why somebody who'd been in such a hurry now suddenly seemed to have all the time in the world. He was hunting, she thought. She stayed where she was and watched him checking every road out from the city centre, one by one. Then he cycled off again down Victoria Avenue towards the river on the left edge of the common. Lois set off again, navigated Four Lamps, no bother, and decided to take her chances across the common 'cos it looked deserted. And she didn't want to pick the same road as the man on the bike. The house lights were on all along Brunswick Terrace, which was practically her backyard. She'd crossed Butt Green and was striking out across the common when she realised that the cyclist had cut across from the Avenue and was making straight for her, bumping over the grass."

"Same man?"

"Yes. Same outline. Hard to tell when someone's on a bike. He had a hat on and a cycling cape, she said. Nothing special. The kind of gear everybody keeps rolled up in their cycle bag in winter. Thick, woolly. Again, she's not a girl who gets frightened easily, but there was something about this bloke that spooked her. She did the sensible thing: ran to the Bensons' and pulled on the doorbell.

"I calmed her down and, suspicious type that I am, I said, 'Look here, Lois — have you been up to something? Ditched some poor bugger in town and he's trailing after you?' I was quite near the mark, as it turns out. Well, there was this bloke — varsity type — she'd annoyed. Left him in the lurch at a pub, though she'd paid for the drinks and didn't owe him a half-penny. He followed her on foot as far as the marketplace. She'd spotted him in the crowd round the Sally Bash band. He could have picked his bike up from where they leave them against the railings by the church and tailed her, but he was a bit of a goof. She didn't think he had it in him — the determination that is. I told her it's not that, it's the snub, the humiliation that gets them. Even a weed can get really riled when a woman turns him down. I made her tell me his name. Thomas Tyrrell, Inspector. Music student or something at St. Barnabas. That's who you're looking for."

"I'm aware of Mr. Tyrrell. Thank you, Vaudrey. But tell me — why the fandango from the Bensons to establish an alibi?"

"It was what happened next that caused that. They were listening on the stairs. Both of 'em. They do a lot of hole-and-corner stuff." He shrugged. "It's their house. No reason why they shouldn't have come down at the sound of Lois's voice. Practically family, she was. Except she couldn't stand them. 'Good gracious!' they said. What was dear Lois doing parading about in the dark on the common? They wanted to know. 'No — don't bother to ring and disturb your parents — you know how your mother gets overexcited. Expected back by ten o'clock? Plenty of time for a cup of cocoa, and then Vaudrey can escort you the short distance to de Montfort Avenue.' "

"Made a lot of sense."

"Yes. But I was quite surprised when Benson suddenly struck up and started making the decisions. The upshot was — yours truly could make the cocoa while *he* put on his galoshes and overcoat. He'd take Lois home and give Bruno the unexpected treat of a second walk that evening. No trouble at all! He'd lost the plot of the play they were listening to, anyway. Would enjoy a bit of fresh air. I thought he was just doing what he did quite a lot of — getting out from under Mrs. B's feet using any excuse. So I made the cocoa and put the dog on a lead. Lois had recovered by then and was keen to return home. With Bruno in one hand, she was as safe as houses. She knew that. That hound would have torn the throat out of anybody putting a finger on her. She set off into the dark with her boss, and that's the last I saw of her."

"Did you note the time Mr. Benson returned?"

"Oh, yes. All this malarky'd made me late for nipping out for my usual, so when 'er indoors dismissed me and went off back upstairs to her play, I went to my room. Couldn't settle. Worried-like. I was keeping half an eye on the clock. He was back by twenty past ten." He looked earnestly at Redfyre. "Bloody fool! All he had to do was drop her off on her own doorstep! Are we missing something, Inspector?" And finally, "What time did she die?"

"Let's say she was dead by the time Benson got home."

Into the silence, Redfyre offered, "Can I get you another pint? Or a scotch? I'm having a scotch."

He returned, two Johnny Walkers in hand, to find Vaudrey motionless, chin sunk on his chest, holding back his emotions. "She was a good 'un, Inspector. Caught me having a quick ciggie on the common on her first day. The Missis can't abide tobacco smoke in the house. No smoking on pain of instant dismissal. 'Cripes! I'm for it!' I thought. But, 'Got another one of those, Vincent?' she says. 'Half a day in this madhouse and I'm back on the gaspers again. By next Tuesday I'll be on the booze. How do you live with it?' " He gave a watery smile. "She brightened the whole house. And she was sharp. She sussed out what was going on with the master and that streak of whitewash he calls his office manager."

"George Philpott?" Redfyre tried to keep his voice steady.

"That's 'im. George Discretion Philpott. No one else has a clue. I mean, well, women have no idea, do they? But Lois had lived among — what did she call 'em? Bohemian? — families. Posh, arty folk who tried a bit of anything they fancied. Thought themselves a cut above morality and the law. And she'd been to Paris." He rolled his eyes as he delivered this last unanswerable argument. "It didn't seem to affect her; she took people as she found them, without any of their nastiness rubbing off on her."

"She kept her uncomfortable knowledge

to herself?"

"Yes. Never breathed a word, even to me, though sometimes we'd catch each other's eye, grin and look away. But a word in the wrong ear, and she *could* have had him arrested and sent to jail. You know how it is! It's worse in London . . . bloody witch-hunt going on down there! A mate of mine on the fabrics in Liberty's got caught chatting up a customer — a male customer. Police were called in. A year of hell in jug, poor bloke." His mouth clamped into an unforgiving line. "They tacked a sign up over his cell door to announce his crime. 'Buggery,' it said. And he never! He never! He was lucky to get out of that hellhole alive. And you coppers wonder why people hate your guts."

"I don't. I know very well why. Some of us struggle against a bad system and even manage to change it. Look, Vaudrey, I have a proposition to put to you — no, this isn't a trap! You have your bag packed, you said. Go and pick it up. I'm offering you a lift to the station and a night's free lodging. I'll guarantee that you can jump on the first train north tomorrow morning. I wouldn't be quite easy thinking you were spending another night under that roof. Come and meet my sergeant. He'll show you the way to the nick."

CHAPTER 16

Shivering in the bleak chill of a Sunday morning, Redfyre, still bleary-eyed from his late night, shone his torch briefly onto the face of his old army watch. Six o'clock. He leaned back against the bark of an ancient chestnut tree, his rough dark serge coat blending seamlessly with the bark, and fixed his eyes again on the front door of the Benson house. Vaudrey had told him that the dog had to be taken out onto the common at six precisely every morning or it would howl the place down. The manservant's task, of course. He might at any moment catch sight of Mr. Benson performing the duty himself, since his man was tucked up in solitary state in a cell at headquarters, probably being handed a cup of early morning tea by the duty sergeant.

Lights flicked on in a satisfactory way, and moments later the front door swung open. His targets appeared on the top step, sniffed the air and ventured forth. Redfyre gathered himself and moved silently forward, gratifyingly taking Benson by complete surprise. The man would have liked to shoot back indoors and pretend he hadn't seen the policeman, but Redfyre fixed him on the spot with a cheerful bellow.

"Ah! Good morning, Benson! And good morning, Bruno!"

His friendly greeting elicited two suspicious growls.

"What the hell are you doing here, Redfyre?" came the astonished and grumpy response. "Not still combing the common for fag ends, are you?"

"Let's say I've found a few ends and am now busy tying them together. I've gathered nearly enough to knit a noose."

"Ha! And you're sizing up necks to fit it? Well, let me offer you another. I'll tell you something very odd. The bloke who works for us, Vincent Vaudrey — you saw him yesterday — has done a bunk. Never bothered to hand in his notice, just disappeared in the night. Are you wondering why, Redfyre? I am!"

"I have my theories. I even have the man. He spent the night enjoying police hospitality in St. Andrew's Street."

"Good Lord! That's impressive! And

you've come to inform me? At this unholy hour? That's impressive, too. But it's all a dashed nuisance. I didn't get my early morning cup of tea. He was a good worker. We'll miss him. Still . . . Mrs. Benson would have been somewhat agitated by his presence about the house in the circumstances, I fear. Hysterics might well have ensued."

Redfyre smiled and with a gesture invited Benson to step down and join him. "Shall we walk? Your dog seems quite desperate to get onto the grass."

"Inspector. I have a confession," Benson began again slowly. "We fobbed you off, the wife and I, yesterday. Told you less than the truth. No malicious or devious intent, of course. We were just trying to avoid attracting an unnecessary police attention to the household and business. When an employee gets herself murdered practically on the doorstep, tongues are bound to wag. Isn't that so?"

"I was not unaware of the attempt at fabrication and wasting of police time. Would you now care to enlarge on or correct your story?"

Redfyre's tone was stiff enough to make Benson drop his blarney and confine himself to the bald truth. He began briskly. "You have perhaps realised that Miss Lawrence and this wretch, Vaudrey, were close. Closer than a girl of her status had any right to be with a servant. And a Londoner, what's more! One of dubious background. You should — perhaps you already have — looked into it?"

He waited for Redfyre to acknowledge with a nod and continued. "Manservants are like gold dust these days, and they don't apply for jobs in the provinces unless they have a very good reason for avoiding the capital. It was clear that Vaudrey was impressed by Miss Lawrence — a pretty girl — and perhaps he fancied his chances, got the inevitable rebuff and couldn't stomach it. She turned up on our doorstep on Friday night with a cock-and-bull story about being followed from town by some stranger. Vincent was very eager to accompany her back home across the river. Suspiciously eager. I smelled a rat and stepped in. 'No,' I said, 'leave it to me. I'll take the dog with us. He'll enjoy the walk and see off any ruffians.' "

"Considerate of you, sir. And did you deliver Miss Lawrence safely to her home?"

Benson stopped and moved the dog lead from one hand to the other with irritation as they walked along. He seemed to be having such difficulty holding back the dog that

Redfyre, overcome by good manners, was on the point of offering to take the lead himself.

"Of course I did!" Benson snapped. "We went over Cutter Ferry Bridge. It's a fifteen-minute walk for me. Would have been five at the pace Bruno and the girl set. I don't walk with the easy grace of youth any longer, Inspector. I took the trouble to keep looking about me and, I have to say, I saw not a soul. There was definitely no man on a bicycle for half a mile in any direction. What was she up to? At any rate, she couldn't wait to be rid of my company. It wasn't an easy conversation. We didn't get on as well as I would have wished, Inspector."

"Would you like to confide the reason for the bad feeling?"

"I wouldn't call it that. She's of a different generation. She is — was — demanding, overconfident, manipulative and damn clever, Inspector. Mrs. Benson and I have not been blessed with children. And I do mean blessed. We would have welcomed them, sons or daughters. If we'd had a son with Louise's qualities, we'd have thought we'd died and gone to heaven!"

He stood for a moment, commanded the dog to sit and spoke earnestly to Redfyre.

"Louise did not know, nor would she ever have guessed, that I intended to pass the business on to her upon my death. My wife would be quite unable to cope — she can barely manage the household accounts — and when I began to look at the situation in an unbiased way with my lawyer at my elbow, it occurred to me that the solution was obvious. She was right there in front of me. Redfyre, I was about to make Miss Lawrence the heir to my business concerns. The disposition would have caused much distress to Mrs. Benson, though I would always have left her well provided for. I leave to your imagination the scenes that would have ensued on the reading of my will, Inspector! Oh, the shrieks and screams!"

The twinkle in his eye encouraged Redfyre to comment indiscreetly. "Shrieks that would have fallen on dead ears, however! You risked little as long as both ladies remained unaware of your intentions until you were safely away in your box."

"My reasoning exactly! Redfyre, a further disgraceful satisfaction I had planned but would never have enjoyed was to cock a snook at Lawrence, her father. We work well as business colleagues, but I have little respect for the man. He mistreats his wife, sets aside his daughters as worthless. He never valued Louise's talents."

Time, Redfyre thought, to reveal a strong card. "Talents, sir? Would you consider an ability to extract money from her boss a talent? In my book, blackmail is a crime, not an admirable character trait."

Benson resumed his walk. "The Friday envelopes? Is that what you're referring to? None of your business, of course, but no! I won't allow you to blacken Louise's memory with the most sordid of police aspersions. She asked me for money one day, Inspector. Oh, not for any substantial amount. She wanted to borrow it in advance of her wages — an undeclared bank loan sort of arrangement. I had the cash, she said she would work off the sum. Gents' agreement. It would have been impossible to set up such a loan with her bank. Being a woman, and a young one at that, any transaction would have necessitated the involvement of her father, which she was at great pains to avoid. She wouldn't tell me what she wanted it for, but knowing her as I did, I trusted her in her intentions. We worked out our pay packet arrangement. Probably incurring the wrath of the Tax Inspectorate, if anyone would be so vindictive as to inform them . . ."

"They will not hear from me, Mr. Benson."

"I was going to reveal my plans for the business to Louise as we walked. It's hard in the office to find a quiet moment when four or five pairs of ears aren't wagging. But the mood wasn't right that night. She was tense, eager to be getting home.

"When we'd crossed the bridge, she told me there was no need to escort her any further. She was within sight of home and admitted that she must have imagined the follower. She began to give Bruno his orders to go or turn around — whatever it is she says to him. But, 'No, no, my dear!' I said." He hung his head and looked aside. "I fear I spoke out of a spirit of mischief. I wanted to annoy her. 'I undertook to deliver you safely and that's what I shall do. Every slow step of the way, don't you fret!' "

He paused again to massage his left hand, wincing with pain. "This dog is too much for me. It will have to go. I only kept the wretched animal on as a favour to Louise."

"And where exactly did you say goodbye to her?"

Benson pointed across the river. "Right there, at the bottom of de Montfort. Thirty yards from her house. Her father was standing on the porch watching out for her. He must have caught sight of us approaching when we were lit by that gas lamp over there on the corner. Louise shouted, 'Yoo, hoo!' and waved at him. He waved back. 'Well, there's daddy!' she said. 'Duty done, Mr. Benson. Thank you so much, and good night.' And off she skipped."

"You didn't attempt to speak to Mr. Lawrence?"

"Lord, no! Keep him out, freezing on his porch exchanging pleasantries when all he wanted to do was haul his daughter inside and tear her ears off? Not kind or necessary. I showed myself in the lamp light and did a bit of gentlemanly gesturing, made a rather exaggerated bow and gave her a theatrical shove in the back, saying 'Over to you!' I was glad to be rid of her by then. I pulled old Bruno off in the other direction back across the bridge as fast as I could — he seemed all set to perform that awful whining he does when she moves out of his sight, pulling frantically to get back to her."

"I'm not sure, in these circumstances, how you think Vaudrey could possibly be involved."

"Must I do all your work for you? He wasn't about the place when I returned. I didn't expect it. He used to go off to the pub, returning at closing time — about eleven. He could have left the house shortly after we did — I've checked with my wife and she hasn't a clue. She dismissed him and went straight back to the play on the wireless after the interruption. There are more ways than one of reaching the bottom of de Montfort Avenue. Longer ways around, but he could have run and got ahead of us. As you've noticed, I walk annoyingly slowly. He could have intercepted her before she reached the house, couldn't he?" he finished, querulous and uncertain.

"Benson, you should hear that Mr. Lawrence told me — and I believe him — that he did not see Louise arriving back. He was working in his study and she did not interrupt him. He was unaware that she was absent from the house, let alone dead, when I brought him the news the following morning."

Benson was aghast. "God help us! It was Vaudrey. The figure waving from the porch was Vaudrey, lying in wait! I've known Oliver Lawrence for thirty years, but I couldn't swear it was him I caught a glimpse of. Still, I never questioned it — who else would have been on that very spot and waving? The brain accepts what the brain expects, you know, Inspector."

"Quite. And my brain is reminding me

that Louise Lawrence knew your secret — secrets, indeed — and was taking money from you. Overstuffed pay packets every Friday? You offer an explanation and I will consider it. I consider also the fact that the girl had knowledge that any man might have killed to keep hidden. How convenient was it for you that she disappeared that night? Was strangled to death only yards from the place where you declare you left her?"

Benson was quivering in terror. He spluttered and protested his innocence. All to be expected, and Redfyre had encountered such emotion on the part of the guilty many times, but he was alarmed by the unnatural movements the man was suddenly exhibiting. The left side of his body appeared to crumple and sag. He seized his left hand in his right, abandoning the dog lead and cursing with frustration. Redfyre swiftly put a foot on the lead and shouted at the dog to sit.

"Show me your hand," Redfyre said firmly and took hold of it.

The hand was a twitching, trembling claw, and the shuddering of the muscles continued all the way up to the shoulder.

"What in heaven's name is going on?" Redfyre asked. "Are you having a fit? A heart attack? Can I get you help of some sort?"

"Nothing you can do but stop bothering me! It's the shaking palsy. *Paralysis agitans,* or as my medic calls it these days, Parkinson's disease. Incurable and progressive, I'm afraid. Even I do not have the pills to combat or even alleviate it." He bared his teeth in what might have been either pain or a sardonic snarl. "My only respite from it is massage, expertly and devotedly administered by my employee, George Philpott. As the attacks are sporadic and never predictable, I pay him a retainer to work on the premises and be present whenever I need him."

"Does Philpott have medical qualifications?"

"He did. He is — was — a doctor of medicine, but he was struck off in circumstances that do not concern you. An act of spite and injustice. We have long been friends, and when he found himself unemployable in his own profession, I offered him the chance of working for me in a not-unassociated capacity. He remains able to use his experience and skills in the business and on his one remaining private patient."

"You felt you needed to conceal his role?"

"Of course. Secrecy in such matters is

important to me. I run a business that is in competition with several rising young outfits who would be circling like vultures if they knew of my condition."

Redfyre looked again at the left hand, gnarled and useless, and remembered Doctor Beaufort's summary: "Left-handed? Right-handed? Impossible to say. Equal and great pressure exerted by two strong thumbs." And on the throat of a very strong girl. A girl who only had to whimper to call up the savage protection of a fierce and devoted dog.

He picked up Bruno's lead and offered his arm to Benson. "I do apologise, sir. Allow me to get you home in time for breakfast. Can you manage if we crawl along? And, as we crawl, perhaps you would be so good as to tell me what I may expect to discover when the results of certain lab tests land on my desk. Tests being carried out to establish forensically the composition of medicaments produced by your company."

Chapter 17

Sunday Morning. Before Dawn.

PC Toseland shivered under his thick police cape and kicked an empty fag packet into the gutter while he waited in the Market Place to hear the six o'clock chime from Great St. Mary's Church. A stickler for routine and cussed with it, he made a point of starting his beat on the first stroke and finishing it on the last eight hours later. Old Mary was well into her count before some of the lesser college bells woke up and joined in the clamour, and by then, Toseland's long stride had carried him halfway down Market Hill. Not that there was anyone around to see him moving into action or to note how meticulously he performed his duties this morning. No one would remark the freshly pressed uniform, the smooth-shaven cheeks, still ruddy and glowing from the porridge his old ma always got up early to cook for his breakfast.

A deserted square, filled with litter from last night's Christmas jollifications, presented no challenge to an officer of the law. This was a dull shift, but he rather enjoyed his solitary condition. It gave him a feeling of power, or something very like it, to stride about the city as though he owned it. And he wasn't all that alone. One blast on his police whistle would be heard at a surprising distance across the quiet town, and two or three of his fellow coppers would be at his side in seconds. There'd be Gilligan on Trinity Street, keeping an eye on the colleges — always quiet on a Sunday morning — and Edwardes over by Parker's Piece, freezing his balls off in that exposed acreage of wilderness. Whichever way you turned in that godforsaken desert, you got the blast of the wind in your face.

He was thankful he hadn't been given the King Street-Maids Causeway duty. That always went to the more experienced uniformed coppers, anyway. Pubs and houses of ill repute every few yards. Every chance of favours in kind handed out, of course, to officers willing to take advantage of the hospitality. It used to be looked on as a perk, that beat — before the war. Not so much since the police cleanup. That old bugger, MacFarlane, in cahoots with the

Chief Constable, tolerated no slackers. No second chances in the Cambridge force.

There were to be no temptations on the beat he had this morning. No market. Not even a breezy exchange of ribaldry with stall-holders arriving early to set up their striped awnings and pile up their pyramids of apples and oranges. The square looked jaded and desolate. Toseland clicked into motion. Worst first, he reckoned, was always a good idea. Pick the green jelly baby out of the bag first, eat the sprouts from your dinner plate and leave the real pleasures to be savoured later with a feeling of duty done. In pursuit of the glow of righteousness, he marched over to the ornate stone statement that was the canopy announcing the public conveniences: THE GENTS. Stinking underground urinals they were, but sometimes you caught a tramp sleeping rough down there and had to move him out and on. What a lady did if she was caught short in the town centre, Toseland had no idea, and was glad no one had ever had the indelicacy to ask him.

He drew a lucky blank in the lavatories and decided to treat himself to a breath of fresh air by walking down past the Senate House in front of Caius College and proceeding on down Garret Hostel Lane to reach the river.

The narrow cobbled lane between the grey dignity of the Senate House and the forbidding stonework of the run of college buildings he always found intimidating. Quiet, secretive. *Pass through if you must, but be discreet. Be invisible. You are not welcome here,* these walls said to him. PC Toseland unconsciously responded to the spirit of the place, stopped whistling and quickened his pace to make his run through.

The bundle of clothes crammed into the base of the archway on his right alerted him to an unwanted presence and slowed his step.

It was one of his favourite parts of the city, this mysterious little architectural flourish. A strong wooden door, fortified with a pattern of studded nails, was outlined by a moulding that cascaded elegantly from a carved entablature no higher than a copper's helmet. It flowed down to a generously wide sill at pavement level, six feet long and two feet wide, the whole space capacious enough to accommodate a hammock, a coffin or a reasonably sized dosser who'd slipped into the wrong part of town. As far as Toseland was aware, the gate was never used. He had no idea which of the colleges it gave access to, if indeed there was a college behind it. It could well give on to the pigswill bins at the rear of the kitchens; it could equally give on to some magical rose garden. Quiet, sheltered from wind and rain, the space had been cleared at the point of Toseland's boot with a joking, " 'Ello, 'ello, 'ello! 'Oo's left the laundry lying about, eh?" several times since the summer.

The constable shone his torch and peered down at the tumble of garments, trying to work out which end was which. Mostly the sleepers aligned themselves in an unconscious calculation with feet to the east. He looked to the east end and saw a small foot wearing a high-heeled shoe. A female. Toseland drew back in dismay. These confrontations with women never ended well for the investigating officer; they inevitably turned into reportable cases. No respect shown to the law — ever. Men would swear and shuffle off, no bother, but the women — at best, they'd launch spit and abuse at you, and at worst, they'd lodge an accusation of molestation. As if! But the paperwork they threw up could be never-ending.

He peered more closely, keeping his hands behind his back. No manhandling! He'd learned the hard way to avoid trouble. He'd encountered women roughs before now, all right — even escorted some of them all the way to the Salvation Army Reception Centre. Not that he'd noted it particularly at the time, but he knew that they'd all been wearing dirty old shoes. Those that weren't wearing their bedroom slippers, having dashed into the street to flee a violent husband.

None of the women he'd encountered had worn silk stockings and high-heeled kid shoes.

He found a shoulder to shake, swathed in a thick wool coat, damp and cold, and he shook it. "Madam!" he said in his policeman's voice. "I shall have to ask you to move on! Are you in need of assistance?"

He'd never come across a corpse before. Apart from the waxen features of his old granny, glimpsed in her coffin across a crowded front parlour before they nailed the lid down. But there was no mistaking one when you had it by the shoulder.

What was he supposed to do now? He quelled his rising panic and began to think. Perhaps she wasn't dead, but just frozen up because of the weather? Perhaps she was unconscious, drugged, drunk, but still alive. Lord! Suppose this was the master's wife, returning after some clandestine outing and scrabbling unsuccessfully to sneak back in to College through a side gate? Did masters have wives? Mothers? *Always check, never assume,* he told himself. He had to find a pulse, and remembered from training where to hunt for one.

The throat.

He stripped the gloves from his icy fingers and poked about until he'd revealed her face and neck. When he saw the bruising and absorbed its meaning, he shot up in horror. He fumbled at his belt to find his police whistle and, with no thought for the quiet of the place, he gave it a blast. And another and another. Until, in the distance he heard the faint double echo of his own shrill appeal. Two notes, repeated. Notes that told him: *Received and understood. Am on my way.*

Redfyre heard the telephone ringing as he opened his front door and dashed to answer.

"Do you know what time this is?" an irritated voice asked him.

"Seven-thirty. Which is at least two hours before a halfway decent super has the right to call a copper on his day off. And that being a Sunday! Were you afraid I was going to be late for Mass, sir?"

"Some of us have been up for hours fighting crime, Inspector. Listen. I'm booked in to lose a game of golf with the Chief Constable later this morning. Sorry about that! Sorrier than you can imagine. The Chief's preferred partner backed out at the last minute with a nasty bout of the 'flu, so I'm alerting you. As highest-ranking officer left in charge — gawd 'elp us! — you are to assume overall responsibility until I can get back. Shouldn't be long, what with the weather and the state of my golf."

"Sir, surely this weather will mean suspended play? I'm surprised they don't have a closed season for the wretched game."

"Not on your Nellie! It's a Scottish invention, remember, Redfyre. Those hairy buggers'll play through a blizzard with the wind up their kilts! Still, most of the action takes place in the clubhouse, they tell me. All you have to do, Redfyre, is sit in the station filing your nails and making sure that my arrangements are being adhered to." His voice faltered for a moment, and then he went on more briskly. "You'd think it was safe to just let things take their own smooth course for four hours on a quiet Sunday, but better safe than sorry, eh? Fact is, it's all hands on deck this bright A.M. We, er —"

His indecisive vagueness was driving Redfyre mad. What was wrong with the man?

Finally, "We seem to have got another one

of *those,*" MacFarlane admitted.

"I beg your pardon, sir. Another one of what?"

"*Murder,* chump! Do wake up! Would I call you to tell you that Mrs. Honeywell has lost her Chihuahua for the fourth time? Some poor lass has been strangled to death in the middle of the city in the night, five minutes' walk from you," he added accusingly.

Redfyre sighed. "I seem to be the centre of a deadly vortex lately! But where? When? Who is she?"

"Calm down. It's in good hands — I've put Thoday in charge. He's down there now. Pathologist is on his way. Just be around, will you? Make yourself available, in case the sergeant gets out of his depth. *You've* still got one and a half murders on your books, and pernickety bastard that you are, you've already turned loose two perfectly acceptable suspects. Tyrrell and Vaudrey both blowing freely in the wind, laughing their socks off, they tell me."

"Not that freely, sir! Vaudrey is reporting to the Sheffield police headquarters twice a day and Tyrrell is back in his digs under surveillance." He reined in his objections to challenge once again his boss's annoying prevarications. "Strangled, you say? Any connection with the Lawrence case?"

"Hardly! Lawrence and the trumpet girl — your assignments — are both girls of a certain class and uppity with it. Respectable, with influential friends and family. Need careful handling. But a connection? Not on your Nellie! There's no conceivable link between them and this woman. Didn't I say? This victim is a prostitute, plying her trade in a part of the town where she oughtn't. Thoday can cover it. He'll come up with some answers in five minutes if he goes into the right pubs — King Street's his home turf. And wasn't he in the raiding party that dismantled that brothel on Maids Causeway? Old Ma Mumford's Den of Iniquity? That syphilitic swamp."

Redfyre stirred uneasily. His boss was dangerously near the verge of one of his rants. He decided to cut him short with a rant of his own. "Indeed, sir. To the embarrassment of certain local dignitaries who were discovered in a very undignified posture. The gentlemen were released unscathed and unnamed — escorted, if I'm not mistaken, to the nearest back exit by our helpful lads, while the ladies — and Mrs. Mumford — were subjected to a physical checkup and overhaul. And the madam put in jug for six months."

"Hah! Fat lot of good it did! The enterprise just packed its bags and moved next door under the new management of Mrs. Mumford's daughter. We never learn."

"But *they* do. And they take better precautions against further raids, including shoring up clandestine support from the debagged dignitaries. They continue because the demand never ceases. Their clients take risks in spite of the dire consequences. Perhaps next time, we should attack the problem from a different angle and arrest the customers, sir?"

"What! And bring half the local council, a good slice of the university hierarchy and a fair selection of His Majesty's boys in blue into disrepute? That's enough moralising, Inspector — you're wasting my time. Get down there and instruct Thoday. He can have a modest allocation of the readies for information. Never hurts to grease a palm — they'd turn their granny in to us for a ten-bob note, some of these low-lifers. And the last thing we'd want is a cellful of screeching old biddies. Old age doesn't confer sanctity and a good character, you know, Redfyre."

"Something I notice every day, sir. But tell me, where was the body discovered?"

"Down the Senate House Passage. That

narrow bit of cobbled road some of the sprightlier undergraduates dare each other to jump across, wall to wall."

"I know the one."

"Do you know that little niche under the arched doorway on the right?"

"Yes, a hidey-hole for tramps. Out of the wind and rain, and out of view from either end of the passage. No idea what the door opens on to. If, indeed, it does open. Can't say I've ever seen it in use. I always assumed it was just for show. An interesting bit of architecture to relieve a stretch of rather austere walling."

"Well you said it, Redfyre: 'Just for show.' And that may prove to be a more acute remark than you realise. A common or garden lady of the night in this university neck of the woods? Nah! Traffic all goes the other way. They'd be nabbed right sharp by the college bulldogs if they set foot on hallowed ground. And they fear those bully-boys more than they fear us. If they get brought in here, there's always a chance they'll be given an interview and a cup of tea by one of our nice officers. At worst, he'll threaten to tell their mum. No, they don't risk it. They never stray far from the Four Lamps. And when they do get killed, the body's left right there on the spot where the murder occurred. On Butt Green or some other nasty hole on the common. 1887, it was, a kid of sixteen had her throat cut on Butt Green and the newspapers went to town. Full front-page spread. The perpetrator turned up in a local pub, minutes later, bloodstained and carrying a dripping knife, announcing that he'd done the deed. Now, if DI Redfyre had been on duty that night, the lad would have been given a severe talking-to, handed sixpence for his bus fare home and let loose. Anyway, top and bottom is, I don't want to see an associated front-page spread highlighting police incompetence this time. You were the hero of the hour on Saturday, Redfyre, with your outstretched arms, quick wits, and hifalutin musical tastes. Come Monday, you could be a blundering flatfoot with a tin ear."

"Understood, Superintendent. Six inches below the fold on page four will have to do. I'll make sure the editor is aware of your wishes. Enjoy your golf, sir."

Redfyre put the phone down before he could utter the words that would have him in the police dock for insurrection and impertinence to a senior officer.

Five minutes' walk. He would have guessed seven, but he'd soon find out. He dashed into the bathroom.

The uniformed constable sealing off the narrow alleyway reacted at once. He put up a hand to warn him off before recognising him and calling out a greeting. "Sorry, Inspector! It's a bit gloomy for detecting around here. The gas lamps are still alight, and I've had a word with the bloke who sees to them. Asked him to make sure they stay on until further notice. You all right for a torch, sir? It's thirty yards down on the right. The duty doctor was summoned; it's Doctor Beaufort's week. Also in attendance are Detective Sergeant Thoday and the constable who discovered the body, PC Toseland. The beat bobby. Two other PCs were present, sir, alerted by police whistle, and the sarge has sent them both back on their beats."

Efficiently briefed, Redfyre went to present himself.

Doctor Beaufort looked up as he approached. "Morning, Redfyre! Another cold and frosty one, another cold and frosty victim. A woman. Mid-twenties, killed during the night. You'd think they'd all be at home, filling the mince pies and hanging the mistletoe."

Sergeant Thoday, sensing a familiar and

excluding double act about to break out over his head, hurried to assert himself. He drew Redfyre aside. "Sir! Superintendent MacFarlane has given me orders to —"

Redfyre cut him short. "At ease, Sergeant! I'm aware. He's spoken to me on the telephone and conveyed his instructions. I'm here to check in my interfering way whether there's any connection between the death of this lady who is now your concern, and that of Miss Lawrence, whose death we are both investigating. Fill me in, will, you?"

"Right. Body discovered at six-fifteen. PC Toseland here carried out the minimum of investigative manoeuvring necessary to ascertain that she was not, in fact, alive and in difficulties, but dead. He summoned assistance, and one of the responding officers ran to HQ with the news of the discovery just I was turning up for duty, so I came straight out here. Doctor Beaufort arrived ten minutes ago."

"Tell, me Thoday — the super tells me the girl is a prostitute. How could he possibly know that?"

"I told him, sir," Thoday explained. "I looked through her bag before I called it in." He produced a slim clutch bag from his briefcase and handed it to Redfyre. "Everything would seem to be untouched. There's a money purse with five one-pound notes and a few coins in it. Female effects: mirror, rouge, lipstick. And an address book cum diary. Complete with her own name and address and about fifty more names, some with addresses. All male. Some names clearly false. I mean, Charlie Chaplin? The Maharaja of Poona, Albert Einstein, Charles Darwin, all customers?"

Redfyre considered this. "Not Darwin. He's dead. But remember — this *is* Cambridge, Sarge."

"Some are even more discreet — just initials. But — hard to believe — some of them have a telephone number to them. How stupid is that! What kind of burk gives his telephone number to a tart?"

"Young? Inexperienced? Uncaring? No shortage of those around. But how very useful to us."

Thoday sighed, thinking presumably of the hours of police work about to swamp them. "Evidently there was no robbery. And that's the funny thing, sir, almost as if . . . Well, I found the bag when we were handling the body — me and the PC. It was underneath her. Why? So no passing light-fingered lad would spot it and nick it?"

"Underneath?"

"Yes. Not chucked away, not thrown over

the nearest wall. Tucked up under her bum, it was. Whoever *placed* her body after killing her, he wanted us to know who she was."

"Thank you, Sarge. Let's take a look at her, shall we? Doctor, if we may?"

Her face had been hidden below a fold of her muffler, a respectful gesture the doctor usually employed, not for his own comfort but to lessen the unease of those gathered around the body.

"Two in two days, Inspector. And the same method of killing seems to have been used. It's a strangulation from the front. Quick, clean, decisive — no need for a weapon. No incriminating knives, coshes or ropes. Just two strong hands and a burst of uncontrollable rage."

"Would you say that? I was thinking a controlled, impersonal summoning up of killing energy. The sort of unpleasant but necessary muscle flexing you might find in a chicken-strangler, an executioner or — for goodness sake — a frontline soldier. 'Nothing personal, you understand, but I just have to kill you.' These victims aren't evoking the terrible slashing and disfiguration of a Ripper, a man driven by his devilish urges. In its way, this very control is ominous. Our man clearly has the stamina to recover quickly and move on to the next victim with no time necessary for boiling emotions to calm."

Redfyre added as an afterthought, "Do you know what trench-raiding is, Doctor?"

A mystified Beaufort nodded.

"Some platoons chose to mount trench raids just to relieve the boredom of war. An enterprising young captain would decide almost clinically to go out across No Man's Land after dark and kill the buggers in the nearest enemy trench. In total silence, with a kind of cultivated icy rage, you make your way systematically along the trench with knife, bayonet, revolver. It takes considerable nerve and energy. You hardly see the man you're killing, and he doesn't see your blade flash. A few lucky ones you may haul back as prisoners for questioning. If you get back safely, you prepare for a tit-for-tat incursion into your own trench the next night. It helped to pass the time," he finished bitterly.

"So, you're looking for an ex-soldier? An erstwhile trench warrior suffering the boredom of retirement in Ivory Towers, Civvy Street, Cambridge, and inventing his own brand of wide game to pep up his bland life?" Beaufort raised a sardonic eyebrow.

Thoday shuffled his feet in embarrassment. "I can see what you mean, Inspector," he said, clearly struggling to understand and support his superior officer in his wild assertions. "These weren't individuals for him. They're like faceless enemy in the opposite trench. He's working his way along, and then he'll make a dash for his dugout when he's achieved his object."

"Redfyre — I'm concerned. In this close-quarters mêlée you've conjured up, are you prepared for retaliatory action yourself? You may wake up and find him at your throat one dark night if you don't learn to keep your head down. And fat chance I see of that!" Beaufort said. "But there's a factor that doesn't fit your explanation. These girls are hardly the random contents of a trench. They have been carefully selected — they're young and pretty. Why don't you take a look at this one?"

Redfyre pushed the muffler aside and started in dismay and disbelief at her features.

"Good Lord!" he muttered. "I know this girl! I mean, I don't actually know her — this is the first time I've clapped eyes on her. But I think I know who she is."

"Curly blonde hair, you can see. Clean complexion. Well nourished. No physical signs of drugs. I've closed her eyes, but they're blue. Any help?"

"Yes, doctor. It's Venus," Redfyre muttered almost to himself.

Beaufort broke the stunned silence. "Well, as I said, she must have been very pretty, but *Venus*? That's going it a bit far, isn't it?"

"Not her real name. I've seen her — and so has MacFarlane — in a photograph. The one I took from Louise Lawrence's room yesterday. A group of friends taking tea on the Lawrences' terrace one day last summer. 'Venus' was her *nom de guerre.* The girls in this group name themselves after Roman goddesses, I think as a sly reference to their roles in society. They see themselves as a sort of pantheon of deities, though precisely what their divine purpose in regard to the rest of us humans is, I really don't know yet."

"Venus, eh? Goddess of love? Poor child! Bit near the knuckle, isn't it? A callous jibe, do you suppose? Or did she accept it as a devil-may-care acknowledgement of the truth? What on earth would a girl like Miss Lawrence have had to do with a woman of the underclass? Where would she have met her? I know it's all the go these days for women to band together for social reasons . . . jam making, knitting socks for sailors — my wife's in a Save the Suffolk

Squirrel group — but these are genteel pursuits. Ladies who socialise are more likely to form a club dedicated to stamping out women like this, not invite one to take tea with them. Were the Lawrence parents aware of who was sipping Earl Grey from their Worcester china, do you suppose?"

"The father, no. At least I don't think so. I'll check. The mother? Yes, I believe even through her drug-induced state, she suspected something of the sort."

"Inspector, how many girls did you say there were in that photo, and how many have been attacked?" There was an urgency in Thoday's voice that focused Redfyre's attention.

"If I include Miss Proudfoot, who escaped — and I think I should — that's three women out of a total of eight present that day. But you should know that one of those photographed is my innocent Aunt Henrietta, who strayed into the shot wielding a large teapot. I think the timing of one of the meetings of the pantheon must have clashed with my aunt's usual Wednesday errand of mercy. She's an old friend of the Lawrence family. Her presence would have turned the would-be suffragist meeting into an informal — and very jolly, I'd guess — tea party. Whoever was behind the camera would have felt sufficiently at ease to take a photograph recording the event."

Finally, he searched in his inside pocket and produced the photograph. "Don't touch, either of you. It's the only copy I have." He held it under each interested face for a moment. "See what I mean?"

Beaufort gave a nostalgic smile. "Takes me back to my student days. In that golden time, you couldn't have a drink or a bite to eat without the presence of a professional photographer capturing the moment."

"No need to book in advance these days. Pocket Kodaks are everywhere. And now, before you ask, I'm planning to see my aunt as soon as I can arrange a meeting. Probably for tea. And I shall have thumbscrews in my back pocket. Not that Hetty ever needs much encouragement to gossip."

"Three victims out of a possible seven, then. That's nearly half. At the rate of one a day, he should be done by next Thursday. Are you able to identify and warn the remaining four deities, Redfyre?" the doctor asked brusquely. "I don't want to spend another morning freezing my kneecaps off staring at extinguished beauty. Defenseless young creatures! This has got to stop!"

The unprofessional remark was exceptional, and the outburst a good measure of the doctor's distress.

So was the hand that reached out and clutched Redfyre's arm. "I mean it, Redfyre! You're doing your best, but I have a feeling the playing field is tilted against you in this affair." He looked about him at the sculpted stone, the ironic resting place for the pathetic bundle of limbs and clothes that belonged to another part of the town. "I'll see if there's something I can do to restore a balance . . . Whatever the professional cost . . ."

Puzzled by his remark, Redfyre told him, "We'll be thankful for any help, doctor. Sergeant Thoday and I will combine our forces and won't have another night's sleep until we've made a date for this bugger with the gallows up on Castle Hill. May I speak for you, Sarge?"

"Right on, sir! I'll help haul up the black flag. I've got this girl's address. It's a new entry for us — not on our books. As soon as I've notified the master of whichever college owns these premises, I shall be off straight down King Street to rattle a few knockers and bash in a few doors."

"Take a couple of our heavies with you. You'll need some muscle to shake that clientele out of their sleep. I'll see you back at the nick or come in pursuit when I'm done here. Toseland! Forget the beat. I want you by my side as runner for the day."

"Glad to oblige, sir!" The voice was eager but controlled. Redfyre knew that a man discovering a body usually felt some strange but compelling attachment to it, unable to struggle free until the murderer was behind bars or dead. Toseland would work like a Trojan to come up with answers to the puzzle of the second murdered girl.

Doctor Beaufort drew his attention back to the corpse. "The ambulance has arrived, and I'd like to send her off to the labs as soon as we can. Lights are beginning to go on in the colleges, and it would be good to be clear here before men in gowns and shining morning faces start flocking down the passage to Holy Communion at Great St. Mary's or out into town."

Redfyre looked at him sharply.

"Don't pull that face! I'm not in any sense suggesting we cart off the rubbish so as not to give offense, if that's what you're thinking! I don't care whether this is a tart of the town or the King's cousin! She's dead and has little enough dignity left, whoever she may be. I don't like my corpses gawped at by the public. She can tell me her story in the seclusion of the lab."

Redfyre nodded. "Just tell me what she's

whispered so far, will you? If it will help us find this devil."

"I'm only sharing my first impressions, but it appears to be the same method as Miss Lawrence. I'd say she died between ten and three. There'll be a better estimate on offer after the autopsy, of course. She may have been killed elsewhere, and her body brought here and, um, laid out. I have a way of establishing that. Along with the evidence of her identity, placed with such precision and it seems to me, a touch of mockery, under her bottom. Miss Rosalind Weston of Cromwell Court, King Street, will be accorded the very best attention I can offer. I'll get the stretcher crew and take her away now. What have you got on your busy weekend schedule, apart from your tea party with your aunt?"

"Oh, I thought I might nip up Trinity Street and call on the next victim. Warn her that her life is in danger," Redfyre said with a tight smile.

CHAPTER 18

Minutes later, Redfyre was ducking underneath a carriage-wide archway and following a cobbled road into — a rarity in Cambridge — a charming piece of largely Georgian domestic architecture. The small square was elegant, withdrawn and secretive. Once, it had been a thoroughfare that sandaled Roman feet might have taken if business sent them east and north into the fenland. Some of the rooflines, soaring upwards in acute angles above the more squat profiles of seventeenth-century buildings, gave increasingly rare evidence of the fast-disappearing ancient town. The cobbles were set to the width of a carriage and dated, he supposed, from the time of the Regency, as did one or two of the prettier houses.

Though smoking chimneys told him that fires had been lit early against the sharp cold of the morning, he was relieved to see that most of the curtains at the windows were still closed.

Nevertheless, it was with a tingling between his shoulder blades, warning him that he was being observed from all sides, that he made his way to the steps leading up to the front door of a charming villa on the far side of the square. He paused to caress the curlicues of an iron balustrade whose handrail had been worn ribbon thin with the passage of the years.

He climbed up to the glossy black door and looked back over his shoulder.

The small house had a clear vision of the comings and goings of its neighbours and, Redfyre conceded, was itself in the view of anyone ready to twitch a curtain and peer out. He stood, hand raised to grasp the knocker, and hesitated. He checked his wristwatch. Five minutes to go before nine o'clock. If this was a social call, there was no possible way he could justify a bang on her door before midday on a Sunday morning without having previously telephoned to announce himself. If it was a professional police knock-up, the question of etiquette did not arise, of course. But then she would never speak to him again, and he realised how very sad that would leave him. He'd been looking forward to taking up her invitation to toast a crumpet or two before an open fire, to hearing her voice, low, warm and ready to break into laughter.

The knocker was suddenly wrenched from his hand as the door was flung open.

"How much longer were you going to loiter on my doorstep?" Dark brown eyes shone with amusement and a smile widened in unmistakeable welcome. He'd forgotten from one meeting to the next how very attractive she was. "No, I haven't got second sight. I was watching you through the window, creeping along rather furtively, I thought. Try not to look so shifty! Canon James, two doors down on the left, has you in his crosshairs, and Mrs. Professor Alexander, first on the right, has been tracking you every step of the way. Good morning, John! I was hoping you'd come, though I hadn't expected you so early on a Sunday. I was just sitting down to breakfast. Have you had breakfast?"

"Er, no. Early call out, I'm afraid."

She gave a merry wave to . . . Mrs. Professor Whatsit, he could only suppose, and closed the door behind him. As she turned and stepped close to take his hat, he felt a jolt of surprise, as he always did, to find a woman's eyes on a level with his own. What had MacFarlane said when he'd drooled crassly over the photograph? "What a smasher! Big lass! Look at those muscles!" Redfyre risked a glance at those muscles and looked away immediately. But there was no denying that the lady was worthy of attention. Even, or perhaps particularly, when he'd caught her still glowing from her morning's exercise. Rowing? In this weather, surely not? Running? It was rumoured that women were spotted charging about on the towpaths early these mornings. She was wearing a man's rowing vest, which emphasised the well-rounded arms and the narrow waist. Her exercise trousers, casually tied up at the waist with a bright silk scarf, could not disguise the long, muscled legs beneath. He decided not to comment or trip over his tongue by referring gauchely to her outlandish state of dress — that was her business. And she struck him as perfectly capable of throwing him back down the steps if she were so minded.

Her eyes narrowed and her lips pursed in concern. "Poor you! Look, in that case, why don't you slip into the bathroom, freshen yourself up and join me for breakfast? I was just about to struggle into a more suitable Sunday getup. If I know Mrs. Alexander, she'll be ringing the Ladies' Morality League right this minute to denounce me for receiving a single gentleman while dressed in my underpinnings."

She spoke lightly, but Redfyre was alarmed. "Would you like me to go over and show her my warrant?"

"Good heavens, no! She'd have an attack of the vapours. Look, I'll see you back here at the table in five minutes. It's all very simple, I'm afraid. Just porridge cooking in the bottom oven. My mother was Scottish, and I always serve it well cooked and with salt. But I have cream and sugar if you prefer. There's boiled eggs, toast, honey, strawberry jam. And the coffee's good. You do drink coffee? I'm sorry, it occurs to me that I really don't know you very well, John. Perhaps tea would . . ."

To his sly satisfaction, he noted that the table was laid for two, and that the coffee pot was a large one. Perhaps she knew him better than she was pretending — better than he knew himself?

"Coffee would be wonderful, Minerva," he said. "And all those other things, in any order. I'm ravenous."

He watched her closely to gauge her reaction. "Minerva." He'd said it clearly enough, but she appeared not to have heard it.

"Good! There's some Lifebuoy soap in

there and a fresh towel or two on the shelf. Help yourself." And, over her shoulder, with a decided twinkle, as she headed for the staircase, "Perhaps you'd like to make up the fire before you do that? Visiting gentlemen do usually enjoy executing a few slick moves with a poker to announce their presence to the household gods. Lares et Penates, would that be? Or Vesta, Goddess of the Hearth? How these old Romans haunt us!"

She allowed him to make inroads into his bowl of porridge and companionably refilled his coffee cup before she spoke again. "Now, John — or Inspector — if this is really that kind of visit, shall we agree to remember we're grown-ups and skip the frivolity of using silly nicknames? I am — you must choose — Suzannah or Headmistress. Or plain Miss Sturdy. How did you know I would be staying here?"

He looked with renewed appreciation at the soberly dressed and rather imposing figure. A nut-brown woollen day dress echoed the colour of her shining and unfashionably long hair, now scraped hastily back into a knot in the nape of her neck. A long string of ivory beads attempted disconcertingly to settle itself on one side or other of her bosom.

"I'm sorry, Suzannah, to barge in on your quiet morning. I rang your school yesterday to enquire after you. We had a pencilled-in arrangement to take tea, if you remember, and not knowing the date for the end of your term, I thought I'd better check whether you were still in Cambridge. Your deputy head was manning the phone and told me you were here taking the weekend off to celebrate the end of term. I was in the neighbourhood, and —"

"Always a pleasure to see you, John. And you're not incommoding me in the slightest. I always dress neatly on Sunday mornings. My habit is to go to evensong so, early on Sunday, I'm free to receive calls." She spoke with the exaggerated care of a Victorian lady, laughing at her own formality. "Being in the centre of things, I have to expect visits. My neighbours pop in, my gardener calls for his wages, my landlord makes his weekly visit to check that all is well. Sadly, I don't own this wonderful little retreat. It's on Barnabas land. We're firmly in the realm of Academe here — every square inch belongs to some college or other.

"But, 'Minerva,' eh? If we're to have a conversation, you ought to know that I've never much liked the name anyway — my eyes are not grey, I have no particular fond-ness for owls and I'm not especially wise. Just a bit older than my sisters in the group and much bossier, so they occasionally al-low me to have the last word, though I'm not the oldest. Your aunt Henrietta claims that status. It was impossible to find a Ro-man name for her — they tend to be rather hidebound, the Romans, and limited in the range of attributes they revere. Hetty settled for the more adventurous grouping of Norse mythology and called herself 'Elli,' Goddess of Old Age."

It was a moment before he could master his surprise. "Don't be deceived. My aunt is a shape-shifting mischief-maker! Though I love her dearly, I fear that 'Morrigan' is nearer the mark." His lighthearted tone, he thought, just about covered his dismay at discovering once again that his aunt was a tricky old so-and-so.

He decided to play one of his aces and produced the group photograph.

Her eyes flicked over it without much concern. "Ah, yes. Ellen Lawrence told us you'd wormed a copy out of her. Hetty did warn us about you. She agreed that it would be a good piece of insurance to have the friendly eyes of the law keeping a watch from the front row of the stalls at the concert. We needed an impartial witness, of course, to the college's bad treatment of Juno Proudfoot. And who better than the rising star of the Cambridge CID? We calculated that his evidence, taken with that of the crime reporter for the *Oracle,* would be compelling, even unchallengeable. Devastating indeed for the college authorities! And so it proved in Saturday morning's article." She flashed a speculative smile and tilted her head. "You came out of that well, John, but you should have left it there. You weren't supposed to take it further. Too zealous by half. Busying about with crime scene tapes and interrogations of innocent girls, involving the master when, if anything, you should have been tearing out the toenails of the *dean.* I'm of the opinion that it is your fervent attempts at exposure that provoked someone to kill Lois Lawrence — to ensure her silence."

"Hang on a minute! That's grossly unfair. In fact, turn back two pages, will you? Are you telling me you and your colleagues knowingly and carelessly exposed Juno to a murder attempt — two, in fact — on Friday evening? If sensible Earwig hadn't snatched back that inhaler, I don't —"

"Wait! What are you saying? *Two* attempts?" Suzannah had turned pale and put down the cream jug with extreme care.

Reining in his outrage, Redfyre went succinctly through the events of that evening, explaining the presence of lethal mercury cyanide in the smelling salts container so conveniently on hand, a split second from delivering an excruciating death. And these attempts on the life of the first girl, he told her, had been followed within a couple of hours by a successful attack on a second.

"Oh, my God," Suzannah breathed. "Earwig was right. There *is* someone tracking us."

"Tracking! I'd say he was doing something much more active than prowling about after all of you, observing. He's knocking you off the chessboard one by one at a quick rate. He seems set on eliminating your group. That's why I'm here, Suzannah. To warn you that you're in danger. You'll understand that I'm not exaggerating when I tell you that a third one of your members was murdered last night."

He pointed to the small blonde girl smiling so brightly on the front row. "She was strangled, and her body placed in the archway in Senate House Passage."

"No — not Venus!" She was unable to voice her emotions, but her stiff, expressionless features betrayed the depth of her shock. Her strong hands began to fidget and her breathing quickened.

Fearing an outburst, Redfyre reached for the coffee pot, poured another cup and held it up to her. To his gratification, she accepted the gesture as he had intended, a wordless sympathy, and acknowledged it by taking a symbolic sip.

"I shall need all the help you can give me if I'm to lay hands on the monster who's doing this, Suzannah," he said quietly. "He is no creation of mine, but I shall un-create, by which I mean destroy him."

"I know what you're implying. We dreamed him up, didn't we? Conjured him up."

"Children say that if you give the Devil a name, he will come when you call him. Yes. I think you gave him flesh and a voice. I believe in evil in my old-fashioned way. I've seen enough of this world to know how easily and thoughtlessly it can be let loose. Though you're not to report that to my superintendent, who already thinks I'm too whimsical by half. Three innocent, well-meaning girls have challenged this killer, awakened his anger and paid the price."

She reached across the table and clutched his hands. "Should I apologize? The word means nothing! I'm left with no words but words of resolve. I'll grieve for my friends later. Tell me what I can do — I'll answer any questions you ask."

"I think I've grasped the significance of Juno's fall down the stairs, but the second attempt by mercury cyanide is still a puzzle. Equally puzzling was the arrival of a poison pen letter from the same hand as the first collection, sent to her in hospital, along with a lugubrious death wreath. And a crowing message of the 'Pride goes before a fall' nature. I've suppressed that — no need to scare her further."

"Juno's all right. She's way out in the country, staying with Earwig's family, and she has friends looking out for her."

"No such good fortune for Rosalind Weston — Venus. What have you to tell me about her? Why was she chosen — rather than you, or Hetty, or the two remaining unknowns in this photograph?"

"We loved Rosalind. She went out of her way to talk to people you would never have expected her to want to know. She was witty, resilient, cheery and suffered her dreadful life — which she'd led from the age of fifteen — with enormous fortitude. Her story is the usual one — betrayed at an early age by the one she loved, degraded and made homeless. But she had spirit, and until she was twelve and her schooling finished, she had a thirst for learning. Lois was doing volunteer evening school teaching for deprived adults when Rosalind turned up as a pupil in her class. They got on well. I think Lois learned more from Rosalind than vice versa."

"So there was just the element of friendship in play here?" Redfyre asked, his brain beginning to whirr.

"More than that. Rosalind confided that in her profession, she came into contact with some eminent men about Cambridge. One or two of their names struck a spark with Lois and Earwig and Juno. Men who were guilty of some pretty dreadful acts against the female sex, apart from the abuse they paid for. For them, in their conceit, a prostitute had no more thought processes than a pillow, and if they were asked in the right way, answers to some telling questions could be eased out of them. Lois listened to what Rosalind had to disclose and made notes. She had acquired scurrilous evidence against some powerful men."

"Blackmail?" Redfyre asked wearily.

"No. She was building up cases against several villains, but to my knowledge, she never made use of it. She was saving it up for the right moment."

"And what was that?"

"You have little idea of Lois's quality, John."

"You'd be surprised. People are very keen to sing her praises. A girl who had influence beyond her class and far beyond her age, it seems to me."

Suzannah smiled. "It helps to know who her heroines were."

"I know she was inspired by Emily Davison."

"Weren't we all? But the one she revered was Joan of Arc. Joan was seventeen when she led the French army in a successful assault on English-occupied Orleans. Seventeen! The youngest commander of a national army we know of. Much younger than Alexander the so-called Great. Vainglorious, egotistical sot that he was! And the same age as Louise when I first met and recruited her. Joan was nineteen when she was burned to death. Lois celebrated her nineteenth birthday last month. She would have said, along with her heroine: *One life is all we have and we live it as we believe in living it. But to sacrifice what you are and to live without belief, that is a fate more terrible than dying.*

"I don't believe the world will ever produce another such as Joan, but Lois set out to emulate her. Her fight was not against foreign occupation, but unfair male domination. The lesson she learned from Joan was to use — and skilfully — their own weapons against them. Joan had donned armour and wielded a sword; Louise used cunning, intrigue, persuasion and the voice of the press. Given a few more years, John, she would have built up the power to launch herself onto the political stage. She would have become the first female Member of Parliament for Cambridge. And now we shall never hear the fine speeches she would have delivered, never see the social changes she would have brought about."

Redfyre sensed tears were not so far from the surface. "I'm guessing from those chapter headings you've just treated me to that history is not your discipline?" he said mischievously as an antidote to the welling sentimentality. "But go back a step, will you? You say you 'recruited' Louise? To what organisation? Who is its head?"

Suzannah Sturdy sighed. "We have no name. There is no head. The moment you take on an identity, you become a target. But there is a movement, and it's widening and gathering strength. Like a tide turning or a storm brewing, we are a natural force. Unstoppable. The suffragettes? Everyone knows their names and where to find them. Their every escapade is signalled in advance and thwarted. The press barons delight in portraying them as mad and destructive. The window smashers, the banner wavers, the prison protesters are consigned to history. They've played their part — and a brave one — but most have happily settled into domesticity. This is a new age, a new generation. Lois was, for me and many others, the personification of this new generation."

"How did you meet her? She was never a pupil at your school."

In short, crisp sentences to counteract her emotion, Suzannah told him of an evening at the end of the last summer term. In concern for the two younger Lawrence sisters, who appeared to be going into academic decline, she had fixed an appointment to see either or both of the Lawrence parents to establish a reason for this. To her surprise, it was Lois who turned up for the interview. Her father, she explained, could not spare the time from his Masonic duties, and her mother was doped out of her senses. Lois declared that she was the only one who could tell the truth. A hideous story followed. Suzannah had done her best to help. She soon realised that Lois was an extraordinary girl, and one who might well join her and a few other like-minded ladies in Cambridge — no, they were not all on that photograph, and no, she would not name them.

"But a schoolgirl?" Redfyre questioned. Was it fair, was it moral for a woman in Suzannah's position — head of one of the most prestigious girls' schools in the city — to recruit in this way, he wanted to know.

She replied with a smile that she doubted Lois had ever been a schoolgirl. She was not, in any case, one of her own. She called shame on Redfyre for entertaining the thought that she would have been so unlicensed and so unprincipled in her behaviour as to take advantage.

The steely headmistress, incorruptible and fierce, was suddenly on show, and Redfyre backed down.

"This generation — Lois's generation — must succeed, John," she summarised firmly. "Inch by inch, if necessary. I may not know much history, but I intend to help to write the next chapter."

"And many strokes, though with a little axe, Hew down and fell the hardest-timbered oak," he suggested.

"Shakespeare, *Henry VI, Part 3,* Act 2," she said with a smile. "Are you now testing my English? Since you're familiar with this play, I'll draw your attention to a line in the first act which I've always thought summed up Lois: *O tiger's heart, wrapped in a woman's hide!*"

"More flattering to refer to the heart of a *tigress,* I think. I understand the female of that species vastly outdoes the male in courage and stoicism." Was he appeasing her or drawing her out? Neither, he decided — just showing off his knowledge.

"And loyalty. Have you hunted tigers?"

"No, but I've yarned the night away with blokes who have. Hunters who sing the praises of the tigress. Much smaller in size than the male, of course, but she's quite capable of seeing him off. He knows he will always win a stand-up fight to the death, but why risk losing an eye in the process? He usually slopes off at her warning smile."

"Well you're spot-on. Lois had that tigress quality. The man who got close enough to her to kill and escape unscathed, John, must have very special qualities or standing."

He felt this might be the right moment to make the point he'd come to make. "Exactly. And, Suzannah, you may be next on his menu, along with the remaining women in this photo or the group."

"And you want me to name them?"

419

"Please. For your safety and theirs."

She shuffled round the table and sat next to him, the better to study the photograph he'd left at his elbow. "Eight of us. The camera was in the hands of Juno, of course. She'd just bought it and was demonstrating her skill with it. Hetty is at the tea table. That's Earwig, or Luna if you prefer, showing her knickers doing a Fragonard on the swing. There I am on the left, trying to hide behind a teacup, and at my feet are Lois and Venus. That leaves this pair." She pointed to two girls in tennis skirts sitting next to Venus. "They're friends of Lois from her school in Surrey." She breathed a sigh of relief. "Vesta and Diana. Both, like Lois, had finished at boarding school. No need to worry about that pair. You can come off watch, Inspector. Their ambassador father has taken them off to join him and his wife in their next posting. Though as it's to Turkey they're headed, perhaps we should be screwing our concern *up* a notch. Stirring times in the Caliphate, I understand. Or should I now say Republic?"

It seemed to Redfyre that her relief was entirely genuine. Her mood was certainly elevated as she went on. "Rest easy! Just three left on the list. Now, Hetty. He can't possibly know about her. If her own nephew

420

didn't know — and you didn't, did you? Ha! Gotcher! Then there's me. He's welcome to try! Earwig? She's heavily protected! Have you seen those brothers of hers? They were all in the war and came out of it staggering under the weight of medals for valour or skulduggery of one sort or another. And they're all home for Christmas. Let's have a second pot of coffee, shall we?"

As she bustled out into the kitchen, Redfyre got up and gave the fire an encouraging poke, then went to stand by the window, enjoying the sunshine streaming into the room and the elegant architecture it slanted over outside. There were few enough pretty houses in the city, so it was a treat to see evidence of age, style and generosity of finish.

A movement at the end of the cobbled alleyway caught his attention. A figure emerged from the archway and strode purposefully towards Suzannah's house. He watched with amused sympathy as Richard Henningham was detained by a call from — what had Suzannah said his name was? Canon James? — from a house on the left. Frozen in stride and clearly eager to be on his way, the master of Barnabas paused to greet a dog-collared, bible-carrying gent. He allowed himself to be engaged in a conversation, which seemed to be heavily one-sided, with the chatty cleric before tearing himself free and continuing. He arrived on the doorstep and banged heartily with the knocker.

Redfyre called to Suzannah. "Your landlord's at the door! Are you sure you're fully paid up?"

She dashed from the kitchen, put the coffee down and tore off her pinny. "Oh, Lord! Richard's early."

The flush on her cheeks and the slight smile spoke to Redfyre, and he didn't much like what he was hearing. "So sorry, Suzannah! I'm afraid I've intruded and really have messed up your Sunday routine, haven't I? Look, I'll grab my hat and be on my way."

As he made his way to the hatstand, he heard Suzannah greet her visitor and ask him to come in.

"Can't this morning, my dear," came the answer from the doorstep. "I'm on a mission. Look, Miss Sturdy, would you think me very impertinent if I were to ask you to pack your things and return to the school for this next bit?"

He overheard Suzannah splutter in surprise.

"I wouldn't ask, but I've been notified — just an hour ago — by the police of a most appalling crime. A detective sergeant has apprised me of a murder committed just a few yards away in Senate House Passage. A woman has been strangled to death. Yet another!"

Suzannah responded with exclamations and a question.

"She was discovered in the doorway the college uses to take the rubbish from the college premises in a discreet way. There will be panic, no doubt, when the story leaks out, and I know you are not one to be unnecessarily afraid. But all ladies in the vicinity are to be alerted — particularly ones living by themselves. The sergeant has enlisted the assistance of the college in this. You and old Mrs. Handley at the tobacconist's are the only solitaries I know of in my bailiwick, so I'm doing my civic duty in warning you. Though his old mother is most unlikely to be on the murderer's shopping list, Mrs. Handley's son has kindly agreed to come and calm her nerves, and my duty is to account for you. You will be more secure in your apartment at the school, where there are always staff on duty. Porters on hand to repel boarders. Please, assure me you will leave! Today."

Suzannah laughed. "I already have an element of the Praetorian Guard at my disposal this morning, Doctor Henningham! Come in and meet Detective Inspector Redfyre, who I think comes bearing the same message."

"What? Oh, Redfyre! We've met. Good Lord, man! Good to see you so swiftly off the mark once more." He changed his mind about rushing off and came inside, reaching for Redfyre's hand. "What on earth's going on in this town? I hope you have some idea. There's much speculation about. Is that coffee I smell? Wouldn't mind a cup, if you have one . . ."

They went through into the breakfast room, where Henningham helped himself to a cup and saucer from the dresser.

"Glad to see you're able to keep down the fluids, sir," Redfyre commented as he took the pot and poured out a cup for the master.

"Fully recovered! You've no idea what a vivid experience it is to be able to eat and drink again! You know, it probably does the body any amount of good to be purged in that way. Not that I'm tempted to repeat the smelling salts experience in a hurry! Oh, and thank your superintendent for keeping me *au fait* with the lab results on that matter," he said carefully with a quick glance at Suzannah. "Very interesting, and rather satisfying to have worked it out before the scientists. Well done, us!"

Redfyre decided he would take his leave as soon as good manners permitted. The table had been laid for two, and the second place had not been for him, as he had arrogantly assumed. Ah, well. The master, though a good decade older than Suzannah, was not a married man. He remained lithe and purposeful and seemed to have all his teeth, hair and limbs. Redfyre could quite imagine that an intelligent, mature lady like Suzannah would find much to admire in him. But he did wonder how Professor Alexander's wife across the square categorised the master's clearly regular Sunday visits to the headmistress.

Just as he was about to rise, his socially delicate situation was resolved for him when a uniformed constable cycled down the alley, counting the numbers of the houses. He stopped in front of Suzannah's house, dropped his bike and hammered on the door. Redfyre hurried to answer.

"Sir!"

"Ah, Toseland. What have you got for me?"

"Two things, sir. This 'ere. Personal. Envelope addressed to you and delivered by city messenger ten minutes ago." He put a white envelope into Redfyre's hand.

The envelope was of good quality, the ink

Stephens' blue-black, and the handwriting forceful and masculine, but rather ill formed. Not the hand of one of his colleagues or friends but, in an intriguing way, not quite unknown.

"The second, Toseland?"

"I left it at the station, sir. Large file of reports from the forensics lab. I thought that had better be left on your desk rather than carted through the streets."

"Quite right, constable. I'm on my way back right now — using your bicycle. I'd like you to go on foot to the porter's lodge at St. Barnabas. Know where? Good. Just deliver the note I'm about to write, will you, and then come back to HQ."

He returned to the breakfast room and interrupted a lively conversation on tropical diseases. "Suzannah. I'm called away at once. But before I go, may I beg of you an envelope and a sheet of writing paper? I have to scribble a note for my officer to deliver."

The requested equipment was quickly put in front of him, and Suzannah and the elder picked up their conversation.

His note was blunt and short:

Detective Inspector Redfyre of the Cambridge CID would be obliged if you would meet him at the gate in Senate House Passage at

426

noon today, Sunday, equipped with the key to the gate.

He folded the sheet, put it in the envelope, licked the gum and sealed it, then he wrote the recipient's name across the front: *Doctor Felix Herbert, Dean of St. Barnabas College, Cambridge.*

He watched as Toseland set off down the cobbled way at a fast clip, then, before returning to the breakfast room, "Excuse me for a moment, will you, Suzannah? I have a note from the office to read."

He tore the envelope Toseland had handed him and read the contents of the single sheet it contained. Just a couple of lines.

Henningham watched without comment, but Redfyre caught his increasing concern as his own expression changed from enquiring to horrified.

"I say, Inspector, is there anything I can do?"

"No, no. Thank you, but no. It's just an invitation. One I desperately don't want, but which I am honour bound to accept."

He looked again at the stark note and knew that he hadn't misinterpreted it.

"John! Greetings! I understand you have a fondness for Laundress Lane when it comes to resolving matters of honour. Tonight at 6 p.m. Yours, W"

He could not ignore the curiosity and puzzlement directed at him from the table, and made an effort to sound lighthearted when he delivered the response they were obviously waiting for.

"Well! What a morning. I begin to feel that, like d'Artagnan, I may have booked rather too many duels into my day!" He tried to smile but was afraid the result must have been something of a grimace. "Noon, teatime and now cocktail hour."

Chapter 19

The station was deserted, apart from the reception sergeant on duty and the odd coppers coming in and out at change of shift. Redfyre was glad to have an hour at his desk with the reports before he made his way back over to Barnabas to meet the dean for the first of the confrontations he had so optimistically laid himself open to.

He dealt with his officer's report on Tyrrell's bicycle first. Clipped and straightforward. The bike had been found exactly where the student had said that it had been left. There was indeed a puncture in the back wheel, and the condition of it — even spider's webs had been noted — indicated that it had not been in use for several days.

Reminding himself that a determined man in pursuit of a woman who'd spurned him could easily, fired by his emotions, have helped himself to one of the many bikes that were always lying about the streets, Redfyre was, all the same, pleased to put one approving tick by Tyrrell's story. After a moment's consideration, he put a question mark by the side of it.

The laboratory reports from the different sections of fingerprinting and pharmacology were revealing.

He opened up the more straightforward account, fingerprinting. He'd delivered the black satin ribbon trailing from the funeral wreath sent to Juno in the hospital to the lab with a deprecatory laugh. More in hope than in expectation. But again, scientific technique astonished him. A kindly young man in a white coat had taken it from his hand and looked at it with interest. Well, it would be a first for them if it succeeded, he'd declared with affable honesty, but that was the way, the only way, to push back the boundaries. The Indians, who'd been at it for decades longer than the Met, were saying they could even raise a fingerprint from the dead skin of a victim. It sounded pretty improbable today, but next week — well, who could know? Here in the lab, they were able to get prints from glass, leather, bakelite — any shiny surfaces. And this ribbon definitely offered a shiny surface. He could even make out smudges with the naked eye, he'd said, eager to carry off his new challenge.

And here were the results. Spectacular ones! Photographic and schematic representations of the two thumbs of a killer — a killer who'd had no idea that he would be leaving his calling card by the simple gesture of tying a bow. Redfyre lingered with satisfaction over the clarity of the hoops and whorls and ridges on display before reminding himself that the evidence was no use at all unless he had under arrest the perpetrator with his fingers on the ink pad in the interrogation room. Still, it formed a valuable part of his reserve armoury.

A short note had been added on a separate sheet. Interestingly, the young scientist had uncovered some traces of a bodily substance in addition to the expected greasy human skin secretions. Blood. Spots of blood, possibly from a thumb or finger pricked by the spikes of the holly element of the wreath? They'd tested it according to the methods of the Institute of Pathological Anatomy in Vienna, which now recognised four different blood types, and pronounced it of human origin and type A. Useful, but only for elimination purposes.

Nonetheless, holding the prints and the blood sample in his hand had a galvanising effect on Redfyre. It was the moment the hounds caught the scent of the fox in the next field. He was hunting an identifiable presence whose two strong, murdering thumbs were on record. It was only a matter of hours, surely, before he saw the face that went with these telltale traces.

A piece of information to be filed alongside the fingerprints, only to be brought into play when a suspect was in detention. But, Redfyre conceded, in this modern world, it was the scientific approach that brought results in the courtroom. A jury of twelve men responded warmly these days to a bespectacled, highly qualified expert who would patiently take them through the scientific evidence. Intuition and reasoning of the Sherlock Holmes type were old hat. Entertaining, of course, but discredited as having no place in a modern trial. Above all, the juries wanted to arrive at a just and secure verdict with no blame for a wrong decision attached to their names; a guilty finding would result in the hanging of the accused, and that was a significant burden for most jurors. They welcomed laboratory reports, which in their eyes did not lie.

The pharmacological report was more challenging, and Redfyre had to read through the detailed findings twice before he felt he had grasped the essentials. He was glad of the résumé of results couched in less formal language that appeared at the end of the presentation. Sharp fellows they had down there in the forensic department — sharp enough to realise that their colleagues in the CID could always do with a helping hand over the challenging parts. He smiled, pleased to accept and learn from whatever help came his way.

He felt that he could now present a very cogent case to MacFarlane. A case for a root and branch inspection of the work being done at Lawrence's laboratory and at Benson's factory in Frog End.

The collection of pills Lois Lawrence and her mother had put together in the matchbox had been pounced on, categorised and stripped down to its alarming essentials by the scientists.

Lawrence had spoken flippantly of Benson's output of "Perk-You-Up Pills for the Pallid," Redfyre remembered. And the five pink samples in the box had been identified as similar in appearance to the famous and much consumed Dr. Williams' Pink Pills for Pale People. A sample of these was produced for his information.

A home pharmacy favourite. Small, egg-shaped and rosy as a cherub's cheek, they were boosted by advertising that assured the customer of their innocence and efficacy. The label listed all the ailments the product would deal with at once: *nervous depression, watery blood, tuberculosis, anaemia, hysteria, change of life and* — most mysteriously — *loss of vital forces.* "Read what you like into that!" Redfyre muttered suspiciously. He read again, interpreting the last three as menstrual tension, menopause and low libido. But so seductive was the fulsome literature, so enthusiastic the letters of commendation that the assiduous forensics bloke had included with his findings, Redfyre was on the point of sending out to Lloyds the Chemist for a bottle for his own use. But then he read the analysis of the contents as discovered on the bench: iron sulphate, magnesium sulphate, powdered liquorice and sugar coating stained pink with cochineal. Mmm . . . He might just as well chew a few of Mr. Basset's Liquorice Allsorts.

Not so with the pink pill of interest supplied by the Lawrence women. Powdered flavouring and sugar coating were very similar, and there was an element of iron sulphate present, but the main constituent here identified raised Redfyre's eyebrows. Opium in its solid state. As a liquid, a tincture of laudanum, this had always been commonly available over the counter at the chemist's shop, but as the addictive properties of the drug became more widely understood, efforts to regulate its sale had been made.

Again, the thoughtful scientist had drawn his attention to France's *Loi des stupéfiants* in 1916 and Britain's 1920 Dangerous Drugs Act.

The second jelloid formula produced similar results. This time, the offending constituent was cocaine wrapped in an innocent-looking green sugar shell.

Benson and Lawrence were flouting the law of the land, it seemed. Or were they? Presented in the matchbox without the original packaging, there was no way of dating the wretched things. The pills could all have predated the 1920 drugs act. The two purveyors of a mindless, addictive nirvana to females would laugh at any accusation he might make and refute it using the full force of their lawyers, no doubt.

He filed the information away in his top — for immediate action — drawer. This would be taken further. And the information remained, as far as he was concerned, a cogent motive, wrapped in chemical formulae, for stopping Lois Lawrence in her tracks.

The appearance of Sergeant Thoday hurrying in with news of the body in Senate House Passage jolted him back into what he looked on as the third attack.

"I'm just about to go and meet our mysterious dean. The bloke who lurks behind the locked door — who gave permission for Juno Proudfoot to perform, against the known wishes of his superior, in the concert at the chapel. Have you noticed, Thoday, that all roads and all clues seem to lead back to that wretched college?"

"I'm beginning to think so myself," Thoday said, eyes gleaming with the excitement of information about to be imparted. "The doc and I were helping — well, standing around observing — when the bearers came with a stretcher to collect her. No bother up to a point, and then one of the lads says, tugging at her coat, 'This 'ere's stuck. It's caught under the gate.' And it was. We had to clear her out of the alcove in her fancy frock and leave the coat behind. Nice, warm thick serge, it was. But the hem of it, a good two inches, was trapped under the wood panel of the gate. We had to send someone round the front to the bursar for the key before we could investigate. The doc stayed on as witness, as he could see that it was important. Well, the wooden gate opened easy-like. Well oiled. We went to look at it from the inside — there's a nice little courtyard in there with a covered way — and anybody could see that she'd been pushed through and set out in the space from the inside because the door had been slammed shut again, trapping the fabric. It didn't show from the inside when it was shut because the gate is oak planks this thick." He demonstrated with his fingers. "There's no way anybody could have just dumped her as they passed through the passage on the outside."

Redfyre smiled in satisfaction. "They're pulling together, our two ends of this puzzle, Thoday. Well observed! You've just put the bullet down the spout of my investigation! I have an appointment to see a dean about a doorway in half an hour."

He began to scoop up his pens and notebook.

"Sir, sir!" Thoday was wriggling with excitement. "There's more! And better!"

"Do go on, Sarge! And would you like to take a seat?"

"No, no! I'm halfway down King Street and have to be off again in a sec. I nipped back because I thought you ought to know.

437

This diary of hers." He brandished it. "I worked out some of her shorthand. It wasn't a code, sir. She wasn't hiding things — just reminding herself. The one we're interested in — the assignation she'd put in for 10:00 P.M. last night was with a certain S.B.D. Now how about that being St. Barnabas, the dean? I tracked back and found he's a regular. Goes back a year at least. Usually midweek. A Saturday night was exceptional."

"Were the meetings always on college territory?" Redfyre asked dubiously. "Or were they conducted elsewhere?"

"Elsewhere, mostly. I found her centre of operations — not what you'd expect. It's on Maids Causeway, but city-side and rather chi-chi. Clean, no expense spared on the furnishings and décor. Run by a woman. A lady, you'd say, rather than a madam. I broke the news of Miss Weston's demise and sketched in the circumstances. She was horrified and upset. Eager to help, so I caught her while she was in shock and found out some interesting things." He waved his notebook. "It'll keep, sir. You ought to be pushing off. But the main thing is, the university folk are all up to it. This call-ahead-using-the-telephone stuff. The nobs have the phones, and that makes it all the more impersonal, harder to get caught out. They can just pick up the phone and order it out like a . . . like a fish and chip supper!" Thoday stammered in disgust.

"Think ahead, and you could arrange delivery of both at the same time," Redfyre suggested whimsically. " 'Delilah for eight, and could she pick up two cod and chips on her way? How very enterprising! Oh, I'll be needing that diary to bash him over the ear with, Sarge."

The moment Thoday had left, Redfyre picked up the receiver of MacFarlane's telephone. He looked at his watch. Just into sherry time. If he was lucky, he'd catch his old college friend in the bosom of his family before they all shot off to Scotland for their Christmas. Freddy, a don at St. Luke's, was in a division above even Aunt Hetty when it came to gossip, but his confidences were always based on facts and relayed with discretion.

His friend's hearty voice, shouting against a background of shrieks and children's laughter, reassured him that this was in no way an unfortunate time to ring up. No, he was just about to sharpen the carving knife before lunch, so ask away . . . St. Barnabas, eh?

■ ■ ■ ■

The figure standing at ease in the alcove, feet apart, hands behind his back was not the dean. Redfyre had never met the dean before, but he knew that this dark-suited, heavy-shouldered man could not be the college don he was expecting. A bowler hat jammed on low over a ridged forehead signalled his lowly status and emphasised the truculence of his expression, turning the features — quite deliberately, Redfyre judged — into a caricature of a flat-nosed English bulldog.

"Good morning! I have an appointment to meet Dean Herbert here at noon," Redfyre shouted above the clamour of the local bells tolling out twelve.

Impassive, Mr. Bowler took the warrant card offered for his inspection and he examined it with not exaggerated but professional care. His insolent eyes fixed Redfyre's in a further, more personal, assessment. "The dean does not attend backdoor callers in person," he said smoothly. "Hawkers, beggars, rat-catchers and other riff-raff are required to move on."

That was quite obviously the end of his official speech. The sentence that followed, being delivered *sotto voce* out of the corner of his mouth, came straight from the man himself and reflected his scorn for the plain-clothed posh boys of the CID. "So shift yer arse, nancy boy!"

Smiling pleasantly, Redfyre took a step closer until he stood invasively close, broken nose to broken nose. His hands whipped up one on either side of the bowler hat and rammed it down over the man's eyes. Instinctively, and with a yell of, "Oi! What the 'ell's this then?" the man raised both his hands to reinstate his hat.

Redfyre's right fist immediately punched into the undefended midriff, releasing a burst of used air and cutting off further speech. Into the rasping and gobbling noises that ensued, he spoke cheerfully. "This is one rat catcher who won't be moved on. I never leave the premises without a rat between my teeth."

Then, in a crisp officer's voice, he rapped out, "Name! Rank! Number!"

The spontaneous reaction to the command, still powerful, had the man trying to raise himself from his doubled-up posture and begin to mouth words. Redfyre thought he made out "Dooley . . . Sergeant . . ." and a run of indecipherable but clearly well-remembered numbers.

"Right. Sergeant Dooley! Stand to attention!" He waited for the man to attempt this, while still whooping for breath. "Cambridgeshire Regiment, were you?"

And, rasping: "First Division, sir."

Redfyre took a step back and observed the man for a moment. "The storming of the Schwaben Redoubt . . . Commendation from Earl Haig himself, I remember. Hmm, you've gone a bit soft, Sarge. Too many good college dinners! I thought my fist was going through a pavlova pudding before it reached a backbone. Glad to see that's still in position, at least. Now, before you take me up to meet your boss, just show me around this gateway, will you?"

By nods and grunts and shakes of the head that developed with recovery into sentences, Redfyre established that the solid gate swung open with oiled ease when one of the two copies of the key was used. One was kept in the bursar's office, and the other was in the charge of the dean, since his quarters were the nearest and he sometimes used the gateway as an exit. His own house was over the river in Grange Road and, if on foot, he would make off through the side gate and across the river. Yes, sometimes he used his bike. He kept a Raleigh in the sheds.

The gate was used as a discreet channel for the college's rubbish, a tradition left over from medieval times when a short path straight down to the river had facilitated the dumping of refuse straight into the Cam. Modern regulations forbade this, but the practice lingered. College servants would daily clear away items of unwanted linen, broken tennis racquets, empty bottles . . . At the ends and beginnings of terms, when the young gentlemen were coming and going on holiday, it was in constant use by the porters. At this point, a challenging yell and a creaking of wheels announced such an operation. Two porters bearing down on them called out a warning to clear out of the gateway — they were coming through. A trolley piled high with students' trunks on their way to the railway station thundered through and turned left onto Trinity Street.

"And whose duty was it to check that the gate was locked for the night?" Redfyre wanted to know.

The domestic bursar's staff, usually a senior porter, did a walkabout, checking all doors and windows and gates. This one was checked routinely at eleven o'clock. Any vagrants would be sent packing, and then he'd close and lock the gate. The key would be hung up in its usual place in the bursar's office at about midnight when the inspection came to an end. Nothing untoward had been reported last evening.

"Thank you, Dooley. Reconnaissance over, I think. Time to engage the enemy! Lead on, will you?"

Dooley escorted him along the covered way fringing a sheltered and surprisingly green courtyard, which appeared to be completely frost free. A scene utterly charming to Redfyre, who lingered to examine with admiration one or two of the evergreen shrubs as they passed through. Dooley, impervious to the attractions of horticulture, pressed on to reach and climb a stone staircase. They arrived at a thick oak door marked *Doctor Felix Herbert.* Dooley knocked, put an ear to the door, pretended to hear a response and threw the door open.

"Ah, come in. You must be the policeman."

The dean of the place. The fellow responsible for discipline and good order in the college. He who would ensure that the junior members of the college were respectful to authority and each other, quiet and abstemious. Undergraduates arriving from public schools recognised that the dean performed the same function as their past

444

headmaster. Though he did not wield a cane, he had the authority to make your life hell and even send you down in disgrace if you really did something to get up his nose.

Redfyre studied the dean as the dean studied Redfyre's warrant card.

Begowned, pale, nervous and waspish was Redfyre's first impression as the man rose reluctantly from his armchair by the fireside. His second, seeing the man on his feet, was that he seemed rather young to hold such high office. Late thirties, perhaps? But then, the master himself, brought in from outside the college some four years ago, was on the young side and unlikely to appoint a man older than himself to the position of dean. Redfyre's friend Freddy had just reminded him by phone that the winnowing wind of war had blown with exceptional savagery through the university. The older men, the dons, who had joined up, had been made officers and inevitably placed in the forefront of battle, had suffered exceptional casualties. One in seven of the dons and students had died, many thousands more had been wounded. And now, these days, to a policeman's eyes, all the fellows looked young.

"Dooley, where have you been loitering? Stir up the fire, will you, and check the scuttle's full." He resumed his seat, leaving Red-fyre standing in front of him. "Now, er, Inspector, I understand you have some questions to put regarding the side entrance to the college, which was the fortuitously chosen deposition spot for evidence of a piece of town tomfoolery last evening? You may interview Dooley, who is *au fait* with the locking procedures and all that sort of domestic business. Take the seats at the table over there." He waved a pale hand towards the distant window of the large wood-panelled room. "The effects of the fire should extend as far as that if Dooley does his job, though there is always a draught between the windows. I advise you to keep on your coat and muffler."

He picked up his book from a side table, adjusted the spectacles on his nose in a marked manner and began to read. A languid hand reached out and grasped the glass of pre-lunch madeira on the table at his elbow. He took a warming sip of the sticky, fragrant and comforting wine.

Dooley kicked the fire about a bit, then sloped off to take his place at the table indicated. Redfyre joined him, a quizzical smile on his face.

"While you're still on your feet, Dooley, why don't you refill Dean Herbert's glass?

Then we can settle to our business without interruption."

Dooley responded truculently to the suggestion. His frown and exaggeratedly slow reaction to obey told his boss that he regarded this as puzzling behaviour — but that everything this copper seemed to do and say was puzzling. Duty done, he returned and sat down waiting for his chance to give pre-prepared answers to anticipated questions.

Police enquiries were clearly backdoor business for the dean. They could safely be left to the butler to be dealt with. And yet, he wished to be within earshot when that business was being conducted. Redfyre decided to be annoying.

"Well, well, well! Dooley — Sergeant Dooley. First Regiment of the Cambridgeshires, eh? That gory interlude, on the Ancre, was it? Where your lot made a suicidal attack on the Bosche. No cameras to record the action, alas, but a solitary plane overflying the field dropped a message off over HQ. What did it say? 'Cambridgeshires going over the top, as if on parade.' Do I have that right?"

He listened to Dooley's awkward response and continued to chat about the regiment's part in the war. Dean Herbert stirred impatiently. He called over his shoulder. "Dooley! You will please confine yourself to informing the constabulary as to the routine associated with the locking of the gate."

Redfyre again addressed the old soldier. "No need for that. I've seen everything I wanted to see down in the passageway. But really, if we're not to chat about our shared experiences, what is there left for me to do here? I shall have to get on and perform the task I came specifically to do — namely, to arrest your boss for obstructing a police officer in the pursuit of his enquiries into a homicide. The murder of Miss Rosalind Weston of Maids Causeway, Cambridge. A young lady with whom the dean has close connections of a disreputable nature. There will follow, subsequent to enquiries being put in the interrogation room, a warrant for Dean Herbert's arrest on a charge of that murder. Now, what did I do with my handcuffs? Shall I cart him off through the side gate or the front entrance, Dooley?"

Herbert was on his feet, knocking over his side table and spitting with rage. "Dooley, leave us. You! Redfyre! Cretinous, bullying public servant who does not know his place —"

The invective flowed as Dooley shot off, leaving Redfyre obligingly to pick up the spilled glass and replace the table.

"There, there," he said, falsely soothing. "I see and quite understand that you have managed to keep Miss Weston's visits secret from Dooley — and from all here in the college, I would assume. You have the key. You dismiss your servant for the night and can come and go and entertain as you wish in complete privacy. As you did on the nights of October the third, October the twelfth, November the —"

"How dare you peddle such lies! Suggest such infamies!" Herbert spluttered, on his feet and very angry.

Redfyre didn't want the dean on his feet. Standing up and delivering lectures was a don's natural posture — superior, dominant. He would counter it.

"I don't *suggest.* I quote from Miss Weston's immaculate recording of her encounters." He took her diary from his pocket and held it under the dean's nose. "Encounters which are confirmed by the, er, company records of a Mrs. Lilian Jellico of Maids Causeway. Now, do resume your seat and answer my questions."

Glowering, the dean obeyed.

With the man's guard down, Redfyre pressed his advantage: "Whose persuasion led you to grant permission for Miss Proudfoot to perform in concert on college premises last Friday?"

The man gobbled at him in confusion, unable to summon up the right words.

"Standing in for the master who was aboard His Majesty's steamship *Ulysses* at the time, you granted her a permission that you knew very well would have been refused had the master been present. He had refused on four previous occasions, I believe. Had they been consulted, a committee of the fellows would have upheld the master's position I understand." (He understood no such thing. He was merely calculating.) "So, unless you were having a sudden and complete change of heart regarding females performing on college premises in anything other than a menial role, you must have been coerced. By whom?"

"Who do you expect, you fool? Who else would know? The wretched girl herself! I haven't set eyes on her since she started blackmailing me. That November date you have in your record is the last time I had any dealings with her. She took her cash, tucked it away in her bag and then said, almost as an afterthought, 'Oh, by the by, Dean. I have your wife, Honoria's, address. I intend to tell her about our encounters unless you do me a small favour.' And that

450

was it — the favour. Granting licence for the trumpeting. Not what I was expecting. Rather a cheap price to pay and easy enough to oblige. In some people's eyes, I even acquired a certain kudos, a tinge of daring modernity by making it!" He shook his head in a gesture of disbelief tinged with amusement. "But she had made the threat. Blackmailers never give up — you must know that. I was in constant alarm waiting for her next demand. And upon receiving one such, I had determined to do the right thing — the only thing — and make a clean breast of it to the police."

"And was this demand made? What did she require of you last night, Herbert?"

"Nothing. No further demand was ever made. And she never came to see me yesterday. I did not approach her with a request for an assignation, Inspector. I have been staying here in my set in college over this last bit. Ends of terms always a demanding time, don't you know. With my wife's encouragement. Naturally." He gave a swift, ironic grin. "Honoria leads a busy life on her own account."

Very busy, indeed, reflected Redfyre. According to his friend Freddy's wife, Honoria Herbert was rumoured to be spending a good part of each day devoting herself to

451

her new passion for gardening. And most of her nights to her passion for the new gardener.

The dean sank deeper into his chair, exhausted. "I have no idea how she came to be on college premises last night — if indeed she was, Inspector. Hasn't it occurred to you that anyone from the town could have abandoned her body on that doorstep, deliberately to cause problems for the college? My evening was a busy one, and I fulfilled all my engagements. I dined at high table, where the master presided. I joined him and about ten other fellows in the combination room where one of our number — Aitchison, I seem to remember — was offering a bottle or two of the best claret. He usually does, to mark the going down of the students and the start of the Holy Season. I retired to my rooms having eaten and drunk more than was good for me. I went to bed early with Gibbon. Edward Gibbon." He pointed to his book. "At nine-thirty. Dooley cleared away my cocoa at nine forty-five and retired for the night himself. I didn't see her, let alone kill her. I couldn't have killed a mouse, Inspector, had it climbed on my pillow and thumbed its nose at me."

He looked at Redfyre not in defiance, but

in bewilderment. "The river is only a few strides away, Inspector. An open sewer-cum-cemetery. It carries away evidence and guilt in seconds. If I had had the carelessness to kill her here on the premises, it is most unlikely that I would have left her body out on the back doorstep with the empties. I'm an intelligent man, and perfectly capable of planning a good and tidy outcome to any murder I might consider committing."

Redfyre breathed deeply and was momentarily at a loss for words. Awkwardly, he prepared to take his leave and managed to trot out a few formulae, amongst which was the baleful one where he advised his suspect not to leave town without notifying the police. As a parting shot, he couldn't resist quoting the Latin motto of the university to him in what MacFarlane would have called his "clever-dick" way. "Well, Doctor Herbert, I think that's all for now. Though I shall be back with the thumb screws if subsequent doubts are raised. Meanwhile your motto speaks for me: *Hinc lucem et pocula sacra.* 'From this place we gain enlightenment and precious knowledge.' Eh? What? I'll see myself out."

He closed the door behind him and breathed in deeply the scent of the damp stone and the wet earth and the green odours of the shrubs. Enlightenment? Not so much of that. But precious knowledge? That was another matter. He felt the bulk of the wine glass he'd picked up from the carpet and hidden in his pocket.

Two sets of fingerprints would be there. Dean Herbert's and Dooley's. For purposes of elimination or accusation? For information only, he reprimanded himself. The capturing and removing of fingerprints from private premises without permission of the owner gave a new meaning to "lifting prints." MacFarlane would have his hide if he found out.

As he passed through the courtyard, he broke off a twig from one of the bushes. A berry-bearing twig. Black, evil-looking berries. An emetic for the Anglo-Saxons, Doctor Beaufort had said. Also within hand's reach were holly, laurel and ivy.

Redfyre didn't imagine the sudden gust of cold air that raised the hackles on his neck. It was real enough. The old yew tree in the southeast corner was stirring in similar discomfort. He eased his old cashmere scarf up to fill the gap between trench coat collar and hat brim. He was very close. As close perhaps as a trapped mouse to the watching cat.

CHAPTER 20

"Here you still are, Johnny!"

"Aunt Hetty! How lovely to see you again. Come in, come in! Let me take your coat. Kettle's just beginning to sing —"

"Oh, good! My dear, the day I've had! I'm in need of sustenance, and I'm rather hoping for some of your Mrs. Page's Victoria sponge."

She stood on her toes and kissed him on each cheek. "My best stockings would seem to be unscathed after a whole minute on the premises — I take it you've got rid of your awful dog?"

"It's chocolate cake today, and no — Snapper's taking a walk through Fen Meadows with Billy next door. I say, Aunt, I'm a little behind this afternoon, could you possibly lay the table?"

With a token sigh of displeasure at the informality, Hetty peeled off her gloves and began expertly to set out plates, cups, saucers and cutlery. She went to the cold slab in the pantry and sniffed suspiciously at a bottle of milk.

"Fresh this morning, Aunt! Straight from the cows on the fen," he called cheerily.

"I'd be very surprised," she said. "They were yearling bullocks on the meadow when I passed this morning, fattening for the Christmas market. Still, I remain always open to new experiences and wonder daily at the advances of science."

They settled at the table, pausing to look with anticipation on his housekeeper's notion of Sunday tea.

"Let me show you round, Hetty," Redfyre said with quiet pride. "We've got potted crab sandwiches, scones with strawberry jam and a dish of thick cream, crunchy cheese something-or-others and, in pride of place, what Mrs. Page calls a 'gateau.' It's from the Black Forest, and it's got chocolate and cherries in it — cherries that have been bottled in kirsch in your honour. A Christmas treat."

Pouring out her third cup of Darjeeling, Aunt Henrietta made a grave observation. "Johnny, I've decided to make an unrefusable offer to your Mrs. Page. I shall take her into my employ from the first week of January. As long as she remains within a rolling pin's distance of you, you will never take the trouble to marry. You are well aware that you, being not only my favourite nephew but the sole penniless one of an otherwise fortunate bunch, are my heir. Before I make myself known to St. Peter, I'd like to be assured that the large amount of cash involved is going to pass eventually to a great-niece or nephew, not a Jack Russell terrier. Tell me — what progress are you making on this front? Earwig a likely starter, is she?"

Delivering a bulletin on his marital prospects was a routine, almost a ritual that had to be got through before he could have a serious conversation with his aunt. He picked up her racing image and decided to run it into the ground.

"I've had four girls circling in my paddock this week, Aunt," he began helpfully. "So, you see, I remain open to possibilities. Earwig will tell you — she's appearing in a different fixture completely. She's not entered in the marriage stakes at all. Surprised you didn't know that. There was a trumpeter I loved for all of five minutes. But she mistimed her takeoff and fell at the first fence. A certain mature lady whom you would have approved of, I discover is already wearing the colours of another stable. And before my racing metaphors strain a fetlock and because distress drives out flippancy, I'll simply say, of the fourth: she's dead. I never met her, but she will always haunt me. I grieve to have missed her."

His aunt was silent for a while, recognising that the conversation had taken its expected turn to the serious. "Ah! You're talking of Louise."

"Yes. Your young friend and fellow conspirator, Louise Lawrence. I've talked to her mother, her father, her employer, her friends and others who had dealings with her. One of her circle strangled her to death, and I mean to find out which one. You must tell me everything you know, Aunt. Because he's not stopping."

He knew that his next piece of news would shock her out of whatever complacency remained to her. "Your friend Venus — Rosalind Weston — also has fallen victim. Her body was discovered dumped at a side exit from St. Barnabas College this morning. The same manner of death was in evidence. Strangulation."

Hetty sat back in her chair as though smacked by an invisible fist. She fished about in her sleeve and found a handkerchief. No ladylike dabbing at eyes and sighing followed — she covered her face, hiding her crumpling features with it, and howled in distress and anger.

When she had calmed a little, Redfyre went on more gently, "Juno, Louise, Venus. There are motives individual to the attempt on Juno and the killing of the other two girls. It's not impossible that each was attacked by a different hand. Venus was engaged professionally in activities that do lead, all too frequently, to violence and death, and she was engaging in blackmail, with all the dangers that entails. I have fingerprints of two men who could easily have done for her. Louise had an enemy for each day of the week! Starting with her own father, her employer, her employer's butler, a jilted undergraduate, a local ruffian whom she humiliated in public and whose dog she stole . . . There may be more that I am as yet unaware of. No one, it seems, was indifferent to Louise. She aroused hatred and admiration in equal measure — sometimes in the same person and all for the same reason: that tiger's heart of hers."

Hetty surfaced, sniffling and shaking, from her handkerchief and gave him a strange look.

"And yet — and yet, Aunt, I look at their smiling faces, caught together on that photograph. You know the one I mean?"

Hetty nodded.

"And I have the feeling that some strong web connects them. A web you would appear to be at the centre of. Perhaps you're the one spinning it?"

Hetty shook her head.

"At any event, I'm not blaming *you* for the fatal consequences — just trying to understand and ward off any further horrors. But please share your thoughts — there's something that's eluding me. Louise and Venus — both bodies were symbolically placed, I think. Louise was thrown into the river only yards upstream from the place where the sewerage works performs its gruesome task of straining out the effluent, the rubbish, the contaminations, before the cleansed water is channeled away. Venus was left for all to see in the place where traditionally the discarded items of college life are dumped. A message, are we thinking? But it's the double attack on Juno that puzzles me most."

"Double? *Double,* John? What are you talking about?"

"Prepare yourself for another shock, Aunt." He filled in as unemotionally as he could manage the events he'd witnessed in the chapel. The offering of the sal volatile to the master, Henningham's experimental sniffing of the contents and subsequent striking down with suspected Delhi Belly, Earwig's deft gesture and firm control, which had prevented Juno's certain death.

"Smelling salts?" his aunt said faintly. "My God! I could do with some now! But — laced with cyanide? How simply awful! And what a sneaky way of administering it! Tell me again, Johnny, what woman do you know of who could have handed such a lethal device to the master?"

She shook her head in confusion when he gave her the description. "A spray of holly in her hat? Oh, you're wasting your time running round the modistes of Cambridge looking for such a thing! This is Cambridge. At Christmas time! Lighthearted, enjoying a seasonal joke. There were probably a dozen ladies who'd picked a spray of holly leaves from a tree in the front garden or from a green garland and popped it onto their hats at a jaunty angle. The naughtier ones choose mistletoe. But, Johnny, would I be assuming too much if I —"

"No, Aunt. I'm sure Juno is still in danger. We're looking for a man intent on exterminating all those infected — in his thinking — by Louise Lawrence's new and muscled brand of feminism. For one reason or another — and for me, the word 'reason' strikes me as a bad choice — he's afraid and angry and implacable. He wants your group stamped out."

"He must be mad, Johnny! Don't you think? What other cause could there possibly be?"

"Must he? I wish I could be so certain. I can't tell you what madness is, Hetty. I'm not sure how it differs from evil. I can't bring myself to trust the theories of the mind-scientists who observe behaviour in consulting rooms or laboratories. There are the officially mad — those unfortunates having had a disease of the mind since birth, a condition which has always been common knowledge to their family and medical authorities. And then there are those who are mentally diseased through their own folly. Drugs, venereal diseases. The few who have suffered mental trauma to their head in war . . . All these will be labelled 'mad' by the public without argument or qualification."

Abandoning his police-lecture voice, he turned to her in appeal. "Aunt, I pick up the dead and the desecrated. The battered, the poisoned and the strangled. I see them, I smell them, I mourn for them. And I vow to find and deal with the person who has killed them. As part of that, I have to guess at the state of mind as well as the physical condition of the guilty, and it's never straightforward. There may be two knifings-to-death of a woman in one night. One will have been killed by a stranger in a sexually-driven attack and left for dead on the common. The other, after a lifetime of provoking and bullying her husband, may have been stabbed by him when — as he hopelessly tells the police — 'Something just snapped, officer.' "

"These crimes occupy the ground somewhere between the two?"

"No. I fear this is something worse. On entirely different territory. It's more akin to a military manoeuvre. There are no qualms about killing a woman. Equally, there seems to be no perverted relish taken in the killing. Silent, sharp and inescapable. Hetty, I want you and Earwig and anyone else you can think of who may be a potential victim to —" At the sight of her hardening expression he paused. "I'm wasting my breath, aren't I?"

"Yes. I'm afraid we're going nowhere, Johnny. We're staying put. If we give in and flee — what then? He's won whatever battle he imagines he's fighting. And do we stay away? For how long? Besides, I'm sure we've all made our plans for Christmas. No one can live with such a threat over them.

And the women you have become acquainted with, the nameless bunch of to-the-core feminists, are hardly likely to run away. We haven't given up. And you don't know of half the membership, my lad! The fight will go on. In the same spirit of clandestine conniving, confusion spreading, bribery, incitement, blackmailing, seduction and mayhem. Each woman has her own strengths and talents. No one is expected to do more than she is capable of or is willing to do. Some of us are in powerfully manipulative positions."

"Don't I know that! You, Aunt, seem to think you have the Cambridge CID in your dainty pocket! Tell me, what are you trying to achieve?"

"I could bore you silly by delivering the usual polemic on equality and votes. But I'll just say: without the unfurling of a single banner, by next year we want to see the University of Cambridge, which has slighted many of our members, agreeing as Oxford has already done, to allow our brightest girls to be awarded the full degrees they have worked for. We want at least two hundred more female undergraduates and access to courses which are at the moment open only to men. We want equal pay for equal work. We want suffrage for all women over the age of twenty-one. Whether they have cash in the bank or not. We want to see the first female MPs taking their seats on the benches of the House of Commons —"

"Enough!"

"You see, you are horrified at what you consider my stridency. Because I list complaints and injustices and demand change, you consider me noisily capricious and unreasonable. And that is exactly why you have never heard me express these sentiments before and will never hear them from me again. We are working towards certain ends, but *sub rosa*. And one by one. We won't shout from the rooftops or go about the place breaking windows. But you will hear about our achievements in the press."

"Oh, good Lord! You've seduced a press baron!"

She considered this for a moment. "No. No one fancied that task. But we have access to one, and a potential noose around his neck."

"And what about the dramatic but just-this-side-short-of-fatal tumble down the stairs by Juno — her grande finale. Did Juno volunteer to perform her acrobatics in full view of a witness planted in the front row? Had she any idea what danger she was running into?"

His aunt wriggled with embarrassment. "You must refer your question to Earwig and Juno. That arrangement was none of my making. They simply asked my help in ensuring you were present. We do not involve the whole group in each project. A cell of six, a hexagon, would seem to be the ideal for strength and security. The bees understand that. It's the only way of keeping careless gossip to the minimum. Inform only those who need to be actively involved. Compartmentalise. It seems to work for the Secret Intelligence Service."

"Oh, my God! You've infiltrated the SIS?" His tone was teasing, but with an undercurrent of concern. Redfyre sighed. "And now, tell me: Elli, Goddess of Old Age! Is she by any chance related to Loki, God of Mischief, I wonder? His aunt, perhaps? I want to know where and how you're thinking of spending your Christmas."

"Not quietly! I'm hoping to have a riotous time in the company of old friends and family. Watching the young folk fall in and out of love, break each other's hearts . . . the usual Christmassy things. And it's almost upon us! We're rather hoping you can join us, Johnny. In fact, I'm delegated to invite you to a jolly Advent party at Earwig's. She's putting on some Scandinavian candle-lighting celebrations to mark the midwinter solstice. That's the twenty-first, next Friday. Apparently, our ancient ancestors were doing this thousands of years ago. Much slaughtering of pigs and oxen, feasting and drinking and dancing around in stone circles."

"Human sacrifice an item on the programme, Aunt?"

He could have wished her pause to consider this flippancy had been shorter.

"Not on the one the Strettons are drawing up. Nothing more alarming than apple-bobbing, I believe. Earwig's arty lot would always be willing celebrants of any ceremony of that kind. Did you know that one of the brothers — Alf, I believe — has turned into an archaeologist and is digging away at Stonehenge under the direction of Colonel Hawley? Ghastly little Alf! He's now quite the distinguished professor figure — exchanging correspondence with Howard Carter no less."

"Alf?"

"Elf-helm, spelled: A-E-L-F-H-E-L-M. You don't imagine he would allow that to be shortened to 'Elf' do you? The brothers will be there in force."

At his frown, she changed tactics. "Earwig's father has declared he is dying. This will be their last Christmas as a family. Certainly their last one in that lovely house. Death duties are crippling, and to pay our rapacious government's taxes, it will have to be sold. If indeed there is anyone left in the country who can afford to buy it. But, always ready to cock a snook at fate, they are filling the house with guests — not all fuddy-duddies like me and your uncle — oh, no. The smartest young things in the county — like you — will be there. Earwig has asked for you particularly. There's going to be a dance band up from London . . ."

Correctly reading his expression, which told her he would rather have his toenails pulled out to the sound of Wagner than be present, she shrugged. "Oh, well . . . I tried."

Redfyre managed a grin. "Two conditions! So long as I can do a tango or two with the prettiest girl present. And so long as I still have the use of all my limbs." He looked at his wristwatch and sighed. "I have an engagement to fight a duel. In half an hour." His grin widened. "I begin to regret my second slice of chocolate cake."

"What on earth are you talking about? Where are you shooting off to in the dark?"

"Can't tell you! Discipline of the Hexagon and all that, don't you know! Let's just say I'm summoned to settle a long-standing difference of opinion with an old friend."

"Oh, no! Not fisticuffs!"

"There may be an outbreak of fisticuffs. Ambush and attack by catapult may occur."

Hetty raised her eyes to the heavens, seeking help and understanding.

Inspiration followed. "Darling, let me write you a sick note."

Leaving Hetty to clear the table while she waited to be picked up by her chauffeur, Redfyre put on his strong, thick-soled Oxford brogues, equally suitable for running or crotch-kicking, and tucked a skull-splitting heavy torch into his pocket. He pulled on his hat, buttoned up his coat and stepped out into the already pitch-dark lane. The stars were bright, but the moon had not yet risen. He would have to grope his way the short distance to Laundress Lane steering by the haloes of light surrounding the gas lamps strategically placed at the street corners.

In hunting — or was it hunted — mode, he paused to listen as well as accustom his eyes to the gloom. His challenger, if he had any wit at all and serious intent, would by now know where he lived and the path he would take to Laundress Lane. With the roles reversed, Redfyre would have mounted an attack before the whistle blew, right here on his doorstep. He looked across at the Saxon burial ground — now disused churchyard — immediately in front of him. The thrashing boughs of the taller trees were silhouetted by the lights shining at the windows of Peterhouse college fifty yards away, but the lower layers of shrubbery, the ancient mounds of earth and the grave-stones crouching at a drunken angle were invisible, shrouded in darkness and rising wreaths of ground mist. Redfyre couldn't see them, but he knew where they were, every hump and obstacle. He'd spent many hours quietly reading in this spot in summer. He'd relished the delight of sitting on sun-warmed fallen tombstones, wandering about deciphering the eroded names carved on them, chatting sporadically with the down-and-outs who washed up in this forgotten place.

A skilled hunter would have lured him here and cracked him over the skull with a fallen branch, then disappeared, leaving no trace of his presence behind. His body could have been taken for a sleeping tramp and remained undisturbed for days.

Absolutely still and quietly listening, he detected a slight rustling from the graveyard. A rustling that was immediately cut short.

His sixth sense was telling him he was being watched. Another furtive noise was followed by the clink of a glass bottle on a tombstone and a beery belch. Redfyre waited ten more seconds, then turned to the right and set off for the river.

He didn't feel embarrassed at the amount of care he was taking. Four years of war and five years of policing had turned him into a professional survivor. He left nothing to chance. Many men would have felt foolish to be observed sniffing the air, straining an ear, or lurking in doorways. Redfyre cared nothing for many men and their feelings. He didn't have much time for accepted notions of chivalry, either. If he knew that shots or blows were to be traded, he would always try to deliver the first. The one that always counted. And, if it proved not to be a clincher, follow up with a swift one to the privates.

So why the hell, he asked himself, hadn't he taken the station Browning from its drawer in MacFarlane's desk? He was a vociferous supporter of the rule that British policemen went about unarmed. It was the thought of the notoriety and scorn that would ensue and the questions that would be asked if he were seen to use a pistol on the streets of Cambridge, possibly wounding or causing the death of some idiot, that stayed his hand. No, he'd get the better of "W" without the aid of so much as a catapult. Caution again reprimanded him: Chances were that this was a childish dare, a silly game he'd been invited to play. But chances were chances, and he never counted on them. What he ought to beware of was a temptation to *enjoy* this threat in the dark. The ancient spirit of Celtic mischief was a useful warmth flowing through his veins, sharpening his mind, and it could be a life saver for a man caught up in a spot of trench raiding in the enemy's front line, but this was Laundress Lane, for goodness sake!

He stayed his step again, in sudden doubt. Laundress Lane. The sinister little alleyway leading from the town to Laundress Green. Often flooded in winter, this was the small grassy area on the riverbank where the washerwomen of the town had spread their linen out to dry. Pretty as a picture and buzzing with life in the summertime. Sinister and deserted on a December evening.

Why on earth had it come to his mind? Why had he mentioned it to Earwig and — more importantly — why had the wretched, deceitful, lying girl passed it on to a villain who ought not even to be in Cambridge?

The lane was not so much the place for a

duel as an assassin's killing ground. A narrow cobbled way, not two swords' width, with high walls on each side. Once embarked on it, there was no way of avoiding anyone approaching from the other side. You had to greet them, friend or foe and pass on. But which side was the "other" one? He'd miscalculated. "W" would be expecting him to take the direct route from his home to the lane. Indeed, that was exactly what he had done. He decided to do an about-turn, put on some speed, retrace his steps, circle round and join the bustle of Silver Street, then enter the lane from the town side. If he was lucky, he might well come upon a furtive figure lurking about looking the wrong way down the lane. With some satisfaction, he'd tap him on the shoulder and with a comedy police greeting — "Allo, allo, allo, what's all this, then?" — and send him on his way with a flea in his ear.

The lamp at the entrance to Laundress Lane opposite Queens' College was alight and, as he walked straight past he noted that the lamp at the far end also was glowing. He managed to make out that between the two, for its full length, the alley was empty. As a nearby college bell struck six o'clock, a band of raucous students gathered at the entrance to Queens' called farewells to each other and shot off in smaller groups, some into the college, some striking out up Silver Street. Three men in green and white striped Queens' College scarves laughed together and crossed the road, making, no doubt, for the bright lights and flowing beer of the Anchor pub on the river bank.

Returning to the lane, Redfyre found it still deserted. He flashed his strong police-issue light the length of it. No crouched assassins. No obstacles of any kind underfoot.

He loitered for five minutes more before he decided he'd been the victim of a crude joke and gave up. Frustration, anger and embarrassment were chipping away at his caution. He was going home. By the most direct route. Straight down the middle of that bloody lane! Anyone getting in his way would regret it. He switched on his torch, set his shoulders as though for a scrum and started out.

He'd taken five steps when he felt the tap on his back.

"Allo, allo, allo!" said a cheery voice. "This is a funny place to find a policeman."

Redfyre whirled, torch raised ready to smash at the face of whoever had sneaked up on him.

"Whoa! Easy! It's only me, you twerp!"

Panting with surprise and alarm, Redfyre stared at the stranger. "Only me" was a man he'd have sworn he'd never met before in his life. An impressive man. Taller than Redfyre by about two inches, he was wearing a dark cashmere overcoat with a black slouch hat pulled down low on his brow. He took off his hat in a courtly gesture and grinned. Fair hair lit up in the torchlight, and blue eyes crinkled against the brilliance with humour as he peeled off the college scarf and pushed it into his pocket.

"Good Lord!" Redfyre managed at last to exclaim.

He put out his left hand and shook the left hand that the other offered him.

"You're a hard man to keep sight of, Redfyre! I lost you right at the start. By the time I'd got out of that bloody cemetery, you'd beetled off in the opposite direction! I had to backtrack and bustle along a bit to get here before you."

He peered down the lane and shuddered. "Godawful places you choose to frequent when you have the choice of this fair city. Graveyards and killing zones? What traps have you installed down there? Pincer gate? Machicolations? *Chevaux-de-frise?*"

"You never know — there might well be a *trou-de-loup,*" Redfyre suggested with a tight smile. "Even Caesar found that digging a wolf hole or two brought results. How do you do, Wulfie? Or are you still calling yourself Oberstleutnant Stretton?"

He responded to Redfyre's challenge with another grin. "So much to talk about! It must be twenty years or more, eh? Why don't we finish this reunion in the Anchor? There's a little back door into the pub, straight off the lane down here on the right. Did you know? I discovered it just this afternoon on my reconnaissance. The beer's not bad, and I suppose it passes for your local, so you can buy the first round."

Wulfie Stretton was not a man who could creep about in disguise hoping not to be noticed for long, Redfyre thought as he made his way, tankard in each hand over to the corner table Stretton had settled at. Large, blond, commanding, and surveying the world about him with an affable eye, he attracted attention. When they'd settled in and taken a thoughtful swig or two of their draught bitter, Stretton grimaced and began to make conversation.

"Doesn't begin to compare with the litres of good Löwenbräu the men enjoyed in the trenches. Or the Rhine wine and schnapps they served in the officers' mess. Who was it who said, 'You can fight a war without women, horses, even bullets, but you can't fight a war without tobacco and alcohol'? It remains a surprise that the Germans failed to win, so superior was their drink. Schnapps has a soul, you know," he confided.

"Oh, yes? We managed very well on Woodbines and rum," Redfyre said pleasantly. "Rum is far too coarse to have a soul, I'm afraid, but it does fire up the old cockles. And it seems to have worked." In a colder, crisper tone he added, "Very bad form, Stretton, to be fighting the war over again. Five years have passed. This is a different country and a different world. I have a pair of handcuffs in my back pocket, and I'm itching for the opportunity to use them if I don't like the answers to certain questions I have for you."

"Fire away, old boy!"

"Just for fun and to humour you, I'll start with an easy one: The scarf, Wulfie? I hadn't realised that the Herr Oberstleutnant was a Queens' alumnus."

"He's not! I pinched it from a bike basket. Who's going to look twice at one of several chaps in a college scarf rioting about with his fellow roughs outside his own college? Protective colouring! I've learned to use it."

"Hmm. And what steps are you using to

melt once again into English life? We had a brisk way with traitors in the war. A green and white scarf won't save your neck."

"Perhaps not, but a blue and gold book might do the trick."

He reached into his inside pocket and produced a familiar small, slim, dark blue book with gold lettering.

"A British passport?" Redfyre asked in surprise. "I wondered how you'd managed to get back into the country. How on earth did you get your hands on this? Is it forged?"

"Perfectly genuine. Take a look. Wherever I go, I use the front door and expect it to be opened for me," Stretton smiled easily.

"Tipping the doorman a hefty sum, I'd guess?"

"Inevitably some greasing of palms or exchange of favours is required in these cases. This arrived for me in the diplomatic bag. Seems to work, though I must confess to a nervous moment at Dover. You can never trust the British Foreign Office one hundred percent. They enjoy their little games and they don't always stay bought."

Redfyre thumbed through the document, checking the stamps dating entry and departure across the countries of Europe and noting in particular his date of admission to the United Kingdom.

"You must have seriously expected a one-way traitor's ticket straight to the Tower of London," Redfyre commented. "You certainly earned it. I think I should arrest you and take you there anyway. Let whoever will, argue about it after the event."

"Always the scrapper, Johnny! But no! You have this all wrong. Didn't Earwig explain? The last thing the British government wants is a fuss. The postwar mood is all for recovery and reconciliation."

"Some might think there was a price to pay for destroying a continent. What about remorse, retribution and restitution?"

"So old hat! And the spectacle of a scion of English county stock dangling from a rope would horrify the nation. You can imagine what a banquet the press would have . . . the front-page headlines. The memory of Sir Roger Casement is still raw and uncomfortable — he suffered a traitor's execution for colluding with Germany. Irish he may have been, but he was a good-looking bloke and an inspiring speaker. The press managed to denigrate his name and his character in court, but some Englishmen, politicians, writers and poets made a huge fuss. The national conscience was put to the question. A nation writhed with indecision and guilt. Oh, no! They couldn't risk going through that again!"

"You found the right heartstrings to tug on?"

"It was decided — and at a level so high it would make your head spin! — that Britannia's morale would be dented by a show trial at the Old Bailey or by a ceremonial military execution involving the severing of buttons or heads. There was no need even for the publicity of issuing a pardon. Because no sin was committed, you see."

He leaned closer and said, "Confidentially now, old boy: I was a British agent, working for King and Country all along. Yes, indeed. In the pay of British Military Intelligence. I have in my possession a document certifying exactly that, a document signed by the highest authority in the Secret Intelligence Service."

"Ah! At last you impress me. It was signed in green ink with the letter 'C' for 'Cumming'?" Redfyre enquired sarcastically.

Stretton shook his head. "No. The much admired head of — what are you calling them these days — MI6, would it be? Mansfield Smith-Cumming did not have the honour of fixing my reinstatement. He died last June. My document is, indeed, signed in green ink, but you'll have to address your queries to Admiral Sir Hugh Sinclair if you must check my bona fides. But I'm sure you know that. A naughty wolf trap, Redfyre?"

Redfyre leaned close and said quietly, "Confidentially now, old boy: Bollocks to your bona fides! To borrow and mutilate a phrase from the Afridi tribe, 'Trust a rat before a snake and a snake before a Stretton.' There are two things I want to know before you leave here with my boot up your treacherous arse: How did you lose your right hand, and what is the nature of your relationship with your sister's friend, Juno Proudfoot?"

CHAPTER 21

Monday Morning, 17th December.

MacFarlane had summoned his inspector and sergeant into the privacy of his office to await delivery of three copies of the *Cambridge Oracle.*

They seized on the papers the moment a constable brought them up and read in silence, absorbing the contents of the front page. It seemed to be as bad as each had feared. Sebastian Scrivener had done his damaging worst again.

The headline reminded the readers of the news they had already read the previous Saturday. FALL OF AN ANGEL was followed, on this Monday morning, by MORE ANGELS FALL! and the subheading: TWO NEVER TO RISE AGAIN. WHERE WILL THIS SLAUGHTER OF THE INNOCENTS END?

The main body of the copy, taking up two-thirds of the front page, was devoted to the death of Louise Lawrence, the remaining

482

third to the more recent discovery of the body of Rosalind Weston.

Redfyre felt obliged to break the silence. "There's nothing here in the account of Louise's death that he didn't hear along with the other journalists at your press briefing, sir," he commented.

"No, you're right," MacFarlane agreed. "The facts are all there and not, for once, exaggerated. I'll give him that. It's the interpretation he puts on them that concerns me. And that he's drawing a connecting line between the two deaths, extending back to the attack on Miss Proudfoot. He's working to an agenda, this bloke."

"An agenda that might well have been dictated to him down a telephone wire," murmured Redfyre.

"Time I had him in for a chat." MacFarlane was growling and blustering and holding the pages by the edges as though attempting to avoid contamination. "Three poor girls attacked in the space of a weekend . . . These sharks must think all their Christmases have come at once!"

"It's the way he gives the unquestioned details but uses them to sort of . . . plant a suggestion . . . that gets me," Thoday ventured. "I mean, look at this, halfway down."

Parents of young girls, accustomed to allowing their daughters to range freely over Cambridge city, will be minded perhaps to draw for themselves a mental map of the city and pinpoint the places where these dastardly crimes have been committed. A pattern will be seen to emerge.

The first angel to fall — the one lucky survivor — very nearly met her end in the heart of the university, in the middle of a college chapel (St. Barnabas), surrounded by crowds of concertgoers. The second was found dead in the river, only yards from a boathouse (St. Barnabas); the third, at the very doorway to one of the colleges (St. Barnabas).

"And he's a bloke who understands the strength of the number three," MacFarlane said. "Once is chance, twice is happenstance, but three times it's: Lock up your daughters. It's out in the open now — he's definitely going for the college. The next sentence says it all. That's the nub."

The young ladies of Cambridge — and their concerned parents and guardians — should perhaps plan their journeys about this fair and hitherto peaceable city with added care and circumspection.

"In other words, it's a sink of iniquity, and any girl going near this college risks life or limb. He goes on to invoke God and the Cambridge CID in his call to arms."

This paper does not relish the thought of reporting the deaths of any further innocents snatched prematurely from the bosoms of their families, and we pray that our daughters may be kept safe in this holy season of Christmas. Moreover, we would urge the concerned guardians of our peace, the Cambridge police force, to do their utmost to uncover the person responsible for these appalling crimes and render him incapable of causing further sorrow for Cambridge families. We would urge our law officers to strain every sinew to prevent our quiet courts and gracious ways descending into the filth of Whitechapel.

"Can't say he's wrong. But no prizes for guessing who I'm going to have on the phone shouting into my earpiece any minute," MacFarlane said gloomily.

"Not your fault, sir, if someone's got it in for St. Barnabas," Thoday said stoutly.

"It's not the college I'm expecting to hear from," said MacFarlane. "They've got the sense to either ignore it, knowing it will all be forgotten by the new year, or else they'll take it up with the editor. Students and staff at the colleges have mostly gone down for the vacation anyway. No, it's the chief. He was turning my ear red yesterday in the

clubhouse, rattling on about the usual —
town-gown relationships. Souring by the
minute, he thinks. And of course, it's all
down to us to sort it out."

"In Saturday's paper, Inspector Redfyre
was a hero — stalwart, music-loving law
officer who saved the life of a potential
victim," Thoday grumbled. "Now this
bloke's needling us just a bit. Isn't he?"

"And tomorrow, he'll go for the jugular.
That's their *modus operandi,* Thoday.
Bloody press! They build you up one minute
— quite deliberately — then tear you down
the next, revelling in the drama of the fall
from grace. And don't believe all that rubbish about 'this paper does not relish the
thought of reporting further deaths'! Huh!
They're licking their lips! They know very
well that Jack the Ripper sold more newspapers than the Battle of Waterloo and the
death of Queen Victoria put together."

He surveyed his small team. "Right, now
lads! Back to real business. Anything to add,
Thoday?"

"About Miss Lawrence, sir. I followed up
the thug with the dog she took from him.
He's a Ronald Johnson from Newmarket
Road. A regular at certain sporting events
that take place behind the Wrestlers pub on
Onion Row. Within spitting distance of old

Mr. Benson's pill factory. In fact, our Mr. Johnson is — was — an employee there. He was sacked last month for bad timekeeping. He could well have known Louise Lawrence by sight, even if she didn't know him."

"Sporting events? Not more bare-knuckle boxing dos! I thought we'd stamped those out."

"No, sir. In fact, these are very unsporting events. Dog fights. Not casual stuff — professional organisers, specially bred animals and heavy betting."

"Investigate Ronnie Johnson. Take a posse, including a veterinarian. Arrest him on a count of animal cruelty, then question him about the Lawrence killing. Well done, Thoday! And well done on little Miss Weston. All that footwork down King Street kicked up some dirt! And it was a sharp-eyed PC on overtime who worked out that she could only have been dumped where she was left, in the gateway, by some bugger pushing her through from the inside."

"Inspector!" He turned to Redfyre. "You also investigated the Weston matter further. Gained access to the ivory tower, but I don't see anyone in cuffs yet?"

"There are two people who could have done the killing, and one has a very strong motive," Redfyre supplied, and gave an account of his interview with the dean. He concluded by admitting his sleight of hand with the wine glass and its two sets of fingerprints.

"Yes, I know it's an irregularity, but —"

"Never mind that! How did you account for it? Did you cover yourself with a good story for the forensics boys?" MacFarlane demanded.

"I entered it as a suspected sample of the *victim's* prints, sir. Attempting to link her with a presence on college premises. I've asked them to print out what they have and compare them with any prints they can lift from the metal clasp and frame or shiny leather surface of the bag found with the body. They'll find that they have, not the girl's prints on the glass, but two unrecorded sets. If one of these then proves to be identical with prints on her bag, then we've got him!"

"How soon can they get back to us?"

"They wouldn't commit themselves to a particular time, but they hope for tomorrow."

"What are your expectations?"

"Not much. Don't get excited, sir. The dean has a very strong motive, either for a premeditated or spur-of-the-moment killing. He had good reason to fear that the girl was about to wreck his domestic life and possibly his professional career with her blackmail demands. He seemed to me not the violent, quick-tempered type at all, but he is quite capable of planning ahead to the extent of involving his manservant as his strong pair of hands. Dooley is an ex-soldier, a man inured to killing. He could have done it for the right incentive. Money probably. And the foolish dean would have dug himself deeper into a pit of death and blackmail."

"Yes, blackmail," MacFarlane frowned. "Seems to be a lot of it about. You say the dean was puzzled by the light, even frivolous, demand the girl made? Granting permission for the trumpet performance? I'm with the dean on this! It's ludicrous! That's not what tarts do. They work for cash in hand, not musical favours. And they have their code — not of honour, but survival. They don't piss off a good regular client. I'm more puzzled than he is! How about you, Redfyre? Making sense of it, are you?"

"More sense than the dean, I think. I had tea with my aunt yesterday, and this was quite illuminating . . ."

MacFarlane mulled over what now sounded even to Redfyre's ears a far-fetched piece of female intrigue. "Mischief," he concluded. "Can't you have a strong word with these wimmin, Inspector? I can see what they're up to. They've targeted Barnabas. Why? Easy pickings? A more approachable master than most — Henningham, you say, doesn't seem actively to dislike females, and even has some sort of relationship going with a local schoolmarm, one of their own group, in fact. Their group — they don't have a name for themselves? Am I getting this right, Redfyre? But these shenanigans represent an expression of some sort of special hatred. And they're not letting go until they've achieved their end. Can we calculate what this end might be?"

"It's hardly the overnight granting of suffrage to all over twenty-one — that's still well below the horizon. It's small, their goal, but achievable. A carefully calculated victory. And it's the first of a series."

"The breach in the dam?"

"Think ahead, sir. If this comes to a boil, and with Scrivener, their honorary member (or their victim?) stoking the fires, the town might react. In a predictable way. The chief himself seems to have noticed what's going on. Sneaky thought — has he, too, had inside information? Has he been approached and alarmed by some wild-eyed Cassandra foreseeing doom? Ultimately, the college will find itself the subject of public suspicion and scorn. To polish up its image it could well take a bold step of proving to the world that it has been maligned. Its only way to reinstate itself as far as I can see would be to open its doors and its lecture rooms to women. This would no doubt be welcomed in the press as a bold and forward-looking gesture. The dean had a taste of that warm praise when he was undeservedly assumed to be responsible for the granting of the concert licence. He had the nerve to confess that he rather basked in the glory."

MacFarlane was hearing him out in silence. "So? Are you ever going to come clean, Inspector, and tell us where your loyalty lies?"

"Very well. I'm a suffragist, sir. Veering to the Millicent Fawcett rather than the Emmeline Pankhurst. I have very simple thoughts on the matter. Women are the equal of men. Always have been. It has just not been acknowledged yet in thought or in law. I'm also an officer of the peace and I cannot tolerate the abuse of the law by either sex to achieve even a worthy end."

"Well now we know where we are. I've got my eye on you, lad."

Redfyre concluded his account of his talk with his aunt by saying, lamely, to an openly scathing audience: "So, I'm adding to the list of suspects a shadowy presence who is targeting these ladies for their beliefs and the energetic way in which they are carrying out their suffragist crusade. He first made himself known to them in the late summer by means of a poison-pen letter. His latest communication is the holly wreath, with a message that can be interpreted as unfinished business with Miss Proudfoot."

"Mmm . . . it's hard to put cuffs on a shadowy presence, Redfyre. Firm up or give up on this."

"Right, sir. Oh, there is just one more thing arising from investigations yesterday. Were you aware of the presence in the city of a man with a dubious history . . . well, dubious to me. The older brother of the Miss Stretton who is a friend of all three victims. He found himself fighting on the German side in the war . . ." Redfyre filled in the unpleasant details and concluded, "I wondered whether anyone had thought to inform the authorities of this man's presence on our patch?"

He could tell by MacFarlane's hardening expression and suddenly abstracted gaze that someone had.

"We have been notified. Yes. He resumed domicile rights — all perfectly legal and acceptable. We are advised no action and no surveillance of any sort is necessary in the case of Mr. Aethelwulf Stretton. I do hope this man is not your shadowy presence, Redfyre. You'd be wasting your time chasing him."

"No, sir. There is one obvious drawback to a suspicion of Wulfie Stretton as our strangler. He has no right hand."

"I beg your pardon!"

Redfyre grinned. "Oberstleutnant Stretton tells me he never actually came to grips with the British army. Pretty early on in the proceedings, the Uhlan lancers he was serving with were engaging a French cavalry unit the old-fashioned way — with sabres. Caught up in a skirmish in eastern France, Wulfie had his sword hand lopped off by a French dragoon. He was lucky not to bleed to death or to contract a disease. He survived, but was clearly not available for further fighting. With his native language being English and knowing some French, he was diverted to intelligence service behind the lines. He interrogated mostly English prisoners. Lord knows what shifty business he became involved with! His story is that he worked as a double agent. Double? Triple? Just a plain self-seeking blackguard, I'd guess! But his story was strong enough for HM's gov and the military to accept and promote it."

MacFarlane broke his silence to comment shrewdly, "There must be more to it than a forgiving government smoothing the path of a prodigal son whose father is on his last legs. What's he not telling you, Redfyre?"

"As you say, sir. I pressed him further."

"Two professional interrogators going head-to-head! I'd like to have been a fly on the wall!"

"As luck would have it, I had him at a slight disadvantage!"

Redfyre decided to squash his elation and save it for later. He'd deal with the facts first. "He hinted that he'd come upon information of a delicate nature during his sessions with certain English officers being held captive. In a threatening situation, these men had been seduced by the friendliness of a man speaking their language — a man of their class, a fellow soldier. Indiscretion on their part is understandable, though not to be condoned. Released and repatriated, these ex-prisoners of war are now occupying influential positions in the government and the military, and either acknowledge a debt of gratitude to Stretton or are obvious subjects for blackmail. In addition to this stick, there is a carrot. Stretton, with the luck of the Devil's own, is now a very rich man. The Prussian family who took him on with their own warlike sons saw their own boys killed off one by one, and Wulfie was the only survivor of the group. They focused all their parental attention and generosity on him. Recently dead, they bequeathed him their extensive properties and wealth. He has translated himself back into a desirable British citizen."

"Desirable? Says who?"

"Desirable in that the authorities prefer to see him over here, putting his wealth to good use. And keeping his mouth shut. In a safe place where closure — *permanent* closure, should it come to that — can be ensured."

"Good Lord!" MacFarlane's voice was faint but admiring. "He wasn't persuaded by a sense of honour to his adoptive parents to stay over there? Why's he back here bothering us in Cambridge? He could go anywhere. South of France. South America."

"Ah! This story has a romantic ending, I'm afraid! I mentioned that he was at a disadvantage during the interview. The man's in love."

Redfyre weathered the cold disbelief directed at him by two pairs of eyes.

"He's suffering from brain fever and overexcitement, the treacherous benevolence towards one's fellow man that leads one to say, 'These drinks are on me!' Or, 'What do you want to know? Fire away!' "

The disbelief was intensifying. Neither MacFarlane nor Thoday gave a sign that they had ever experienced the euphoria that comes with the state of being in love. Redfyre sighed and struggled on. "Stretton's sister, who devotedly kept him in communication over the years, told him her best friend, a trumpet player, was undertaking a concert tour of the cities of northern Germany, accompanying Christopher Coote, the organist. Yes, Juno Proudfoot. She was scheduled to perform at Dresden in the summer, and Earwig encouraged her brother to travel there, go to a concert and meet her. And swap family gossip, no doubt. News from home . . . They must have found a lot to talk about and remember."

MacFarlane groaned and muttered.

"A smasher like Miss Juno — she wouldn't be needing nostalgia to attract his interest," Thoday said. "Question is — why would she notice him above all the other stage-door Johnnies, especially with his past?"

"As you say, Sarge. Juno is a taking little thing and has many admirers. Wulfie is unattached. Good-looking, if you don't mind the duelling scars and the broken nose. He's rich, romantically inclined, and indulges in the generous gesture." Redfyre sighed, remembering the expensive flower vase from "A" of the outstretched arms. "Why are girls so easily taken in?"

"Oh, I don't know," MacFarlane said doubtfully. "It sounds to me as though the lass has her head screwed on the right way. I hope she wrings every last German mark out of the shit. Redfyre, is this leading anywhere?"

The appearance of a large evidence box delivered to their table in the inspectors' room made MacFarlane's eyes gleam where the accounts of female hysteria and male emotion had not raised a spark. His favoured suspect remained the undergraduate Thomas Tyrrell, and he welcomed the appearance from the labs of a plaster cast taken from the sandy surface of the pipe repair works on the common, a few strides away from the sanctuary of the Bensons' front door. He reminded his small team that Tyrrell's own bike was not involved. Punctured and the tyres clean of all trace of the bright orange builder's material, it could be discounted.

Not so the jilted student himself, however.

"We can't comb the whole of Cambridge for a tyre with this stuff caught in its grooves, so let's narrow the search area down a bit," MacFarlane suggested. "Go to the map, Thoday, and talk us through the lad's itinerary, subsequent to the push off she gave him in the pub."

Thoday obliged, with a minimum of commentary to move the end of his pen representing Tyrrell from the Trinity Street pub down to the Market Place. There it circled about confusedly and, finally coming to a decision, it took off again, returning to Trinity Street and Barnabas College. There, Tyrrell engaged the suffering master's sketchy attention for ten minutes and came out again — in and out, as logged by the porter. "And he *says* he went straight home," Thonday concluded.

"Suppose he helped himself to another bike? I like the idea that Louise was pursued. We have two accounts that verify that and from men with conflicting views of the lady, so probably worth hearing. Waggle your pen about a bit, Thoday, and show us where he might have come across a bike in the environs of Barnabas."

"Um . . . Sometimes you come across them leaning against the railings outside on the street. Here. Inside? Dunno, sir. Do they have bike stores? Could he have been bold enough to just walk into a college bike store?"

"He's bold."

"Yes, sir. Would you like me to —"

"Right after the meeting, if you wouldn't mind. And here — take this with you, just in case."

He passed him a small specimen jar containing sand with the colour and consistency of orange sherbet.

"Chances are, with that degree of fineness, it will have worked its way up into the grooves and still be there. It won't have been cleaned out because our lad would never have noticed in the dark what he was cycling through. Be sure to take gloves, Thoday. And take a copy of the tyre pattern while we've got it here on display."

"I already did, sir. It's a Dunlop, like ninety-nine out of every hundred bikes in Cambridge. I had it looked at by Bert himself of Bert's Bikes in the City Road. The only thing he could tell me was that it was hardly worn — nearly brand-new."

"Right. Hang on a tick! Let's make no mistakes at this juncture, shall we? Mistakes of a *'Police Raid Private Premises'* nature. I'll ring the college and tell them you're coming."

He emerged from five minutes of conversation with a satisfied smile. "Nice to have a bit of good news when we need it. The college has officially 'gone down' for holiday. The master himself won't be breathing down your neck, at least! He's still recuperating, of course, from the effects of his nasty inhalation. And doctor's orders send him off into the Washlands to shoot at geese 'at dawn or under the moon.' Pinkfeet, whitefronts or some such poor bastards just winging their way in from Siberia. Sounds like an unhealthy spot for man and bird, if you ask me. The master could well land himself with a dead goose for his table and a case of pneumonia. Ugh! But that's where we are. The domestic bursar who spoke to me just now, bless him, seemed sane enough and pretty dismissive of all that holiday nonsense. He remains on duty, and if you have a problem, you're to chuck it in his lap. Well, there you go! Do your worst, lad. The porter will sign you in and out. Blimey! It's easier to get in and out of Pentonville Jail!"

He rumbled on. "Next exhibit? That suffragette scarf. Results of examination." He read and summarised: "Everything we might expect. Horse and human hairs . . . soil profile consistent with the Epsom

Downs . . . Aha! Ox blood, not human! Gotcha, Redfyre! If the scarf exists, it's still out there somewhere.

"And the smelling-salts inhaler?" He hunted around in the box. "Funny! Not here. I hope this hasn't gone missing . . ."

"No sir, there's a covering letter from the labs. They have it and are retaining it for the moment. Here we go . . . Too many fingerprints for any to stand out. Too blurred. Solid silver. So of course it has hallmarks. Identified as a London stamp and date. Manufacturer's mark identifies it as an *objet de vertu* supplied by Messieurs Asprey of London, New Bond Street, some fifty years ago. Also engraved on there — and we missed this in our concern to keep our mitts off the lethal item — initials! CR. No use at all! CR was probably very pleased to be given this, but it could have been handed down to someone with completely different initials. Or sold off, most probably. No one uses these much nowadays, apart from a few elderly ladies who are fixed in their invalid ways. And, being of silver, it'd be worth a few quid if you melted it down. The writer of the report, a Doctor Philips, requests an interview with the investigating officer in private, sir. Well, what do we make of that?"

"Probably wants to make you an offer for it on the quiet. Go along, Redfyre, and ask him. When you're up to scratch with your notes."

The porter didn't exactly smile on seeing him, but he was not unhelpful, Thoday noted. A touch of the seasonal spirit filtering through? Thoday put it down to the relief of seeing the backs of those pesky undergraduates.

The porter produced his gate book and, creaking with condescension, offered it up to the police for a second viewing. There they were: the entry and departure of Thomas Tyrrell last Friday evening. Purpose of visit: unscheduled interview with the master. Just as Redfyre had reported.

"Tell me, sir — did Mr. Tyrrell arrive on foot or on a bicycle?"

"On foot, of course. No bikes allowed in the front court past this gate."

"And can you confirm that he was still on foot when he left?"

A look of disbelief crept over the granite features. "I just said, officer. Came in without, left without."

"If your young gentlemen arrive seeking entry but are in possession of a bicycle, what is their procedure?"

"They take it to the bike shed, park it and come and declare themselves. Those who don't hop straight over the wall."

"I'd like to see the bike shed, if I may."

"If you like. Nip down Barnabas Passage over there." He pointed to a small entrance that Thoday hadn't even noticed. "Twenty yards down on the left. It's open."

For a bike shed, it was remarkably well ordered and clean. Hardly a shed. Not at all the tatty corrugated iron roof, wooden walls and earth floor ankle-deep in fag ends that he remembered from his school days. The walls were of stone, en suite with the rest of the college building, the floor paved; above his head was a whitewashed ceiling. A converted stable block? Many of the slots were empty, indicating that some cycles had been taken home on the train. About fifty remained. Ah. A problem they had not anticipated. Nevertheless, Thoday was going to set about it. He first marked for future reference, with a chalk mark, each bike that he passed in review and noted the number of its stall.

He knew exactly what he was looking for. He took out his torch and flashed it over every wheel. Many tyres were quickly discounted, being in a state of poor repair or even dangerously worn down. The one or two that were evidently recent, showing crisp Dunlop grooves, he subjected to a minute examination, hopefully holding the bottle of orange sand in one hand as a check. After a fruitless hour, he straightened his back and sighed. They were assuming Tyrrell had thought to return the piece of property to its place after going on a killing rampage. How likely was that? And yet — queer folk, these students. They had their code. If he'd borrowed a bike from a friend, he might out of natural loyalty have done just that. Even berserking Vikings looked after their mates.

Thoday fought back unsettling notions that he'd been sent out of the station on a wild goose chase and scowled.

As he was leaving, his eye was caught by the gleam of a silver mudguard at the end of what, in the gloom, he had taken to be an alcove. Further inspection showed it to be a sort of annex. If you pushed your bike a few yards down straight ahead instead of turning left, you found yourself in a smaller version of the previous space. There was room here for twenty bikes. Ten were present. Thoday discounted three staid old sit-up-and-beg bikes from before the war. Though well maintained, they had 28-inch wheels, and their tyres did not fit his profile.

A quick glance over the remaining seven told him that he was in the presence of thoroughbreds. Almost all were new, or at least postwar. Some still bore the metal tag of the distributor — a well-known Cambridge supplier. The models made Thoday's mouth water: a Rudge-Whitworth — "Britain's Best Bicycle" — a Coventry, three Raleighs, an Imperial Triumph Roadster. Lastly, he ran an envious finger over a French Peugeot of the kind that had won last year's Tour de France with 36-year-old Firmin Lambot aboard.

So this was where the dons hid their secret longings away! Except that they weren't longings. They were very real. Tyrrell, a mere student, would never have dared help himself to one of these. He almost walked away, but the thrill of being in contact with the shining speed machines held him back. He took out his torch and bottle and set to work.

The newest of the Raleighs was a last year's model, a Raleigh Superbe Roadster with Dunlop tyres. And trapped in the indentations of the brand-new rear tyre were a good number of grains of sand the same colour as the sample he held in his hand. Thoday realised he was panting with excitement. He took a sample bag from his pocket and carefully scraped half of the deposit into it. With that safely back in his pocket he took the time to think. This bike had been ridden closely behind the girl who was found murdered very soon after. Whose fingerprints were on the handlebars? He knew that he would have to report it and a crew would be sent along to lift the prints. But whose bike was this?

The dealer's nameplate was still attached. Varsity Cycles. He took down the details, including the stock number, and prepared to speed along to the Mill Road to make them turn out their records. Then he could, with a modest smile, place the name of the murderer on the desk right under Redfyre's nose.

Moments later he was bidding a smiling farewell to the porter.

He must have been exuding more charm than he was aware of, he thought, when the porter called him back.

"Sergeant! You were asking about bikes just now . . . I don't know if it's worth mentioning, but after young Mr. Tyrrell had left me — on foot — and set off back down Market Hill, a cyclist came steaming down the passage about five minutes later. He turned up the street away from the market. I would never have taken notice of some young tearaway on a bike round here, but this one was going like the clappers. On a slippery road. Maniac! I was going to shout a warning, but he'd already disappeared. Type of bike? No idea. Just the usual two wheels and a saddle job."

Thoday thought joyfully, *It doesn't matter! It doesn't bloody matter!* and clutched his pocket. Tucked away in there was a notebook, the last page of which contained a series of numbers, and an envelope containing a few grains of sand that could hang a man. *This is what matters!*

"Doctor Philips is expecting me."

Redfyre was recognised at once and shown through to the lab where the scientist was at work. The young man smiled in welcome.

"So glad you could come. I'll make this swift. Under some pressure at the moment. Over here, if you wouldn't mind . . ."

He picked up a steel specimen box and led Redfyre to a microscope. "Take a look at the object I'm going to display. It's the silver inhaler. There, do you see the marks? Wonderful bit of design and engraving. The assay office has stamped it carefully to intrude as little as possible on the design. Luckily, the design itself is pretty florid and you could easily miss it. You can see the

London stamp — the leopard's head, next to it the lion passant, which is a guarantee of quality, and on the right of that, the head of Queen Victoria."

"The initial 'S'?" Redfyre asked. "I don't carry the dates table in my head!"

"I looked it up. It's 1873. And next to that, you've got the maker's mark — Charles Asprey and Son, as they were in that year."

"This plunges us back into Victorian London, with its ladies swooning from heat and tight corsets. This would have been made for a lady, I expect."

"I've never heard of a gentleman using one," Philips agreed. "But there's a clue as to the identity of the owner. Wait a minute." He took off his green lab coat, the gesture revealing a tweed jacket and Fair-Isle jumper that made him instantly less intimidating. "Take a stroll with me in the court, will you?"

They went to sit on a bench in a sunlit corner. A thoughtful and suddenly reticent Philips took out a pipe and began to fiddle with it, to Redfyre's annoyance. He recognised this time-wasting activity as a device to put off embarking on a distasteful or difficult subject and looked on patiently. After two unsuccessful attempts to raise a glow in his wad of tobacco, Philips gave up and began to explain himself. "I exceeded the directions, I'm afraid. Strayed into the area the detective occupies. Hope you don't mind, but I'm about to mark your card. Doesn't have any significance for me, but you may well be able to put an interpretation on it."

Redfyre made encouraging noises and took out his notebook.

"You'll have noticed the bit of engraving that wasn't meant to be hidden under an Art Nouveau curlicue? The initials?"

"CR, I think."

"That's right. I took the liberty of ringing up Aspreys and discussing it with them. Frightfully helpful. And their records go way back in time. They said they'd investigate and call back. To my surprise, they did."

At this point, his flow seized up and he hesitated. Redfyre remained silent.

"Well, upshot is — they found the order and a record of payment. Fifty years on, and I can tell you that the lady it was crafted for was a Miss Clara Rumbelowe. I don't have an address for her, but I can tell you who commissioned the design and manufacture and paid the bill. For a sum so large I can only suppose it must have been an engagement or a wedding present."

He took a sheet of notepaper from his

pocket. "I jotted down the name and the London address of the generous donor. You'll see why I'm indulging in all this hocus-pocus, hole-and-corner stuff. Not my style at all! But the way things are turning a bit ugly in Cambridge . . . well, I thought you might prefer a bit of discretion when it comes to bandying about a well-respected local name. I say — are you all right?"

Redfyre gazed blankly at the page he held in his hand. "It's getting a bit cold of a sudden," he said with a shudder. "Shall we go back inside?"

CHAPTER 22

Redfyre had borrowed the station Riley to drive himself out to Melford. In the end, he hadn't needed to ask. MacFarlane had pressed it on him. He would sign it out, he declared, as a "necessary tool for the conveyance of arrested murder suspect in custody" back to CID headquarters. The superintendent had even offered an undercover officer to accompany him.

"Look, I know it's a bunch of wimmin you're tangling with, and you tell me they're going to be present in force at a sort of saturnalian rout. Music? Dancing? Jazzing even — you know what those Strettons are like . . . Strong drink will doubtless feature, heightening emotions and reducing inhibitions. You'll be needing some backup. Don't ask for Thoday. They've clocked him. And that moustache of his has an admiration society of its own. Take Toseland. He's not yet had the pleasure. Stick him in a penguin suit and tell him to mind his manners."

"Let's not get carried away! They're hardly raving worshippers of Bacchus, sir! They won't tear me to shreds. And it's not them I have to be wary of. It's the predator who's trailing them. Juno, Earwig, Suzannah, my aunt — they could all be on his list. In fact, if what my aunt suggests is correct, his list could well be longer than ours. We're restricting ourselves to the characters in the photograph, but remember, 'cloud of midges' was the phrase Hetty used to hint at its form and extent. They could be anywhere and everywhere. Mrs. Mac — do you really know where she spends her Thursday evenings? But I have to decline, Toseland. A copper would stand out and be uncomfortable in that company. *I* feel uncomfortable in that company!"

"Well at least, thanks to some sharp forensics work, we have an idea of this tiger's identity. We have a name! Even though I can't quite square it with some of the known facts. We seem to have a candidate who cannot, according to the physical facts, be responsible, but who, according to the forensic evidence, definitely is. There's something we're missing, Redfyre, but I've bowed to your pressure and I've obtained an arrest warrant, duly signed. And that was bloody hard! The duty magistrate took one look at the subject and had to be revived. If we've got it wrong, Redfyre, we'll both be queuing at the work exchange next Monday morning."

For once, the inspector didn't charge his superior with exaggeration. His grim smile said that he was well aware of and accepted the prospect of instant dismissal. He was more concerned about the future of his boss, a married man with several children, and he admired — as always — the man's gruff readiness to do the decent thing.

MacFarlane handed over the document as though it were the last remaining copy of the Magna Carta, his eyes not leaving it until it disappeared into Redfyre's inner pocket.

"Anyhow, I'm saying we're going with the evidence we have in hand and under our microscopes. When this one comes to court, I want a series of gents in white coats passing through the witness box, telling the jury what's what with benefit of Science. Thanks to a bit of good bookkeeping and a print in the sand, we've got this joker by the tail!"

"Let's not forget the medical insight and advice from Doctor Beaufort, sir."

"I don't. I just don't mention it, Redfyre. And I require you to do the same! This must be the last reference, even between ourselves. The doctor opened a door for us that I don't normally dare knock at. I think he twigged what was going on before we did."

"He was heartily sickened by the succession of girls to the slaughter. He took a risk, though."

"Don't I know it! I haven't even pressed him on the favours he must have called in or the pressure he must have exerted on his intractable colleagues to come up with one name on a very short list. He could be wrong, Redfyre. We could all be wrong. But I'll tell you this — no egg ends up on the doctor's face. Got that?"

"You don't need to say that, sir. But, if he's right, we've got the killer and we know his motive. We've got a box full of forensic evidence. We have the warrant. We have the handcuffs. All we need is the customer."

MacFarlane's doubt bobbed to the surface again. "How certain can you be that he'll be there at the party? This is a smart feller. Is he likely to just walk into a trap? Is it even a trap? And is my best officer the tethered goat?"

"I'm pretty certain he'll turn up. His job is not done. I know that he's close to at least one of the girls. Consciously or unconsciously, one of them has been keeping him abreast of the group's strategy. It's clear that our man suffers from a visceral misogyny, loathing women to the point of destruction of individuals whom he sees as a threat to his ordered masculine world. Has this been an aspect of his psychological nature all his life, or has it just come to the surface, triggered by the provoking behaviour of one particular girl or group of girls?"

"A bout of visceral misogyny, eh? Is that to be preferred to a dose of Cambridge cholera? Gerraway! He's just gone up the hill to Doo Lally! Nutty as a fruit cake!" MacFarlane calmed himself and suggested more soberly: "I'm no expert, but I'd guess what we have to deal with is something akin to neurasthenia. Would you say? Battle and shell shock? Changing his personality and freeing him to indulge in hitherto submerged impulses and skills? Chaps come out of neurasthenic attacks speaking in foreign tongues to their nurses and composing symphonies, I hear. Strange things happen when the brain rots. Our bloke probably isn't all-out gaga. This is a man who can control, or at least *time,* his urges. He's suppressed them for years. He may decide to delay his next outburst, keep us waiting another decade?" MacFarlane was suddenly sounding uncharacteristically doubtful.

"Better to call the whole thing off, Red-fyre?"

"You can try telling that to Earwig, sir. I was unsuccessful. She claims that the madness will just erupt again at a later date when they're less prepared to resist. Why not lure him out in the open?"

"I'm not happy about any of those girls — young Juno especially — being used as bait. She's suffered enough."

"She knows what's what, sir, Earwig says, and will do whatever's necessary for the cause."

MacFarlane had groaned and signed the chit for the Riley.

Redfyre glanced back over his shoulder at the back seat reserved for the guilty party and the stout steel ring and chain fixed to the left side partition. He could not bring himself to conjure up a picture of the prisoner. He distracted himself by checking that the statutory handcuffs (two pairs) and the big, ugly station Browning 1910 semi-automatic (loaded) were in their place in the glove locker and drove on.

He approached the house slowly. He always did. It took his breath away in any season, but there was something especially dramatic about its lines when they were freed from the leafy canopy of bosomy oaks and set against a winter sun sinking in blood-red wreaths of cloud below the horizon. The shortest day of the year. And it was certainly going to be the longest night.

Earwig had telephoned him in great excitement after his aunt's visit to say how thrilled she was that he was prepared to "put old quarrels aside and help out the family in its need." He was unsure which quarrels and which need she had in mind, but he let her gush on. She'd asked if he would come out early. The invitations had proved wildly popular and people were bringing friends, arriving early, arriving late, she explained. It was turning into a lunch party, followed by tea and finishing with the evening celebration they had originally planned for. "You know how it is!" she said. "Open house, I'm afraid. We'd so love it if you could arrive at teatime and be here ready to help with the party guests when they come flooding in. Oh — on your way, could you possibly call by daddy's wine shop and collect an extra crate of champagne? The one he likes. They're putting one out for you, but they'd like you to pick it up before four o'clock. We probably have enough, but . . . well, with the announcements and the toasts and all that, you never know! And Madame Flora Fontaine drinks it by the bucket."

Redfyre didn't ask.

And here he was, dramatically evening-suited, perfectly tied white-tie, gardenia in buttonhole, Beretta 418 tucked up in his inside pocket next to the arrest warrant and a dozen merry widow Clicquots nicely chilled on the back seat.

He patted himself down, checking again. Spare handkerchief in left trouser pocket? Yes. Cigarette case in right jacket pocket? Yes. On second thoughts, he fished out the Beretta. An Englishman's tailcoat was simply not designed to accommodate a gun, even one so unemphatic as this Italian-designed piece. It had been a birthday present from his well-meaning but whimsical mother. The year before, he'd received a sword stick. It was a worrying business, having a youngest son who'd insisted against all good advice on fighting crime. He looked scornfully at the tiny ladies' gun, barely as big as his hand, and imagined himself drawing it on Wulfie. The man would catch the bullets in his teeth and die of laughing. He slipped it into the glove locker with the Browning.

He reminded himself that whatever disfavour the old Riley did to the eighteenth century façade of the grand house, he must insist that it stayed parked by the front door, facing outwards, starting handle at the ready. He had just managed to convey these instructions to a manservant when he was swept down upon by Clarissa Stretton.

Earwig's mother, the soon-to-be-widow, enveloped him in a cloud of eau de cologne, warm arms and a voluminous stole of cloth of gold. Phantom pecks on his cheeks confirmed him a member of her close circle; this was something she had never done before, and he wondered if his status had changed in some way since they last met. If it had, the change was due to Earwig or her brother Wulfie's information. Neither prospect filled him with joy.

"My darling boy! Don't worry — I'm not going to say how you've grown! I said that the last time we met. I will say how you have matured. Oh my! Quite the handsome young man about Cambridge. Earwig, for once, did not exaggerate! . . . Put the champagne with the others in the still room, will you Frank?"

Clarissa was a tall, fair woman. Her blonde hair was thick and showed not a sign of grey. Redfyre remembered it as always hanging in plaits, one over each shoulder in a defiantly bohemian flourish. The plaits were still there but now coiled around each ear, giving her a medieval air. Add a wimple and you'd have something approaching the fairy Lady of Shalott, he thought, waiting for death among whitening willows and shivering aspens.

But this was no melancholy soul, enfeebled by impossible longings. She put out her strong potter's hands and held him up by the biceps for inspection. She tweaked his tie this way and back again that way, looking at him in a teasingly critical and decidedly proprietorial way. He had an awful feeling that her next words would be, "He'll do!" though for what purpose he could not be sure.

"You know Gerald's dying?" she said.

He mumbled that he was aware of the family concern for her husband insofar as Earwig had revealed it when they met last week.

"He has deteriorated since then. We're just hoping he will get through the evening. He turned his face to the wall some months ago in the best Viking tradition, but it didn't take. He had to get up to tend his droopy gloxinia. I can't tell you how his hothouse blooms are suffering! He's upstairs, saving his strength until it's time for the announcements and the toasts, when he will join us.

We didn't think it at all suitable for one of the boys to stand here at the door greeting our guests while his father was on his last legs — imagine the gossip! — so we all agreed you'd be the perfect person to help me out. Do you mind? All you have to do is smile! I'll tell you who's coming at us. Ah! I know who this is," she said as a Rolls Royce slid towards them. "Sir Nicholas and Lady Crawley. Dash forward and help her out, will you, John? She's a martyr to arthritis."

Earwig had said it: "They're flooding in!" Dozens of people arrived, all with smiles on their faces and a clear determination to enjoy the occasion with an appropriate pagan gusto. It was the winter solstice, after all. If they wanted that dying sun to rise again in the morning, they had to play their part in its resurrection. Give the sun god a taste of what he would be missing if he refused to get out of bed the next morning. Feasting, jollity, music, dancing, song were all on the programme. Consciences — though none were much in evidence — were easily appeased by the thought that sober Christian devotions would be given full rein in the week to come.

After half an hour of bobbing out onto the chilly forecourt and back into the warmth of the hall, Redfyre realised that he had been deserted. Clarissa had disappeared, probably gone to find a fur stole.

"We're about halfway through the list," a voice said cheerfully at his elbow. "I'm taking over from mother. She's been called away to the kitchen. Here, I thought you might be ready for this!"

"This" proved to be a glass mug of hot and fragrant cider punch.

"Ah! Not a moment too soon. Here comes the Lord Lieutenant. Take a quick swig and push him indoors quickly."

They worked on, smiling and merry, glad to hear behind them a jazz band letting rip on a few well-known, loved by all, rags and syncopations. A high level of noise and regular bursts of laughter from the reception room made Redfyre, tense though he was, wish he could go through and join in. Earwig caught his thought and reassured him. "We'll do two more and then go inside. Lots of people you know in there. Many left over from teatime. Your aunt? She's already installed. And some chaps from Cambridge claiming an acquaintance? Old college chums of yours, I think, queuing up to book the first waltz. Suzannah's expected, but she hasn't arrived yet."

The final couple, a young married pair Earwig had met in the war, greeted them both warmly. The girl of the pair tugged Earwig excitedly aside and whispered in her ear. The sideways look she slid at Redfyre spoke volumes. The young man gave him an open, bluff and approving stare.

"I say, old chap," he said hesitantly, "so much going on in this family, it's hard to keep up. I'm always the last to hear. Could it be that, er, congratulations are in order?"

"Congratulations, commiserations and farewells, all in order and in that order tonight, but none of 'em for me," Redfyre said with a disarming grin. "Do go through and take a glass of this excellent toe-curler from Frank's tray, er, Edwin."

"Earwig!" he called her to his side. "The two people I most want to see tonight haven't arrived. Aethelwulf and Juno. Where are they?"

"Oh they're about the place somewhere," she said vaguely. At his ice-cold stare, she began again. "You passed by the gatehouse on the way up the drive . . ."

"Is there any other way to get here?"

"Well no. But that's where they are."

"Are you going to explain?"

"It may look — deliberately — like a medieval ruin."

"I'd always assumed it to be a bit of a folly. Romantically covered in ivy, sawn-off

tower, window overlooking the forest —
when I was last here, it was the lair of a
band of brigands. Wulfie's pack! He'd
declared it his headquarters. I used to run
past it very fast, hoping not to be snatched,
taken in and tied up for instruments of
torture to be applied to my most sensitive
parts. Which is what he routinely promised
his little playmates."

"Well, it's been tiddled up and put back
into use again. The only instrument of
torture down there is the trumpet, and the
sensitive part it's applied to is Father's ear.
He can't bear the noise of it. When Juno's
staying with us, she has to practice twice a
day, and for two hours at a time. Father
banished her to the gatehouse. In fact, it
was her suggestion. In London it's impossible to find somewhere remote and sound-
proof, which is why she likes it so much
here. When it comes to music, she really is
a disciplined young woman and never
neglects her practice. It also rather suits her
to escape the Strettons for hours on end."

"Apart from one Stretton in particular,
apparently?"

"Wulfie is very protective of Juno. Has
hardly let her out of his sight since that
nastiness with the staircase at Barnabas. He
didn't want her to appear at such a well-

attended gathering with a raving lunatic at large, and he's holding on to her as long as he can. He's taken to keeping her company down there. In fact, he's actually bought himself an instrument and she's teaching him to play."

She caught his sardonic expression and added, "To put a good face on things, of course. And after all, they are about to become engaged. Tonight. I expect you'd guessed. They've been told to present themselves hand in hand in blushing mode before the feast starts. Father is coming doddering down to make the announcement, and then we'll all drink a toast. Wulfie was a bit shy about making much of an appearance . . ."

"I can understand. We called it 'sticking your head above the parapet.' There's always someone out there to shoot it off. Oh, here's a latecomer. Who's this?"

A stately Daimler was approaching unhurriedly down the drive. The driver braked, paused and dipped his headlamps in salute on catching sight of Redfyre arm in arm with Earwig.

Suzannah Sturdy leapt from the passenger seat, not waiting for the attentions of her driver. Richard Henningham stepped out, laughing and pointing with mischief at Redfyre. Leaving the motor running, he limped up the steps and announced, "Not staying! Not invited. Just delivering Miss Sturdy, who is. Her taxi didn't turn up and she had the good sense to call on me. Just back from a duck shoot. I've been flat on my front in a leaky punt for four days, scaring birds out of their wits. I just had time to have a swift scrub and find the starter handle. Luckily the old brute is easier to fire up than I am." He waved at his motorcar.

While Suzannah chatted with Earwig, he took Redfyre by the sleeve and murmured, "Must go before she overheats. I say, could you possibly organise a taxi or a lift for Miss Sturdy at the end of proceedings? I'm a bit the worse for wear, don't you know. The fens are never kind to joints. Don't worry; if you can't, I'm sure I shall rally. Or send my butler — he understands the motor. Just give me a ring when she's had enough." He started to slip away down the steps with a gallant wave to Suzannah.

But he had reckoned without Earwig. "What's this? Stop! I won't have it. Master, you must stay for the party! Evening dress? Who cares? This is a pagan celebration you are being invited to join! A bearskin would be very authentic, a toga appropriate. Your dark suit will go unnoticed. Suzannah, make him change his mind!"

Henningham took one look into Suzannah's warm, inviting eyes and signalled to the waiting Frank to take the car to the rear. He risked a shrug of the shoulders and a fleeting glance at Redfyre that said: "Women! What can you do?"

Redfyre sighed in relief at his decision. He was reassured to know that he would be able to catch the eye of the master with amused conspiracy across the room crowded with revellers. "Keep tight hold of that one, Suzannah," was Redfyre's silent advice as they went, arm in arm, as two couples in to the heated, candlelit and pine-scented jollity of the old banquet hall.

Any misgivings he'd had about the character of the occasion vanished the moment the hum of lively chatter and laughter enveloped them. So many of the guests knew each other well but did not meet as often as they would have wished, and there was a good deal of gossip to be exchanged. Distant members of the Stretton family were noisily rediscovering each other. Redfyre found himself being shaken by the hand by Earwig's three older brothers, his erstwhile tormentors. Stan (of the Cambridgeshires) had stayed blond and handsome and was

almost the twin of Wulfie. In Alf and Godric the fair hair had dulled to a light
brown, but Redfyre would have known them
anywhere. Friendly and witty, they had
memories of the past that were very different from his own and were trotted out with
warm nostalgia.

He spent some time speaking to old
friends from his college days, trying to account for his connection, until today un-
guessed at, with the Stretton family. Dis-
turbingly, he found that Earwig was
accompanying him everywhere, hanging on
his arm and finishing his sentences. Increasingly there were mentions of "Earwig and
Johnny." Had he mistaken the trap the
wretched girl was setting tonight? Was it
made of silk not steel, and was he already
enmeshed? He squashed the thought with
the recognition that there were also present
at this jamboree about a dozen men far
more eligible than himself who would have
snatched at the offer of Earwig's hand. He
noted the admiring glances she collected as
she swayed her way with a sinuousness he'd
not noticed before amongst the guests. A
slender shape in silvery, almost see-through
silky fabric trailing to the floor. Lord! Was
she spinning the sticky stuff as she moved?
Laying down a web to catch him by the

ankles? Her thick hair had been tamed and slicked down with something shiny, and restrained over one ear with a diamond and pearl clasp, her already generous mouth was — perhaps unwisely — accentuated by red lip rouge. Nervously, he rubbed at the side of his face where he remembered her planting a greeting.

At a word from Earwig, the chief steward nodded and summoned his staff to circulate, ensuring that all the guests' glasses were topped up with punch, ready for the next event. Alf stepped forward and made a dinging noise on his glass. He announced the appearance of the famous opera star, straight from Sadler's Wells, Madame Flora Fontaine with her piano accompanist for the evening. Slumming it on the keyboards tonight was a distinguished organist, also a friend of the family: Doctor Christopher Coote. Madame Flora had generously offered to thrill the audience with a medley of songs from the London stage. They were to be given a selection from *The Gipsy Princess, Sally, The Merry Widow* — all their favourites. Would they please gather round and make themselves comfortable?

Redfyre noted that even here in the musical offering there was evidence of careful planning. The promised cascade of romantic tunes would bring a lump to the throat and a flutter to the heart, and everyone in the audience would be predisposed to welcome news of a real-life love story and be yearning for a happy ending. But Coote? Juno's alter ego when it came to the musical world, of course he would. Redfyre had guessed at their closeness. And the man had a practised charm that would grace any entertainment.

Guests hurried to fetch chairs and squeeze onto sofas. Some of the gentlemen settled cross-legged on the floor at the feet of the ladies they were squiring. To energetic applause, Christopher strode on stage left, arm outstretched to welcome Flora who came out with improbable shyness from behind a thicket of potted palms stage right.

Taking advantage of the stir-about and glad to escape the throbbing delivery of "To Love and Be Loved," Redfyre grabbed Earwig by the arm and, holding onto her tightly, marched her out of the room and into the entrance hall.

"What's the nearest quiet space? The library?"

"No, that's upstairs. There's my little reading room," she said, puzzled but intrigued.

She led him into a small wood-panelled room off the hall. An old butler's redoubt, Redfyre guessed, where he had kept an eye and an ear on the front door whilst polishing the silver. Decommissioned in these straightened times and made over to suit the needs of a girl who read copiously, judging by the full bookcases overflowing into piles on the floor. A desk bearing a telephone was neatly arranged with writing paper, inkwell and blotter and a filing system had been placed to hand by its side. Two comfortable armchairs filled the rest of the space. Redfyre realised that this was not only a retreat but a strong point, and its regular occupant could well be running the estate and the house from here. Earwig. Life would change significantly for her when the heir, Aethelwulf, took up his inheritance. No need to sell on if he was as rich as was hinted. He could merely pay the government-imposed death duties out of his own resources and take up life here again as the master in the company of his glamorous new wife. Earwig risked being banished to the dower house with her mother. A penniless old maid who would have to find other, more menial duties to occupy her time and energies. She was about to be displaced from the position of de facto mistress of the house by an older brother of doubtful worth who'd come swanning back into her life like the Prodigal

Son. Redfyre looked at the eager, vivid face and looked away sharply. Emotion must be effaced from his next actions if he were to get this right.

Crowded though it was, room had been made for Christmas decorations. Green garlands were draped along the cornice, and a handmade hooped mistletoe kissing bough hung in the centre of the room. A bowl of last autumn's apples, polished to a red brilliance, sat on a low table.

With a flash of mischief, Earwig closed the door on the Gipsy Princess and her heartache and led him over to the mistletoe hoop. She turned to him, holding his hands, still puzzled but with what he feared might be a hopeful smile beginning to quiver on her lips.

Moving to block her exit from the room, Redfyre adjusted his grip so that he was grasping both her wrists and spoke crisply.

"Are you ever going to tell me, Miss Stretton, exactly why you made an attempt on the life of Juno Proudfoot last Friday evening?"

Chapter 23

"Oh, Lord! Is that all you want to know? Crikey! I thought I was going to have to fend off a proposal of marriage."

With one swift upward movement, she had broken his hold and was using her released hand to point at one of the armchairs. "Why don't you just sit yourself down there and I'll put you out of your obvious misery?

"First, no, I won't marry you. There — thought I'd get that out of the way.

"Second, yes. Guilty as charged. I did plan Juno's fall down the stairs at St. Barnabas. But I was not alone. 'Conspiracy' is the word the coppers would choose, I suppose. Juno herself was a conspirator, as was Louise Lawrence. Venus played her part. Your aunt Hettie had a walk-on role."

"I understand that these cells comprise six members, you've given me five."

Earwig gave out a noise which he could only have written down as "Pish, tush!" Not for the first or tenth time, he had the feeling he was failing to come up to expectation.

"How you stickle for detail! We have no constitution, written or understood. We don't count members. It's not a Brownie Brigade we're running, you know. If you want a sixth, you can count my mother. She did the cutting and pasting to make the first of the poison-pen notes. She refused to do any more on the grounds that it was too fiddly for her big fingers and too inconsequential for her big mind to be bothered with. I had to compose the rest myself, in capital letters."

"And the point of all this craftwork was to impress the crime reporter of the *Oracle*, are you telling me? To spin him into your web?"

"Yes. He's a good sort, Scrivener."

He sighed. "The man's a journalist, Earwig. They have no loyalties. They play one side against the other. And if there are no sides, they'll create them. Listen — this is important. Did you show him the notes? In his article, he referred to them . . ."

"Yes, we did. At least the first four. But it's all right — Scrivener's fixed."

"Fixed? What do you mean?"

"We know where he spends his Sundays. Louise found out, expressed her disapproval in the sweetest terms, and threatened to share the salacious gossip with his editor if he didn't oblige us. Louise knows — knew — some surprisingly dark people in unhealthy holes and corners. She made many enemies."

"And me — why did you think it necessary to involve me? You wanted a copper-bottomed, gold-braided witness?"

She nodded and began to bite her lip, showing some tension for the first time in the interview. "There was more to it than that. Look, John, I'll apologise later. Properly. Not much time now. The dates of the letters were the sixteenth, seventeenth and thirtieth of November. Number four — *ENTER THE ORGAN LOFT ALIVE* — I sent on the third of December. The last one to arrive, number five —"

"The really nasty one about Jezebel thrown from a height and eaten by dogs?"

"Yes. I must say you spotted there was something wrong with it the moment you saw it, John. I didn't write it. It arrived on Tuesday the eleventh of December, the day before your aunt rang you. It threw me into a blue funk for a minute or two. I mean — a note in the same design, uttering the same warnings but much more horrid — it was startling. It felt as though a malign stranger had suddenly turned up at the gaming table and was playing an unknown hand. A man who seemed to know what cards we were holding. Hetty thought the best thing was to drag you aboard. The sight of your clever ferret's face and broad shoulders — not to mention your copper's bottom, sitting on the front row, would deter all but the most hardened of criminals, she said. I think you're more of a sheepdog. It's those brown eyes that laugh at you all the time."

She got up, took a sheet of paper from the desk and handed it to him along with a pocket calendar. "I expect you'll want to jot down the dates."

"Yes indeed. It's the details of a case that pin down the guilty," he said, scribbling. "I've worked out how you played the trick. Juno isn't the smartest of witnesses and gave away rather more than she realised when I talked to her on her hospital bed. Oh, by the way, I have at home in safekeeping a gem of a tiny French vase I shall pass back to her at the first opportunity. The flowers I rescued from the ward died of the cold on the back seat of the Riley, I'm afraid, though I managed to salvage your English roses and they're doing as well as can be expected. But could you confirm what Louise Lawrence's part was in all this?"

"Right-oh. She brought in a curtain tie that we checked was long enough to bridge the stairwell. It was Louise who lured away the front of hall man who was supposed to light the stairs. She took him across the road to the pub until it was all over. Juno smuggled the tie upstairs in her trumpet case, and when she was ready to come down again, she twisted it round her arm. No tying up was necessary. You weren't supposed to go scrounging around, peering into corners."

"I did notice there were no modifications to the carpentry."

"We calculated that if Juno came clattering down, banging on the stairs with her trumpet case as she went and screaming, it would be very dramatic. If she just took a nosedive for the last few steps on her front — like a doing a front roll in the gym — it would be very convincing. No one in his right mind was likely to go looking for extra hooks or screws."

"It was certainly convincing," he said simply. "Even to one in the forefront of the action. And her performance, the spell of unconsciousness, was utterly persuasive."

"That's because it was very nearly a real unconsciousness!" Earwig smiled. "Silly girl misjudged the distances in the dark, tripped over her case and tumbled down far more steps than we had ever intended. Whew! It could have been all too real an accident!"

"Earwig," he said gently. "Juno narrowly escaped death that night from quite another cause. It was *you* who inadvertently saved her from a very painful death. Do you remember the silver smelling-salts inhaler?"

She had not known. She listened, growing increasingly pale, horrified and angry as he explained. Finally, in a quiet voice, she asked simply: "Are you saying that the son of this Miss CR, as she was before marriage on the engraving, the presumed inheritor of this deadly bit of equipment, is here tonight? Under my roof?"

He nodded. "Waving his wine glass and joining in the chorus of 'I'm off to Chez Maxim's' by now."

"Where would anyone come by this mercury cyanide stuff?"

"You could get it from a pharmacy to kill your household rats, but you'd have to sign for it, and the transaction would be traceable. You could buy it at any pharmacy in France, six ampoules to the pack, without declaring your name. In that case, we are unlikely ever to come up with an identity. The net is simply too wide. The third — and for us the most productive — line of enquiry is that you could even, in very special circumstances, have it prescribed by your own doctor."

"What circumstances?"

"A very tiny, very specific dose, I've discovered is actually being administered to two select groups of patients, one in London and one here in Cambridge."

"Why Cambridge? Is this significant?"

"Yes, when you understand that the supplier of this new experimental 'cure' is based here in the city. Louise's own father and his sidekick, Benson. Working hand in glove with the medical profession. And, believe me, I wish them the best of luck in their endeavours. I haven't yet got the proof that Louise discovered how her father was involved, but it's likely that with her nose for sensation she had snuffled up information of the sort and was proposing to make some sort of illicit use of it. If a list of sufferers were to be made public, reputations, marriages, lives would be ruined. I wondered if she had confided in you?"

"She hated her father and disliked her boss, and I think wouldn't have hesitated to hand either one of them in, but no — she left me no cryptic messages, no delayed letters in the post revealing all. She was a girl who chose to bank her secrets. Sorry. Are you ever going to tell me what these patients are suffering from and what this supposed cure is?"

Once again, Redfyre knew that the interviewing rules had been turned on their head.

"Syphilis," he said simply.

He watched closely for her reaction as he continued. She'd been a nurse in the war; she must have encountered cases and understood the horrors.

"The scourge of the century. In every country of Europe. There is no known cure for a disease that lingers painfully, that comes and just as mysteriously disappears for months on end. That makes a man decay from his vital parts outwards and upwards until, last of all, it reaches the brain. A brain that is telling the sufferer that the disease has been passed on to him by a female prostitute. Female. Eve. Jezebel. The source of all turpitude. The fact that the unfortunate woman caught it herself from a dastardly *man* doesn't enter many men's heads."

Earwig was trembling with shock and rage. "You're telling me that this creature tried to kill Juno and did kill Louise and Venus?"

"That's what I have to fear."

"Then I hope you find him before I do. John, who are those monsters who used to terrorise the ancient Greeks?"

"The Furies?" he suggested. "Very old deities with snakes for hair, bats' wings, blood-shot eyes. They used to carry brass-tipped scourges and whip their victims until they died in torment. Female, of course. Three of them."

"If he encounters *me,* he'll wish it was all three Furies he was confronting instead," she said, and he believed her.

CHAPTER 24

"The music's stopped. Hasn't it?"

They dashed to the door and opened it to be greeted by the happy sounds of fading applause, laughter and chatter. Back in the banqueting hall, the performance seemed to be halfway through, and the crowd was stirring about, refilling glasses, munching on canapés circulating on silver salvers. Guests were shaking their limbs and finding a more comfortable perch before Flora let rip on the promised *Merry Widow* selection.

Clarissa seized Redfyre's arm. "There you are! Where on earth have you been, John? Look, we have a problem. Wulfie and Juno should be here doing their duty by now. They should have been here at least half an hour ago, but we can't find them. Someone's dressed my husband and given him a shot of whisky, and he'll be produced the moment Flora finishes her last song. We thought 'A Dutiful Wife' would hit just the right note before the couple are given the family's blessing. Earwig's missing too; even Suzannah's drifted off."

"Suzannah!" Redfyre raked the hall. "Where's she gone? When?"

"Oh, ten minutes ago . . . fifteen? Such a thoughtful woman! She told me her escort — that impressive chap Henningham — was a little the worse for wear and she thought it would be better to drive him home while he could still stand. Luckily, Suzannah is able to drive motorcars and was perfectly ready to have a go at the Daimler . . . John! Eadwig!"

Redfyre was racing for the door, Earwig scampering behind.

Once outside on the steps, they stopped to listen to a sound that filled Redfyre's heart with despair and temporarily made his limbs feel as heavy as lead. The wail of a five-note lament ending with a soaring screech he recognised at once. The "Hejnal Mariacki." The last desperate call of a medieval trumpeter sounding the alarm. Too late.

Redfyre gathered himself and made a swift calculation. To run or not to run? It was a very long drive. The trumpet call had barely reached them. He dashed down the steps to the Riley, knowing that if it failed to start, he'd gambled badly. Earwig forced the passenger door open and swore as the awkward beast coughed and spluttered when he swung the handle. On the second try the engine caught, and the car surged forward down the drive under Redfyre's urging.

He drove it within an inch of the gatehouse wall, Earwig sounding the hooter all the way. They both jumped out, staring up at a distraught Juno in evening gown, trumpet in hand, leaning dangerously out of the window high above their heads.

"I've put the door bar up, but he's beating it down," she managed.

A loud splintering crash from inside made her scream again in terror.

Redfyre climbed onto the bonnet of the Riley and flung his arms wide. "Jump!" he ordered. "I'll break your fall. We've done this before! Now!"

A second later, he was rolling about on the frosty ground, trying to keep the weight of a squeaking, sobbing Juno away from the hard surface. He was winded, but all his limbs seemed to be in working order. He assumed the same condition for Juno as he helped her to her feet and opened the car door.

"Get in and keep your head down! I'm going into the tower."

He reached over to the glove locker and found it hanging open. "Shit! Bloody girl!"

The Browning had disappeared, along with Earwig. Fumbling and cursing, he extracted the Beretta and checked it over. He slipped it into Juno's hand. "Use it. Point and shoot at anyone you don't like the look of. Back in a sec."

The indecently loud boom of a Browning going off in a small space had him charging inside the gatehouse. He'd no idea what the layout could be — he'd successfully managed to avoid any acquaintance with the interior in his youth, but a building with a footprint so small was hardly offering him an entrance to the labyrinth. Not wired for electricity, evidently, but there was an oil lamp struggling against the shadows in a wall socket and the remains of a fire in the hearth that took up the whole of the far wall.

Slumped in front of the hearth, facedown on the Afghan rug, was a body. Redfyre turned it over.

"Wulfie!" He shook him. A groan was all the indication he needed of life still flowing, though sluggishly, through the large form. Bleeding from his mouth, incapable of speech, he managed to open his eyes and stare in horror at the stairs. A ridiculously out-of-proportion staircase but this was a folly, a flight of the architect's imagination, a harking back to medieval times. Redfyre guessed that up there would be a landing spacious enough to accommodate a pair of duelling swordsmen in front of the upper living room. A landing where someone was attempting to gain entrance by battering down the thick oak door.

Until he had fallen silent a minute ago.

Stairs to the upper floor would of course take a twist to the right to inconvenience a climbing attacker who would find his right arm and any weapon he held in it obstructed and useless. Would Earwig have known that? He couldn't remember whether she was right- or left-handed. Could she even manage the weight and heavy trigger of that old blunderbuss of a pistol?

Redfyre had no weapon, but his left fist was quite useful. Against what, he had no idea.

Clinging to the wall as closely as he could, his back to the central stone spine, he eased his way upwards.

"John? Is Juno all right?" whispered Earwig's voice from somewhere above his head. "Has he killed Wulfie?" And, with sick humour, "Where are the Furies when you need them?"

Three more steps and he reached the

landing. And a scene of horror. He reacted as he had done when seeing Rubens's *Massacre of the Innocents* for the first time. The sight of the dark red of blood against pale flesh, the contorted shapes in the shadows, the atmosphere of uncontrolled violence, were all there and given an extrasensory dimension by the stench of gunfire and freshly spilled blood. It stopped his breath.

Nothing was where it was supposed to be. Disoriented and dizzy, he shook his head and took in the scene again. A long, low oak bench — used, he presumed as a battering ram — lay askew and barring his way, legs sticking upwards. It had been thrown, he calculated, at Earwig when she emerged onto the landing, gun in hand. The girl was on the floor facing him, barely recognisable. Two wide eyes in a blood-smeared face stared up at him. Her silvery dress was mottled with dark matter.

She was sitting across the shins of what Redfyre feared was a corpse. Earwig's left hand still clutched the Browning, which was trained with rock-solid steadiness on the throat of the man she'd just shot. Blood pooled from his chest. A huge area of whitewashed wall next to the door was splattered in blood.

"He's still breathing," she went on. "But

not for long, I think. Just in case, I thought I'd better immobilise him. Sit on their legs or neck, I was always taught." She glanced at the red-soaked upper torso and shuddered. "I'm not hurt. Just very messy. He sort of . . . exploded. I suppose I was too close. Can I get up now, John?"

He helped her to her feet and told her to go down and tend to her brother, explained that Juno was safe and sound but armed in the Riley. "Be sure to identify yourself before approaching," he said unnecessarily, obeying his safety routine. "Please — give me the gun, will you?"

She handed it over and he switched on its safety before stowing it away in his pocket.

As soon as she'd embarked on the staircase, he gave his attention to her victim. She'd aimed a little high for the heart, one shot, and there was a slight chance that he would survive, though Redfyre wouldn't have put money on the outcome. At such close quarters, the Browning delivered a blast that could stop a rhinoceros in its tracks.

The victim shared his doubt, apparently. The eyes opened and smiled at him sardonically. "Can't imagine why I'm still alive! Shot by a woman! I'd rather counted on it being your cool eye and steady trigger finger that did for me, Redfyre. Soldier to soldier. Funny, isn't it? I survived a war with the mighty Germans, but the one against the weaker sex has done for me." He paused to catch his breath, then expelled it at once in a single vituperous word: "Harridans! They attack you through your weaknesses and fill you full of poison. They want to have everything you hold dear for their own use." He closed his eyes and gritted his teeth as a wave of pain shook him. "I say, I suppose an explanation is owed . . . Can you bear it? I won't keep you long. They were trying to dismantle Barnabas, you know. Using blackmail, slander, lies, flattery and bribery — all the evil arts they possessed. For the trivial reason that I'd denied them access to the music school. Or any of the other schools, for that matter. They have their own female colleges, why can't they keep their acquisitive fingers off what has never been theirs? Was never intended to be opened up to them?"

"Henningham, you're ill. I mean, apart from the hole in your chest. I am aware of —"

"You know about that?" The master smiled again. "No excuses! Because you're a terrible old softie, you're about to put the blame on the nasty little spirochetes, the invasive, killer bacteria that have taken over my body and are now laying siege to my brain. In this clear moment, before they storm in through a sallyport and I have to surrender, I'll say — nonsense! I declare: Spirochetes, not guilty! I have *always* despised the female sex and loathed their impurities."

He coughed and spat out a gout of blood. "You just don't see the reality of what's happening, do you? Sir Bloody Lancelot! Titupping about on your white charger with your plumed helmet. You're a traitor to your sex, man! It's *they* who are the spirochetes! The women! Deadly as any bacterium, every last one of them, and they're on the move. Their march is unstoppable. They're climbing inexorably up to the brain. The only thing that slows them down, ironically, is their own tenderness for men! And their own gullibility. Even the most intelligent of them is so easily deceived. Suzannah . . ."

Was that a sob, a gasp or a laugh that followed?

"I'm leaving you here to die alone with your evil thoughts," Redfyre said. "I'm going to find Suzannah, the hem of whose gown you are not fit to touch. Oh, my God! Suzannah!"

And he slipped away, shaking with disgust and fear.

CHAPTER 25

"Shame about the party!"

Aunt Henrietta's declaration startled Redfyre. She enlarged on her frivolous thought. "I don't know when I've been so engrossed in a gathering for ages. Though it took on quite a different character once the bodies started to be carted inside. The police were very discreet, Johnny, I must say, but everyone quite lost their appetite for roast pig and haunch of venison. Clarissa tells me they were glad of the leftovers the next day, however, when so many called to pay their respects and enquire after Wulfie and Juno."

She was unhappy with his continued silence. Henrietta had never quite believed in the virtues of a stiff upper lip. She'd insisted that he come out on his bike to spend Christmas Eve with her and his uncle in their own warm little home in the country in Madingley village, deliberately to make him open up.

"Have you seen Suzannah? How is she taking it all?" she persisted, handing him a cup of tea and a plate of mince pies. "Does she realise how very lucky she was? Dancing a tango with a cobra would have been a rather safer activity than keeping company with that man!"

Redfyre smiled. "She's fine. Like me, she's gone very quiet. Licking wounds. Not all of them visible."

"The ones that *are* visible are bad enough! Have you seen her wrists? Cut to shreds! She struggled, poor child! He tied her to the door handle with fishing wire that he'd brought in his pocket and abandoned her in the Daimler, a hundred yards down the road. She heard all the awful noises — the trumpet call, the hooter, shots and screams — knowing she was next. I want to tell you, John, that her — um, friendship with the master was not cultivated at our request. We had no idea. I can only hope that she hadn't got too fond of him."

"We may never know. I suspect she did have regard for him. So did I. He was a likeable man. His students all respected and admired him. But he was certainly spying on her, using her as a source of information. She may tell us how much she did let slip when she's had the chance to recover and give it some thought."

"She survived. That's enough."

"Only just. In fact, she very nearly did die at his hands. I haven't told her, and I don't want her to know . . . Aunt! Do you hear me? It didn't strike me until later, nearly too late. That Sunday morning when I went to tell her the news of the discovery of Venus's body, he was coming to visit her. I'm sure now that he intended to kill her that day and arrange that her death would be assumed to be the work of the man who'd killed Venus the previous night. Getting reckless! But a nosy cleric neighbour stopped him for a gossip. Telling him, I'm sure, that a policeman had called and was still with her. He was a man who could put on quite a performance, the master."

"And he gave a particularly good version of a man suffering the effects of a close call with a poison."

"Yes, all that hocus-pocus with the inhaler! His faked sniff at the salts and the subsequent attack of the collywobbles! He was well aware of the symptoms of accidental poisoning by mercury cyanide — as a patient being prescribed the noxious stuff, he must have had warning enough from his doctor. The cyanide was his plan B, in case the fall down the stairs that he knew the girls had planned proved not to be fatal."

"Plan B, you call it? How do we know that he didn't carry it always with him on the off chance?" Henrietta said, her tone scathing. And, chillingly, "How do we know he hadn't used it before?"

Always the one to stop him short with a thought going off at a tangent, Aunt Hetty.

Redfyre went on uneasily. "He may have been fooling people for longer than we're aware . . . He fooled young Tyrrell as well. Tyrrell would have been very surprised to see the charming master, who'd agreed to see him and hear his complaints though supposedly suffering from Montezuma's revenge at the time, spring into action the moment he left and make off on his bike in the direction of Louise Lawrence's house. The house whose location Tyrrell had just revealed. He followed her to Bensons', where she took refuge. He lurked about a bit, and when she emerged, escorted by her boss and her dog, he cycled off ahead of her down the main road and had installed himself right in her own front porch. She came running up thinking the gent who waved at her was her own father, looking out for her."

Hetty shuddered. "How appalling! To be taken by surprise like that, and by a man of some consequence whom you respected! No wonder she didn't fight back."

"I thank the lord for our sharp-eyed coppers on the common and the fingerprint department, who lifted his prints from the handlebars of the bike they enabled us to find."

"You knew when you turned up at the party that he was responsible? And why?"

"Yes. Though stupidly and sentimentally hoping against hope that I'd got it all wrong. There were ends I had to tuck in or cut off before I could slap him with a warrant."

"All satisfactorily resolved?" she asked, sensing his hesitation.

"One end is still sticking out. Henningham can no longer tell me, but there is a man who can. Scrivener. I didn't have time to engage Henningham in a discussion of the press, but apart from the hexagon of plotting women, Scrivener was the only person who'd been shown the poison-pen letters and had an inkling of the plot. I believe he couldn't resist speaking to the master to hear his views. Probably mouthing some nonsense about striking a balance. 'This is their point of view, now would you like to give the readers your riposte?' You can imagine! Henningham was a smart man. He'd have extracted whatever information he needed with flattery and a disarming smile. It was in Scrivener's interest to foment discord between the town and the university. It sells newspapers. That's all he cares about. He measures his ego in numbers of copies sold. Today's fish and chip wrapper, oozing with grease, was yesterday's stunning news."

"The girls trusted Scrivener. But if Henningham knew what was being planned, why didn't he just put a stop to it? Cancel the concert? It would have been difficult and embarrassing for the college, but he could have done it."

"It suited him wonderfully for it to go ahead! It played right into his hands! It was his alibi. He was away in India at the start of the plot when the dean succumbed to blackmail and gave consent. The supposed attempt on Juno's life was already arranged by others before his return. The first of the poison-pen letters had been delivered, and he'd had an account of them from Scrivener. Any subsequent missives of his creation would be ascribed, of course, to the original plotter. When it came to the delivery of the thoroughly nasty funeral wreath for Juno, he had merely to step outside into the court and help himself to a selection of seasonal vegetation. He took great care tying the bow by flattening it, as you do, with his rather large ex-artilleryman's thumbs. The black satin ribbon gave us two beautiful prints whose hoops and whorls corresponded exactly with the prints we found on the handlebars of the cycle sold to Doctor Henningham two years ago."

"So he was clear of all suspicion of the first murder attempt. And the thickheaded police — that's you, darling — would assume the second, the third, the fourth were by the same hand and therefore unconnected with him." Henrietta touched her throat briefly, eyes widening in horror.

"It's all right, Aunt. You were very low on his list, I should imagine. Wouldn't you say there was a sort of hierarchy of hatred about his choice of victim? Juno was the instigator, the one who was throwing a direct accusation of prejudice at him. The one who challenged him in public, thrilling an audience in his own chapel by exercising what he regarded as a man's art. She came in for his most concentrated hatred, I think. He was determined to kill her even though he had to beat his way through Aethelwulf to get at her."

"And that's a puzzle. Wulfie may be one-handed these days but he's no slouch with his left. What ever happened to *him*?"

"He, er, isn't keen to talk about it. Relying on the 'concussion resulting in lapse of memory' excuse, I think. He did divulge to me, however —"

"Under duress, would that be, darling?" she asked with a touch too much eagerness.

"You might call it that," he said with a smile, not wishing to disappoint. "Wulfie was standing whistling to himself and warming his bum downstairs at the fire, wondering if it would be acceptable to shout up a third time to Juno telling her to get a move on, that they risked missing their cue, when in strode Henningham. A bluff and breezy presence introducing himself as the master of St. Barnabas who had been present when Juno had had her accident was not in the least troubling. A bit of a nuisance perhaps, as they were in a hurry, but no more than that. The master extended his left hand, grasped Wulfie's only hand tightly and promptly clouted him hard with his own free right."

"Oh, dear!"

"More harm done to Wulfie's pride than his skull, I think. Though the master had hands like sledgehammers. His strong thumbs certainly squeezed the life out of poor Louise Lawrence, who was no pushover. He quickly identified her as Juno's ac-

559

complice, thanks to Thomas Tyrrell. By subjecting the dean to a grilling, he discovered it was Venus who had engineered the granting of permission for the concert."

"Urgh! We were unravelled bit by bit."

"I'm afraid so."

"It makes me feel old and useless. How far would he have gone?"

"I daren't think. He was growing less controlled. The effects of the disease are unpredictable. Sometimes the sufferer has a surge of energy, physical or mental, sometimes at the same time and, on these occasions, he believes himself to be a hero, a demi-god, a god even. Henningham wanted to use his surges of remaining physical strength to do as much damage as he could. At least now he's dead, we've been granted sight of his doctor's notes. He was entering the third — and final — stage of the disease, and he'd been informed."

"Why was he so charming to you, John? He really seemed to like you."

"I could have liked him. Funny thing, Aunt. He was playing a game with nothing to lose. I think he was enjoying the skirmish. Though it was probably not the *man* I was fighting, but a myriad ghastly little killer bacteria. I'd rather think that was so. And that's what I shall tell myself and anyone else who speaks of the master in terms of horror and evil. He too was a victim, confused and ultimately consumed by the very worst that nature has to chuck at man or woman."

The cheerfully amateur sound of a band of Christmas carollers, performing to the accompaniment of handbells under the lamppost at the end of the street, chased away the nightmare and brought him back down into a blessedly mundane place. "Ouch!" he said, and, quoting with mischief from Rupert Brooke:

"And things are done, you'd not believe,
At Madingley, on Christmas Eve!"

"I could arrest them for grievous auditory harm and wilful assault on the herald angels!"

He finished his tea and asked casually, "Is Earwig all right? I haven't heard from her."

"Ah! That's because she's in Paris, darling. Aethelwulf got himself patched up — it takes more than a smack on the head to lay out that thug for long. He gathered up Juno and Earwig and a nurse from an agency and took them all off to stay at the Ritz to take their minds off the unpleasantness. Though Earwig did have time to wrap up a present for you and ask me to hand it over!"

He decided to unwrap the small parcel then and there because he sensed his aunt's bright-eyed curiosity was stronger than his own need for discretion. "Well, it's very nearly Christmas. We'll take a look, shall we? Ah. It's a book. A novel by H. G. Wells. His latest. I haven't got it yet. So — good thought, Earwig! Yes, a good thought. Probably a good read, too — she seems quite the reader. I shall enjoy this on my one day off!"

"*Men Like Gods*?" Hetty read out the title aloud. "Isn't that a bit unclear? 'Like' — is that a verb or a preposition? What can it mean?"

"Haven't a clue! Science fiction is my guess. It seems to be all the rage at the moment. I'll let you know when I've read it. There's a card. On it she says, um . . . 'When you've found your Utopia, I'll join you there. Possibly sometime in the New Year.' Puzzle this! She's making a date with me in the snug at the Pike and Eel? What on earth does she mean?"

"Oh, I think I can guess," Henrietta said, nodding.

ABOUT THE AUTHOR

Barbara Cleverly was born in the north of England and is a graduate of Durham University. A former teacher, she has spent her working life in Cambridgeshire and Suffolk; she now lives in Cambridge. She is the author of thirteen books in the Joe Sandilands series, including *The Last Kashmiri Rose, The Blood Royal, Not My Blood, A Spider in the Cup, Enter Pale Death,* and *Diana's Altar.*

The employees of Thorndike Press hope you have enjoyed this Large Print book. All our Thorndike, Wheeler, and Kennebec Large Print titles are designed for easy reading, and all our books are made to last. Other Thorndike Press Large Print books are available at your library, through selected bookstores, or directly from us.

For information about titles, please call:
    (800) 223-1244

or visit our website at:
    gale.com/thorndike

To share your comments, please write:
    Publisher
    Thorndike Press
    10 Water St., Suite 310
    Waterville, ME 04901